Praise for *The Eye of the Sheep*

'Full of achingly true insights into family violence and the way trauma passes from one generation to the next. Laguna dissolves the barriers between author and reader, getting the voice of odd, funny, love-hungry Jimmy so right that I still don't quite believe he isn't out there somewhere, spinning and spinning in ever-faster circles.'

　—Emily Maguire, author of *An Isolated Incident*

'The power of this finely crafted novel lies in its raw, high-energy, coruscating language which is the world of young Jimmy Flick, who sees everything . . . *The Eye of the Sheep* is an extraordinary novel about love and anger, and how sometimes there is little between them.'

　—Miles Franklin Literary Award 2015, judges' report

'Sofie Laguna faultlessly maintains the storytelling voice of Jimmy, who is oblivious in some ways and hauntingly knowing and observant in others. There are many places in which such a story could tip over into sentimentality or melodrama, but Laguna's authorial control and intelligence keep the story on track and the reader engaged and empathetic, and she manages both the humour and the darkness of this story with great sensitivity and control.'

　—Stella Prize 2015, judges' report

'The greatest achievement here is making this family's world not just compelling but utterly entertaining. Laguna does this by showing the way her characters are the sum of all the parts that make them . . . It is quite a feat to write characters with such nuance. In harnessing her storytelling facility to expose the flaws in the system with what is becoming trademark empathy, Laguna is an author proving the novel is a crucial document of the times.'

　—*The Australian*

'This book should be impossibly bleak, but Laguna has managed to imbue it with luminosity. This is a story about how to find your place in the world and how to accept what you have been given. *The Eye of the Sheep* will break your heart—a small price to pay to hear Jimmy's story.'

　—*Readings*

'. . . an extraordinary, haunting tale about love, anger and family. Adopting the sweet but manic voice of six-year-old boy, Jimmy Flick, Laguna cleverly navigates the tensions of a struggling working-class family in this surprising, heartbreaking and funny story.'

—*Canberra Weekly*

'By getting inside Jimmy's mind and showing what an amazing place it is, this book goes a long way towards explaining what a library of textbooks could not.'

—*Sydney Morning Herald*

'Jimmy is a tour de force of a character, brilliantly maintained . . . Laguna's great skill is in conveying contradictory human depths.'

—*Adelaide Advertiser*

'. . . [a] tender and delicate novel, rich with sympathy and understanding.'

—*Compulsive Reader*

'Sofie Laguna has perfected the voice of a child. *The Eye of the Sheep* is a dark tale told with perfection.'

—*Culture Street*

'If you liked *Room*, *The Lovely Bones* or *The Rosie Project*, you'll like this too. The main character is a young boy, Jimmy Flick, who has a unique (and unspecified) way of looking at things. It's such a joy to be presented with a character who thinks so differently and feels so authentic. Jimmy lives in a poor family where violence is never far from the surface and life is chaotic. This is compelling and arresting.'

—*Geelong Advertiser*

'Laguna has a way of beautifully illustrating the deepest of emotions, with Jimmy providing an alternative look at the world of domestic violence, love and family relations. Full of both happiness and heartbreak, this novel deals with elements of human nature in a deeply touching way.'

—*Weekend West*

'. . . truthful and beautiful.'

—*Newcastle Herald*

'A beautifully written novel, refreshingly raw, through the eyes of a child. I couldn't put it down.'
—*Launceston Examiner*

Praise for *One Foot Wrong*

'An extraordinary achievement . . . original and compelling . . . compels us to see our familiar world as new and intriguing—no small feat.'
—Jo Case, *Big Issue*

'. . . a book that intrigues and affects every essence of your humanity . . . a dark and terrible tale told in lyrical, poetic language and stark imagery.'
—*Australian Bookseller and Publisher*

'. . . intense, disturbing and hallucinatory.'
—Kerryn Goldsworthy, *Sydney Morning Herald*

'The language is pitch-perfect—it is the light in this dark tale . . . a haunting story of horror, but also of friendship and love . . . Despite the darkness of the subject matter, it is surprisingly uplifting, cathartic and affecting.'
—Louise Swinn, *The Age*

'. . . harrowing, beautifully written, insightful and absorbing . . . unique, forceful and absolutely hypnotic . . . Fresh, honest writing . . . makes this dark journey well worth taking.'
—Emily Maguire, *Canberra Times*

'An authentic voice, an evocation of childhood and memory that, for all its terrors, evokes the sublime, tragic moment when innocence submits to experience. Laguna creates a world and a character and a language that we become immersed within. That she does it with a subject matter of such destructive cruelty, that she does it with such rigour and power, is a testament to her craft, skill and maturity. This is the opposite of what the tabloids do: this is humane, passionate, true.'
—Christos Tsiolkas

Sofie Laguna's second novel for adults, *The Eye of the Sheep*—shortlisted for the Stella Prize—won the 2015 Miles Franklin Literary Award and was long-listed for the International IMPAC Dublin Literary Award. Her first novel for adults, *One Foot Wrong*, published throughout Europe, the US and the UK, was longlisted for the Miles Franklin Literary Award and shortlisted for the Prime Minister's Literary Award. Sofie's many books for young people have been published in the US, the UK and in translation throughout Europe and Asia. She has been shortlisted for the Queensland Premier's Award, and her books have been named Honour Books and Notable Books by the Children's Book Council of Australia. Sofie lives in Melbourne with her husband, illustrator Marc McBride, and their two sons.

SOFIE LAGUNA

THE CHOKE

ALLEN&UNWIN
SYDNEY • MELBOURNE • AUCKLAND • LONDON

First published in 2017

  This project has been assisted by the Australian
Government through the Australia Council,
its arts funding and advisory board.

Excerpt on pp. 113–14 taken from 'Eldorado' by Edgar Allan Poe, first published in 1849.

Allen & Unwin
83 Alexander Street
Crows Nest NSW 2065
Australia
Phone: (61 2) 8425 0100
Email: info@allenandunwin.com
Web: www.allenandunwin.com

Cataloguing-in-Publication details are available
from the National Library of Australia
www.trove.nla.gov.au

ISBN 978 1 76029 724 4

Set in 13.25/17 pt Adobe Jenson Pro by Bookhouse, Sydney
Printed and bound in Australia by Griffin Press

10 9 8 7 6 5 4 3 2 1

For Marc, with love and gratitude

In memory of Aileen

Sapere aude

Horace,
First Book of Letters

Part One

1.

Kirk turned his slingshot over in his hand. 'This thing is going to hurt, Justine.'

'Really hurt,' said Steve.

'Don't smile, or I'll aim it for the hole.'

I closed my mouth. Some of the teeth were taking a long time to grow through the gum.

Kirk pulled the elastic strap tight. 'You've got ten seconds. One . . . two . . . three . . . four . . . five . . .'

I took off through the trees as the numbers faded behind me.

I ran beside the river, sometimes looking ahead, sometimes at the currents. Soon I heard Kirk and Steve following. We kept the same distances between us, not trying to run away, not trying to catch up. We knew where the branches came low and close to our faces, where the roots crossed the path like rope and where the fallen trunks tried to block the way. Kirk, Steve and me moved through the jungle like Pop and Sandy running from the Japs. Pop never knew what the war was for. *Why a river of blood? Why so many boys? What was it flowed in the veins of those bastards?*

3

We ran and ran—they were not the enemy and I was not the prey. The river ran beside us, muddy and high, eating at the sides.

'Coming, Justine!' Kirk called.

One day I'd have a boat ready. A raft of branches I'd weave together with Pop's towrope. I'd hide it at the top of The Choke, in the trees that stood underwater.

I turned and saw Kirk closer behind me now. I ran faster. I felt a sting in the back of my knee.

'Got you!' Kirk shouted.

I turned and Kirk held up his slingshot. I kept running. I felt another sting on my leg. I screamed, and the galahs flew up out of the branches screeching and screaming at the same time as me. I turned again, and saw Kirk pick up another stone. I stopped, my face throbbing as I scraped up a handful of rocks and dirt. I ran at Kirk. 'No!' I shouted. 'No!' All the cockatoos shrieked and blasted from the branches in sprays of white. I threw my dirt and rocks at Kirk.

Kirk cried out, dropping his slingshot, hands to his eyes. I picked up another handful of rocks, as he stood spitting dirt, wiping it from his face. Then he turned and left the river trail, running through the trees to our hideouts. Steve followed and I was close behind.

They tore at the branches of my hideout. They pulled away my bark-and-leaf walls, my towel-and-branch roof, my chimney of twigs. I threw rocks and dirt at them, then I ran to Kirk's hideout and kicked at the top of the log. The log fell away, breaking into pieces. Kirk threw me on the ground and sat on me. I kicked and bucked, pushing up and down, twisting my head from side to side so that I saw the sky in pieces, dirt to sky dirt to sky dirt to sky.

Steve held the blade of his pocketknife to my face. 'Better close your mouth,' he said. I spat in his face.

'Ugh!' He wiped his cheek and I pulled my arm out from under Kirk, knocking the knife from Steve's hand. Steve tried to take hold of my ankles but I kicked my legs too fast for him to get a grip. Our faces were red and hot, our breath hard and fast as we fought and struggled against each other as if it was the same war Pop and Sandy fought. If you lost what was it flowed in your veins, for what reason?

Kirk pinned my arms under his knees; I could only wriggle like a worm under the weight of his body. I pushed and grunted against him.

'Enough,' said Kirk and suddenly, as fast as we started, we stopped. Kirk put his hands in the air. 'Smoko,' he said, climbing off and sitting beside me.

Steve let go of my ankles and looked for his knife in the leaves. The knife only had one small blade, eaten with rust, but Steve said Dad gave it to him. That the knife could kill. Steve carried it with him everywhere. I sat up and we shook dirt from our hair and faces and out from under our clothes. We pulled off our shoes and tipped out the stones. I lay beside Steve, his shoulder against mine.

Kirk stood, hands in his pockets, looking up. The red gums leaned towards each other, as if they wanted to touch, the same as the banks of the river at The Choke. Kirk, Steve and me were held by the trees and their branches in the shapes of heads, faces trapped inside, pressing to see through the bark. Our three worlds joined. Our mothers were different but we all had the same name—*Lee*.

Kirk walked into the triangle of our hideouts, where there was a ring of stones like the one around Pop's fire. Steve and me followed. Kirk sat and pulled a wad of White Ox and a crumpled cigarette paper from his pocket. Steve and me sat too, watching as Kirk licked the shiny edge of the paper and rolled the tobacco into a cigarette. Stray pieces of tobacco stuck out each end, like a cigarette for a scarecrow. Kirk pulled a box of matches from his pocket. The cigarette glowed orange and Kirk coughed. He blew out the smoke and it billowed around his face. 'Fuck,' he said, coughing into the smoke. He passed it to Steve, who closed his eyes when the smoke went down, then blew it straight into the air in a stream, as if he had always been smoking and was good at it.

I said, 'My turn.'

'You're too young,' said Kirk.

'No, I'm not.'

'You're only ten.'

'How come Steve is allowed?'

'He's eleven.'

'Yeah,' said Steve.

'And you're a girl.'

'I can still smoke.'

'No, you can't,' said Kirk. 'And don't tell Pop.'

I kicked at the dirt. But I didn't want to smoke.

Kirk and Steve passed the cigarette between them until it was so low it burned Kirk's fingers. 'Ouch!' He flicked it into the air, then stubbed it out in the dirt with his boot. I scraped more dirt over the top. 'Cigarette cemetery,' said Kirk.

We got up, walked down to the river and sat on the edge. We threw sticks as far as we could, then stones to sink the sticks. The Choke was where the river was at its thinnest, the banks like giant hands around a neck. After the rain the Murray couldn't hold, and it flooded, so the trees stood underwater. They stayed living until The Choke dried out and you could see the black water stains left behind on the trunks. You could see the cod moving across the river bottom, slow enough to spear.

We each picked up a stick and aimed. Kirk said, 'If we had Pop's Mauser we could shoot one and bring it home.'

'Cook it on Pop's fire,' I said.

'Yeah,' said Steve and Kirk.

'Eat it with egg,' I said.

Kirk aimed his stick at the water. '*Kapow*,' he said, jerking it back. 'Sorry, fish.'

Steve raised his stick and did the same. 'Sorry, kangaroo,' he said. '*Kapow*.'

'Sorry, Mr Fisherman!' I said and shot my stick.

Kirk and Steve laughed. We threw our guns out across the water and watched them fight the surface, then sink. Kirk said, 'How about we leave you here, Justine? We could tie you to a tree. We could winch your mouth open so an owl could make a nest.'

Steve said, 'Yeah, how about it?'

I said, 'Yeah, how about it?'

'Maybe next time,' said Kirk.

'Yeah, maybe next time,' I said.

Kirk looked at the sky. 'Better get back.' We walked to our hideouts. Kirk came over and helped pick up my biggest branches, propping them against the pole-tree. Steve threw bark across the branches and pulled the towel tight for the roof. He took his knife from his pocket and cut the living branches for my shelf and Kirk shaped the esky. From inside my hideout I saw the forest between the branches. While Kirk and Steve fixed their hideouts, I scraped up piles of rocks and dirt as ammunition.

Soon Kirk said, 'Come on. Pop will be waiting.' We stood and looked at our hideouts, at the ring of stones, at the trees and the sky. Then we walked slowly, away from the Murray, along the path back to Pop's Three.

2.

Pop's house stood at the top of three acres that he bought when he came back from the war. He got a job at the mills where he cut trees into sleepers for the railway. *I'd rather cut the bastards then lay 'em*, he said. When Pop was a prisoner in the war, the enemy made him lay a track between Burma and Siam for the Eastern Bullet. *We were the living dead*, Pop told the Isa Browns. *We were ghosts.* The house on Pop's Three was pale green, stained with a line of dirt that rose up and down like a wave around the fibro. It was if the house had once stood underwater, like the trees at The Choke.

When we went through the back gate Pop was sitting at his fire, smoking. He threw a small stick into the flames. 'Tea's in half an hour,' he said. He got to his feet and crossed the yard to the kitchen.

I never left Pop's Three after Donna split. It was me that split her. I was breech, waiting inside her on my knees. I thought that was the right way to come out. Pop and Dad drove Donna to the hospital. *Who comes out on their knees? Who comes into this world begging?* I heard Pop ask the chooks. *Poor bloody Donna.* The doctor and the nurse put their hands on Donna's stomach, trying to turn me, but I wouldn't turn. I thought it was the right way. The breech nearly killed her. Donna stayed with Dad and me for three years, in the house in Moama, but she was sewn up so badly the stitches couldn't hold; one by one they came apart, then when I was three years old she split for good. Pop asked Relle, Dad's first wife, to take me. She said, *Any kid but Donna's.* So I stayed with Pop.

It was Pop who found me at the bottom of the yard the night after my mother left. There was a barbecue. All the Worlleys and the Lees were there, drinking, listening to music. *Saw you were gone,* said Pop. *When I found you at the bottom of the yard you were cold as bloody ice. Christ knows where you were going.* I was looking for my mother. Was she at The Choke? Did she have a boat hiding in the trees? *That was the night you met the big man,* Pop would say. *You remember that, Jussy? The first night you met him, when he was Ethan Edwards?* Pop had taken me inside and sat beside me on the couch, holding my hand as John Wayne crossed the television on his horse, hunting down the Indian. 'So we'll find 'em in the end, I promise you. Just as sure as the turnin' of the earth.' *Only thing to stop you crying was the big man, Jussy.* I heard John Wayne as Ethan Edwards blasting the enemy. Pop said, *You get 'em, big man,* and then I slept. Every time I woke, Pop and the big man were there; Pop holding my hand while the big man cracked his whip at the Comanches.

Dad said my mother got on a train to Lismore to see her sister. He said she kicked up a stink because she didn't want to do what a wife signed up for. When Pop asked the sister, the sister said Donna never got off the train and she didn't blame her. If someone doesn't want to be found, there are places they can hide; they can make a shelter in the trees, from branches, from rocks and things people don't want. Tyres, milk crates, piles of bricks. They can use camouflage; they can hide in old cars, in skips, they can make a house from a couch or two doors. Dad said he had an idea where Donna was, a bloody good idea, but Pop said, *Leave it alone, Ray. Donna is gone.*

———

Kirk and Steve and me and Pop sat around Pop's fire with plates of sausages and fried eggs on our knees. Corn and peas rolled to the edges. The coals in the fire glowed orange. Everything on our plates was sticky with yolk and sauce. Pop said, 'Eat the bloody peas.' We stole looks at each other and let the peas fall to the ground, kicking dirt over the top. Pea cemetery. Beyond the circle of light, trees moved in the wind and crickets called to each other. Pop's fire held us together, burning with invisible flames that wrapped around us like arms.

Down at The Choke the river pushed its way between the banks. The water knew the way it wanted to go. Past our hideouts, past our ring of stones, past the red gums leaning close enough to touch—it flowed forward all the way to the sea.

3.

After I had taken the dinner plates to the sink, the telephone rang, its sound cutting the quiet. Kirk sat up straighter in his chair. Steve turned towards the house. Pop grumbled as he got to his feet. 'Al-bloody-right,' he said as he walked slowly back to the kitchen—Pop had to keep his gut in one straight line or he woke the bug. The telephone kept ringing. Kirk and Steve and me waited to see if it was Dad. 'Right,' said Pop. 'Where are you? When do you . . . Yeah, son . . . Reckon? Yeah . . . Yeah . . . How's she running? Check the fanbelt? You looking at three hundred mile you want to know it's tight . . . Yeah, son, see you Friday.'

Kirk said, 'It's Dad.'

'What day is it?' I asked.

'Tuesday,' said Kirk.

Dad hadn't been home since July and now it was nearly the Christmas concert. I had lost my two top and bottom teeth since he last saw me, and there were no new ones at the top yet. I was the last one in my class. If I showed my teeth there was a hole. I stuck my tongue in and out of the gap, feeling the sides.

Steve took out his pocketknife and pulled out the blade. He turned it in his hands before closing it and putting it back in his pocket. There was only one blade, smaller than the one Pop used to cut my fingernails. Relle said it used to be Dad's but Dad said bullshit. Relle said, *It was yours, Ray, don't you remember?* and Dad said, *I'd remember a knife as useless as that.*

Pop came out with a can of beer. He sat down on his chair and pulled back the ring. The can hissed as if a small snake had escaped. He said, 'Your old man's coming home.'

Your old man's coming home. When Pop spoke the words I felt our worlds—Kirk's and Steve's and mine—shrink and separate. The mother half was different. Ray had left one for the other. Relle found Ray and Donna in the truck. Donna was in Relle's seat, with her arm on the handle where Relle's arm went, her feet up on the dash where Relle's feet used to go. Relle knew what Donna and Dad had been doing before she found them, as if her eyes had stolen away, climbed through the window into the cabin, hidden behind the mirror and seen everything that happened, then went back and told the head. I was eating Weet-Bix at the kids' table not long after I moved to Pop's, when I heard Pop and Dad talking.

You should have been more careful, Ray.

Accidents happen.

Yeah, and now I'm stuck with your bloody accident.

The table was so low it kept me at the height of their knees. If they didn't look down they forgot I was there.

I can take her.

Not where you go, son.

Where do you think I go?

I know where you go.

Where's that?

Leave it alone.

Just saying, I can take her.

Drop it, Ray.

Where would he take me? Where would we go? Nobody knew exactly where Ray went or what he did.

Behind us, the back-house stood dark and locked. The flames of Pop's fire and the lights from the kitchen didn't reach far enough to show it, but you could see its outline. It was another sort of black. The back-house was where Ray lived when he was home. The only thing missing was a shower. Ray filled up a bucket with warm water from the tap at Pop's sink, then he hung it over a pipe with a funnel. When Ray was away the back-house was locked, the curtains closed. If you looked in the window you saw your own reflection. After the phone call the back-house seemed to grow bigger, as if Ray was pressing out the walls from the inside, reminding us, like the heads inside the red gums.

———

After dinner Relle came by to pick up Kirk and Steve. 'Ray's on the way,' said Pop. Relle didn't look at me. She never had. Not once. *Any kid but Donna's.* She couldn't identify me, as if I was an accident that hadn't happened. I felt the hole in my mouth with my tongue. Who is born on their knees? Who doesn't know the right way out?

Relle had black hair in a ponytail and her eyes were narrow like Steve's—she kept the edges tight. Every day she drew dark green lines around them. 'Oh yeah?' she said. Her eyes gleamed. 'When's that?'

'Friday,' said Pop.

'He's going to teach me how to shoot,' said Kirk.

'No, he's not,' said Pop.

'He said he would.'

'No, he didn't.'

'Danny's uncle is going to show us if Dad doesn't. When he gets back from Gympie.'

'Bloody Gympie,' said Pop. 'Want a beer, Relle?'

'No, Dean's at home. And I'm on the early shift tomorrow.' Relle worked at the bakery in Nullabri. She started at four thirty in the morning when it was still dark. Just before the bakery opened she painted all the tops of the donuts with the flavours. But she never ate a single donut. The donuts could sit in shining rows—pineapple, lime, chocolate, strawberry—and she didn't care. She didn't even need a taste.

Kirk said, 'Damn.' Dean was Relle's new boyfriend.

'We got to go, boys,' said Relle, jangling her keys. 'Get in the car.'

'Can we stay here?' said Kirk.

'No.'

'Why not?'

'Because there's shit to do at home. Dean wants you to help him move the rubbish from down the side.' Kirk and Steve groaned. 'Get a move on,' said Relle. 'I want to pick up dinner for Dean on the way.' The boys got up and followed Relle through the house. They wanted to stay the night at Pop's, closer to where Dad would be coming to, closer to where he would park his truck, closer to where he would sleep and drink and be.

⌒

After they left I went down the back and checked on the chooks. I hooked my fingers through the wire of the run, leaned in close and saw the shadows of the girls sleeping on the roosting bars. Cockyboy was keeping guard at the top. He made a small warning cluck in his throat. I breathed in and smelled them there, the Isa Browns alive behind the wire, heads turned into the warmth of their feathers.

I went back inside, sat on my bed and looked through *Road and Track*. I saw a white Ford F100 with the same long aerial as Dad's, the same bull bar. I cut down one side, and along the bottom. Now I was ten I cut the edges smooth and straight. I'd been doing cut-outs since I moved to Pop's. I had to hide the good ones; if he needed paper to light the fire he came to my room. I got off the bed and put the truck on top of the pile in my cupboard. Dad would be home on Friday. It wasn't enough time for the teeth to break through the gums. I pushed my tongue in and out of the hole. Kirk said, *You could stick Brian Chisholm's torch in the hole and go to work in the mines. You could get paid.*

Friday was three more days. There wasn't time.

4.

The next morning the sun came in through my window, yellow and bright. My room was the only one at the front of the house; I was the eyes of Pop's Three, and could see the end of the road. I looked in my shelf and found my school skirt and a t-shirt. I got dressed and went into the kitchen. Pop was making his tea, his dressing-gown hanging loose around him. I poured Rice Bubbles into a bowl. The radio played the news. Pop rolled himself a White Ox. 'Bloody Vietnam. It's 1971, for Christ's sake, and we're still getting them out . . .' He sighed and shook his head at the radio. 'Jesus, Lizzy . . .' Lizzy was his wife; she died in Ballarat Hospital in 1952. That was nineteen years ago, but for Pop it was only yesterday.

The smoke from Pop's cigarette and the steam from the tea curled around each other, searching for an exit. Pop took another suck, and looked at his White Ox. 'The kindest animal,' he said.

I said, 'Pop, what day is it?'

He took a sip from his tea. 'Wednesday.'

'And tomorrow is Thursday,' I said. 'Then it's Friday.'

'Well done, Justine,' he said. 'I knew you went to school for a reason.'

After breakfast Pop rolled another smoke and passed me the egg basket. The Isa Browns were waiting in the run. Pop stood at the open gate as Cockyboy stepped out first, looking from side to side, his red comb wobbling. There were long claws on the backs of his legs, like hooks. 'Hey, Cockyboy? You taking care of the ladies?' said Pop. The girls came next. 'Hello, ladies; morning, girls; here, chook chook chook.' The White Ox on Pop's lip bobbed up and down, like a tiny waving arm.

Pop passed me the old water, full of seed shells and dirt. I tipped it out and carried the dish to the tap. I filled the dish with clean water and brought it back to the run. Then I took the egg basket to the chook boxes. The eggs were warm and smooth in my hands.

'How many?' Pop asked me.

'Five,' I said.

One time a hen wouldn't move out of the box. 'Nesting,' said Pop. 'Leave her alone.' When at last she left the box to peck for seeds I looked in her nest. There were six eggs sitting in the straw. I heard the babies tapping on the shells from inside, squeaking and chirping, as if they were calling for help. I picked up one of the eggs and cracked open the shell with my fingers, but the chicken inside wasn't ready. I could see right through its skin to its bones. Its eyes were closed and its neck was loose. It wasn't big enough. I pushed the chicken back in and turned the egg around so Pop wouldn't see the hole I'd made, then I put it back into the nest. But a fly must have flown into the nest and found the hole. Five chickens hatched from the eggs and one didn't hatch at all. When Pop turned over the last egg he found the baby chicken with a maggot in its guts. Pop's face turned red. He said, *Leave my chickens alone, Justine.*

I carried the basket of eggs up to the kitchen, then I put my empty schoolbag on my back. 'See you, Pop,' I called, but he'd gone into the chook house. I could hear him talking as he cleaned the run. *Natural! Hell! Jesus! Lizzy! Right!* Pop talked to the chooks and the radio and the television and the big man, he talked to Cockyboy, to the fire and the beer cans and his White Ox. And he talked to Lizzy. Lots of the words were just sounds, spoken under his breath, so I couldn't tell one word from another. Then a word would be spoken loud. *Fault! Sandy! Know! Blood!* I didn't know where the words began, what came before and what came after. It was like trying to read; I could only guess.

I walked along the Henley Trail to the bus stop, stepping over the puddles that were there, even in summer. In Yolamundi the grass and the roads and the bush were always damp and shining with the Murray. It lay in long shallow puddles under the trees, it darkened the roads and filled the potholes. The red gums knew how to grow in the river. They didn't care how deep it got, how wide, how fast it flowed, they dug in and held on and kept growing.

As I walked I sang carols for the concert. *I'm dreaming of a white Christmas, just like the ones I used to know.* My school shoes pinched my toes at the top of every step. *Where the treetops glisten and children listen.* The concert wasn't far away now. *May all your Christmases be white!* Before the fall-out with the Worlleys I never walked the trail alone. I would cut across the paddock to the Worlleys' farm, and walk along Dray Road with whichever of the Worlleys was going to school that day. There were six cousins. One was a girl called Kathy and the other five were boys and some were brothers. Kathy wasn't a cousin; she was a sister. Kathy was small with one eye that looked far into the distance.

Jamie, the oldest Worlley, used to walk out in front as if he was Cockyboy and we were the chooks. Before the fall-out we would be together on the school bus. The cousins made a lot of noise. Jamie always sat in the middle of the back seat; he stretched out his arms on both sides and said, 'Ah, all mine.' Nobody knew if I was a Worlley or a Lee. We were all together.

The Worlley farm had three caravans in a circle, like a town. Geese guarded the circle, hissing and biting if a car drove in. They watched over Mother Margy's pansies, and the wrecked cars, and the piles of planks and the calves that were born too soon. The geese had their own island in the middle of the Worlley dam. The foxes tried to swim across but the geese made a line, joining their wings one to the other, hissing and honking. There was a rusted car with no windows coming out of the dam. Uncle Ian said, *That's where you end up if you drink and smoke pot at the same time*, and Dad said, *As long as you had fun on the way down*.

Before the fall-out, when we were friends with the Worlleys, Pop and me and Kirk and Steve went to the Worlley farm for barbecues. One day Pop found a long piece of yellow plastic at the scrap yard. He rolled it up and took it under his arm back to the Worlleys. Pop and Uncle Ian lined bricks across the top of the plastic and laid it out so the plastic ran down the hill. 'Turn on the bloody hose!' Pop called out to Uncle Ian.

We were all there, waiting for the water to come from the hose: Jacky and Lachie and Kathy and Jamie and Tyler and Ee Worlley and some more of their cousins from Wodonga, and Steve and Kirk and Kirk's mate Danny and me. Water came blasting from the hose and Pop pointed it at the plastic. The kids screamed and shouted.

Jamie Worlley went first. Shouting as he slid, both hands in the air. Then we all went down; we went down alone and we went down together, screaming and laughing as we slid. Pop and Uncle Ian stood on the sides shouting, 'Go, you beauty, go!' The Worlley farm was so full of Worlleys and Lees and cousins and friends it felt like the whole town was there. We belonged together.

Jamie went into the caravans and came out with bottles of shampoo and detergent. 'Don't tell Mum,' he said. He squirted the bottles over the yellow plastic slide then he turned the hose on as hard as it would go. Bubbles rose up in clouds. Jamie shouted, 'I am the bubble man! Watch me fly!' He slid down on his stomach, his arms out wide, and the bubbles covered him and flew up around his head and into the sky. Then the rest of the cousins and the brothers and the sister and me slid through the sweet-smelling bubbles.

Back then, two years ago, Jamie was already fourteen. He took off his t-shirt and I saw muscles like water currents on his shoulders and chest. There was a long red scar down the middle of his back that that was raised at the sides. When he saw me looking he said, 'Somebody dug it.' Then he said, 'Nah, it was from a knife.' Then he said, 'The truth is it was from a dogfight.' All the cousins wanted to touch the scar but he said, 'Justine first.' The cousins made a line behind me. Jamie said, 'Go on, Justine, touch it.' I stared at the scar. Jamie said, 'Go on, it won't bite.' The scar still looked sore, as if the dogfight wasn't long ago. He said to me, 'Justine, you'll be the first person to touch it.' The scar was long and thin and red down his back. Jamie looked over his shoulder at me. He said, 'Go on.' He stepped back, so we were closer and I reached out and put my fingers on the scar and it did bite me! It leaped from his back and bit my fingers and I jumped away and screamed. Jamie laughed and then all the kids reached for it with their bubble hands, touching it quickly then jumping away when the scar tried to bite.

Every day that summer we went over to the Worlleys. The uncles had beer for Pop, and Mother Margy gave Pop food. *Eat, you skinny bastard,* she said. Pop ate up the steaks and the chops, the potatoes and bacon and bread and corn. He took sips of beer between bites and raised his glass to the uncles and his smile opened his face so I could see inside where the Japs got him.

On the night of the fall-out we were all sitting in the middle of the Worlley caravans, by the fire. Only Ray was missing; he hadn't been home for a long time. Pop said it would be any day now, that he was finishing up a job in the Territory and he'd be back in time for the Yolamundi muster.

'He never makes the fucken muster,' said Ian Worlley. 'Ray knows better.' When it was time for the Yolamundi muster the forest filled with cows charging in every direction, their bellowing as loud as the branches that crashed and broke around them. The men charged through the trees on their horses, rounding the cattle up to the yards where they were branded and cut and drenched. The kids hung off the fences and shouted 'Giddup there, giddup there!' as the cattle ran into the crush.

Uncle Ian drank from his bottle then he spread his legs apart as if there was a horse between them. 'Remember the last one?

Big bloody bulls,' he said. 'Must have been five hundred head, and every one of them white.' He held out his bottle. 'Yah, yah, get up there, you white bastards!' He tipped back the bottle and opened his mouth. The men had been drinking from cans all day, while the kids played, but when it turned to night they drank from big bottles.

'Jesus,' said Belinda, shaking her head.

Uncle Ian used a pretend whip, cracking it high over the heads of the bulls. 'Every one was white, but it made no difference, they were on the way to the same place.' He laughed and drank. 'The same fucken place.' He picked up a tyre that Belinda's baby used as a seat and threw it into the fire.

'Jesus, Ian!' said Belinda.

'What did you do that for?' asked Mother Margy.

'I like the smoke,' said Uncle Ian.

'Fool,' said Pop.

'What did you call me?' Uncle Ian said to Pop.

'A fool,' said Pop.

'A fool?' said Uncle Ian.

'That's right. A fool who owes me money.'

'Tight bastard,' Uncle Ian said.

'You owe me money, Ian. I found the bloody tanks. I helped you get them into the ground. Now you have to pay me for them.'

Uncle Ian was on his feet. 'What are you talking about?'

Mother Margy said, 'Settle down, Ian. Have something to eat.'

'Don't you tell me to settle down. You're her mother, not mine.' He held his bottle out to Belinda.

'Shut up, Ian,' said Belinda.

'You owe me money, Ian,' said Pop.

Uncle Ian said, 'The Japs really did a number on you, didn't they, Bob?'

'What do you know about the Japs?' Pop spat.

'I know enough.'

'You weren't bloody there. You know nothing. Bloody nothing!'

'I know the Japs took your balls, old man,' said Uncle Ian.

Pop lunged at him across the fire, his hands like a rabbit trap around Uncle Ian's neck. Uncle Ian staggered back. He pulled Pop off him then he punched him in the face. Pop fell to the ground. Kirk and Steve tried to hit Uncle Ian in the guts. Steve screamed, 'Get off him! Leave him alone!' Then Lachie and Jay hit Kirk and Steve. They were on the ground, their arms and legs thrashing in the dirt. I couldn't tell who was Worlley and who was Lee.

Belinda and Mother Margy rushed to Pop, and Margy put his head in her lap. There was blood on her skirt and hands. Belinda screamed up at Uncle Ian to fuck off.

Pop was groaning.

Belinda held the cloth to his forehead and said, 'You're a fucking idiot, Ian!'

Mother Margy said, 'Kirk, take Steve and Justine and go home.'

'What about Pop?' said Kirk.

'I'll take care of your pop,' said Mother Margy. She unhooked Pop's keys from his belt and passed them to Kirk. 'He'll be home by morning.'

———

Pop's keys clinked in Kirk's pocket as we walked across the Worlley paddocks in the dark. It was cold in our faces and under our clothes. 'Will Pop be alright?' I asked Kirk. We had never seen anyone hit our Pop before or talk to him about the Japs. Only he talked about the Japs. They belonged to him.

Burma and the war in 1940 and the tracks that led to Siam belonged to him.

'I'm going to shoot Uncle Ian,' said Kirk.

'Me too,' said Steve.

We'd always been the Worlleys and the Lees; it was other people we wanted to shoot—not each other. My teeth chattered with the cold. I searched the whole sky from one end to the other as we walked but there wasn't a single star. Only Kathy could see the stars, with her other eye.

It was even colder inside Pop's house then outside. We turned on the lights and stood blinking at each other in the kitchen. Kirk said, 'I'm going to get the Mauser.'

'How?' I asked. Pop kept the Mauser in the gun cupboard; it was always locked. He never let us near it.

Kirk dangled Pop's keys in front of Steve and me. 'How do you think?'

We followed Kirk to the door at the top of the stairs. The stairs only led to the gun cupboard. Pop built it when he first moved in. *A bed for Mrs Mauser*, he said. Kirk pulled the door to the stairs open. The stairs going down were so dark you couldn't see the bottom. Steve took my hand and held it tight. Kirk stepped through the door and Steve and me followed. We hadn't been down before; Pop didn't let us. *I catch you kids anywhere near the gun cupboard and there'll be trouble. You understand?*

Every step it seemed to get colder. The only thing warm was Steve's hand in mine. We didn't talk. We stayed close, as if hearing each other's breath and feeling the heat from each other's skin would keep us safe. At last we came to the bottom.

'Fuck,' said Kirk. I heard his hands brush the wall.

'What?' Steve asked.

'The cupboard—it's too high,' said Kirk. 'We can't reach it.'

'Hook your hands together and I can climb up,' I whispered. 'Then I'll put the key in.'

'Good idea,' said Kirk. 'You take the keys, Steve.' I put my hand on his shoulder and my knee in the cup of his hands. We leaned against the wall. 'When I count to three,' Kirk said. 'One . . . two . . . three.' He pushed me up and I took hold of the narrow cupboard.

'Pass me the keys,' I whispered.

Steve passed the keys up to me. I had to let go of the cupboard with one hand to take them. 'Which one is it?' I asked.

'I don't know. Not the big one,' said Kirk, his voice breathy and strained from holding me. 'Not the one for the truck.'

I felt for the smaller keys and then I felt the gun cupboard for where the lock was. I stuck in the smallest key but the lock didn't turn. And then I dropped the keys.

'Ouch!' said Kirk, letting me go. I came down on top of him. Steve started laughing and then I did, and then Kirk did. Our bodies shook with laughter harder and faster than they shook with the cold. I felt my brothers against me, their bodies warm and laughing in the darkness.

When we were quiet, Kirk said, 'Try again.'

We got up, our bodies looser and warmer. Kirk hooked his hands and I put in my knee and Steve pushed me up too, his hands under my bum. We worked together; this time we knew what we needed to do. Steve passed me the keys and I found one that wasn't as small as the one before, with sharp edges, and I stuck it into the lock, turned it and the door of the gun cupboard opened.

'Take the keys,' I said to Steve, passing them down.

'Are the guns there?' Kirk asked.

Pop kept two brother-pistols with the Mauser. *Company for Mrs Mauser*, Pop told the Isa Browns. *Those pistols never bloody miss. If I had them in my hands in Burma it would have been a different bloody story.* I felt for the guns inside the cupboard. Pop never even let us open the door to the stairs. *You keep clear of my guns. I catch you bastards anywhere near that cupboard and you'll know about it.* I felt something long and cold and metal.

'Is it the Mauser?' Kirk asked.

'Yeah,' I told him.

'Get it,' he said.

As I lifted the gun out of the cupboard, something hard clattered across the ground, raining down on Kirk and Steve.

'Fuck,' said Kirk. 'Bullets.' The Mauser was heavy in my arms as Kirk helped me down.

'Pop'll kill us,' I whispered.

'Pop's not here,' said Kirk. 'You and Steve pick up the bullets. Give me the gun.' Me and Steve got on our hands and knees and scraped up the bullets, stuffing them in our pockets. Kirk said, 'Let's get out of here.'

We followed Kirk upstairs into the living room. Cold came off the windows in waves. Outside the night was black. Kirk put the Mauser on the coffee table and we sat on the floor around it. None of us knew how to load it or shoot it. Pop never showed us. He didn't want Dad showing us either. We had only ever seen it when Pop took it out to clean it. Pop hovered over it like it was a baby he didn't want us to hold.

We touched the trigger and the black handle and the barrel. Kirk picked it up and aimed it at the window. He made the Mauser jump as if a bullet had shot out of the end. '*Kapow.* Sorry, Uncle Ian.'

'Gotcha, Uncle Ian,' said Steve.

We took the bullets out of our pockets and rolled them across the table. They were shiny with sharp heads to pierce the skin. The Mauser held us to it and to each other, as if it was a magnet and we were the metal. We sat a long time, leaning back on our hands when we didn't need to touch it anymore. When we heard a noise we didn't care, we had the Mauser, we could shoot that noise and we could shoot the bastard that made it.

—

It was our first night in the house without Pop. Kirk helped me pull my mattress into the boys' room and put it between their beds. He laid the Mauser beside me, its butt on my pillow. 'She can sleep with you,' he said. I pulled my blankets over me and the gun. Kirk hung his hand down so he could touch it in the night.

Early in the morning, when the light was still grey, I opened my eyes and Kirk was holding the gun. 'Putting it back,' he whispered.

'Don't forget a chair.'

—

Mother Margy dropped Pop home in the Dodge later that morning. 'Took him to the hospital in Echuca,' she said, when I came out the front.

I said, 'Are you okay, Pop?' There was a row of black stitches on his forehead.

He said, 'Fucken money.'

'Forget it, Robert,' said Margy. 'It was the booze talking.'

'Bullshit. It was all Ian.'

'Give it time.'

'Fuck time,' said Pop.

Mother Margy got back in the Dodge, shaking her head. She drove away and Pop went inside and rolled a White Ox. 'It's always fucken money,' he said, putting a match to his cigarette. His skin was puffed around his eyes, and he looked pale. There was blood crusted under the line of black stitches. 'That's it, Justine. You don't go there again. Same goes for your brothers. The prick owes me.' He sucked back on his smoke. When Pop spoke to me, it was the same as when Dad did. The words were there, but it was as if they were speaking to themselves. I was just an excuse.

———

That was two years ago. Now the Worlleys and the Lees were different sides of a war, like the one Pop fought in 1940. *Me and Sandy against the bloody monkeys. They weren't made of the same stuff; God knows what flowed in their veins, but it wasn't blood.* Now I walked the Henley Trail alone.

5.

I could see the forest on one side all the way to the bus stop as I walked. Down there, through the bulging red gums, was The Choke, and my hideout. *Come all ye faithful*, I sang. A cockatoo screeched and I raised my pistol. *Crack!* Down came the bird. *Joyful and triumphant . . . Crackcrackcrack!* Down came a tree and a cloud and the sun.

When I got to the rock that Pop put by the side of the trail to show me where to stop, I gave it a kick. I stuck my tongue in and out of the gap in my teeth and looked down the road. There would probably be Worlleys on the bus. Before the fall-out, all of us kids used to sit together. Now the Worlleys left me alone on the bus, as if I was invisible.

When I saw the bus coming I stepped closer to the edge of the road. The bus slowed down and drew in, mud sloshing around the wheels and splattering the sides. The Worlleys looked away when I stepped between the two rows of seats. They never knew if Dad was home; it was safer to leave me alone. They knew about Pop's Mauser too; they'd seen him cleaning it. They'd heard him talk about the brother-pistols and how far they could shoot, how it only took one bullet.

I kept my eyes down and chose a seat at the front as the bus turned out of the Henley Trail into Yolamundi Road. The sun was warm through the glass. I heard the Worlley cousins talking and laughing at the back, but soon a lot of other kids came on at the different stops, and they were between me and the Worlleys, and I couldn't hear them anymore. I pressed my nose to the window. One more day and Dad would be home. I put my tongue in the gap—in out in out in out, even if it hurt.

6.

Soon the bus arrived at the school. I stepped down without looking behind me and walked up the path. Nullabri Primary School had yellow play squares, a green patch for the monkey bars at the front, and an oval at the back with bushes for a fence. Lots of kids were coming in through the gates. Dawn and Noreena leaned on the monkey bars. Noreena had long hair with a green headband to match the uniform and she was the main friend.

'Hi, Justine,' said Dawn.

'Hi,' I said.

Noreena said, 'Did you brush your hair this morning, Justine?'

I pulled at the knots at the back of my head. 'Yeah,' I said. The bell rang and we walked up to Mrs Turning's classroom.

———

Mrs Turning stood at the front, waiting for us to sit at our desks. I sat next to Kathy Worlley. She looked away.

'Good morning, class,' said Mrs Turning.

'Good morning, Mrs Turning,' everybody answered.

'I hope you have all completed your homework because we are going to begin with spelling practice.' Mrs Turning came from England; she showed us on the map with the class pointer. *A great distance from here and different in every way!* 'Please take out your workbooks,' she said.

Kathy and me took our books out from under the desk.

'We shall begin with the A list and work our way through. Please choose a clean page to begin.'

Everybody was quiet for Mrs Turning. She had been at the school since the start. Her hair was grey and pulled back into a tight ball at the bottom of her neck. I put my pencil to the page and pressed. Mrs Turning said, 'Spell *animal*, please, class. *Animal.*'

Kathy started to write. I pressed my pencil into the page. I saw letters backwards. S came before Q, T came before D, E came before B. When I started at Nullabri Primary my teacher was Mrs Bettsbower. When Mrs Bettsbower said, 'Who wants to go first?' I put up my hand. Mrs Bettsbower said, 'Justine, can you find the word *girl* in the box?' I got up from the floor and went to the box in front of the class, but I couldn't find the word *girl*. Mrs Bettsbower said, 'Justine, open your eyes.' But my eyes were open, and I was looking. Where was it? Mrs Bettsbower said, 'What does *girl* begin with, Justine? Think. Can you find the word that begins with *g*?' I looked and looked but I couldn't see a single word that began with *g*. I saw other words: *Ma. Tac. Yob. I. Nus.* But there was no *girl*. Mrs Bettsbower frowned. She said, 'Sit back down, Justine.' I felt a hot wave flush over my face as I went back to my place on the floor. I looked at my feet. Mrs Bettsbower said the word was there, in front of my eyes, but I couldn't find it. I didn't put up my hand after that.

It was because I was born back to front. My words were breech, like me. Every year finished and I never caught up.

Anything that had a word, or numbers in a row, I had to guess. I watched other kids for clues. I stood back in the line, I noticed the way the pencil moved, I heard the start of an answer and sometimes that was enough for me to know how to finish. But not always.

I looked at Kathy's paper. She drew the line going around, and then the straight line going up, like a back for the circle. I did the same. I waited for the next letter and I did the same line going down, then back up.

'Justine!' said Mrs Turning. My pencil jumped across the page. 'Are you looking at Kathy's page?'

I couldn't speak. I stared at the leg of the desk.

'Are you? Can you answer me, Justine?'

But I couldn't.

'Is that what you are doing? Is it?' Mrs Turning pressed her lips tight, waiting for me to answer. 'Do you know what looking at somebody else's work is called, Justine? Let me tell you: it's called cheating. Get up and go and sit beside Michael Hooper.'

I stayed where I was; I always sat next to Kathy.

'Justine? Can you hear me, or must we have our ears checked? *Move!*'

I turned to look at Michael Hooper. His head rolled on his neck like a flower too heavy for its stem. His chin was wet; there was a bib around his neck. His crutches leaned against his desk. Nobody had ever sat beside him.

'Didn't you hear me, Justine? I said get up and sit next to Michael.'

Everyone was quiet. Nobody went near Michael. If he tried to speak he groaned.

'Justine!' Mrs Turning said. 'Move!'

I got up, pushing back my chair.

'Take your workbook and pencils with you. You can stay next to Michael for the rest of the term.'

I walked slowly to Michael's desk. I put my workbook on the table beside him and sat down. He tried to turn his head to look at me, his eyes rolled. 'Read to your husband,' whispered Matt Dunning. Brian Lawson snorted.

Mrs Turning said, 'Class! Attention, please. Spell *ancestor.*'

I sat on the furthest edge of the chair. I looked towards the window. Down at The Choke the banks would press in, but the water would keep flowing; it couldn't be stopped. I heard Michael breathing as I put my pencil to the page. He was trying to write, his arms shaking, his legs jerking. I drew lines going up and down, over and over.

Soon it was free reading, with a no-talking rule. I chose a book with a truck on the cover. The man in the mobile library said, *Every book contains a dream.* The truck had silver fenders and four lights. It had too many wheels to count. There was an aerial out the top so the driver could hear the news of the road. I traced my finger over the cover. I wished I could drive the truck wherever I wanted to go. At night I would pull over on the side of the road and play, 'You're My Best Friend' by Don Williams. If I woke in the night the song would still be playing. 'You're My Best Friend, You're My Best Friend,' over and over.

Before I opened the book, I closed my eyes. *I wish.* I wanted the letters to make words I could understand. I wanted to find out where the truck was going, how long until it got there, what it was carrying, what the driver put in his cabin. But when I opened the book the words didn't make any sense. What was *ngis?* What was *leewh?* What was *ilesm?*

⌒

I sat beside Noreena and Dawn in the lunchtime block. Noreena said to me, 'Does Michael smell?'

I shrugged. I looked across the yard and saw him sitting at the benches, his crutches leaning against the table.

'His brain isn't the right size,' said Dawn. 'He didn't get enough oxygen.' Her mother was a nurse on the night shift at Echuca.

'I can't believe you have to sit next to him, Justine,' said Noreena, wrinkling her nose.

'At least he doesn't always come to school,' said Dawn, unwrapping her sandwich. 'Maybe tomorrow you'll have the desk to yourself. Sometimes he has to go to hospital.'

'What for?' Noreena asked.

'They train him to stop shaking. He gets tied to a railing and every time he shakes he loses a point. Do you want my banana, Justine?'

'Yes,' I said. My stomach growled.

She said, 'Be a gorilla.'

I got on my feet and dropped my arms so my hands hung low to the ground. I stuck out my chin.

Noreena said, 'Go, Justine!'

'Ooh-oooh-oooh!' I was a gorilla. 'Oooh-oooh-oooh!'

Dawn and Noreena leaned back with their mouths open, laughing like the black lorikeets over Pop's Three; *crackcrack!* and down they came with Mrs Mauser.

'Here,' said Dawn. She gave me her banana.

Over at the benches Michael sat by himself, shaking and jerking as he looked down at a book open in front of him. His body was always moving, like someone you couldn't see was pulling the strings.

The afternoon was carol practice with Sabine. Sabine wore a scarf that trailed over her shoulder like a wing. You could see the sunlight through the scarf. She smelled of soap and her hair was loose around her face. Sabine came close to us when we were singing, to hear if we should be in the high group or the low. When Sabine came near I stopped singing. I breathed in her smell of soap, from her neck the colour of cream. She said, *Articulate!* She sang, *Deck the halls with boughs of holly, fa la la la la!* I heard Michael groaning beside me. When he sang his face stretched, his mouth wide as if there was another Michael Hooper on the inside, trying to come out.

———

At the end of the day I walked out of school with Dawn and Noreena.

'Let's go to the bakery before the bus comes,' Noreena said.

'I'm going to get a raspberry crown,' said Dawn.

'I'm going to get a strawberry tart,' said Noreena.

Dawn and Noreena sang carols as we walked down the street. *The holly and the ivy, when they are both full grown, of all the trees that are in the wood, the holly bears the crown.*

A bell rang when Noreena pushed open the bakery door. The smell of bread and pies and sausage rolls made my mouth water. I looked into the kitchen and saw Relle at the ovens. She wore a white cap over her dark ponytail. When I came in she looked away.

Mrs Mulvaney was behind the counter. 'Hello, girls,' she said, smiling.

I looked at the shelves behind the glass. There was rocky road with cherries. Dawn and Noreena jangled money in their pockets. They always bought something. Sometimes Dawn gave me the last bite.

'What would you like, ladies?' said Mrs Mulvaney. Her chest was a warm mountain with the red-and-white stripes of her apron rolling over the top; her cheeks were pink. She was new—it used to be Mrs Reeves. 'What takes your fancy?'

Dawn chose a raspberry crown cupcake and Noreena chose a strawberry jam tart. We had turned to leave when Mrs Mulvaney said, 'Well, miss, what about you?'

I turned hot. Dawn and Noreena looked at me; they knew I had no money, but Mrs Mulvaney was new in the bakery and didn't know. She used to work at the stock and feed where Pop bought his egg grit; I came with him sometimes and waited while he spoke to the boss. She said, 'Come on, Justine, wouldn't you like a custard tart?' She pointed to the tray and smiled. 'I do battle with them from the minute I get here.' The custard tarts sat in rows and above them were peach slices in the shape of a heart.

Dawn stepped forward as if she was sharing a secret with Mrs Mulvaney. 'She has no money.'

Mrs Mulvaney frowned, then she leaned over the counter, her chest broad and full against the glass. 'Tell you what, Justine,' she said. 'You choose something that you'd like and I'll cover it for you, hey? I'm a millionaire this week.'

I looked up from my feet into her warm pink face and she said, 'Go on, what would you like?'

I swallowed. I didn't know what to do. I looked up and down the rows as my stomach burned and growled. There were too many to choose: rocky road, lamingtons, hedgehogs. I'd looked at them and wanted them too many times. Dawn and Noreena were watching me, waiting. Relle could see me from the back, holding up the line. *Any kid but Donna's.* The whole shop was waiting.

Then Mrs Mulvaney said, 'How about we start with a pie, then I'll put an eclair in a bag and you can eat that for afters. How does that sound?' I nodded. My throat felt tight. 'Good, that's what we'll do, then.' Mrs Mulvaney took a pie out of the warmer with her tongs, squirting sauce in the crack at the top, then she took the eclair from the cake tray behind the glass. She put them both in brown bags, and when she passed them across she squeezed my hand. 'You enjoy those, pet.'

Dawn nudged me. 'Say thank you.'

I looked up at Mrs Mulvaney. The bags were heavy and hot in my hands. I couldn't speak.

Noreena frowned. 'Justine,' she whispered.

'Leave her alone, Noreena.' Mrs Mulvaney smiled at me. 'Go on, pet, you enjoy every bite.'

Dawn and Noreena and me sat on a bench and ate our pies and cakes, swinging our legs. After I ate my pie and then my eclair, everything inside came down like an anchor, into the ground. When I walked to the bus stop, I sang the words too. *The holly and the ivy, when they are both full grown, of all the trees that are in the wood, the holly bears the crown.* If I could have spoken the words to Mrs Mulvaney they would have been, *Thank you, Mrs Mulvaney.*

—

When I was getting on the bus I saw Mrs Hooper, Michael's mother, going down the school steps beside him. Michael's crutches were under his arms, his schoolbag on his back. When he came to the kerb he put the crutches down first, then he used them to swing himself towards the car. He leaned forward and opened the car door. Mrs Hooper didn't help him get into the car. She left him alone and went around to her side. I watched as they drove away.

—

On the bus on the way home I felt full and warm. Outside of the bus window I saw trees with black cockatoos in the branches. There were Worlleys at the back but nobody said anything to me. Nobody knew when Dad was coming home; there was no warning.

Before the fall-out Dad was friends with the uncles. Mother Margy used to say, *Handsome Ray*, and give him apple pie when we were at the caravans. Everybody drank beers and ate steaks and the caravans stood around us in a circle—each caravan for a different Worlley family, all glowing with light and television, all loud with kids and babies and music from the tape recorder. Mother Margy piled up the pie for my dad, poured on the cream and said, *The girls can't stay away from handsome Ray, can they, Ray? Lucky I'm old, hey?* Stacey Worlley sat on her camp chair by the fire, her eyes never leaving Dad; every step he took, every sip he swallowed, every word he spoke.

Before Stacey Worlley got married and changed her name to Chisholm, Dad and Stacey used to go together. When we went to the Worlleys for barbecues, Stacey sat on Dad's knee. She turned her body round and kissed him and both her legs were over one of his, as if he was a horse. Her jeans were so tight they were like pale blue skin. Soon Dad and Stacey would get up and go into one of the caravans. When they joined the fire again Mother Margy said to Stacey, 'You know he's a heartbreaker, don't you, Stace?' Mother Margy's hand was on Dad's leg, like she was trying to hold him to the chair. 'He comes and he goes.'

'That's why I'll never marry him,' said Stacey, kissing my dad.

'That's why he'll never ask you,' said Mother Margy.

Relle said Stacey was a slut even after Stacey married Brian and changed her name. Brian Chisholm worked in Goonyella where he dug coal with a machine that had five levels. It took a team to work it. Relle said, *Bloody Stacey, it may as well be written across the back of her skirt.* Goonyella was in Queensland.

Stacey found Brian around the same time as the fall-out. He asked her to marry him, and then it was over between her and Ray. The same as it was over between Pop and the Japs. *If I ever saw one round here I'd get out the Mauser,* Pop told the chooks. *Don't worry about that. I'd take his head off without looking back.*

———

The bus stopped at the rock. As I walked down the trail to Pop's Three I looked up at the trees leaning over me. *O the rising of the sun, and the running of the deer, the playing of the merry organ, sweet singing in the choir,* I sang to the highest branches. Dad was coming home tomorrow. I stopped my singing. In out in out went my tongue.

7.

I saw smoke rising at Pop's Three. I walked through to the yard. The fire was lit, and Pop was on his knees at the chook run tightening the wire. The chooks pecked at the ground around him. 'Hellfire alright . . . not human! And after all that, what for?' The chooks tilted their heads as they listened to the rise and fall of Pop's words.

'Hi, Pop,' I said.

'G'day, Jussy.' He turned to me, a White Ox balanced on his lip. There was chook shit on his cheek, caught in the cracks. 'Doing a bit of a fix-up.' He looked towards the back-house. Then he took the rake from against the wall and held it out. When Dad was on the way home Pop cleaned, trying to get ready.

I put down my schoolbag and raked the grass, dragging butts and chook shit and bottle tops to the fence. Pop put the old straw from the chook run into the wheelbarrow, wheeled it out and tipped it at the far edge of the Three. He got shovels from the shed next to the run and we scraped out more shit. I broke up the bales and we spread new straw across the run. I filled up the chicken drips at the tap and put egg grit into the plastic bucket, then I brought it down to the feed tray.

Pop leaned on his shovel. 'Ladies, your new home awaits,' he said, tipping his head.

The chooks gathered around him, pushing against each other, hoping they would be the one he would pick up and hold and stroke when he sat in his camp chair.

'Going to pull in a bit of fuel from down the back,' he said, getting into his truck.

I walked towards the fence; Cockyboy watched from the rail, his eyes like hard black pips.

When I first came to Pop's Three, seven years ago, Cockyboy scratched my face. I was chasing the hens. I wanted to pick one up and take her into my room. Pop said, *If you can catch one she's yours.* I chased the hen one way, and then another. Kirk and Steve and Dad called, *Go, Jussy, go!* They laughed and cheered. *Go, Jussy! Go, girl, go!* Cockyboy came for me, his feathers gold and red and gleaming, his red comb and black eyes coming for my face! I screamed and my cheek stung. I don't know if it was his beak or his claw that drew the blood. I cried. Pop said, 'He's just showing you who's boss.' Later, in the bathroom mirror, I saw a long red hook line under my eye, like the scythe that hung in Pop's shed.

I put down the rake and went into the chook run. I picked out three eggs. Everything Pop cooked had the yellow yolk, like a sauce. I sat down by the hen boxes, holding the eggs carefully in my hands. The chook run smelled of clean straw and feathers. It was quiet in there. I leaned against the boxes. One more day then it was Friday.

Dad never said what he did when he was away. When he'd been home a while, resting, having a beer with Pop, talking on

Pop's telephone, the secrets started to cook, like bread in the pan, its crust breaking as the secrets rose, pushing his guts up to his throat. Dad's skin was a layer stretched tight. That's when he needed to go away, to let out the secrets where Pop couldn't see. Things he wanted, things he didn't have a name for.

Then he came back home, empty. To rest, keeping still in the back-house, sometimes coming out for a beer, sometimes saying, *Good to see my special girl again, hey, Juss.* Talking on the telephone, holding it close to his mouth so you never heard whole words. If you came into the room when he was on the telephone he showed you where the door was with the angle of his head: 'Out.'

When Pop came back with the wood I helped him unload it from the trailer. The shoes pinched my toes every time I bent to pick up another piece.

—

'*Red River*'s on the box tonight, Jussy,' said Pop. We carried our egg and potato and corn into the living room. 'The big man as Tommy Dunson.' Pop turned on the television and the picture fuzzed and snowed. 'Fix it, Jussy, darlin',' Pop said, sitting on the couch. I left my dinner on the coffee table, got up and moved the aerial. I twisted it and turned it until the picture stayed steady, then I let it go and slowly stepped back. There was John Wayne as Thomas Dunson, riding his horse to Red River. 'I knew I took you in for a reason, Jussy,' said Pop. I was the only one who could fix the aerial; nobody else.

Pop and me sat on the couch balancing dinner on our knees. Thomas Dunson's help was Groot, but what could Groot do? He had a limp and spoke in a voice too soft to hear. Pop said, '*We brought nothing into this world and it's certain we can carry nothing out,*' at the same time as Thomas Dunson. '*Every time you turn around, expect to see me, 'cause one time you'll turn around and I'll be there. I'm gonna kill ya.'* Pop knew all of Thomas Dunson's words as if he had lived another life as Thomas Dunson.

When the movie finished Pop said, 'Wish you were around when Sandy and I were in Burma, big man. Would have been a whole different story, Duke. Bastards.' He turned off the television and the room was shocked with the quiet, as if Thomas Dunson had left without warning. Pop rolled a White Ox and drank from his beer. 'Your father's coming home Friday,' he said, but it wasn't me he was talking to. They were just words. He could have been telling Thomas Dunson.

———

At school on Thursday morning, I was about to sit at the desk beside Kathy Worlley.

'Don't forget your husband,' said Matt Dunning. He turned to Michael.

'Piss off,' I whispered. I looked at Michael, shaking and jerking at his desk. I wished I could sit beside Kathy and copy her straight lines. Michael's head rocked back and forth. All the time I had been at Nullabri Primary he had been there, shaking and jerking in his seat, but I had stopped seeing him. Everybody had. I went to Michael's desk and when I pulled out my chair, I knocked one of his crutches to the floor. Other kids laughed as Michael bent down, jerking to the side as he picked it up.

Mrs Turning said, 'This morning is the multiple-choice comprehension test.' She walked around the class, putting the test on every desk. 'Please place a tick in the circle beside the correct answer.'

I heard Matt Dunning and Brian Lawson laugh. Brian said, 'Give your husband a kiss.'

I closed my eyes and said, *I wish*, but when I opened the test and looked at the words the letters had changed places. I saw *ecided, tnagele, esponser*. I saw letters in a row, *DCAB*. I couldn't read the sentences. Michael kept moving and pulling, his arms jumping, his neck going stiff then loose, stiff then loose. I put my pencil to the paper. It didn't matter which circle I ticked. Michael scratched at the page—his pencil missed the paper and marked the desk. I ticked inside some circles then stopped. Michael and me were the same. That's why Mrs Turning put me with him; we couldn't do anything.

After the test the reward was free reading. I took my book with my dream of the truck on the cover but I didn't make a wish to understand the story. I didn't open the book. I put my fingers on the truck and looked through the window at the light coming from the sky. I closed my eyes and saw the truck waiting for me under the light, 'You're My Best Friend' playing on the stereo.

Michael took a book from his desk. He opened it and smoothed down the pages with his shaking hands. There was a lot of writing on every page, little letters, lots of words. There were maps. There were photographs next to the maps; pictures of animals, snow, trees, whales. Men with sleds and dogs. Boats. Arrows going up and arrows going down. Michael turned the pages of the book until he came to a big blue country. Then he went as still as he had ever been and leaned over the page.

—

Michael went home at lunchtime that day. His mother was at the door waiting. She smiled at him. They walked out together and she didn't help him.

8.

That night, I lay in bed and my tongue found the gap, in out in out. The teeth were there when Dad left and now they weren't. I closed my eyes and watched scissors cut the air above my head into pieces. My bedroom was on the top level of a truck that could travel over land and sea. I brought the food up with a pulley; hot pies and chocolate eclairs and orange juice.

———

'When will Dad be here?' I asked Pop the next morning.

Pop sat in the sun that was coming through the kitchen window and smoked. 'He'll be here when he's here,' he said, turning his cigarette in the light as if he liked the clothes it was wearing. The news was playing on the radio. 'Bloody communist, Whitlam,' said Pop.

I stirred sugar into my Rice Bubbles. You never knew when Ray would come. Sometimes he'd call Pop and let him know; other times it was a surprise. A year ago, when I was nine, I was walking along the Henley Trail back to Pop's. It had been raining and there were deep puddles on the road. The

Murray was high, spilling over the sides. The grass under the trees glowed green. I sang as I walked. *Red and yellow and pink and green, Purple and orange and blue, I can sing a rainbow, sing a rainbow, sing a rainbow too.* Sabine was teaching us. *Listen with your eyes, listen with your ears, and sing everything you see.*

I saw the Worlleys come out of Dray Road and watched as they turned into the trail. Jamie, Lachie, Kathy, Jacky, Ee, Tyler and a new one I didn't know. It had been a year since the fall-out. A year since we'd been friends. Jamie called out to me, 'Justine! Justine!'

The cousin I hadn't seen before said, 'Meow.'

Kathy had her head down.

'Justine! Justine!' the cousins sang out.

I kept my eyes on my feet. There was nobody else there, only the Worlleys and me.

Jamie called out, 'Hey, Justine, can you hear me?'

The other cousin said, 'Meow, meow.'

Jamie said, 'You know what a pussy is, don't you, Justine?'

I walked faster.

'Do you, Justine? Do you know what a pussy is? Have you learned yet? Has Pop taught you?'

I looked around for cars or people but there were none. I wished Kirk and Steve were with me.

'You know you were the first one to touch my scar?' said Jamie. He was catching up to me. 'You remember that? It's my turn to see your scar.'

'What scar?'

'You know—your scar,' he said, close to me now. 'The one every girl has.'

'I haven't got a scar.'

'Yes, you do. Can I have a look?'

48

The other cousins—Lachie, Jacky, Ee, Tyler and the new one—stood behind Jamie. Only Kathy stayed on the other side of the road. Jamie stepped closer to me. He was taller now. 'Here, puss puss,' he said. He used to go so fast down the slide. He went down on his front, on his back, he went down sitting, he went down face first, then feet first, over and over, laughing in the bubbles. He was faster than all of us, his scar from the dogfight red and glowing. 'Here, puss.' He flicked his fingers at the front of my skirt, between my legs.

I pushed his hand back. He would have been fifteen by then and bigger than me.

Jamie said, 'Easy does it.' He grabbed at my skirt again. 'Show us your scar.'

The other cousins around him laughed and then they stopped. They looked at each other. It was quiet outside of the Worlleys and me. It was a flatness that stretched and spread all the way to the line that joined the sky to the world. Was this what Kathy saw with her other eye?

Jamie stuck his hand up the front of my dress and pinched.

Lachie said, 'We better go, Jamie.'

Kathy started to walk down the road on the opposite side. The cousins were backing away, following her.

Jamie didn't notice them—he was only looking at me.

I said, 'Fuck off.' I was shaking.

He said, 'What did you say?'

I said, 'Fuck off.' I wished I had a weapon. Steve's pocket-knife—I'd hold it to Jamie's neck, I'd stick it in.

'That's what I thought you said.' He nodded towards the river. 'Let's go for a walk in the trees over there.'

'No.'

'Come on, just over there.' He took my hand and tried to lead me towards the trees.

I pulled away. 'No!'

He pushed me onto my back on the wet grass. When I looked up I couldn't see the other Worlleys. I tried to get away. Jamie pushed me down and sat on me. 'No! No!' I bucked and kicked out my legs but he leaned forward and pinned my arms to the ground. The grass squelched underneath us.

'How old are you now?'

I twisted my head from side to side as he leaned over me. 'Fuck off!' I said.

He put his face close to mine. 'Don't talk to me like that—I'm fifteen,' he said. I kept wiggling underneath him, bucking up and down and kicking. 'Keep going, that feels good, Jussy.'

'Get off me!' I said. Jamie reached back, lifted my skirt and touched me under my pants. I tried to kick him and push him away. 'Get off me!' I struggled against him. Then I heard a car coming down the highway. Jamie turned around to look.

It was a white truck with a single blue door. The bull bar was hung with pieces of orange twine and there was rust along the bottom of the tray. It was my dad's truck.

Dad slowed down when he saw us. He stopped the truck. I hadn't seen him from the start of the second term to the finish. He came around the front, his long legs fast, and Jamie scrambled away from me. My dad grabbed him and held him against the side of his truck by the front of his shirt. 'Jamie fucken Worlley.' Dad spoke the words slow, with space between each one, as if he had all the time in the world. His face was set without lights; you couldn't go inside it. Jamie didn't say anything. His eyes were wide, and there was breath coming hard in and out of his nose. He was trying to look away from my dad but Ray's face was too close. 'What were you doing to my little girl?'

Jamie said, 'Nothing.'

'Nothing?'

'Nothing. Just having fun.'

'That's what I'm going to do now,' said Dad. 'Have myself some fun. Get in the truck, Justine.'

I didn't move; I stood by the side of the road as if I was frozen.

'Do as you're told and get in the truck,' said Dad over his shoulder.

I ran, stumbling in the dirt, to the truck.

Had Jamie and me been having fun? A year ago we had gone down the slide with bubbles in our hair and down our legs, across our backs and in our hands. Jamie Worlley had a scar and I was the first one to touch it. Everyone made a line behind me. There were so many of us I didn't know who was a Worlley and who was a Lee. Then Pop had the fight with Ian Worlley and we didn't have fun anymore.

I watched as Dad smashed Jamie into the bull bar of the truck. Jamie's head shot back. Dad slammed his fist into Jamie's gut, and Jamie groaned. Dad hit him hard in the face and dropped him in the ditch. Then Dad spat on him. Jamie turned his face away. As my dad came towards the truck I saw his eyes, like black and shining glass.

Dad got in the truck beside me. 'Fucken behave yourself,' he said, before turning the key. He wasn't looking at me when he said the words. *Fucken behave yourself.* He was looking through the windscreen. Was it me he was telling, or the road ahead?

Dad was angry with Jamie Worlley, but he was angry with me too. What was Jamie trying to do to me? I knew shadows of things; I could see the letters but didn't know the order. I stole a look at Dad's face as he drove; it was a door that wouldn't open.

———

I finished my Rice Bubbles and put the bowl in the sink. Outside the sun was shining. But it never dried Yolamundi. As I walked the trail to the bus stop I could still see the water leaking up through the ground, filling the ditches as if the Murray was looking for new pathways. I practised the hymn on the way. *The holly bears a blossom as white as the lily flower, the holly bears a berry, as red as any blood.* When Michael sang he pulled at the ends of the words, stretching them, tugging at their sides. *Hollee-ee, bea-ears, berry-erry, b-b-b* . . . I sang the way he did as I walked, I made the same sounds. *As re-e-e-d! Re-ee-ee-d!* Did Michael live on the inside of his body, or was his body him? Was I my body, or did I live inside it? I stepped around a puddle in the road. Michael's eyes were green. I didn't know any other green eyes, did I? When the bus pulled up to the stop I saw Worlleys looking at me through the windows.

———

At school Dawn and Noreena were playing hopscotch at the front. Noreena threw the stone into the farthest square. *'I like coffee, I like tea, I like the boys and the boys like me,'* she sang as she jumped.

'Hi, Justine,' said Dawn.

Noreena gave the stone to Dawn and pointed at my skirt. 'When did you last wash that?' she said.

I shrugged. Pop had to turn the spanner in the machine to do a wash. If he got the time wrong it stuck.

Noreena shook her head.

I looked down at my skirt. There was a dribble of yolk aiming for the hem.

———

In class with Mrs Turning we had to write the word on a line under the picture. I knew the pictures. *Castle. Soldier. Bridge.* Michael's pen scratched and jumped as he looked from the pictures to the lines. He started to write. Castle like my hideout. Soldier like Pop. Bridge over the Murray at Moama. I closed my eyes and saw the letters for the words, but when I tried to write them they were backwards. It was the breech. There was no way to undo it. I picked at the yolk on my skirt. I noticed Michael staring at my page. His arms and neck and leg shook and swayed but his eyes stayed steady on my work.

When the playlunch bell rang Michael put the crutches under his arms, then he pulled himself to standing. One of his legs worked better than the other. Dawn and Noreena waited for me in the corridor. I watched as Michael swung towards the door.

'Coming, Justine?' said Dawn.

'Coming,' I said.

Noreena said, 'Elastics?' She took a long white elastic from her bag. Dawn and me stood opposite each other at the play squares while Noreena put the elastic around the backs of our legs. *'Jump, jump, knees up high, jump, jump, kick the sky, jump, jump, who's the best? Touch the band and fail the test!'* I looked across at Michael, sitting at the benches by himself, eating from his fruit box, his book open on the table.

———

In the afternoon we had to write words on the blackboard and join the sounds. Mrs Turning was at the front of the classroom with her wooden pointer. She said, 'The first sound is *c*—what is the next sound, please?'

Lots of the kids put up their hands. Michael wrote something on his page. Sarah Lockey said, 'The next sound is *on*, Mrs Turning.'

'Correct, Sarah,' said Mrs Turning.

Michael had already written something; N first then O. I changed it the other way so the O came first. O N. It zigzagged and jumped, but I could see what it was. *On*. Michael knew the answer. I looked at him; he looked back at me, his eyes steady, while the rest of him jerked and shook, as if the person pulling the strings was excited.

9.

When I came home from school I found Pop out the back breaking up boards. 'Where's Dad?' I asked him. 'How should I know?' He threw a plank into the coals, and sat down on his camp chair. I sat on the back step. Pop said, 'Here, chook chook; here, Missy.' The chooks came close. Pop bent down towards them. 'Here, chook chook chook.' He picked up one of the girls and smoothed its feathers. 'Hey, chook; hey, Lady; hey, little Lady,' he said. He made a soft kissing sound. The chook clucked and its head moved in tiny jerks, this way and that way, in Pop's lap. I took off my shoes and wiggled my toes. 'I gave up waiting for your old man a long time ago,' Pop said to the chook. But I knew that wasn't true; I knew he was waiting, just like me.

That night Pop's gut trouble came early. He lay on his bed, a hand across his stomach. Pop didn't know the bug was there when he left Burma; it was hiding in his lining, feeding on the layers. The bug liked to feel Pop's small tight gut around him, holding him in like a blanket, a cocoon. I wish we could let Cockyboy at it. He'd peck it like a worm and swallow it whole.

When Aunty Rita visited she said, 'See a doctor, Dad, and stay off the booze.'

When I've drunk the same amount of beer as the blood that flowed, that's when I'll give it up, that's when, that's when, not till then, goddamn it! Pop told her to piss off and leave him alone.

Tonight he lay on his bed with his face turned to the wall. When it was dark I said, 'Are you making dinner, Pop?'

Pop said, 'Bugger off.'

There was still a whole night to go. I went into my room and cut out a car with a double exhaust. Later, when I walked past Pop's room on the way to the kitchen, I heard him talking to the wall. 'You bastards. Christ! You monkeys! You black-haired scum. For what?' He groaned and drank from his beer, trying to drown the bug.

I walked out to the back-house. I looked in the windows and saw my face in the glass. I walked all around it, dragging my hands along the walls. It felt cold. Pop told me Aunty Rita, Dad's sister, used to live in the back-house, before she left home. Now Aunty Rita worked at Tarban Creek as an electrical nurse. I met her once, when I was four, after I had been living at Pop's Three for a year. She came to visit from Sydney. She was tall like Dad, and she had the same shining black hair and white skin. But her eyes were different, as if the circles were only covers. If you lifted them, you would find the electricity from Tarban Creek, balanced inside her.

The time she visited I was out the back collecting feathers. Cockyboy was perched on the top rail, watching me. Aunty Rita stepped through the kitchen door into the yard. Dad was just behind her. 'Oh, Ray . . .' she said, her eyes on me. She shook her head as if she couldn't believe something. She looked over her shoulder, back at him. 'What did you bloody do to get so lucky?' She walked down to me. 'I'm your Aunty Rita,' she said to me. I thought she was going to cry. She put her fist to her mouth and knocked it against her lips. 'I can't believe I never met you before.'

Dad said, 'Whose fault is that?'

Aunty Rita kept her eyes on me. She said, 'Nobody's, Ray.' She kneeled down in front of me. 'I brought you a present, Justine.' She pulled a parcel wrapped in paper from her bag. She said, 'I didn't know what to get you.'

As I took the present from her, some of the brown chook feathers fell from my hand and stuck to Aunty Rita's sleeve.

Dad said, 'What do you say, Justine?'

I didn't know. What do you say? I looked at Aunty Rita's boots on the dirt.

Aunty Rita called back, 'What do *you* say, Ray?'

Dad went inside. Cockyboy jumped down from the gate.

'Pop's still got a bastard rooster, I see,' said Aunty Rita. 'Want to open your present?'

I nodded. We tore off the paper. It was purple pyjamas inside with a train driving across the front. The train had a smile, half its wheels were off the track, as if it was dancing. I looked up at her. Could I wear them? Could I wear them now?

'You want to try them on?' my Aunty Rita asked me.

'Can I?'

"Course you can.'

I ran inside and took off my skirt and my jumper and pulled on the pyjamas. They felt soft against my skin. The train danced against my chest. I went back out and saw Aunty Rita in the kitchen talking with Pop.

'You get used to it pretty quick,' she said. 'You learn the signs. You know who to watch out for . . .'

Aunty Rita saw me and said, 'Hey! Justine, they fit you perfectly.'

Pop raised his eyebrows.

Dad came in. He sat down and pulled out his pouch of White Ox. 'They're pyjamas, Justine,' he said. 'You can wear them tonight when you go to bed.'

I didn't want to wait until it was night. I wanted to wear them now.

Aunty Rita said, 'Oh, come on, let her wear them now.'

I turned to Pop. 'Can I, Pop?'

'Wear what you like,' said Pop, looking at Dad.

Dad lit his White Ox. 'How's the nuthouse?' he said to Aunty Rita.

'It's not a nuthouse.'

'Not after you use the pads, hey?' said Dad, blowing out smoke.

I ran my hands down my new pyjamas, then I took some steps, like the dancing train. I sat on the kitchen floor and spun. I put one leg in the air. Aunty Rita clapped. 'What a show,' she said. 'What a great show! More!'

I looked at my dad.

Dad took a long smoke, then he said to Aunty Rita, 'How's Naomi?'

Aunty Rita frowned at Dad.

'That's her name, right? Naomi?' said Dad.

Pop drew in breath. Aunty Rita's face turned red and the electricity that travelled with her from Sydney came out from under her clothes, at her trouser bottoms and around her collar. 'She's fine,' said Aunty Rita.

'She's a doctor, right?' said Dad.

'Yeah, she is.' Aunty Rita glanced at Pop. His face was tight, his mouth hard, like he was trying to bite down on something. He looked hot, as if the flames from his fire had singed his cheeks. Pop got up and stood at the sink, trying to get closer to the taps.

'You met at the hospital, didn't you?' said Dad.

Aunty Rita nodded. 'Yeah. Yeah, we did.'

The smoke from Pop's White Ox rose above his head.

'Hospital romance,' said Dad.

On the floor I saw brown chook feathers that had come inside. Caught on my clothes and Aunty Rita's.

'Ray,' said Aunty Rita. 'Don't.'

'What sort of doctor is she?' said Ray.

'Fuck off, Ray,' said Aunty Rita.

I saw Pop's hands spread, holding the edge of the sink, knuckles white.

'What sort of doctor is she?' Every time Dad spoke it was light, like a ball being thrown into the air, easy, like a breeze, but under it was heavy as lead.

Aunty Rita turned to Dad. 'Just an ordinary doctor, Ray. She works with the women at the hospital.'

'Really?' said Dad. 'You're in good hands, then. Nice. Sweet.' The smoke Dad blew in a stream to the ceiling pressed its way into the corners. 'You're doing alright for yourself, Rita. She hot?'

'She is hot,' said Aunty Rita. 'She's really fucken hot.'

Pop turned around from the sink. 'Bugger this,' he said.

'Bugger what, Dad?' Aunty Rita snapped.

'You know what. This bloody business.'

'What business?' I could almost see Aunty Rita's heart pounding behind her shirt.

'Bloody unnatural, Rita! Jesus! What's wrong with you?'

'What is, Dad? What's unnatural?'

'I'm off to the pub. You guys want anything?' said Dad, standing.

'You're a fucken prick, Ray,' said Aunty Rita.

'You're welcome,' said Ray.

'What's not natural, Dad?' Aunty Rita asked.

'You know what I'm talking about,' Pop said.

'Say it, Dad,' said Aunty Rita.

'Don't make me say the bloody words. It's bad enough . . .'

'What words? What won't you say?' Aunty Rita said.

'Not in this house!'

'Are you ashamed? Is that what it is? You're ashamed of me?'

'You're dead right, Rita. I am ashamed!'

'That's what you're ashamed of? After what you did!'

'Don't talk to me like that in my house!'

'You're worried about the way I talk? This house has more to worry about than the way I talk!'

'Shut up, Rita!' Pop was shaking.

'Don't talk to me about what's natural, Dad! Until you can bring Mum back from the dead!'

Pop spluttered as if Rita had made the pathways of his words crisscross and tangle; he didn't know which one to choose. 'Get out of here! You're a bloody monster! Shame on you.'

'Fuck you, Dad. You're the monster!'

'Get out of my house!'

'I'm leaving!' Aunty Rita took her bag off the table and went down the hall to the front door, her boots loud against the floorboards. I heard the front door open and then she came back.

Dad hadn't left yet. He said calmly, as if the fight hadn't happened, 'Forgotten something?'

'Fuck off, Ray,' said Aunty Rita, grabbing her keys from the table.

'Take it easy, Rita,' said Dad.

Aunty Rita stopped. Her hair was dark and swept back like his, and her eyes were the same black, but just behind them was the light that came from the hospital, the light she gave to the patients. She was his big sister; she seemed to loom over him, as if she was the one who was taller. She wasn't scared of him. She said, 'Pop's little man. Little Ray. Little bed-wetting Ray.' Dad didn't speak. He shrank. It was the only time I had seen him small, the way he was when he stood beside Lizzy's hospital bed in 1952, thirteen years old, not much older than Kirk. He was losing something he needed, and there was nothing he could do to stop it.

I followed Aunty Rita down the hall towards the front door. Pop called out, 'Leave her, Justine.'

I kept following. The dancing train clung to my chest, as if it was afraid it would fall. 'Aunty Rita,' I said.

She turned and saw me. She kneeled down in the doorway, pulling back tears. She took my hands and kissed them. 'Justine, it was so good to meet you. I'm so sorry.'

Then she got up and left.

⌣

Aunty Rita wouldn't be scared of the patients. She would see the handcuffs, she would read the signs, and say, *Are they necessary?* Pinpricks of electrical light would come through her eyes. When she used the pads she would say, *It won't hurt, I promise.*

Aunty Rita saw what happened the time Pop exploded and Lizzy was in the house. Ray and Rita both saw it—they were holding hands when it happened—but Ray only opened his eyes some of the way, to shield himself. Aunty Rita let herself see it all. Aunty Rita wanted to be with Pop, to talk to him and be his friend and tell him about the hospital and the pads and drink his tea and see his chooks. She wanted to—but she had seen too much. Like John Wayne as Rooster in *True Grit*, she had seen the killing.

But why did Pop say she was unnatural? Why should Pop be ashamed?

It didn't matter how loud the grown-ups shouted, they never gave names to things.

———

I moved away from the back-house and crossed to the chook run. I stood at the wire and listened for sounds from inside. I heard rustling. I breathed in the smell of straw and feathers and Isa Brown. 'Hey, girls,' I whispered. 'Hey there. Hey, ladies, hey there, here I am, it's Justine.' The chooks were quiet. I wanted to go inside but Pop didn't like me to wake them. 'Dad's coming home soon, girls,' I said. Cockyboy clucked a warning. I left the run and went back into the house.

I could still hear Pop from the bedroom. *If it wasn't for Sandy. Hungry? Christ!* I went into the living room and stopped at the photo. There was Dad, Rita, Pop and Lizzy standing together outside the house the day Pop bought his Three. The line of dirt that marked the fibro was there even then, encircling the house. Dad wasn't much older than me. There was a small flower in Lizzy's hair. I touched her face and her dress. Lizzy was buried in the cemetery. She got pneumonia; it clogged her lungs. They took her to the hospital. One day, after Dad and Pop had drunk all the beers, Ray shouted, *Rita's fucken right. It wasn't the pneumonia, you cunt.*

I didn't know what to do next. I looked at the photo again; Pop, Lizzy, Dad and Rita all together. But I didn't know what to do after that. What was there to do?

10.

In the middle of the night I was woken by the sound of an engine. I looked out of the window and saw Dad's truck stopping out the front. I watched as Dad opened his door and climbed out of the driver's seat. He was tall, his hair shining black in the moonlight, his legs long, his shoulders wide. He was the reason the Worlleys left me alone; they never knew when he was coming home. It could be now, it could be tomorrow, it could be Christmas—there was no warning. I stayed at the side of my window in the dark and watched my dad pulling out his bag. He stopped to look up at the stars. He was as tall and strong as Thomas Dunson. *Every time you turn around, expect to see me*, I whispered at the glass. *I'm gonna kill ya.*

Dad mustered in Queensland. He worked at sawmills. He went to the city. He went to Sydney. He could rope cattle. He could get them into the crush, and bring them to their knees. He could fix his own truck. He could shoot. When Pop wasn't home he talked on the telephone. He said, *How many? How much?* He said, *When, mate?* and *What time?* and *Shouldn't be a problem.* He said, *I'll do it.* He'd laugh close to the telephone.

No fucken problem at all. Then he came into the kitchen, drank milk from the bottle, spat in the sink and didn't talk. Soon he would leave and do his jobs and help his friends and let out his secrets. Then, when everything was done and he was empty with nothing to spend, he came back to Pop's Three—to Kirk and Steve and me. We were where he came to have a rest.

I heard him come into the house and go to the kitchen. After a while I heard the back door slam. I lay down in my bed and closed my eyes. My wooden truck-ship and my scissors were waiting for me. I cut more layers; I put my bedroom higher and higher. I made the path going up smooth for Michael and his crutches. I cut out a holder for the crutches so they didn't slide. We looked down and saw the forest beneath us—the leaves on the trees swirling in the wind. I kept cutting until the truck-ship reached the clouds where everything was soft and white but still I couldn't sleep.

———

In the morning, before Dad woke up, I followed Pop out the front to look at Dad's truck. Pop lifted the bonnet. He leaned in and muttered under his breath. He ran his hand over the body, feeling for the damage he couldn't see. I looked at the doors for new scratches and at the tyres for nails. I put my hand on the treads to see how smooth they were. I ran my hand around the front and looked at the bumper. The truck knew the story of where my dad had been; it was only the truck that could tell it.

———

Pop got the fire going, and Relle dropped Kirk and Steve at the house. Pop cleaned the barbecue with steel wool. A cool wind moved the branches on the trees and shook the leaves. The fire crackled as the flames jumped. The chooks turned to look at the back-house door, then at Pop, then at Cockyboy on the edge of their circle. *When when when* would Dad wake up?

Kirk put rocks on the fence posts and we took turns knocking them down with our stones. When Pop wasn't looking Kirk shot a stone at Cockyboy. Cockyboy jumped into the air and squawked.

Pop said, 'What are you up to?'

Kirk said, 'Nothing, Pop.'

'What time did he get home?' Kirk asked me.

'I don't know. Some time in the night.'

'Were you awake?'

'No.'

Kirk threw another stone. 'This time he's going to teach me how to shoot.'

Steve took his knife from his pocket and said, 'Wonder if he'll want this back.'

Kirk said, 'It wasn't him that gave it to you. It was Mum.'

'It used to be Dad's.'

'Bullshit, it was never Dad's.'

Steve closed his mouth tight. The knife was the only thing he didn't have to share with Kirk.

There were spuds and corn boiling in Pop's billy on the fire. The sausages and chops were on ice in the esky. Pop had cold beers in the laundry. Everything was quiet, as if a movie was about to begin on the television. The branches, the birds, the fire and Pop, Kirk, Steve and me were waiting for it to start.

At last the back-house door opened and there was Dad.

He stood tall in his jeans with no top on and the belt in its loops undone. My tongue sped up in out in out of the hole, lips shut tight. Kirk threw another stone. 'Got it,' he said, as if he hadn't noticed Dad standing on the back-house step. Once, just after Dad and Relle had a fight, Dad turned to Kirk and said, *The worst of both of us rolled into one, you little bastard.*

Steve looked at Dad, then he threw a stone too.

Pop stopped scouring the barbecue. 'G'day, Ray,' he said.

Ray nodded and said, 'Dad.' He yawned and stretched his arms to the sky. I saw dark pockets of hair spreading open underneath. His shoulders were strung with muscle, and there was a line of hair down his stomach, leading to his jeans hanging loose around his hips. Shadows of stubble crossed his cheeks and chin. 'You've grown,' he said to me. 'Going to give your old man a kiss?' I walked across the yard and Dad bent down to me. I stood on my toes and kissed his cheek. He smelled of sweat and sleep and ash. I didn't open my mouth. I didn't want him to see the hole.

He looked past me, at Kirk and Steve. 'G'day, boys.'

Kirk threw another stone. Steve waited.

Dad said, 'You fellas are getting big. I better do what I'm told around here.'

Kirk stood as straight as he could. He said, 'Danny's uncle is going to teach me how to shoot.'

'Good on him,' Dad said.

Kirk seemed to go smaller. 'When he gets back from Gympie.'

Dad came down the back-house steps and went to Pop's fire. He sat on a camp chair and said, 'Got a beer?'

'Sure,' said Pop, and walked across the yard into the laundry. He kept his beers in an esky beside the washing machine. Soon he came out carrying two cans.

Kirk said, 'What about me?'

'What about you?' said Pop. 'Go and get the bread and the plates.'

Kirk grumbled and went into the kitchen.

'Help him, Justine,' said Pop. I got up and followed Kirk.

In the kitchen Kirk picked up a pile of plates. He said, 'When I learn to shoot you'll be my first target.'

I looked through the kitchen window and saw Dad throw a piece of wood on Pop's fire. 'You'll never learn how to shoot,' I said. I picked up the knives and forks.

'My first target.' Kirk pointed his finger at me as if it was a gun.

'If you could shoot,' I said.

When we came back out into the yard we heard Dad say to Steve, 'What are you up to?'

Steve kept his eyes on a small stone in his hands. 'Nothing,' he said. When I looked at Steve it was as if there was a ditch all around him too wide to jump. If you shone a torch into it, you'd never see the bottom. Steve couldn't get across by himself; it was only Dad who could help him. Every time Dad went away—to Bathurst or Sydney or the Territory or Melbourne or Cairns—the ditch around Steve deepened and grew darker.

I remember the first time I saw it. Steve was seven and Dad was just home, just through the door. He'd been away a long time and Steve ran to Dad, and shouted, *I've grown. Look at the mark on Pop's wall, Dad. Look!* and he pointed to the mark. His face was so light, his smile so wide, his cheeks pink. *See how tall see, see!* and he put his arms around Dad's legs. I watched as Dad set him back. *You got your mother's height, poor bastard,* he said, and laughed. He turned away from Steve and I saw the ground split open around him.

Dad said, 'How old are you now? Started high school yet?'

Steve said, 'Eleven. Fifth class.'

'Want an arm wrestle?' Dad said.

Steve looked up from his hands. 'Yeah!' He sat in a chair next to Dad and Dad pulled over the card table.

'Arm up,' said Dad.

Steve put his arm up against Dad's. Steve's was thin and white, and Dad's was strong with dark hair.

Pop got up from his chair and put his hand over theirs. 'On the count of three,' he said. 'One . . . two . . . three!'

Steve tried as hard as he could to press Dad's hand down onto the table. He strained and pushed and his face turned red.

'Go, Steve, go!' said Kirk.

Pop said, 'Go, Steve! Go, mate!'

Cockyboy squawked from the fence.

'Push, Steve, push! Go! Go!' we shouted.

Dad's hand was at the bottom, hovering just above the table, as Steve tried and tried, then Kirk put his hand on Steve's and now it was two of them against Dad.

Pop said, 'You help too, Justine!'

I put my hand on top of Kirk's. Now it was me and Kirk and Steve against Dad, trying and trying to get his hand down, pushing as hard as we could.

Pop shouted, 'Go, kids! Go, kids!'

Then, as Dad's hand was about to hit the table, just the smallest distance to go, too small to see, Dad flipped us. He pressed us all to the table. He leaned back, hands in the air.

Pop said, 'You almost got him! You were this close!' He held up his fingers in a pinch.

But Dad beat us; even with all three of us together, it was Dad who won.

Pop put the sausages on the barbecue and Dad fixed the stereo in his back-house so it played guitar music into the yard. *When you're with me, baby, there's nobody else, when you're with me . . .* Pop and Dad drank beers and we threw stones and hung around them. Kirk pretended to shoot the fence posts. *Pchoo pchoo!* He blew smoke from the top of his fingers. Dad held his two fingers up and pointed them at Missy and Lady and Madame and all of them as they pecked and clucked. *Bang bang bang*. Kirk and Steve never took their eyes off Ray; they spoke the way he spoke, they sat and ate and stood and leaned and laughed the same way.

Dad said to me, 'How's my girl?' There were empty beer cans at his feet. He said, 'Come here.' I went to him and he said, 'You're getting big. Still skinny. Pop feeding you? Pop, you feeding this kid?'

Pop said, 'Where do you think all the eggs go?' He took a sip of his beer.

'Hey, Jussie,' he said, 'still hanging with that Dawnie?'

'Yeah.'

'How's Dawnie's mum?'

Pop frowned at him.

'What?' Dad raised his eyebrows at Pop. Dawn's mother wore high heels every day, as if her feet under the heels had long spikes that needed hollow shoes. The shoes made a *tap-tap-tap* sound when she walked along the street. 'She okay?' Dad asked. 'What's her name? It's Julie, isn't it? Or Julianne? How is she?'

'Good,' I said.

'Dawn still your friend?'

'Yeah.'

'Nice,' said Dad, nodding. 'Nice.'

Pop frowned at Dad again, then passed him another beer. Dad nodded his head to the music, moving his lips to the words. *I'll be there, baby, until the end of time, if you're gonna look so sweet, so sweet . . .* Pop and Dad rolled cigarettes and Kirk said, 'Can I have one?'

'You can smoke White Ox after you've been to war,' said Pop. Dad snorted. 'And not before.' Pop lit his cigarette. 'It'll be the only thing to get you through.'

Kirk picked up Pop's tobacco pouch and looked at the ox that stood under the bow. 'I can't go to war unless I learn how to shoot.'

'Got Danny's uncle for that, haven't you?' said Dad. You could never tell what my dad was going to say. There were no clues. Every word he spoke was a surprise. I kept my eyes on him, trying to guess.

'Not if you show me first,' said Kirk.

'Sixteen you can learn,' said Pop. 'Give me back my tobacco. I'll show you myself. The Mauser is the best teacher.'

'Bullshit,' said Dad. 'The bloody Mauser. It's a relic. You still got the pistols?'

'What do you think?' said Pop, his White Ox glowing hot. I saw them in each other, Pop and my dad, the way they held the White Ox between their finger and thumb, the way they took in the smoke, the crack of their voices, their eyes narrowing when the smoke went down. Pop was the first call across the hill and Dad was the echo.

'I think you do. And I think they're rusting in the bloody cupboard. You should let us take them out, Pop. Give them some fresh air. Have a talk to 'em, let 'em know the war's over.'

Kirk looked excited. 'Yeah, Pop. They need fresh air.'

'Forget about my guns,' said Pop. 'They stay where they are. Sixteen, Kirk.'

Kirk whined. 'Danny's uncle is going to show me and Danny with a rifle.'

'Danny's uncle . . .' said Pop, shaking his head. He crushed his cigarette butt under his boot. 'Pass me the snags.'

———

When Dad was home Pop's Three was charged, as if Aunty Rita had put her electrical pads to the roof and pulled the lever. Kirk and Steve never wanted to leave. If Relle hadn't made them go home they would have hung around the yard all day, waiting for Dad to see them or speak to them or shoot the air with a pistol and say, *Bullseye, boys.*

11.

When Dad was home I took a long time to fall asleep. I turned and turned and cut the air above my head until it fell to the floor in messy slivers. On Saturday night, instead of trying to sleep, I got out of bed and went into the kitchen. I could hear Dad and Pop talking outside. I stood beside the back door and saw them in the yard, sitting by the fire. The flames jumped high, lighting up the yard in orange.

Dad's and Pop's voices fell from loud to soft, then rose again. I sat on the step, hidden by the shadows. The cold from the step came through my balloon pyjamas.

Aunty Rita sent the pyjamas to me two years ago. Pop was lying in bed with gut trouble and the radio playing. *Why land a man on the bloody moon? Bloody Yanks. The bloody moon!* I heard him tell the radio. I walked out of the front door. Every time I saw a daisy-head I bent to pull off the petals. I kept going up Pop's drive, bending and picking and pulling off the petals, singing as I went. *I know the colours in the rainbow, I know them very well, I'd say. So if any colour is missing, I'd know it right away.* Sabine was teaching us. *I'd know it right away!* There was nobody on the trail, nobody near the Three, nobody anywhere. I came to the letter box at the top of the road. The letter box was Pop's business. He didn't like me going near it. *After it rains look up to the sky, There might be a rainbow way up high,* I sang. I saw something wrapped in brown paper peeking from the box. I pulled it out and headed back to the house. Pop was in the kitchen making tea. I said, *Look, Pop,* and held out the parcel. *You leave my letter box alone, Justine. That's not your business.* Pop took the parcel, turning it over in his hands. He read the name on the back. *Rita Lee.* He muttered words I couldn't hear and tore open the paper. He lifted out the balloon pyjamas. Coloured balloons floated over the arms and legs, the chest and back. I said, 'Pop, are they for me?' He said, 'Go near my letter box again and there'll be trouble.' Then he gave me the pyjamas.

⌒

I watched from the doorway as Dad drank from his beer. 'Some bitch up in Dubbo,' he said.

'Who?' Pop asked.

'Does it matter?'

'What happened?'

'Nothing. She wanted a fuck.'

'And?'

'And then she didn't.'

'Right.'

'Bit late by then.'

'And they took you in?'

'Yeah, they did.'

'What happened?'

'She withdrew her statement.'

'Why'd she do that?'

'I don't know. Must have been love.'

'Christ, Ray.'

'Silly fucken woman.'

'Cops know you're here?'

'I never told them.'

'Good. Behave yourself for a while. Go and see Relle. She'd have you back.'

Dad said, 'She would too. Relle. Christ.' Their laugher rose with the flames.

Pop got to his feet and went to the fire. He rolled a White Ox. 'How about sticking around?' he said.

'For what?'

'There's work here. The sawmill. You could come back. There's always the muster.'

'I got things I'm doing.'

'What things? Where?'

'Bathurst. I been working for a bloke there.'

'Bathurst? Doing what?'

'Leave it, Dad.'

'What are you doing in Bathurst?'

'Not your business.'

'It is my business.'

'It's not.'

'You got money?'

'Don't worry about my money. I never ask you.'

'You come back here broke. I wouldn't see you otherwise.'

'I come here to see the kids.'

'You come here to see the kids. You see the kids when you run out of money.'

'My money's not your business.'

They drank from their beers as if it could dampen the heat between them.

Pop threw more wood into the flames. 'It is my business. I got your kid here. Do you forget that?'

'If you don't want her I can take her.'

'You can take her?'

'Yeah.'

'She'd live with you?'

'Yeah, why not?'

'Because you're up to no good, that's why.'

'No good. What would you know?'

'I know you're up to no good.'

'What do you call no good?'

'A lot of things. The shit you been up to. The guns. It's no good.'

'You know a lot about *no good*, don't you, Dad?'

'There's nothing I haven't seen.'

'If Mum was here, she'd agree with that.'

'What do you mean?'

'You know what I mean.'

'Then say it.'

'You fucken say it, Dad. You were there.'

Every fight led back to Lizzy. Their words were like picks, digging a tunnel that ran through the earth at Pop's Three to the cemetery in East Nullabri where she was buried. When Pop came back from Burma he was packed with dynamite. The same explosives that felled the trees and broke the rocks and tore open the ground between the jungles. He had to get rid of them or they would split him apart. Lizzy was in hospital for broken bones but when she was there she caught pneumonia. Pneumonia was in the toilets and the cups and the towels and the hospital corridors. It stuck to her hands and climbed inside her, the same way Pop's bug did to him in Burma. When Lizzy died my dad was standing beside the bed, holding her hand. She took some of him with her as she left. Lizzy held the missing piece where she lay underground, and it was too deep under there for Dad to get it back. The missing piece was the key to the lock of Dad's face, the light in his eyes, the words for his secrets.

———

In the morning, when Dad was still asleep, Pop and me went out to the chooks. Pop made tiny dry kisses in the air. 'Here, Lady; hello, Madame; how are you, Missy, my Missy? Going to lay eggs for your old Pop, your old Poppy and Miss Jussy? Hey, little girls, little ladies; here, chook chook; here, chook chook chook.' Pop picked up the new water dish from the stock and feed. 'Where do we put it, Jussy?' he asked.

I said, 'In the corner.'

'Here, Jussy?' he asked, putting the water feeder in the corner. The chooks helped Pop talk to me; they helped him to see me and ask me things.

'Yeah,' I said. 'They won't knock it over there.'

'Good thinking, Jussy, good thinking,' he said. The chooks' smooth feathers and round bodies and wings softened Pop's edges. They smoothed him down, gave him something warm to hold and eggs for his breakfast.

Pop stepped out of the run for the grit. 'Telephone,' he said. I stepped out and heard it too. Pop left me with the chooks to answer it.

When he came back he was saying words under his breath— the only one I heard was *Rita*. 'Justine, check the fences,' he said.

'But, Pop . . .'

'Go and check them. Get a move on.'

I crossed the yard and took hold of the fence. I had to check the posts, the wires and the fox mesh for holes. Pop didn't run anything on his Three; he kept it quiet—no surprises. I walked slowly, my hand on the wire. As I went up the slope of Pop's Three I could see glimpses of the Murray through the forest, muddy brown, rippling. Then Pop's Three sloped down and I couldn't see anything. I was at the furthest part of the Three. It was only space and empty sky. There was nobody here. There were no sounds. There was nothing. I wanted to run; I couldn't see the house, I couldn't see the forest on the other side, I couldn't see anything. There was nothing in me, and nothing outside of me. It was the same as the ditch around Steve. Like the Japs in the war with Pop, I didn't have a reason. My heart pounded. I started to run, my hand on the fence, until I could see the Murray through the trees again. Down there, the banks of The Choke pressed in on the water from both sides, trying to strangle it. But the water kept going. My heart stopped racing and then I was past the top of the Three and I could see Pop's house again.

When I came back the fire was lit. Pop made us ham and egg sandwiches and we sat in the camp chairs and ate. The yolk dripped down the sides and turned the ham yellow. Pop put enough salt on it to see the crystals sinking into the sauce. I wiped my bread across the butter left on the plate.

'Good, hey, Jussy?' said Pop.

'Good, Pop.'

⁓

When Dad came out of the back-house Pop asked if he could help him pick up a load of wood. 'It's out the back of Sandy's,' he said. 'Your truck takes more than mine.'

'How much?' said Dad.

'Enough to get us through winter,' said Pop.

'It's December,' Dad said. 'How much wood do we need?'

'Winter comes around,' said Pop. 'Give it time to dry.'

Dad shrugged. 'If you say so.'

I sat between Dad and Pop in the truck. The cabin was full of papers and empty pouches of White Ox. A necklace with a cross hung from the mirror. Dad drove and Pop was beside the window. The wind blew across our laps and faces. Pop said, 'Rita called.'

Dad looked across at him, eyebrows raised. 'Oh yeah?'

Pop nodded. 'Yep.'

'What did she want?'

Pop kept his face in the wind as he spoke. 'Wants to visit.'

Dad frowned. 'What for?'

'What for? She's my daughter's what for!'

'Settle down, Dad. Just asking. You haven't seen her for . . . how many years has it been?'

'Not my bloody fault. Jesus. You were there.'

'Take it easy, Robert. Just asking.'

'Nearly six years,' said Pop. 'Jesus.' He shook his head.

Kangaroos lined the side of the road, their grey faces peeking between the trees. I thought I had come to the end of them and then there were more kangaroos, watching, paws raised.

Dad said, 'When's she coming?'

'Soon.'

'When's that?'

'Next week.'

'Right.' Guitar music hummed over the engine. *When you kiss me, sweet angel, when you kiss me, what can I do?* 'Why now?'

'Jesus, I don't know.'

'It won't be because she's getting married.' Dad laughed.

Pop looked across at Dad with his eyes hard. 'Shut up, Ray. That business is finished now.'

'You think so?'

'Just leave it alone.'

'Did you ask her why she wants see you?'

'She's my daughter, for Christ's sake. A father doesn't ask his daughter why she wants to see him.'

'Right,' said Dad. 'She coming on her own?'

'Why wouldn't she be coming on her own? 'Course she's coming on her bloody own.'

'Just asking.'

'Well, stop asking.'

I looked past my dad, through the open window, out to the blue, sunny sky; my Aunty Rita was coming to visit.

12.

Relle dropped Kirk and Steve at Pop's Three on Sunday afternoon. Ray was hammering a nail into the bottom of his boot. He held the boot between his knees, as if he was putting a shoe on a horse. I stood beside him and watched. He never used more movement than he needed; one hit with the hammer and down went the nail. Kirk picked up a stone and pressed it against the strap in his slingshot. Dad looked up as Kirk pulled back the elastic and shot the stone over the fence. Dad put down the boot. 'Give us a look at that thing,' he said.

Kirk and Steve came over to him. Kirk walked with his chest out, like he was a man with a slingshot, a bow and arrow, and a gun, and he could choose which one he wanted to shoot. Steve was behind him, half hidden, in the cool of Kirk's shadow.

Dad took the slingshot from Kirk and turned it over. It looked small in his hands, like it might break. Kirk and Steve and me watched as Dad picked up a rock from the ground beside his camp chair. Light came from his hair, so black it shone. His skin was pale and thick; if you tried to cut it you wouldn't get through, the knife would stick. Dad aimed the rock at the door of his back-house. The sound of the rock hitting the door handle pinged in the air. I felt my mouth drop open.

'Danny's uncle is going to show me and Danny how to shoot,' said Kirk softly.

'You said.' Dad drank from his can.

Steve stayed in the shadow, but I could see the crack in the ground around him.

Dad threw his cigarette into the fire. He got up, crossed the yard and went through the fence. Me and Kirk and Steve stood on the bottom rung and watched him. We never took our eyes off him, as if he was a movie and we didn't know what would happen, who would win and who would be killed. We were waiting to see.

Dad bent and picked up a stick and when he came back to us, waiting along the fence, we saw he was holding a slingshot much bigger than Kirk's. The handle was as long as his arm, and the sides were in a perfect V. It was if the slingshot had been left there for him. Dad walked out the front to his truck. He came back with a piece of rope that stretched the same way elastic did, and he tied it to the sides. He picked up one of the stones from around Pop's fire and went to the fence. Magpies bounced from the wire to the ground, looking for worms and beetles. There was one magpie separate to the rest. It pecked at the ground, then looked up at us, head on the side. Dad lifted his slingshot. The bird didn't move, watching us. Dad aimed his slingshot. My tongue went in out in out of the hole. Kirk looked at Steve, then at me. Dad pulled back the elastic until it was tight, then he let go.

We walked to the bird lying on its back. My mouth felt dry. The magpie was opening and closing its claws, as if it was trying to take hold of something. There was blood from its eye. Dad walked back to the fire and sat down in his camp chair. He tossed the slingshot onto the ground. There was nothing left to matter to my dad.

13.

When I walked into the classroom on Monday morning, I saw Michael at the desk, his map book open. I went over and sat beside him. His body shook; his shoulders, neck, head, arms, legs jerked and pulled, but his eyes, when he looked at me, were two wells, deep and green. Brian Lawson said, 'Elastic spastic.' I saw Thomas Dunson lift his rifle. *Every time you turn around, expect to see me.*

That morning it was assessment to see if we had to go into the slow group next year with Mrs Eddles. My pencil hovered over the page. I had to guess. I put a tick in one of the circles. I didn't know what the letter was beside it. I moved to the next circle. I put my pencil above another letter. As I went to put a tick in the circle Michael knocked my hand. I looked at him. I went to do the tick again and Michael knocked my hand again. I glared at him. *Leave me alone.* I looked back down at the letters. *Echoice, erac, tahw.* Which one? I didn't understand. I looked around the room. Everyone was putting ticks in the circles, their eyes moving down the page. I looked back at the test. What did it matter where I put my tick? From the other side of the room

Mrs Turning said, 'It is multiple choice. Make sure you read every option carefully before making your choice.'

I put my pencil in the one of the circles, and Michael jerked and shook. What was he doing? I put the pencil in another one of the circles. He shook again. He made a sound but I didn't know what it meant. Nobody looked at him; everyone was used to his sounds and his movements, as if he was invisible. I put my pencil in another one of the circles. I looked at Michael. He made a small move, then he went quiet. I drew a tick. By the end of the test I knew his move for *yes* and his move for *no*. I finished the test at the same time as everybody else, with a tick in every circle.

It was a long time till playlunch. Mrs Turning was teaching letter-writing. She wrote a sentence on the board. A piece of crumpled paper landed on my desk. I turned around and saw Matt Dunning and Brian Lawson grinning at me. Michael saw the paper too. I picked it up. Michael tried to shake his head. I straightened out the paper and saw a picture of a dick. It had wee coming out in a spurt to the edge of the paper.

Mrs Turning said, 'Justine, what is that?' She came over to my desk and took the paper from my hand. She looked at the dick and said, 'What do you mean by this?' Her glasses reflected the light; I had never seen behind them and didn't know if there was anything there.

Matt Dunning and Brian Lawson waited for me to say, *I didn't do it, Mrs Turning, it was Matt and Brian, they did it.* But not telling was my only weapon.

Mrs Turning said, 'Justine? Did you draw this?'

I didn't speak.

'Justine?' Mrs Turning held the dick in front of my eyes and nose, its piss heading for my lap. 'Justine?'

I saw angles of colour and light in Mrs Turning's glasses. Her skirt was grey with checks and it matched the top, grey with checks.

'Did you do this?'

I stayed quiet.

'Go to the corner!'

Michael groaned in his chair beside mine. His head rolled. I was the only one who knew what he was trying to say: *No, no, Mrs Turning, Justine didn't do it.* Everyone thought it was just sounds that he made, that they weren't words. But I knew. *No, Mrs Turning, no, no, no! It wasn't her! It wasn't Justine!*

I got up, my chair scraping against the floor.

'Settle down, Michael,' Mrs Turning said.

Michael's arms flew into the air over his head. He was groaning, spit coming from his mouth. *No! She didn't do it! Mrs Turning, it was them who did it. Them! Matt Dunning and Brian Lawson!* But all she heard was groaning.

Dawn and Noreena whispered to each other.

Mrs Turning put me in the corner, where I stood facing the wall.

Michael's groaning sounds filled the room, as if it hurt him to try to speak, hurt him to see me get up and go and stand in the corner, hurt him to see Matt and Brian lie; as if he, Michael Hooper, was my friend.

⌣

The last hour of the day was carol practice. All of third class stood in rows in front of Sabine. Shelley Castles was between Michael and me. '"Joy to the World", please, boys and girls.' Sabine lifted her baton. *Joy to the world, the Lord is come! Let earth receive her King!* Everybody sang—even Michael. I only made the shapes of the sounds—I didn't want anyone to hear—but Michael made the sounds too. Matt Dunning and Brian Lawson rolled back their eyes and jerked their heads trying to copy him. I stepped behind Shelley Castles and stood beside Michael. *Joy to the world, the Saviour reigns! Let men, their songs, employ!*

If there was no one else in the class, if it was just me and Michael, and we were the only two at Nullabri Primary, I would have sung with him. It would be our own concert, and the singing of Justine and Michael would fill Nullabri Hall; it would be so loud the glass of the windows would break and the doors would blow open. The audience would clap and cheer and say, *More more more! While fields and floods, rocks, hills and plains, repeat the sounding joy, repeat the sounding joy.* The singing would go up to the sky and the people driving by in their cars and trucks would stop by the road to listen as we sang, *Repeat, repeat the sounding joy! Sing joy, joy, joy to the world. Joy, joy, joy!*

⌣

At the end of the day Michael's father picked him up. He came to the front of the school where I waited with Dawn and Noreena. Dawn said, 'He's a teacher at the high school.'

'Mum said it's not fair they have to look after Michael,' said Noreena.

'He can't do anything.'

'So unfair.'

I watched as the back door of the car opened. A little boy climbed out. He went to Michael, put his arms around his legs and held him. Michael gave the boy one of the crutches and then he swung himself with the other crutch into the car. Michael's dad didn't help him.

I didn't know why he was my friend. He couldn't move properly or talk properly. Did he think I was the same? Was I? I wanted to look at his book with the maps. I wanted to sit beside him, and when we walked to the shelter sheds or to the yellow play squares or down the path to the gates to his waiting parents I wouldn't help him either.

———

That night, before I slept, I cut Michael a path that wrapped around my truck all the way to the top. I cut it smooth for his crutches. Nobody could open the truck and if I forgot the numbers for the code Michael would groan and stretch and nod when I guessed them right, and that's how I would know. I put his book at the top on a podium the same as Headmaster Prentice used at assembly. Michael pointed at the pictures and the letters were in the right order so I could read every one.

14.

'Justine, you're starting to smell,' Noreena said.

It was playlunch and I was in the square with Dawn and Noreena.

'What?' I said.

'You're starting to smell like Michael.'

Dawn walked along the yellow line, arms out wide as if it was a tightrope. 'It's true, Jussy,' she said.

'What do you mean?' I looked across to Michael, sitting at the benches.

Noreena said, 'You smell like wee. The same as him.'

I felt my face turn hot and red. I watched Michael turn the page, his hand shaking.

'No, I don't,' I said, but I didn't know. Did I smell?

'Yes, you do,' said Dawn. 'We didn't want to tell you. It's not your fault you have to sit next to him.'

'Oh, it's not your fault, Justine,' Noreena said. 'But maybe you need to have a bath when you get home. Wash it off. Does your Pop make you have a bath?'

I shrugged. Pop didn't have much hot water; I only had a bath sometimes.

'Yeah, you need to wash it off,' said Dawn. 'Michael probably can't have baths; his arms and legs would break the sides. His mum probably has to wash him with a bucket. She probably can't get to all of him. But you can have baths, Justine.'

'Yeah, Justine, you definitely can,' said Noreena.

I nodded. But I didn't know why.

As we were going back to class I saw Matt Dunning and Brian Lawson cross to the benches where Michael was sitting. They stood in front of him. Since Mrs Turning put me next to Michael it was as if people noticed him for the first time. Other kids started moving towards Matt Dunning and Brian Lawson. They made a half-circle around the benches so I couldn't see Michael anymore. Dawn and Noreena followed me towards them. I heard Matt Dunning say, 'How did you get like that, spastic elastic?'

I pushed through the crowds and saw Michael's head jerking back.

'Can I have a go of your crutches?' said Brian Lawson. Everybody watched as he picked up Michael's crutches and put them under his arms, then he swung around on them. Other kids laughed. Michael was breathing hard.

I stood with Dawn and Noreena, who were laughing with the other girls as Brian swung around on the crutches, back and forth in front of them. My heart started to race. Michael's body shook, his arm flung out, his eyes rolled back. He groaned. Spit came from his mouth, down his chin. Brian kept swinging. 'Spastic elastic!' he chanted. 'Spastic elastic! Needs his mum to hold his dick so he can do a wee-ee.' The girls screamed and laughed and Michael groaned. I thought my chest would explode. Matt Dunning grabbed Michael's map book from the table. Michael's back arched, spasmed, as pages from the book fell to the ground.

I ran to Brian and pulled the crutches from him. I held one up like Thomas Dunson's rifle and looked down the barrel at Brian Lawson's face. '*Every time you turn around,*' I said, '*I'm going to catch up with you.*' I moved my gun around slowly; I looked in everyone's face—the laughing girls and the teasing boys—right into their eyes, where the bullet would go. My hands were shaking. I kept the gun high. I went up the row and down the row, a bullet for every one. *Bang bang bang bang bang bang.* The bell rang and still I held the gun. Someone made a sound. Like a giggle, but scared. I kept the gun cocked, ready, and looked straight down the barrel at my targets.

Matt said softly, 'Weirdo.' Then Matt and Brian walked away. The girls followed. Only Dawn and Noreena stayed. I lowered the gun. My arms were still shaking. I leaned the crutches against the bench near Michael.

Noreena said, 'Justine, what's wrong with you?'

'Nothing,' I said.

Dawn said, 'Are you coming?' I looked at Dawn and Noreena, green ribbons, smooth dresses, eyes I couldn't see inside.

'No,' I said. I sat down beside Michael Hooper.

Noreena frowned. 'Come on, Dawnie.' They walked away.

Soon Michael's movements and his breathing slowed. I bent down and picked up the torn pages from the map book. I smoothed them and put them back in their place in the book. They were maps of the world, all in different colours—green, blue, pink. I saw a mountain range and a volcano. Michael groaned as if he was trying to speak. I said, 'What?' He pushed words through the sound. But I still didn't understand. 'What?'

He said, louder. 'Stupid idiots!'

Michael took his crutches and pulled himself to his feet. We walked to class. Matt and Brian left us alone in the classroom. They didn't say anything to me about Michael; they didn't call him my husband. When it was lunchtime I sat with Michael and he didn't make me be a gorilla. He spread his lunch in front of us on the bench; there were strawberries and bread and cheese, and a cold sausage. Michael tore the sausage in half and he passed one half to me. When Dawn and Noreena walked past us, Michael pointed to a picture of two sharks in his map book.

———

And then I didn't need other friends; I only needed Michael. I didn't want the school bell to ring; I didn't want the day to end. I learned the code of his sounds and it was an easier language than the one Mrs Turning was trying to teach. In a day I forgot that it had ever been hard to understand what he was saying. He was Michael. I didn't help him to walk or to sit or to stand. I didn't help him do anything. I stood and waited while he picked up his books and his bag and opened doors and took out his lunch. But he helped me—he helped me with the order of the letters, the order of the words, which circles to tick, which lines to join, which numbers to add. There was less and less he had to do for me to know he was helping me. It was in the smallest movement. It was easy. Easier than anything at school had been before.

One morning he didn't come to school. I waited and waited and there was no one to ask, *When is he coming back? When will Michael be here?* The sharks circled and I turned away.

When he did come back on Friday, he said to me, 'I hate nurses.'

'Nurses? Why?'

'They make me move my legs.'

'Bitches,' I said. Michael's head shot back, his eyes went wide and he sucked in air. It exploded from him in snorts. I had never seen him laugh like that before.

Bitches! Dawn and Noreena didn't look at me, as if we had never been friends, and we hadn't; we hadn't ever been friends.

⌒

We walked along the row of pine trees by the fence. 'What do you want to do when you leave?' he asked me.

'Leave where?'

'Here. School. When you grow up?'

I shrugged. I wasn't sure. I didn't know if there was anything I could do.

'There must be something you want to do,' he said.

'I don't know.'

'What if you could do anything?'

'Anything?'

'Yes.'

'Anything at all?'

'Yes, Justine. Anything at all.'

'I'd drive a truck.'

'A truck?'

I didn't want to tell him anymore. Maybe it was wrong. Stupid.

'What sort of truck?'

'I don't know.'

'Come on, Justine. What sort of truck?'

'I don't know.'

'A semi?'

I shrugged.

'A truck to transport things?'

'I don't know.'

'You do know. Come on, Justine, tell me!'

But I couldn't answer. My answer would be wrong.

'Justine, if you don't tell me then . . . I don't know! I don't know what I'll do. I won't tell *you*.'

We walked in silence. His breathing was huffy. He kicked at the pine cones in the grass and didn't look at me. A long time went by.

'A big one,' I said. 'One you can live in. With a cabin behind the driver's seat.'

'What colour?'

'White and silver. It would go fast. A lot faster than any other car on the road. It would be big enough to live in. You could go a long way. You could follow the Murray to New South Wales. You could cook in it. You'd need a ladder to get to the cabin it would be so high.'

Michael turned to me, his face serious. 'Can I come?'

He wasn't laughing at me; my answers weren't wrong or stupid. 'Yes,' I said. 'You can come.'

'We could go anywhere.'

We could go anywhere. A highway stretched out before us. All we had to do was make it through the school gate and there the truck would be, waiting, its fenders gleaming, its big silver body ready and fast, with a slot for the crutches and two seats: one for Michael and one for me.

⌣

When I saw Mrs Hooper driving up to the gate in the morning, I wanted to run down to her car. I wanted to say, *Can I help you, Mrs Hooper?* But I couldn't find the words to speak them.

Can I help you, Mrs Hooper? Please let me help you. Even when she smiled at me, not minding that I didn't help, even then, I couldn't speak or move or do anything except be glad Michael, her son, was there. *Thank you for Michael, Mrs Hooper.*

15.

While he was away Dad had missed Kirk's thirteenth birthday. Kirk had come to Pop's to wait, just in case Dad called on the telephone, but the telephone never rang. Pop said this Saturday night could be the birthday instead. Dad was going to be home at five o'clock for a barbecue. Pop bought steaks and bread rolls and corn on the cob. He poured lemonade into paper cups while we waited for Dad. Kirk and Steve sat against Pop's woodpile; they both held sticks and shot at the lizards and ants that crossed the dirt. I sat beside Pop on one of the camp chairs. Kirk said, 'Dad's going to teach me how to shoot.'

Pop stirred his fire with a stick. 'No, he's not.'

'Yeah, he is. He told me.'

'No, he didn't,' said Pop. Sparks flew from the flames.

'He said he's going to show me on the Mauser.'

'The Mauser stays where she is. You'll learn to shoot when you're sixteen.'

Kirk threw a bottle top towards the chickens. Missy warbled and jumped. 'Danny's uncle will show me before then.'

'Good for him,' said Pop. 'Leave my chickens alone.'

'When he gets back from Gympie. He's got his own guns,' said Kirk. 'He's got a rifle and a .22.'

'Sure he has,' said Pop. 'Get me a beer from the esky, will you?'

Kirk went into the laundry. Pop looked at his watch. We drank the lemonade. It was still hot from the day. Mosquitoes flew around our heads. Pop slapped at his legs. He got up and brought more wood from his pile then he threw a plank into the flame and I watched the nails glow orange. The lemonade left a coat of itself on my tongue. I pushed my tongue in and out of the hole, in out in out.

Kirk came back with the beer. Pop looked at his watch again. Then he went into the chook run. 'Here, chook chook chook,' he called. Kirk made a gun with his fingers and fired it at the chooks as they followed Pop through the gate.

The water from the Murray seeped up through the ground. Even in summer, when it was hot. The trees' branches moved in the warm air. The flames of Pop's fire jumped and danced. 'Cockyboy!' Pop called. 'Get in here.' Pop walked down to Cockyboy and shooed him from the top of the gate. 'Come on, Cockyboy, get in there. Go look after your girls.'

'Get in there, Cockhead, get in there,' Kirk said.

Steve pulled out his blade. 'Run for your life, Cockhead,' he said.

Pop came out of the run and walked up to the house. Kirk said, 'Danny's uncle is going to show us how to shoot as soon as he comes back from Gympie. Danny will come and get me; we'll go straight over. We'll head up to The Choke and shoot at the roos on the other side. Danny's uncle hunts pigs, too. Pigs are harder to see. They're the same colour as the trees.

You have to tell the difference then *kapow*.' Kirk held up his finger and shot the pigs.

It went quiet. Kirk and Steve dug holes with their stick-guns, and I watched the fire as we waited for Dad. It felt like we had always been waiting for him; since we were small, before the fall-out, back when Donna was still my mother, we had been waiting. Even when he was here we were waiting—for him to look at us, talk to us, laugh at the jokes we made, notice the things we did.

Pop came out of the kitchen with the steaks and chops. He spread the fire with his stick, put the grate over the flames, then laid out the steaks and chops. We watched as the steaks sizzled with black lines from the grill.

'Thirteen will be a good year,' said Kirk. He flicked dirt into the air.

'Better than twelve,' said Steve.

'Yah! Yah!'

What was that?

'Yah! Yah!'

Kirk and Steve and me got up and ran down the side of the house, towards the sound at the front.

'Yah! Yah!'

There was Dad and he was riding a horse! A big silver horse!

'Dad!' we called.

Dad smiled at us and lifted his hat. The horse pranced beneath him.

'Dad!' we called. 'Dad!'

The horse was trying to pull him one way, then another. Kirk stood taller beside me; it was better than a telephone call, better than Danny's uncle, it was his own dad on a horse for his birthday! Dad came up on the big silver horse, holding the reins with one hand. He made a gun with the fingers of his other hand and held it in the air.

Where did he get the horse?

'Stick 'em up!' said Dad.

Dad's legs hung low on either side of the horse, his black boots pressing hard into the stirrups, pushing them outwards, as he rode it towards the house.

Pop came out the front. 'What's going on?'

'Ride 'em, cowboy!' Dad said, pulling on the reins.

The horse reared back, its mouth open wide enough for me to see the gleaming metal across its tongue. Its legs and shoulders and thighs were tight with muscle and strength.

'Who does that belong to?' Pop called to Dad.

'She's all mine,' said Dad. He twirled the horse around, with the reins against her neck. The horse went in the circle whichever way Dad pulled. 'What do you think, kids? Do you like her?'

'Great horse, Dad,' said Kirk.

'Yeah,' said Steve. 'Great.'

'Can I have a ride?' Kirk asked.

'Where's she from?' Pop asked.

'Let's just say somebody owed me.'

The horse kept moving this way and that. It threw its head and pulled against the metal in its mouth. Nothing moved in Dad; his body was solid and still in the saddle as the horse pulled and twitched and fought him. The horse was the movement and Dad was the stillness.

'She yours?' Pop asked.

'She is.'

'Can I have a ride?' Kirk asked again.

'She's a wild one, mate. I reckon she might try to run straight back where she came from with you in the saddle.'

'Where's that?' Pop asked, frowning.

'Nowhere land,' said Dad.

'Tea's ready,' said Pop. 'You going to get off that thing and eat? We've been waiting.'

'Can I have a ride?' said Kirk.

It was as if Dad couldn't hear Kirk. He said, 'Coming for a ride, Justine?'

'It's Kirk's birthday,' said Pop.

'What, today?' said Dad.

'Not today,' said Pop, 'but . . .'

'Justine can fit behind. Come on, Justine.'

Kirk's mouth fell open. I saw covers slide over the tops of his eyes, blocking the light.

'Come on,' said Dad. 'Climb up.' He rode closer to me, leaned over and held out his hand. The horse was so big, shining and grey, its eyes so dark. My dad was big too, above the horse, muscles down his arms and muscles down the shoulders of the horse, strong across its back.

I didn't know what to do. It was a barbecue for Kirk's birthday.

'Justine,' said Dad. 'Come over and get on the horse.' The horse smelled of sweat and grass and earth, its breathing heavy as it pulled my dad one way and then another. 'Come here,' said Dad, holding out his hand to me.

Kirk watched. Steve stood, caught, inside the ditch that ran around him. He couldn't move. There was no chance for him. Pop said, 'It's Kirk's birthday, for Christ's sake.'

Dad said, 'Be there in a minute. Come on, Justine.'

'Leave Justine here, Ray,' Pop called. 'She can't ride a bloody horse.'

'She doesn't have to,' said Ray. 'She can sit behind.' Then he sat up in the saddle and called back to Pop, 'Remember when we went with Mum to Swan Hill? Remember that, Pop? We rode that day, didn't we? Mum rode too, remember? You haven't forgotten that day, have you, Pop?'

Pop's mouth shut tight, his lips pressing hard against each other as if they were trying to hold back what happened.

'Get on the horse, Justine,' Dad said. 'Take my hand, then put your foot on mine.'

My dad leaned down. I took his hand. I stepped towards the horse and its dark eyes rolled back in its head so I could see the whites. It stepped away from me as if it was scared. I tried to put my foot on Dad's boot, but my foot wouldn't reach. I could feel Kirk and Steve watching me as I tried. Dad took his foot out of the stirrup. 'Just get your foot on my boot,' said Dad. 'Come on, Jussy.' He wanted me to do it; he was sick of being in Pop's drive and sick of trying to get me on the horse.

A blackbird swooped down and the horse jumped. 'Settle down,' said Dad in a low voice. 'Easy, girl, easy.'

As I lifted my leg to try to put my foot on his boot, he grabbed hold of my hand and pulled me up and over the back of the saddle. I was looking at the dirt on the other side from way up on the horse, as it skipped and swerved. Dad laughed and then he righted me so I was sitting up behind him. The saddle tipped me towards him; I was so close I could smell the cigarette smoke in his jacket.

I watched as Kirk turned and walked back into the house. His head was down. It was his birthday, one month late. But it was his birthday. As he walked, the half that was the same in us shrunk to nothing.

'Hold on, Justine.' Dad pulled my arms around him. 'You right?'

'Yeah,' I said. The horse was trembling and hot and damp, pulling beneath us.

Pop called, 'Ray, leave Justine here.'

Ray said, 'Let's go, Jussy.' He pulled one rein so that the horse turned and headed for the trail. 'Giddup, girl!' said Dad, flicking the reins over her shoulder. The horse started to trot, jiggling me against him.

Dad said, 'What do you want to call her, my special girl?' Did he mean me or the horse? Who was the special girl? He kicked the horse. 'Come on, get up there!' he said.

The horse began to canter along the trail away from Pop's Three.

Dad kicked it harder. 'Get up there! Get up there!'

The horse began to gallop, its hooves clattering on the dirt road. When I looked down I saw the pebbles flying out from under its hooves, like shrapnel. The faster she went the easier it was to ride her. I held on to my Dad as the red gums of Yolamundi rushed past. I forgot the hang of Kirk's head as he turned to leave, I forgot that it was his birthday, his dad, his ride, and that I took it, I took Kirk's ride.

'Silver,' I called out to Dad. 'Her name is Silver!'

'Hi ho, Silver!' shouted Dad, leaning forward.

⌒

The moon in the sky that night showed the tops of the trees on the other side of the fence, the leaves and branches glowing. Pop and Ray drank from their beer cans in front of Pop's fire.

'Reckons he can get a thousand bucks a ton,' said Dad.

'Bullshit, son,' said Pop. 'A thousand bucks?'

'I heard it from the horse's mouth.' Dad tipped his beer in the direction of Silver, in the paddock on the other side. 'A thousand bucks.'

'How much is towage? Did he say?'

'He said it was all-inclusive.'

'Did you believe him?'

'He'd be a fool to bullshit. He wouldn't take the risk.'

'So what are you going to do?'

'Check it out. Drive up there and do a few loads.' Dad drank from his can. 'Got my eye on a block backside of Nullabri.' Dad said one day he was going to build a house on a block and stay put so Pop wouldn't have to look after me anymore.

Pop said, 'Right.' Dad was talking more since Silver came.

I walked to where the horse stood in Pop's paddock. She was eating grass with her head down. Her coat glowed as if the light from the moon was under her skin. 'Silver, Silver,' I whispered, putting out my hand. She sniffed my fingers. I patted her nose and leaned closer. She smelled like the chooks and the grass. Her eyes were made of black water, as if it had been poured into the bowls of her face. I climbed through the wire and sat on the ground in front of her. River water seeped into my pants. Silver smelled my hair. She pushed at my head and snorted her warm breath against my ear. I heard Pop and Ray laughing from the yard. Dad said, 'Bugger that for a joke! Fuck, no!' I put my hands up to Silver's face and stroked her forehead. She pulled at the grass around my feet. 'Silver, Silver,' I said. I stood up and put my arms around her neck. She let me hold her. Her chest was so strong, so wide and warm. 'I love you, Silver.'

⌒

But in the morning when I went out to see her, the paddock was empty. I could see the prints of her hooves in the grass.

'Horse is gone,' said Pop from the back door.

'Gone where?' I said. Pop came down to the fire, his dressing-gown around him, a White Ox on his lip. He threw sticks into the smoke of his coals until there was a flame. 'I don't know.'

'Where's Dad?' I said.

He pulled out a burning stick and lit his fag. 'Don't know that either.'

'Will he be back today?' I asked.

'Your guess is as good as mine,' said Pop.

'Will he be back this morning?' I asked. I picked up a bottle top and threw it into the flame.

'I don't know,' said Pop. We stood, Pop and me, not knowing, waiting in the space left behind.

⁓

When Pop was in town at the stock and feed shop, I went out to the paddock. 'Here, girl; come on, girl.' I held out my hands to her and she came close and I felt her warm breath on my fingers. I closed my eyes and led her through the gate, then I put one foot in the stirrup and swung myself over. I felt her underneath me, stepping one way and then another. She felt hot and I smelled her sweat. 'Easy, girl, settle down, settle down,' I said. Then I kicked her, 'Yah! Yah!' and we took off around the yard. I held on to the reins with one hand; with my other hand I made a gun and shot it in the air. *Pchoo! Pchoo, pchoo! She's mine, all mine!* We galloped through the house, out of the front door and down Pop's road. Faster and faster, Silver's hooves clacking on the road, the stones flying. *Hi ho, Silver!*

16.

You never knew where Ray was when he was gone. He spoke on the telephone and you never knew who he was speaking to. His friends changed. He went out to places to meet them, but he never said where. Pop told the chooks, he said, *Since that day at the hospital. That was when it started. That very day. The hour she left us. A different boy after that. Nothing but secrets.*

⁓

When I came home from school on Friday I saw Dad sitting at Pop's fire with Aunty Rita.

'G'day, Jussy,' said Dad. 'You remember Rita, don't you?' Dad sucked back on his cigarette.

'Hi, Justine,' said Aunty Rita.

I couldn't look up at her. I looked at her feet—she was wearing boots like my dad's.

'Justine,' said Dad. 'Say g'day.'

I kept looking at Aunty Rita's feet; they were almost the same size as Dad's.

'Justine?' said Dad. 'Say g'day.'

'Ease up, Ray,' said Aunty Rita.

'Say g'day, Justine. Go on.'

I kept my mouth closed; I didn't want Aunty Rita looking at my teeth.

Aunty Rita said, 'You've grown a lot since I last saw you.' Her voice was strong like Ray's but soft like a woman's.

'When was that?' said Dad.

'Justine must have been . . . four,' said Aunty Rita. 'Don't you remember? Pop and I had words.'

I could feel her eyes on me. Heat moved up to my face.

'Oh yeah, that time,' said Dad. 'How could I forget?'

'You look like your mother,' said Aunty Rita.

Dad said, 'Like I need reminding.'

'Nothing wrong with being reminded.'

I stole a look at her. Her eyes were the same colour as my dad's but there was light behind the circles. I could see into them. She was tall like Ray, with wide shoulders. She wore almost the same clothes as him: checked coat, boots, checked shirt. She said, 'So, Justine, does that make you nine?'

I said, 'Hmm.'

'Open your mouth when you talk,' said Dad.

'You open your mouth, Raymond,' said Aunty Rita.

Dad looked away.

'Ten,' I said.

'Ten!' said Aunty Rita. 'You're getting there. You want to show me your room?'

'Where's Pop?' I said.

'Sandy's,' said Dad. 'He won't be back for a while. It's okay, go and show Rita your room.'

Aunty Rita got up from her chair.

She followed me into my room. The room was the same length on all sides, one of the walls was light green, one had wallpaper, and the other two had wallpaper that Pop had painted over white; I could still see the stripes underneath. Aunty Rita looked at my bed, and around at the walls, then she went to the window and leaned against it, looking at the road outside. I heard her sigh. She turned around and sat down on my bed, near the pillow. I sat on the other end.

'How is school?' she asked.

'I don't know,' I said.

'If you're anything like me school is bloody awful. The best thing about school for me was that it finished.'

'Do you want to see my cut-outs?' I said.

'Sure,' she said.

I took my piles of cut-outs from the cupboard; trains and trucks, cars and motorbikes, helicopters, caravans and boats covered the blanket. Aunty Rita ran her hand over them. She looked at them carefully, taking her time. She picked up a train made up of a long row of coloured carriages and said, 'This is a good one.' She leaned back against the wall and looked up at the train in her hands. 'You could get to the other side of the world on a train like this. Imagine how much of the country you'd see. Imagine how nice it would be falling asleep at night.' She put it down and picked up a picture of a motorbike. 'Steer clear of these,' she said. She looked at a pile of Ford pick-ups. Some in colour, others black and white. She said, 'Just like Ray's . . .' She put down the cut-outs. She looked up at me, her face worried. 'He been back long?'

'Two weeks,' I said.

'Do you see him much?' she asked. 'How often does he come home?'

'Sometimes. He's away a lot.'

'What's he doing out there? Anyone know?'

I shrugged.

'Kirk and Steve come around?'

'Sometimes,' I said. 'When Relle lets them.'

'Relle . . .' She snorted softly through her nose. 'Do they look after you?'

'Who?' I asked.

'Your brothers.'

'Yeah.'

Aunty Rita got up from the bed and looked out of the window again. She drummed her fingers on the windowsill, turned around to me and said, 'You want to go for a walk?'

'Yeah.'

Aunty Rita helped me put the cut-outs back in a pile. She picked up the photograph of the train. 'Can I keep this?' she asked.

'Yes,' I said.

Aunty Rita folded the picture in half and put it in her coat pocket. 'Remind me of you,' she said.

We went through the house and out of the back door. Dad was drinking a beer at the fire.

'Okay if we go for a walk?' said Aunty Rita.

'If Pop finds out he'll take down the Mauser,' said Dad.

'I can deal with Dad. Come on, Justine.'

We walked across the yard towards the gate. Cockyboy sat on the top rail. 'Bastard rooster,' she said.

'That's Cockyboy,' I said.

'It always is,' said Aunty Rita, picking up a small stone. She threw it at Cockyboy's feet. He squawked and jumped down from the gate. 'Bugger off, Cockyboy,' said Aunty Rita. 'We're going for a walk.' She pushed open the gate.

17.

It was a warm, grey afternoon; the sky was clean and thin. The trees ahead stood knotted and twisting.

Aunty Rita said, 'Do you like it at Pop's, Justine?'

'Yeah,' I answered, my eyes on the path. I had only lived in one other place: Moama, when Mum and Dad were together. Dad had a barbecue against the wall, close to the window. He was drinking from a can of beer and waiting for the barbecue to get hot enough for the sausages. Suddenly the glass of the window behind the barbecue shattered. I watched as a spider's web of cracks spread from the centre. Mum screamed. I ran towards her, scared of the glass. She kept screaming. She didn't stop.

Dad said, 'You fucken better.'

It wasn't long after that she was gone.

'Does he look after you alright?' Aunty Rita asked me.

'Who?'

'Dad. I mean Pop. Your granddad.'

'Yeah.'

'Food in the fridge?' she asked.

'Yeah.'

'Alongside the beers, right?'

'He keeps the beers in the laundry,' I told her. 'Next to the washing machine.'

'Right . . .'

Our feet followed the narrow trail. I could feel her behind me; Dad, but not Dad. His sister.

Soon we came to the trees, their trunks as wide as bulbs. You could see the roots above the ground, trying to cover every direction. The branches moved slowly. Their bark red and pink and cream, peeling back, showing the bones. Their leaves silver-green in the grey light.

Aunty Rita said, 'I forget all this.' She lifted her arm and looked up. The trees made passages that led to the sky. Aunty Rita took my hand. 'Makes me dizzy,' she said. 'So beautiful.'

We kept walking. I heard crickets. Soon we came to the Murray. It flowed wide and brown, tiny waves across the surface.

Aunty Rita said, 'This was where I used to come when I lived here. I came here all the time.'

We walked along the path that followed the edge.

'Do you come down here much?' she asked me.

'Pop only lets me if Kirk and Steve come too.'

'I reckon that might put you in more danger,' said Aunty Rita. 'Relle still giving Pop hell?'

'Yeah,' I answered. 'She's still giving him hell. Especially when Dad's back. She doesn't like Dad, but then she does. Then she really does.'

Aunty Rita laughed. 'You keep quiet, Justine, but you got a lot to say, don't you? Once you warm up.' Then she said, 'I was like that. But I never warmed up until I left home. Even then it took a long time.' She seemed to be talking to herself. 'Not until I met Naomi.'

'Who's Naomi?'

Aunty Rita put her hand against a tree. 'My friend,' she said. 'My good friend.'

We walked for a while more.

'I got a friend,' I said.

'Oh yeah? Who's that?'

'Michael Hooper.'

'That's a nice name,' she said. 'What's he like?'

'He's got a map book,' I said. 'He knows all the countries. And he can read. He can count. He's strong,' I said. 'He's really strong. And he can sing. He's not scared. He could be scared, but he's not.'

'I like the sound of him. How long have you been friends?'

'Not that long. Only this term.'

'It's good you found him. What do you guys do together?'

'Um . . . we talk, we eat his lunch. I don't know . . . he helps me.'

'That's good, Justine. That's really good.'

We climbed over a log in the path. Then I said, 'He doesn't always come to school.'

'Oh? Why is that?'

'He has to go to hospital.'

'What for?'

'To see the nurses. They make him stretch his legs.'

'Why do they do that?'

'He didn't get enough oxygen. His body . . . it doesn't always do what he wants it to.'

'That must be hard,' said Aunty Rita. 'For him. And hard for you when he's not there.'

'Yeah,' I said. 'It's a lot better when he's there.'

'Good,' said Aunty Rita. 'I am glad you have him. And I bet he's glad he has you. Friends can really make the difference.'

'Yeah,' I said. 'They really can.'

We stopped at the tyre swing. It hung from a long rope that was tied to a branch growing out over the river. Aunty Rita pushed at the swing, and the tyre bounced away from her. 'Want to go for a swim?' she asked me.

'Yeah,' I said. Even though the light was grey, the sun was warm behind it.

'I can't look at this river without having a swim,' said Aunty Rita, unbuttoning her shirt. 'Even in bloody winter.' She pulled off her boots and jeans and stood on the bank in her underpants and bra. She was Dad, and she wasn't. She turned to me. 'Last one in is a rotten egg!'

I pulled off my dress and scrambled down the bank. Aunty Rita was already jumping for the tyre. She held on and pulled herself up to standing. She pushed with her legs, leaning back, looking up to the clouds. The tyre went up and up, then down again, her back straight and hard as the statue of the Nullabri soldier, her shoulders broad and smooth, her body alive with the electricity she gave out at Tarban Creek. Up and down she swung, higher and higher. When the tyre was out far enough she let herself fall into the water and screamed.

I laughed.

Aunty Rita climbed out, drops of river water flying from her skin. 'Your turn,' she said.

I sat with the tyre between my legs and held on as my Aunty Rita pushed me higher and higher. I could feel my mouth open wide, wider than the hole in my teeth, and I screamed and laughed, 'Noooooo!' and Aunty Rita pushed me higher still.

'Let go!' she cried. 'Let go, Justine!'

I flew up, up, up into the light, then fell under, into the cool water of the Murray. When I came to the surface, paddling my legs and arms, there was my Aunty Rita, grinning at me. She splashed me, the water spraying up between us. 'Take that! Take that!' I splashed my Aunty Rita. 'Take that!'

'Take that! Take that!'

We climbed onto the bank and sat together, ants crawling around and over our toes and ankles. I drew a heart in the dirt with a stick. Slowly, holding the stick with a pencil grip, I wrote a *J* and a *4* and an *R*. I did it slow as I could. I wanted the letters in the right order: *J 4 R.*

Aunty Rita said, 'Oh, Justine.' She put her arm around me. Aunty Rita outlined the heart with stones.

I looked up and saw someone coming through the trees. Aunty Rita said, 'It's Ray. It's your dad, Justine.' She put her hand over her mouth. 'Yo yo yo!' she called like Chief Puma from *McLintock!*

Dad called back, 'Yo yo yo!' as he came through the trees, his hand up and down over his mouth.

Aunty Rita tipped back her head. 'Yo yo yo!'

When he was close, still running, he pulled his shirt over his head. When he came to the river he pulled off his boots and jeans. He was broad and tight with the muscles that lived under his skin. Aunty Rita jumped to her feet, still in her underpants and bra, and they ran down to the river. They called to each other, brother and sister, back and forth. 'Yo yo yo!' Their hands over their mouths. Both tall and shining. Dad jumped on the tyre and sailed out over the water, his legs pushing the swing high. He came crashing down, his arms wrapped around his legs, and the water splashed up around him in circles. Aunty Rita ran in after him. I watched as they fought, ducking and coming up and going under and splashing. Every drop of water between them was filled with light and electricity.

'Ah! You got me, sister, you got me.' Dad dragged himself up
to the bank as if he'd been shot with an arrow. He lay on his
back in the dirt, not scared of ants, not caring if they crawled
over him, not scared of the sticks and dirt and stones hurting
his skin, not scared of the light in his eyes. Aunty Rita fell back
beside him, and they looked up at the bright, grey sky.

'Your dad could never beat me, Justine.'

Dad said, 'She's right, Jussy. I never could.'

They lay side by side, their chests heaving. I lay beside them
and listened to the trees growing around us. I heard the branches
creak as they lengthened, I heard the roots as they spread, the
leaves as they multiplied.

Aunty Rita sat up, put her face in her hands and cried. Dad
sat up beside her. He sighed and said softly, 'Jesus.' Years passed
through his body, until he was a boy again. He knew why his
sister was crying. He didn't try to stop her. If he touched her
he would have cried too.

I looked past them and saw Lizzy in the trees; before
the broken bones, before pneumonia and the hospital, before the
war in Burma—the way she was in the photograph, with the
flower in her hair.

Dad said, 'You okay?'

Aunty Rita lifted her face from her hands. 'This place . . .'

'Come on, we better get back.' said Dad. *This place* was still
his home.

Dad and Aunty Rita pulled on their clothes. Aunty Rita
stood and held out her hand to me. As we walked she began to
sing, *A gallant knight, in sunshine and in shadow, had journeyed
long . . .* Her voice was deep and smooth. Dad joined in. *Singing
a song, in search of El Dorado.* Then I sang too—we were Cole
Thornton, J.P. Harrah and Maudie from *El Dorado* as we walked

back to Pop's. *Over the mountains of the moon, down the valley of the shadow, 'Ride, boldly ride,' the shade replied, if you seek for El Dorado.*

—

When we crossed the yard I saw Pop in the chook run. 'Here you are, ladies; here you are, Cockyboy; here, chook chook chook,' he said, as he scattered the seed. Aunty Rita looked at me with a spark in her eyes. *Another bastard rooster.*

Pop stepped out of the run.

'Hi, Dad.' Aunty Rita's voice sounded caught in her throat.

There was sweat on Pop's forehead and chook shit across his cheek. Each of his legs was so thin that there was dark space in the shorts around them. He said, 'Rita.'

We stood in the yard: Rita, Ray, me and Pop. It suddenly seemed hotter. Cockyboy strutted around our feet like Pop's guard.

'Good to see you, Dad,' said Aunty Rita.

'You're looking well, Rita,' said Pop.

Something ran between Aunty Rita and Pop, and hurt them.

'How have you been?'

'I've been okay.'

It went quiet. I said, 'Pop, Aunty Rita and me went for a swim. We went on the tyre.'

'Jesus,' said Pop. 'Lucky you didn't break your back.'

'You used to swim in the river, didn't you, Dad?' said Dad.

'I did.'

'Remember that?' said Dad. 'Us and the bloody Worlleys at the river. Wasn't it you that tied that bloody tyre up in the first place?'

'It was.'

'And the first one to use it. Mum went off her nut,' said Dad.

'She did. Then we made her get on it.'

It was quiet. Lizzy was pulling at them from where she lay under the ground. They wanted to see her swinging through the air, holding tight to the tyre for as long as she could, flying higher, seeing the river beneath her. But when they did, it hurt them.

'Christ, that was a long time ago,' said Dad.

'We're all getting older,' said Aunty Rita.

Pop said, 'It's good to see you, Rita.'

'Not what you say to me when I come home,' said Dad.

'You come home too often,' said Pop. 'You thirsty, Rita? You want a beer?'

'I could murder a beer.' Aunty Rita put her arm around me as we crossed to Pop's fire. 'Justine has grown tall,' she said.

'She eats all my eggs,' said Pop. 'You eaten, Rita? Ray fed you?'

'Are you kidding?'

Pop said, 'Can't believe I asked,' and they laughed the same laugh, dry through the nose.

'Hey, take it easy, sister. I offered you a beer,' said Dad.

'You did, brother. You offered me a beer, it's true.'

The feeling was light. The same as the sky over the Murray, warm and grey and light. I wanted to hold on to it. It was as if the hole in my teeth had been filled; I didn't care about it anymore. I had my Aunty Rita! The Lees were a family with different parts—an aunt, a father, a grandfather and me.

Pop put sticks on his fire. I sat beside Aunty Rita. Pop brought out chicken wings and grilled them on the fire. He sprinkled them with salt and put corn cobs wrapped in foil in the flames. He poured honey over the chicken wings.

Dad said, 'Special treatment, hey?'

Pop said, 'Shut up, Ray.'

'Looks good, Dad,' said Aunty Rita, and the smell of chicken wings and honey and butter filled the circle around the fire.

I felt the dry river water on my skin, I saw dirt banked up behind the hairs and I stretched and felt them break apart. We were hot. It was summer, but the fire always burned. *Keep the bloody Murray at bay*, said Pop. The only time he didn't light the fire was if he had gut trouble.

Pop, Dad and Aunty Rita's talking flowed around me like music. Soon it turned to song. *But he grew old, this knight so bold, and o'er his heart a shadow fell as he found no spot of ground, that looked like El Dorado.* They sang and drank beer and said, *Ah, the big man, the Duke, Old Duke, you can't go past the big man.* All of them said it, as if they all knew the big man and loved him and his songs and all knew his search for El Dorado. The grey light darkened and the flames of Pop's fire burned brighter, holding us close.

I don't know who carried me inside. It could have been Dad; it could have been Aunty Rita or Pop. I was laid on the bed. My shoes were pulled off. Someone kissed my cheek. I heard, 'What a little beauty, you are, Justine.'

18.

The next day I woke up to the sun in my eyes. I got out of bed, crossed the hall and stood by the closed spare room door, listening.

Pop came out of the kitchen. 'Leave her alone, Justine. She needs a rest.' The lines on his face were not as deep, as if a pair of thumbs had rubbed them smooth. I smelled eggs frying. I yawned and stretched and went into the kitchen. There was a plate of thick buttered toast on the table, beside the teapot. The teapot wore Lizzy's pink knitted cosy that only came out at Christmas. Eggs and bacon and tomato sizzled in the pan. Pop smoked a White Ox while he fried. The smoke from the kindest animal drifted around the room, mixing with the smell of bacon. My mouth watered.

Aunty Rita came into the kitchen. She was wearing striped pyjamas and her dark hair was in messy knots. She yawned and said, 'Morning, Jussy.' She tousled my hair. 'That smells good, Pop.' She sat down at the table.

'The girls lay more than we can eat. New egg grit and better pellets.'

'Ah, the girls . . .' said Aunty Rita, grinning at me.

Pop put the eggs, tomatoes and bacon on the toast, then he put one plate in front of Aunty Rita and one in front of me.

'What about you, Dad? Aren't you eating?' said Aunty Rita.

Pop raised his White Ox. 'I'll eat later. You start before it gets cold.' He leaned against the bench and watched Aunty Rita and me eat eggs, hot tomato and bacon on toast, and it was as if every mouthful we took fed him something too. Aunty Rita put a lot of butter on her toast and so did I. Then strawberry jam. I drank milk to wash it down, and Aunty Rita drank tea.

When we were scraping the plates Pop said to Aunty Rita, 'How's the Torry running?'

'Alright. I ask a lot of her. Bit of a rattle anything over forty.'

'Want me to take a look?'

'That'd be good, Dad. Save me from getting ripped off at the mechanics. Can I take Justine out in your truck while you do?' She turned to me. 'Want to go out somewhere, Justine?'

'Where to?' Pop asked.

'I don't know. Into town? The bakery?'

'Righto,' said Pop, putting his White Ox out in the sink. 'Bring us back some bread.'

—

I was going into town with my Aunty Rita. I felt light, as if the balloons from my pyjamas were in my chest. I pulled on my skirt and top. Aunty Rita came out of the spare room in her checked coat and jeans. 'Keys?' she said to Pop.

Pop took the keys from his belt. 'Anything over forty in the truck you'll hear more than a rattle.' He carried his tool bag out the front to Aunty Rita's car.

We went down the side to Pop's truck. The curtains were closed in the back-house. 'Get up, Ray, you lazy bastard,' Aunty Rita called out. 'Some things never change,' she said to me.

Cockyboy watched us from his place on the top of the gate. 'A lot of things never change,' I said.

'You got that right, sister.'

'Hey, I'm not your sister!'

'Niece. Close enough.'

We got in the truck. She turned Pop's key and the engine started. 'Shall we run Cockyboy down on the way out?'

'What if he comes back as a ghost?' I said.

'Christ,' said Aunty Rita. 'Imagine that.'

'Spooky.'

'Hey, Justine, got any room in that stomach for cake?'

'Yep.'

'You're funny, Justine. Anyone ever tell you that?'

'No,' I said. 'You're the first.'

Aunty Rita laughed. She turned on the radio, fiddling with the knob until it came to music. A man sang, *Out where the skies are bluer, out where friendship's truer* . . . 'Perfect,' she said. 'Cowboy music.' *Out where a fresher breeze is blowing, out where the world is in the making.* We drove down the road away from Yolamundi.

Song after song played as Aunty Rita drove. *I'm back in the saddle again, out where a friend is a friend, where the longhorn cattle feed on the lonely jimson weed, I'm back in the saddle again.* We hummed along, and when we could guess the words, we sang. In between songs Aunty Rita said, 'Don't trust cowboys, Justine.'

'What about John Wayne? He's a cowboy.'

'Except John Wayne. You can trust him.'

'Just ask Pop.'

'Ha!'

When we came to the turn-off to Nullabri, Aunty Rita said, 'Let's keep going.'

'What about the bakery?'

'Forget the bakery. What if Relle's there?'

'Christ,' I said.

'God, you're funny. Keep going to Echuca?'

'Echuca,' I said, as we sped past the turn-off. Pop never took me to Echuca. *Too much bullshit for too much bloody money.* And he didn't like the crowds.

There were wheat silos as big as castles along the road. There were more trucks. It was a lot busier than Nullabri; there were people visiting from the city, passing through, or farmers coming to town to buy supplies. The roads were wide, there were more shops with things for sale in the windows: shoes, dresses, books, chairs, beds. There was a stock and feed shop bigger than the one in Nullabri. Aunty Rita parked the truck on the main road.

I saw the long bridge over the Murray. On the other side was Moama, where we lived in the house with the barbecue too close to the glass. 'Can we cross it?' I asked Aunty Rita.

'The bridge?'

'Yes. We could walk it.'

'It's a long bridge. You want to do it on foot?'

'Can we?'

'Sure. Why not?' She took my hand and we walked up to the bridge. There was one lane for walkers and two lanes for cars and trucks. The bridge separated Moama from Echuca. Cars rumbled past us. Halfway across, when I could see the Moama caravan park, I stopped and looked over the side. My chest felt tight.

'What is it, Justine? Are you alright?' Aunty Rita asked me. A long way down was the deep brown water of the Murray. She said, 'You lived in Moama for a while, didn't you?'

I said, 'Yes.'

'Before Donna left, right?'

'Yes,' I said. *Ray!* My mum screamed when the glass broke. *Ray, no!* But Dad didn't break the glass, did he? It was the barbecue too close to the window. Why did she scream that way?

Aunty Rita held my hand tight. The bridge shook as car after car rumbled over.

Way below us, the water in the Murray flowed forward. Soon it would reach The Choke, where it would push through and keep going. The traffic kept rumbling across behind us, car after car after car, the wheels rattling the metal in the pylons. Aunty Rita and me stood there for a long time, my hand in hers.

'I'm sorry about your mum, Justine,' said Aunty Rita.

My chest loosened. 'Let's go back.'

'Sure,' said Aunty Rita.

We turned around and walked back into Echuca. We walked along the main road looking in shop windows at cups and plates, dresses and books. 'You want an ice-cream?' Aunty Rita said. We crossed the road to the ice-cream shop. The shop was full of kids and mothers and fathers, and couples as old as Pop. All the flavours were in boxes behind the glass: vanilla and lemon and strawberry and caramel and chocolate. Aunty Rita said, 'Choose whatever you want—my shout.' My face felt hot. There were so many flavours I didn't know if I could choose.

Aunty Rita pointed at the rainbow flavour. 'That one looks good,' she said. 'Let's go two of those. Doubles. How does that sound, Justine?'

'Good.'

Aunty Rita ordered the double rainbows. Even though my stomach was full from a dinner of chicken and corn and a breakfast of eggs and bacon and toast and jam, there was room for the double rainbow.

We sat at a picnic table near the port and watched the paddleboats carry people up the river. If the boats kept going, they'd reach Yolamundi; the Murray connected the towns like a road of water. The people in the boats leaned over the sides, pointing out the birds and the trees, taking pictures.

Aunty Rita said, 'I'm sorry I haven't seen you more, Justine. It gets . . . it's hard . . . with Dad—I mean Pop. But I'd like to visit more. Let's stay in touch, hey? No matter what happens. You are officially my favourite niece.'

'Your only niece.'

'Oh, that's right,' she said. 'You're still my favourite.'

—

When we drove up to Pop's Three, Pop was at the front leaning over the bonnet of Rita's Torry. When he heard us pull in he looked up, oil grease across his forehead, and waved his spanner.

'G'day, Pop,' said Aunty Rita.

'How was town?'

'Good. We ended up at Echuca,' said Aunty Rita.

'Echuca? What the hell for? Too much bullshit,' said Pop, putting his head back under the Torry's bonnet. 'For too much bloody money.'

Aunty Rita winked at me.

We went down the side and saw Dad sitting at Pop's fire, drinking a beer.

'Starting early?' said Aunty Rita.

'Never too early.' Dad raised his beer. 'Where you been, darlin'?' he asked me.

'Getting ice-cream,' I said.

'Oh yeah, where's that?'

'Echuca,' said Aunty Rita.

'Ah, the big smoke.'

'Busier than it used to be,' said Aunty Rita.

'Not as busy as where you came from. Must look small to you.'

'Must look small to you,' Aunty Rita said back to my dad. She wasn't scared of him; whatever he said or did, she wasn't scared.

'How long you hanging around, Rita?' said Dad.

'I'll leave on Monday, if that's alright by you. Maybe I could take Justine to school on my way out.'

'You take the bus, don't you, Justine?' said Dad.

I shrugged.

Pop stepped out of the back door. 'Lunch?' he called.

'Feel like I've been doing nothing but eat,' said Aunty Rita. 'What do you say, Jussy? More?'

'More,' I said.

—

'How do you handle it?' Dad asked. We'd finished lunch and were sitting around the fire.

'What?' said Aunty Rita.

'Bloody Tarban Creek. How do you do it?'

'You get used to it.'

'Dangerous, if you ask me.'

'Nobody is asking you.'

'You watch out for yourself in that place,' said Pop.

'Most of the time the patients are on too many drugs to be dangerous. A lot of them are just sad.'

'Still using the zapper on 'em?'

Aunty Rita put her empty plate on the ground. 'Yeah,' she said. 'Still using it.'

'Fuck. You there when they do it?'

'You ask me the same questions every time,' said Aunty Rita. 'I was wondering how long it would take you. Yeah, I am there. It's over pretty fast. They feel better. A lot of them want more. They come back for it. It's their choice.'

'Not all of them have a choice,' said Dad. 'You zap 'em anyway, right?'

'You know, shock therapy would be good for you, Ray,' said Aunty Rita. 'Take the edge off.'

'You two . . .' Pop warned.

Ray said, 'Where are you living, Rita?'

'You know where I'm living, same place.'

'Oh yeah,' said Dad. 'But you're not living there by yourself anymore, are you?'

The crackle from the fire seemed to spread across the Three. Pop said, 'Get us a beer from the esky, will you, Ray?'

'Some already here,' said Dad, leaning over and picking up a beer from beside his chair. He passed it to Pop. 'Who are you living with, Rita?' Dad asked again. 'What was her name? Wasn't it Naomi? She moved in, didn't she?'

Pop's Three felt loaded; the crickets in the grass and the possums asleep in the trees and the hens pecking at our feet could be blasted into the air and cover us in feathers and blood and chicken eye.

Aunty Rita said, 'Yeah, that's her name. Naomi. It was Naomi who told me I should come. She said to sort things out.'

Pop breathed out hard, got up and walked to the fence. He stood looking at the other side.

Aunty Rita said, 'What are you trying to start, Ray?'

'Not trying to start anything. Just asking. It's polite to ask.'

Pop came back. He sat down. 'Better get on to that pipe by the shed, Ray. Better fix the bloody leak.'

Dad wasn't listening. He said, 'She's pretty, that Naomi, from the picture you showed me last night, Rita. Real pretty.' He nodded. 'I'd ask her out.' My dad was the biggest at the fire. His muscles told the story of his strength; strung around him, under his skin, tying him together. The Worlley brothers and Kirk and Steve did what he said. Everybody did. He could say what he liked. It was only Aunty Rita who couldn't see how strong he was.

She said, 'She is really pretty, Ray. And she's all mine, so don't you ever look at her or I'll rip your fucken head off.' Aunty Rita was the only one in the whole world who wasn't scared of my dad. She was older than him; she had come first and seen more and knew more. Aunty Rita and Ray's eyes were the same colour, but Aunty Rita's sparkled with volts. She knew the supply and it was Ray who was scared of Rita.

Pop stood again. 'That's enough,' he said.

'What's enough?' said Aunty Rita, turning sharply to Pop.

'You know what I'm talking about.'

'No, Dad, what is it you are talking about?'

'I thought that business was finished.'

'What business?'

'That bloody business. I thought it was done.'

'Why would you think that?'

'I thought that's why you came.'

Aunty Rita's mouth dropped open. 'You thought that's why I came? Because I'm straight now?'

'Don't . . .' said Pop.

Ray leaned back in his chair like he was watching a show.

'Don't what, Dad?' Her face was turning red.

'Don't push me, Rita.'

'Or what? Or what, Dad? You going to punch me?' She stood. My heart was racing.

'Get out of my house!'

'Or what? Or what, Dad?' she shouted. 'What are you going to do to me, Dad? What you did to my mother?' Her voice filled the yard, rose up over the river. It reached the crowns of the trees, it travelled the passages and up into the sky. 'Why can't you say it? Why can't you say it, you gutless fuck!'

I was afraid for Pop's Three.

'So why'd you come all the bloody way here? No one asked you. I didn't ask you. Better for us all if you stay there.'

Aunty Rita walked away from the fire towards the house.

I ran after her. 'Aunty Rita!' I called. She swung around and breathed in like she'd been stabbed.

'Oh, Justine.'

'Don't go,' I said.

'Come back here, Justine!' said Pop. 'Leave your Aunty Rita alone. Now!'

I looked at my Aunty Rita. Her eyes were red and there were red patches on her cheeks. She looked back at me and swallowed. She said, 'Justine, I'm sorry.'

My eyes stung and prickled. 'Aunty Rita . . .'

'Justine!' Pop called. 'Get back here, now.'

'Go on,' said Aunty Rita. 'You better do what he says.'

'I want to go with you,' I said. 'Can I go with you?'

Aunty Rita shook her head 'Oh, Justine . . .'

Dad came to us and he said, 'You better leave, Rita.'

'Fuck off, Ray,' said Aunty Rita. 'You're a bastard, you know that? I always think there might be more . . .' I heard tears in her voice. 'But no, there isn't.' She turned away from us both and went to the back door. I tried to follow her but Dad put his hand down hard on my shoulder.

———

Dad kept me by the fire while she packed.

'Can I say goodbye to her?' I asked. I felt as if a weight was pressing on my chest. 'Dad?'

'Christ,' said Dad. 'If it will stop you whingeing.'

I ran through the house into the spare room. Aunty Rita was writing something on a piece of paper. She said, 'Justine,' and put her arms around me.

'Aunty Rita.' My words were muffled in her shirt, against her neck.

Aunty Rita held me tight. 'Justine, I'm sorry. Your dad and me . . . Don't worry about it. We always fight, okay? Ever since we were kids. He's still my brother.' She touched my cheek. 'I wish I could see you more.' Her voice went thick. She sniffed, pulling back tears. 'Justine, I have to go home, but I'm going to give you a phone number, okay? Two phone numbers—one is for where I work, at the Gladesville Hospital.'

'Tarban Creek?'

'That's right. And the other one is home. You don't need to tell anyone. I'm just going to give them to you. I want you to keep the numbers and use them if you need to, okay?' She took my hand and pressed the piece of paper into it. 'It shouldn't be this way, Justine. It's . . . not right.'

She held me to her. I couldn't say anything. I didn't have words.

Aunty Rita looked into my eyes. 'I will write to you, okay? I'll ring you too. You're going to be okay, aren't you?'

I didn't want her to leave.

'I'm sorry, Justine.'

Aunty Rita stood. I held the paper with her numbers. She went out through the front door.

⌒

From my window I watched Aunty Rita's car drive away from Pop's down the Henley Trail. I kept watching until she crossed the bridge and then I couldn't see her anymore. I sat on my bed. There wasn't one thing to do. I sat for a long time. My room was still; it was only the sunroom in the morning—in the afternoon the room was in shadow. What was there to do? There wasn't one thing.

19.

I lay on the bed holding Aunty Rita's numbers. I didn't know what to do with them. I didn't know the order of the numbers. I looked up at the fan hanging from the ceiling. The fan had never worked; it had been still so long there were cobwebs slung between the blades. I stood on the bed, reached up and put Aunty Rita's piece of paper on top of one of the blades. When I sat back down on the bed I could still see a corner. I lay on my bed looking at the corner of paper for a long time and then I fell asleep. In my dream Aunty Rita and Naomi were riding a horse down a road—Aunty Rita was in front, Naomi was behind. Naomi held a baby wrapped in a red blanket. I waved and called to them, but they didn't hear or notice. They kept riding. The road was made of muddy water.

When I woke it was dark. I got up and went into the hall. The only light came from Pop's door. I pushed it open and saw Pop lying on his bed. 'What the hell for? Give me one reason . . . one good reason.'

I said, 'Pop?'

'Ah! Christ!' he said. 'Christ!'

'Are you alright, Pop?'

'Get me a beer.'

'Do you want something to eat?'

'I want a beer.'

I went to the laundry, switched on the light and took a beer from the esky. Then I went back to his room. I smelled something sour.

'Bloody kids,' he said. 'Where's the trust? What was it for? Answer me that, goddamn you! Whole damn lot of you! One good reason!'

'There you go, Pop,' I said, putting the can of beer on the table beside his bed. He rolled over and I saw the tracks that he laid in Burma in his face. I saw the river of blood and the good boys and the Japs. They charged down the grooves in Pop's cheeks and chin and forehead.

I went into the yard. Dad's truck wasn't parked down the side and there was no light coming from the back-house. I stirred the coals of the fire—orange under the grey. I sat on Pop's camp chair. Mosquitoes flew around my face.

I got up and crossed to the chook run. The gate creaked as I pulled it open. I took a breath and smelled the chooks inside, sweet and soft. I breathed them in—shit and straw and feathers. I went closer to the bar where they roosted. I could see the outline of Cockyboy in the dark. He clucked and shuffled. 'It's okay, Cockyboy,' I whispered. 'It's only me, Justine.' Cockyboy was quiet. I sat down close to the boxes where three of the Isa Browns were sleeping. I leaned in. I could see Pop's Missy. I put my hands on her—at first she jumped, so I smoothed my hands over her wings the way Pop did. 'Sssshhh, Missy, it's only me, your friend Justine, shhhhh.' I picked her up. She didn't try to escape, staying calm in my hands as I slid to the ground. I put the hen in my lap. I could feel the bones of Missy Isa Brown's chest through her feathers, and the heart beating behind the bones.

———

On Saturday Kirk and Steve and me were out the front of Pop's Three. Kirk stood on the top beam of Pop's fence, arms outstretched. 'Aunty Rita's a lesbian,' he said.

I tried to pull myself up. 'What's that?'

'A slut,' he said, kicking at my hand.

I looked up at him, shielding my eyes from the glare. 'Is that what Pop said, that she's a slut?'

'Yeah, he did. He said it when he was at the pub with Sandy, and Stan heard and told Mum. He said Rita was a lesbian.'

'But what's a lesbian?' I asked.

'I dunno,' he said, jumping down from the rail. 'A dog.'

20.

The next morning I was in the yard eating Rice Bubbles when the back-house door opened. Dad stepped out wearing only shorts. He came down the steps and sat on his camp chair under the window. He took his leather pouch from his pocket and rolled a White Ox. I could feel him watching me.

'Come over here,' he said.

I put my bowl down and walked across the yard.

Dad pulled back on his cigarette. 'Want to do something today, just you and me?' He blew a stream of smoke into the sky.

'Okay,' I said.

'What do you want to do?'

'I don't know.'

Dad took another drag and blew a smoke ring into the air. 'You used to love these, Justine,' he said, blowing more rings. 'You tried to put your finger through 'em before they disappeared. Remember?' He put his finger through one of the rings. 'Get your shoes on and get in the truck.' He stood and went inside the back-house.

I was on the step doing the laces of my shoes when Pop came into the kitchen. He rubbed his eyes and pulled his dressing-gown around him. 'What are you up to?'

'Going out with Dad,' I said.

Pop frowned. 'Since when?'

Dad came up to the kitchen wearing his jeans and shirt.

'Where are you taking Justine?' Pop asked.

'For a drive.'

'Where to?'

'Nowhere, Pop. Just a drive.'

'When are you back?'

'Won't be long,' said Dad. 'We'll stop by the bakery and pick up something for lunch.'

Pop frowned again. Was I meant to do what Pop wanted or what Ray wanted? When Dad was home nobody was sure. 'Aren't you low on fuel, son?'

'Plenty of fuel.'

Dad drove the truck down the Henley Trail then out onto the highway. 'Where are we going?' I asked him. He didn't answer. Soon he drove off the highway and along another dirt road. I held on to the door as the truck bumped on the stones and potholes. We drove deeper into the bush, shrubs and thin trees pressing in on the truck. There were rocks on the ground between the bushes. The truck bumped and creaked. Dad drove off the dirt road into a clearing. He stopped the truck and pulled on the handbrake, then he opened his door and got out. I did the same. I didn't know why we were here or what we were doing.

Dad went around to the tray of his pickup and pulled out a big box of bottles and cans. I followed him deeper into the bush. Dad stopped beside some rocks. He said, 'Stay here.' He went ahead about the same distance as Pop's yard, before he turned around to face me. 'This is your target line,' he called out. 'Get a feel for the distance.' He put the box down and took out paint cans and bottles. He lined all the bottles beside each other along one rock, then he lined up the paint cans along another. 'Come here,' he called to me and I went down to him. 'When you practise you dig your targets into the ground, see.' He pushed a bottle deeper into the dirt. 'Put 'em in an inch or two, you got it? If you don't dig 'em in, even a missed shot'll knock 'em over.'

'What are we going to do?' I asked Dad.

'You're going to learn how to shoot,' he said.

It was Kirk who wanted to learn how to shoot. If you gave Kirk anything—a pencil, a spoon, a ruler—he'd turn it into a gun. Danny's uncle promised he would teach them. He said he was going to come to Victoria when the shearing season was over in Gympie, but Danny didn't know when that was.

I followed Dad back to the truck. 'What about Kirk and Steve?'

'This is where I learned to shoot when I was a kid.' It was as if he couldn't hear me. Nothing I did or said changed anything. 'The old man showed me. Never told Mum about it, of course.' Whenever Dad talked about his mother he spoke softly, as if he was praying. Lizzy died before he was ready. Before then, Pop told the chooks, Ray was no trouble at all. What a kid. But he left the hospital and that was it, a part of that boy was buried with his mother. *And it was the best part, let me tell you, chook chook chook. The best part of Ray went into the grave that day.*

Dad opened the passenger door and took something from the glove box. He said, 'Come here.' I went over to him and he unwrapped a piece of sacking. There was a gun in his hands.

Dad held it up and turned it slowly in the air, as if it was an old friend who he liked and missed. 'Meet the Smith,' he said. He wasn't saying it to me, but at the same time he was.

'What about Kirk?' I said.

Dad said, 'Hold out your hands.'

He put the Smith in my open hands. They dropped down with the weight.

'Heavier than you think, hey?'

'Yeah.'

'Feel the barrel.'

I touched the gun.

'Not the cylinder. The barrel. Here.' He put my fingers on the barrel. It was smooth and cold. 'Pull the trigger,' he said. 'Feel how much it takes.'

I pulled the trigger. It was hard to pull back. The Smith was smaller than Pop's pistols, and thicker. Kirk and Steve would like to meet the Smith. Kirk would ask questions about where it came from and what did Dad shoot and how did you load it and when did you get it and what sort of bullets did it take. Dad mightn't answer but Kirk would keep asking until Dad gave him something, just one thing, even if it was small, he'd keep asking, Kirk wouldn't give up. Steve would stand behind Kirk and wait for whatever might be left over.

'Turn it round and take a look at it from the other end, Justine,' said Dad.

I turned the Smith around so that I was looking down the barrel.

'How does it feel?'

I shrugged.

'You don't ever want to find yourself looking into a gun from the wrong end.' Dad took the gun from my hand. 'Chances are it'll be the last thing you see.' He pulled at a small lever at the top of the gun. 'That's your hammer,' he said. 'That's what lights her up. Once you know your gun it's pretty simple: you point her at the target and pull the trigger. With the Smith you'll need both hands. The gun kicks back, just to let you know she's done what you asked her.' Dad gave me the gun again.

He went to the truck and came back with a small box. 'Bullets,' he said. He took the Smith from me and opened the cylinder. 'Bullets go in here,' he said, and stuck a bullet into each hole of the cylinder. 'As long as you can count up to six you'll be alright. You can do that, can't you?'

There was nobody here in the bush with my dad but me, and still it was as if I wasn't there. My dad could have been talking to himself, or an audience of a thousand—but it wasn't to me. He closed the cylinder and locked it into place. Then he held up the gun, lifted the hammer and aimed. He said, 'Once she's loaded, only point the barrel at something you want to kill.'

I saw him up on Silver's back, galloping along the Henley Trail, his Smith held high, like John Wayne when he was Rooster Cogburn. *Only point it at something you want to kill,* he shouted as he galloped past the audience.

He took me by the shoulders, stood beside me, and turned me to face the bottles and cans. 'You think the sound'll knock your head off, but it won't, trust me. Bottles first. Watch.'

He held the gun up and out with his arm long and straight, and looked down the barrel towards the bottles and cans. His eyes narrowed.

Then he pulled the trigger. The sound was so loud it felt like it burst my head. I heard glass break. I stepped away from him, holding my hands over my ears as Dad shot five more times. *Bang bang bang bang bang.* The sound of breaking glass filled the bush. My head pounded.

Dad lowered his arms. 'What do you reckon, Justine? Good shooting?' He looked at the jagged pieces of broken glass and shook his head at them, as if they had tried to get away, but he had seen them and they hadn't escaped. *Bang bang bang bang.*

I looked at the row of broken bottles. 'Good shooting.'

'That was your first lesson.'

'Thanks, Dad.'

We walked across to the truck and he lowered the tray. He put down the gun, sat on the tray and took a leather pouch from the back pocket of his jeans. On the side of the leather pouch were the letters R.A.L. with two snakes twisting around them. *Raymond Andrew Lee.* He took out a pinch of tobacco, put the tobacco onto the paper and rolled it into a cigarette. 'Do you good to know how to shoot,' he said. 'Good for when you get a bit older.' The cigarette bounced up and down on his lip, as if it was agreeing with him.

'As old as Kirk?' I asked him.

'How old's Kirk?'

'Thirteen.'

'Yeah, 'bout that old,' he said. 'That's when it starts. Maybe a bit older. Now go down there and put all the broken bottles in a pile. Get 'em out of the way. This time we'll go for the cans.'

'Okay,' I said. I walked down to the bottles. My legs were shaking. It was only my shoes, too tight for my feet, that held them together. I picked up the broken bottles and put them in a pile at the end of the row so that it was just the cans left behind. I walked back up to Ray. When his cigarette was finished he stubbed it out on the rock. 'Time to reload,' he said. 'Get me six bullets from the box, Justine.'

I did what he said, passing him the first bullet. He looked at it carefully, holding it close to his eyes, then away from them. He said, 'You need to know how to look after yourself. So when you say, *Fuck off*, they'll know you mean it. They all want the same thing.' Was Dad telling me or the bullet? He pushed the bullet into the cylinder. I passed him the next one. 'Don't let 'em, Justine. They're all the same. Every single last one, rich or poor, black or white, old or young, they all want it.' He pushed in another bullet. 'Most of the time, that's all they want. Don't give it to 'em.' Dad turned a bullet in his fingers, looking at it from every side, then, as if he'd decided it was the same as the others, pushed it into the hole. 'Make the bastards wait,' he said.

When the Smith was fully loaded, he said, 'Get up and stand in front of me.' He passed me the gun. 'Only point it at the thing you want to kill.' Dad placed his hands over mine. He stood behind me and I could feel the heat that came from his body. 'Look at your target,' he said. 'First can.' I looked at the white can of paint. 'Don't take your eyes off the target. Don't think about anything else. Don't even think about pulling the trigger. Keep your eyes on the can. Just remember, it's you or your target. Which one of you will die today?'

I looked at the white paint can; it had a bend in the middle, as if it had been kicked. Which one of us would die today? I felt Dad's fingers over mine as he pulled the trigger. The sound threw me back against him. The can fell off the rock. A bell inside my head rang like an alarm. 'Shot,' Dad said. 'Ready to go again?'

Bang! Bang! Bang! Bang! Bang! Shot! Shot! Shot! Shot! Shot! Every empty rusted can fell down dead.

———

In the truck on the way back to Pop's Three, Dad didn't talk. He rested his elbow on the window ledge as he drove, looking out from the front to the side, calm as if something had been emptied from him.

When we got home Pop was on the couch watching the dog races. He said, 'You get bread?'

Dad walked out the back without answering.

I went to my room. My ears were ringing and my head ached. I sat on the bed and pulled off my shoes. The bed tipped one way and then another. I knocked against the walls as I walked out of my room to the toilet. I stood over it and vomited. I stayed there, leaning against the wall. After a while I went back to my room. I lay on my bed and looked at the corner of paper that peeked out from the blade of the fan. I kept my eyes on the paper until the room stopped swaying.

Only Aunty Rita wasn't scared; she was strong enough to balance the volts. She knew exactly where to place the pads. If you missed even by an inch you could kill someone but Aunty Rita never missed. She fried the anger until the person was ready for a new start.

21.

On Monday morning, after I got off the bus, I saw the Hoopers' car at the gate. Mrs Hooper opened the door. I stood by the fence and watched. Michael lifted his arm to me. I waved back and then his mother, Mrs Hooper, waved too, but I didn't know how to wave back to her. My arm wouldn't do it. I looked at the ground.

Michael called out to me. 'Justine!'

I could hardly look; his mother was still there.

'Justine, come here!' he called.

I walked slowly towards him without looking at Mrs Hooper.

Michael said to his mother, 'Justine's shy.'

I felt my face turn red.

Michael said, 'Hi, Justine.'

I looked up at him, drew in a breath and was glad it was Monday.

Mrs Hooper and me walked with Michael up to class. He swung his crutches forward, pulling himself along the path, and nobody looked or shouted at us, or said, *Spastic elastic*. It had all stopped now it was Michael and Justine.

We were eating the popcorn his mum put in his lunchbox. She had sprinkled it with sugar and salt, so all the flavours were there. Popcorn fell to the ground at our feet. There was salt around our lips. 'What do *you* want to do?' I asked Michael.

'When?' he said.

'When you leave school.'

'I want to be an archaeologist.'

'What's that?'

'You dig for things. Like fossils. You go to a lot of different places—the desert, the snow, old places. You find things nobody knows about. You discover them.'

'Like what?'

'Like animal bones. There are still new animals to discover. And insects. And birds. We haven't discovered all the birds. You find old buildings, things people used in the olden days.'

'What sort of things?' I asked him, licking sugar from my fingers.

'Cups and plates. Weapons. Shields. You dig them up and find out what happened. You have to do all the work for yourself. Nobody explains it. You look under a magnifying glass, and write down what you find.'

When Michael talked the jerks interrupted him, but he pushed past them to where the bones lay, digging them up, magnifying them until he saw every part and could put it into words.

The crutches leaned against the desk like guns, ready if we needed to use them. Every other kid saw the guns and left us alone. Mrs Turning left us alone too; she didn't ever come too close to Michael. We did our lessons; Michael helped me with the order of my letters, he helped me choose the right words and tick the right boxes. I stood beside him at singing practice. Sabine lifted the sides of her cheeks as she sang, *Deck the halls with boughs of holly, fa la la la la la la la la!,* and Michael and me decked the halls and the rooms and the desks and the walls with boughs of holly.

22.

The next Friday night Pop wasn't home; he was at the Yolamundi Hotel with Sandy. Sandy was a good mate, but he only went out if Pop picked him up. He couldn't drive after the war. *Couldn't find the bloody gearstick after that,* said Pop. *Thought it was under the bloody seat. I told him, Sandy, it's a bloody car. But he wouldn't touch it. Brought it all back, the whole bloody business. No more for me, mate.*

Dad had been home three weeks. He said, 'Fuck, I'm ready to get out of here.' He mixed rum with Coke. He poured half and half into his glass, threw in a handful of ice cubes and lay back on Pop's couch. His legs stretched out across the cushions. Me and Kirk and Steve sat on the floor and drank Coke. We were watching *Hondo* with John Wayne as Hondo Lane. Dad said, *Everybody gets dead. It was his turn,* at the same time as Hondo. He raised his glass to the television.

When the ads came on Dad said to Kirk, 'Your mother got a boyfriend?'

Kirk and Steve looked at each other. Kirk said when Danny's uncle showed him how to shoot he'd put a pillow over Dean's head and pull the trigger. He couldn't wait to see the feathers fly.

'Does she?'

Kirk said, 'No,' and kept his eyes on Hondo Lane. Kirk said even if the cops found out it was him who shot Dean it wouldn't matter because as long as it was before he was sixteen he was too young to go to jail.

Dad said, 'She doesn't?'

'No. I don't think so.' Kirk said if he was found guilty he'd be sent to training school with minimum security and get his forklift licence.

'Bullshit, she doesn't.' Dad took a drink from his glass. 'Good on her. Why not?' Dad's voice sounded as if there was an ocean beneath it that left his voice on top, watery and rocking.

My stomach rumbled. Pop had left sausages, peas, ham and bread on the kitchen bench. He told Dad to fry the bloody sausages. Dad stood up. He was bigger than a lot of the other fathers at school. He was bigger than Headmaster Prentice. He was bigger than the statue of the soldier in Nullabri. He burped when he reached his full height and Kirk and Steve laughed. *But a long time ago, I made me a rule. I let people do what they want to do,'* he said along with Hondo. He left the room. Kirk took a swallow from Dad's drink. He wiped his mouth clean and kept watching John Wayne. Steve did the same.

Pop told us not to touch the stove. Pop didn't like to leave us, even when Dad was home. But Sandy had called and Sandy had saved his life twice. If it wasn't for Sandy there'd be no Pop. *Kids, your old Pop would be under the mud with the leeches somewhere between Burma and Siam. He got me through. The bastard got me through.*

We heard Dad talking on the telephone in the kitchen. 'What are you doing? Now, I mean . . . Nothing . . . The kids are here . . . Later . . . You know how I feel . . . Bullshit, it's not like that . . . Settle down. I told you . . . Nah, I drove her home . . . Nothing . . . Hey, baby, settle down . . .' Dad came back into the living room and lay down on the couch. 'Fucken women,' he said.

John Wayne as Hondo was talking to a lady in the kitchen. *You smell all over like a woman, rich and warm and soft. I could find you in the dark, Mrs Lowe.* The picture began to fuzz, lines crossing the screen. I got up to change the aerial. Pop said I was the best at changing it. It didn't matter how lost the picture was, I could find it. Pop said, *Well done, Justine. You got the knack.*

I could feel Dad's eyes on me as I stood with my hands on the aerial. I moved it one way, and then another. Kirk and Steve were watching too. Kirk wished he had the knack and could find the picture, but he didn't even try because he knew only I had it. I kept moving the aerial but the picture wasn't coming back. John Wayne after John Wayne moved down the television screen.

Dad said, 'Your mother was the worst of the fucken lot.' *Your mother was the worst of the fucken lot.* Dad's words sent volts around the living room. He never talked about my mother. It was Pop who told me I was born breech, that it scared my mother away. I learned about the stitches that broke from Pop, not Dad. He told the Isa Browns: *She should've have been cut out, but it was too late and, breech or not, out she came. Poor bloody Donna. Still, that's no excuse, hey, ladies? No excuse, her own bloody daughter.* Dad never even said Donna's name. I kept moving the aerial but I couldn't fix the picture. *Your mother was the worst of the fucken lot.* It didn't matter what place I put the aerial, the picture wouldn't come back. Dad looked at me from the bottom to the top. I felt hot. 'You do look like her, Justine,' Dad said. 'Rita was right.'

Parts of the picture changed direction; John Wayne was caught in a loop, pieces of him going round and round. 'You got the same legs,' he said. Dad raised his glass at my legs. I could feel Kirk and Steve looking at them too. 'You're like her in other ways,' Dad said. 'Can't tell what's going on, what you're bloody thinking. What are you thinking, Donna?' he said. His eyes were red, his words slurred—was he asking me, or Donna? Kirk and Steve didn't speak or move. Their eyes darted from me to the screen. I couldn't see John Wayne at all; he was blocked out by fuzz and storm. I couldn't move my hand.

'For Christ's sake!' said Dad, standing up. My hands dropped to my sides. Dad took the aerial and turned it. 'She changed when she got pregnant. That was the end for us,' he said.

I sat back down. My stomach felt tight and sick. *She changed when she got pregnant.* Was it the breech? Pop said I got it wrong from the start. Was it me who changed her?

Dad lifted the aerial and put it down again. It wouldn't fix. Dad said, 'Fuck it,' then he kicked the television with his foot and picked up the bottle of rum. He swung it in his hand as he left the room. The picture fuzzed as if there was a blizzard inside.

'Try again, Justine,' said Kirk.

'I can't do it.'

'Yes, you can. Try again.'

'I can't.'

'You can,' said Kirk. 'One more try.'

I turned the aerial and John Wayne as Hondo Lane came back. He was holding Mrs Lowe in his arms.

'You still got the knack, Justine,' said Kirk.

'Yep,' said Steve. 'You still do.'

We sat held together in the space left behind by our dad. We watched right to the end when Hondo killed Silva and the Apaches had to find a new chief.

'Go, big man,' said Kirk.

'Go, Hondo,' I said.

———

Later, we ate Pop's bread with sauce. Kirk said, '*She changed when she got pregnant.* Did you hear that, Justine?' The bread and the sauce turning in his mouth changed the sound of his words. He smiled, the sauce caught in the corners.

'Did you know that Dad taught me how to shoot?' I said.

He stopped chewing. 'When?'

'A while ago.'

His face dropped. 'Bullshit.'

'With the Smith,' I said. 'He took me into the bush.'

'Bullshit.'

'He did. Ask him. It takes six bullets and it's heavier than the Mauser. A lot heavier.'

'He showed you how?'

'Yep,' I said. I held up my Smith and shot Kirk in the face. Then I got up from the kitchen table and left him there. We went from full brother and sister to half, back and forth. Dad pushed us together then he pulled us apart.

23.

Now I wanted school when I used to want holidays. Michael waited for me and I waited for him. He was never in a hurry. It was as if I was a map book and when he opened it he could see all the lands and animals and weathers and conditions and pictures that I was made of, and wanted to know more. As if there would always be another page to turn, another picture to see, more information to learn.

——

Everything was funny that had never been funny. Worlley boys and teachers and blackboards and schoolbooks and spelling tests and bus drivers and maths—all funny. Michael's laugh was full of breath and groan; it blasted from him, and his body shook so hard that he knocked things to the ground—lunchboxes, drink bottles, books and pens and sharpeners fell to the floor. What could I do but join him, as if everything at school was funny and small, and not forever, only for now?

——

We sat in front of a big sheet of white paper at the benches. We had coloured textas from Michael's pencil case. Michael did a line and I made it a square. He added a body going down and I made it into a cabin. He did circles and I made them into wheels, he did steps and I made them the second storey, he did lines going up and I made them into antennae, he made them into crutches, I made them into guns, he made them into an engine and I made the engine into wings and the truck we had drawn could fly. He drew the road underneath and I drew the clouds above, then he drew the frozen sea that led to Antarctica, where no one had ever been before.

24.

The next Friday afternoon, when I came home from school, Dad was in the kitchen.

'Come with me, Justine,' he said, as if he'd been waiting.

'Where are we going?' The smell of something sweet and strong came from his face and from under his arms.

'We're visiting a friend of mine.'

'Who?' Most of Dad's friends were in other places; he saw them when he was away from home.

'Just get in the truck.'

'Justine?' Pop called as we passed his bedroom. I stopped and stood in the doorway. Pop was still in bed. 'Where are you going with Ray?' he asked.

'I don't know,' I said.

'Ray!' Pop called out, his voice croaky. 'Where are you taking Justine?'

Dad didn't answer; he was already out the front. I heard him calling me. 'Justine! Get a move on!'

Pop sat up in the bed, pulling his dressing-gown around him.

'Justine!' Dad called again. 'Come on!'

'I have to go, Pop,' I said.

'Jesus,' said Pop. 'What's the bloody hurry?'

'We're visiting a friend.'

'What bloody friend?'

I heard Dad start up the truck. 'Justine! Get out here!'

'Pop, I got to go.' I left the room and ran out the front door. Dad was already in the truck, his window down.

Pop came to the front door. 'Where are you taking her, Ray?'

Ray didn't answer.

———

Dad sat tall and shining in the truck as he drove along the Henley Trail. There was a White Ox, already rolled, behind his ear. Soon he took the turn-off into Dray Road. Why would he take this road? Nobody lived here but the Worlleys. Dad hummed a song with the radio, the wind blowing back his dark hair. *Baby, baby, nobody going to love you the way I love you, let me show you how.*

'Where are we going, Dad?'

He didn't answer me. *Let me show you my way, baby, let me take you there,* he sang.

'Dad? Where are we going?'

My way is sweet, honey, my way.

'Dad?'

It was as if the open window carried my voice away with the wind. Dad kept going. Dray Road only led to the Worlleys'. Nobody lived out here but them. I felt as if something inside me had come loose, like a screw from Aunty Rita's Torry. It bounced and rattled inside my chest and gut. I didn't want to go the Worlleys'. I didn't want to see Jamie. I didn't want to see his scar, or the cousins.

Dad took the White Ox from behind his ear. 'Light her for me, would you, Justine?' he said. He took the metal lighter from his pocket and passed the cigarette and the lighter to me. There was a girl on the lighter only wearing underpants, lying back with her legs in the air. I held the cigarette in one hand and the lighter in the other, then I flicked the lighter until a flame jumped from the spout. But the flame wouldn't stay, and the White Ox didn't light.

Dad looked across at me. 'Put it in your mouth.'

I put the White Ox in my mouth.

'That's the girl. Now light her up.'

I flicked the lighter under the cigarette.

'Put it under the bloody cigarette.'

I put the flame to the White Ox and Dad nodded. 'Get it going, Jussy,' he said. 'That's the girl.'

I sucked back the smoke. I coughed and smoke came out my nose and mouth. The White Ox was alight.

I passed the cigarette to him and he sucked it back. 'Best ciggie I ever took a drag from,' he said.

I looked out of the window. I tasted ash and smoke. I didn't want to go to the Worlleys'. I wished we could keep going and that the best ciggie wouldn't end.

When he came to the road that led down to Mother Margy's and the circle of caravans, Dad kept driving past the turn-off. I breathed out and my chest went quiet. Maybe we weren't going to see any Worlleys and this was the way to somewhere else . . .

Soon we came to a narrow dirt driveway. Dad turned into it and I saw a caravan, with a table and two chairs set up outside. There was a white plastic horse and a blue sandpit next to the chairs. Dad stopped his truck. There were piles of bricks and silver paper and wood, and rocks and rubbish near the caravan. Away from the caravan, down the hill, I could see a big flat concrete square, and a doorway without a door. It was a half-built house. I looked over the fence and recognised the back paddocks of the Worlleys' farm.

A small white dog came out of the caravan, barking at us. Then Stacey Worlley came down the steps behind it and I knew: this was Stacey Worlley's caravan. Stacey and Brian moved into their own place after they got married. Pop told the Isa Browns, *Bloody Brian Chisholm, what a bloody fool taking on that lot.*

I couldn't talk. I didn't know what to say or how to tell Dad we didn't go to the Worlleys' anymore. Pop said, *No more.* He said, *The Japs didn't take my balls; they took a river of blood. Fucking Ian!* Why had Dad brought me here when he knew Stacey was married to Brian? Dad knew about the wedding. He didn't go—Brian didn't want him there—but Pop told him about it, and Mother Margy told him too. Stacey rode in on a white horse with a veil over her eyes and her wedding dress draped over the horse's back. Dad knew that. He said, *Brian can't ride a fucken horse to save himself,* and Pop said, *It wasn't Brian on the fucken horse. It was Stacey,* and Dad said, *She can't ride either—not a bloody horse, anyway.*

Today she wore a short pink dress—not long like the wedding dress—and she was carrying a little baby girl. I looked around for the wedding horse. Pop said they put jewels in its reins and painted its hooves black. They said the horse was pure white and that's why they paid what they did. *Not a hair on the animal any colour but white.* The stereo played 'Save the Last Dance For Me' when Stacey rode the horse down the aisle. She wore a veil over her eyes so all she saw was mist.

The dog kept barking. 'Here, Honey!' Stacey called. 'Shush, girl.' She bobbed the little girl in her arm, then she went to

Honey and picked her up with her other arm. The dog licked the baby on the cheek. 'Honey! No!' said Stacey, bobbing them both. She wore lipstick the same colour as the dress. Her shoes were pink too, and had a heel that pushed her forward.

Dad opened the door of the truck. 'Get out, Jussy. Go say g'day,' he said.

I sat without moving. I didn't want to say g'day to Stacey Worlley. I hardly spoke to her even before the fall-out. Pop said, *Never again, never a bloody Worlley*. Stacey was older than the rest of us, and didn't go on the slide or ride a bike. She screamed at Lachie and Jamie and the other cousins, 'Bloody boys!', and Jamie called her Longhorn Stacey even though she was his older sister.

Now Stacey was looking at the truck, her mouth open as if she didn't know whether to be excited or scared. I couldn't see Brian anywhere.

'Get out, Justine,' Dad said, his eyes on Stacey.

I got out on my side and Dad got out on his. We stood in front of the truck.

'Go on,' Dad said to me. 'Go say g'day.'

Stacey said, 'What are you doing here, Ray?'

'Go on.' Dad pushed me towards her.

'G'day, Stacey,' I said, looking at her pink shoes. The heels left holes in the dirt around her feet. Before the fall-out Stacey used to sit on Dad's knee. Sometimes they left the party and went for a walk, and when they came back Stacey's face was soft as she leaned back against him. Dad kissed her neck and she said, *Don't, don't*, then he did it more.

'Hi, Justine,' said Stacey. 'You've grown.' She hardly looked at me; her eyes were on Ray.

Dad said, 'Brought Jussy over to meet your little girl. Thought you could do some girl talk together.'

Stacey shook her head at him, a smile playing on her lips. She put Honey on the ground and the dog sniffed around our feet. Dad grinned. He touched Stacey's baby under the chin. 'Who's this little cutie?' The baby wore pink too, matching Stacey. She had a bow pinned to her hair and she was sucking a dummy. In her arms was a torn yellow rabbit.

'This is Sherry,' said Stacey.

'She's gorgeous,' said Dad. 'Like her mother. How old is she?'

Stacey tried to hide her smile. 'She's one and a half. Brian reckons she looks like him.' She straightened the bow in Sherry's hair.

'Nah,' said Dad. 'She's got your eyes. Baby blues. What do you think, Jussy? Isn't she a little cutie? Don't you think she looks like her mum?'

'Yeah,' I answered. The baby sucked at the dummy and watched my dad. Her eyes were like the two blue centres of flowers.

'You going to invite us in, Stace?' said Dad. 'Maybe the girls can get to know each other. Practically cousins.'

'Yeah, right. Just like the good ole days,' said Stacey.

'They were good days,' said Dad. 'Haven't known better.'

'And then you left.'

'Biggest mistake I ever made.'

Stacey chewed at her lip. 'What do you think, Sherry? Shall we invite them in? Give them a drink?' She kissed Sherry's cheek.

'Now you're talking,' said Dad.

'Just a quick one,' said Stacey.

'Just a quick one,' said Dad.

Stacey turned and walked towards the caravan and we followed. Honey ran in circles at our feet.

The caravan was set up inside like a house; there were photos of Brian and Stacey on their wedding day. There was a picture of the white horse as it came down the aisle. Stacey's wedding dress hung over its rump. There was another picture of Stacey holding Sherry, who held the torn rabbit. There were couches and chairs, and in one corner there was a big television. It took up a lot of the room. Everything was facing the television: the photos on the wall, the glass golf trophies on the shelves, the furniture, the baby toys on the floor—dolls, plastic cows and sheep, a small pram—the bar stools and kitchen counter, all faced the television, waiting for Stacey to turn it on.

'Very nice,' said Dad, looking around. 'Brian's really takin' care of you.'

'The house will be built soon,' said Stacey, bobbing Sherry in one arm. 'Going to be three bedrooms, plus a games room. Brian wants a pool table.'

'Good for him,' Dad said. 'Can he play pool?'

Stacey took a bottle of drink from the freezer, see-through, like water. 'You know he can,' she said.

'I know you can,' said Dad. 'I've watched you playing pool very closely.'

'Ray,' said Stacey, shaking her head at him. She took a bottle of lemonade from the fridge, and two glasses from a cupboard above the stove. She did everything holding Sherry. Sherry sucked on her dummy and watched my dad. Honey darted around our feet as if she didn't know where to stop. Stacey tried to put ice into the glasses, but it was hard with Sherry in one of her arms. She said, 'Can you take her for a sec?' to Dad. Dad held out his arms. Sherry started to cry. 'Oh, Sherry, no need for that.' Stacey took back the baby.

'Let me do the ice,' said Dad. 'You hold the baby.' He pulled the ice from the tray and put it into the glasses. 'Teamwork,' he said. He poured a lot of the see-through drink over the ice. 'How long did he leave you for this time?'

Stacey sighed. 'He hasn't left me, Ray.'

'I don't see him anywhere.' Dad pretended to look behind the door. 'Unless you've got him tied up in the bedroom.'

'He's making money,' said Stacey. 'You've heard of that? Making money?'

'I've heard of it,' Dad poured lemonade into their glasses.

'The honest way, I mean.'

'How long is that going to take him?'

'I dunno,' she said, grinning suddenly. 'Ages.'

Dad passed Stacey her drink. He reached out and chucked Sherry under the chin. 'Such a cutie,' he said. He went to the door and looked out. Then he turned back around. 'Must get lonely here. Just you and the little one.'

Stacey sat on an arm of one of the chairs. 'We're okay. Mum drops around. Uncle Ian. And at least I know when Brian's coming home.'

'Yeah,' said Dad. 'At least you know that. Cheers.' He raised his glass.

'Shut up, Ray.' Stacey got up again and took a packet of chips down from the cupboard. Her dress showed her legs as she reached; they were the same colour as the cream Mother Margy poured onto Dad's apple pie. She tipped the chips into a bowl. 'What do you want to drink, Justine?' she said.

'She'll have whatever's going,' said Dad.

'Lemonade okay?' said Stacey.

'Yeah,' I said.

Stacey poured lemonade into a plastic cup. She patted one of the chairs facing the television. 'Sit down,' she said. She put the chips on a small table beside the chair. I could smell baby shit. There was a bottle of milk on the kitchen counter.

'Must get tough though,' said Dad. He leaned against the kitchen counter, his legs, hard and tight in his jeans, crossed one over the other.

'Nothing you can help me with.' Stacey put Sherry onto the floor, pushing one of the dolls towards her, then sat on the chair next to mine. 'Ian comes around if anything needs doing. Belinda picks up stuff from the shops.'

'You used to like my help.' Dad sat down on another one of the chairs.

'Used to.'

'Used to feel pretty good, didn't it?' Dad leaned forward and pinched Stacey's thigh. She pulled away. 'Used to feel real good,' he said, sipping from his drink.

Sherry started to cry. 'Oh,' said Stacey, picking her up from the floor. 'You're tired, aren't you, sweetheart? I have to put her down. Bubs missed her nap today, didn't you, petal?' Stacey kissed Sherry on the top of the head.

'Shame,' said Dad. 'Jussy would love to have a play. Wouldn't you, Justine?'

'Yeah,' I said.

'I won't be long,' said Stacey, carrying Sherry out of the room. 'She's terrible when she's tired.'

Dad walked slowly around the room, looking at the photos of the wedding horse, of Sherry, of Stacey with the veil, of Brian in his wedding suit. He drank from his glass and shook his head. 'Brian fucken Chisholm.' He poured more drink into his glass. 'What do you think, Justine?' he said, looking at the picture of Brian up close.

'About what?' I said.

'Who the fuck knows?' he said.

Stacey came back into the room. 'There,' she said. 'Now I can relax.'

Dad held out his drink to her. 'To us,' he said.

Stacey didn't lift her drink.

'Come on, Stace,' said Dad.

Stacey sighed.

'For old time's sake.' Dad held out his glass. 'Come on, give it up, what's the harm?'

'Alright then, for old time's sake,' said Stacey, lifting her drink.

They touched their glasses and both took a long sip, looking at each other over the rims. 'Cheers, darlin',' said Dad.

'You're a bad boy, Raymond,' said Stacey.

'I love it when you say my name,' said Dad. 'Say it again.'

I looked at the patterns in the carpet. They were brown diamonds.

'Say what?'

'You know what. My name.'

'Raymond.'

'And again.'

'Ray!' Stacey made her eyes wide at him.

'Just one more time, sweet Stacey.'

Stacey looked at me. 'You want to see what's on television?' she said. She leaned over to turn on the television. My dad never stopped watching her; if I'd looked into his eyes I would have seen her there, trapped.

'Television looks good,' he said. 'Big.' But he wasn't looking at the television; he was looking at her legs and her short skirt.

Stacey flicked from channel to channel; when she came to a cartoon she said, 'There you go.' A baby elephant floated down through the sky with its trunk curled around a blue feather. I took a drink of the lemonade. 'How's your old man?' said Stacey.

'Pain in the arse,' said Dad. 'How's yours?'

'Same,' she said, swinging her crossed legs up and down. 'What about your love life?'

'What about it?' said Dad.

'You seeing anyone?'

'I'm seeing you.' He took another long sip.

'You know what I mean. Are you seeing anyone?'

'Like I said—you.'

The baby elephant landed and a mouse wearing a hat came up to him. *There will be a way out of this, my friend—or should I say* new *friend—there will be a way. We just have to think. Think!*

'You're not answering my question,' said Stacey. 'Have you got a girlfriend?'

'I'm here, aren't I, your honour?' said Dad.

'With you that doesn't mean much,' said Stacey.

'Come on, darlin', stop giving ole Ray a hard time. There's no girlfriend. It's good to see you.' Dad took the bottle of see-through drink from the freezer. She put up her hand to try to stop him filling her glass, but he kept going. 'Want to sit outside?' he said.

'Sure,' she said, standing. She looked at the television. Dumbo wouldn't let go of the feather; that's how he floated. He couldn't let go. 'Doesn't the elephant know he doesn't need the feather?' said Stacey.

'I need the feather,' said Dad.

'Ray.' Stacey shook her head at him.

'Come on, let's be out there when the sun goes down,' said Dad.

'Still romantic.'

'You know it, sweetheart.'

They went to the door. Honey followed.

'We'll be just outside, Justine,' said Stacey.

The baby elephant had to save his mother. It was up to him. Otherwise she would die in the cage. Dumbo had to fly. But how could he? I ate some of the chips and drank the lemonade. Dumbo jumped from the basket then he came down slowly, and everybody cheered. There was no way he could do it, but he did it. The movie finished. I sat on the floor and looked at Sherry's teacups and pretend biscuits. I pushed a truck with a bear in the tray across the brown diamonds on the carpet. I got up and looked at the photo of Stacey riding the wedding horse. The horse's eyes were the same shining black as Silver's. It had ribbons plaited into its mane. Stacey was smiling. She wore thick lipstick. The news came on. Outside it was getting darker. The door opened and I heard Stacey say, 'It's in the pantry. Don't forget ice.'

I wondered how long we would be here, visiting Stacey. What would Pop say if Dad didn't take me home soon? What would he do if he knew Dad had taken me to the Worlleys'? Dad came inside and looked around the kitchen. Honey was at his feet. She sniffed me, then went back outside. 'Where's the pantry?' Dad called to Stacey through the door.

'Next to the stove, Dumbo!' Stacey called back.

When he found the cupboard by the stove, Dad pulled out another bottle of see-through drink. He never looked at me, as if I was as see-through as the drink. He went back outside, leaving the door open.

'So what happened with the girl in Shepparton?' I heard Stacey ask.

'What girl?'

'The one who called the cops.'

'You heard about that?'

'Yep.'

'She was crazy. I was always thinking of you. She knew. I think I even called her Stace.'

'Bullshit.'

'No bullshit. Why do you think I'm here?'

'Ray, I'm married.'

'I know, Stace. I know. I missed out. Biggest mistake I ever made. But I can still see you, can't I? Have a laugh. Get to look at you. Where's the harm in that? You're gorgeous, Stacey. Drop-dead gorgeous. I hope Brian tells you that.'

'Bit hard when he's away.'

'That's where I come in, sweetheart. Happy to say it all day long. You still make me weak at the knees. Here, feel 'em.'

I heard Stacey giggle.

'Shaking, right?'

'Yeah, right,' said Stacey.

'You want to take me on a tour of the house?'

'What house?' said Stacey. 'It's taking forever.'

'It'll get there. Come on, take me on a tour.'

Stacey came to the door. 'Go on, Honey, go inside. You can't come or you'll run off chasing rabbits.' Honey came into the living room. 'Back soon, Justine,' Stacey said. Her cheeks were flushed pink, her hair had come loose and hung around her face. She was like a small pink candle melting at the sides. She closed the door of the caravan.

Rio Bravo came on the television. I pulled my feet up under me on Stacey's chair to watch the big man. The caravan was warm with the door closed. Honey lay at the entrance with her head between her paws. John Wayne as Sheriff Chance was keeping the brother in jail. He wasn't scared; he could have been, but he wasn't. *Down in the valley, the valley so low, hang your head over, hear the wind blow,* Dude sang. Colorado Ryan joined him, his voice soft and sweet. I closed my eyes. *Angels in heaven, know I love you. Hang your head over, hang your head low . . .*

——

In my dream, Stacey, carrying Sherry in one arm, rode towards my dad on the wedding horse. He climbed up behind her, holding a long gun like Sheriff Chance. Stacey's wedding dress was all around them, wrapping them in white. Colorado Ryan sang, *If you don't love me, love who you please.* The horse reared up, bucking and kicking as it tried to throw my dad to the ground. Around them was a ditch, like the one around Steve. Stacey said, *No! No!* to Dad and he said, *Yes. You do.* I woke and opened my eyes; somebody was crying.

I didn't know where I was or what I was doing in this room. Who was crying? I looked around at the photos on the wall and the baby toys on the floor, and remembered that it was Stacey's caravan. The television showed white and grey dust crackling and fuzzing. I got up and turned it off. Honey was still at the door. She whimpered at me.

I followed the sound of crying to a door with a picture of a butterfly. Blue light came from under the door. I pushed it open and saw Sherry standing in her cot, crying. There was a light made of a blue star on the wall near the cot. When Sherry saw me she looked scared.

I went back and opened the front door of the caravan. Honey ran out. I couldn't see Dad or Stacey. There were two big empty bottles lying on the grass under the table. The half-built house was in silver piles lit by the moon and the stars.

'Honey!' I called. 'Honey, come back!' I couldn't see the dog anywhere. What would Stacey say if Honey was gone? Sherry cried louder. I went back inside to her room. 'Shhhh,' I said. 'Shhhh, Sherry.' I leaned into her cot and picked up her toy rabbit. 'Here you go, here you go.' I waved the rabbit close to her face. She kept crying. I didn't know what to do. Sherry was so little. There was a mark on her cheek from the dummy she had been sucking. I saw the dummy on the mattress of the cot. I picked it up and tried to give that to her but she cried louder and shook her head.

I went back to the front door. 'Dad!' I called. 'Dad!' The night went on as far as I could see. 'Dad!' I called again. 'Dad!' Honey ran back into the caravan, whimpering. 'Honey!' I said. 'Good girl, good girl, Honey.'

I closed the door and went back to the cot. I leaned down to Sherry and she reached out her arms to me. I lifted her over the bars and held her. 'Don't cry, Sherry, don't cry.' She was heavy and warm in my arms as I carried her out of the room. She stopped crying. I gave her a chip from the bowl and she held it in her hands. I sat down on the chair with Sherry on my knee. Honey sat at my feet, as if she had given up on the world outside.

It was like I was the mother and Sherry was my baby, Honey was my dog, and this was my home. If I wanted I could hook the caravan up to Dad's truck and drive it away. We could go down the Henley Trail, past Pop's Three and out onto the highway. We could keep going until night turned to day and Yolamundi was far behind us. Everything and every person and every place would be new, like a present never opened.

Sherry started to cry again so I got up and bobbed her in my arms the way I'd seen Stacey do. We went around the room looking at the pictures. 'Who's that? I said to her. 'Who's that?' I pointed at the photo of Stacey on the horse. 'Horse,' I said. 'Horse.'

Sherry said, 'Mumma,' and then she pointed at the dog and said, 'Unny. Unny.'

I said, 'Honey. Honey.'

Honey followed us around the room. She came with us to the trophy and the sink and the photo of Brian holding Stacey in his arms.

We walked to the door; I pushed it open and we stood in the doorway—this time Honey stayed inside the caravan. I pointed at the sky. 'Look, Sherry, stars. Stars.'

Sherry pointed and said, 'Star. Star.'

A scream came from the half-built house. The skin at the back of my neck prickled. 'Mumma, Mumma,' Sherry said.

'Shhh. Shhh, Sherry,' I said. The scream came again. Sherry started to cry. I bobbed her up and down, faster than before. The screaming kept going. What should I do? I didn't know. I went inside the caravan and shut the door. I was shivering. Sherry cried louder. I went down to the other end of the caravan, away from the door and into another room. I kept the lights off, rocking Sherry in my arms. 'It's alright, it's alright,' I whispered. But I didn't know if it was alright. I sang to Sherry, *Down in the valley, the valley so low*, over and over. *Hang your head over, hang your head low*, until she stopped crying. *Roses love sunshine, violets love dew. Angels in heaven know I love you.* I lay back on the bed in the room, I don't know whose it was; there was no light—I was too scared that someone would see it. I lay holding Sherry against my chest, until we slept.

When I woke, Ray was standing over me, shaking my shoulder. 'Get up,' he said.

I felt sleepy; I didn't know where I was again. I didn't know why my dad was there. He didn't come into my room. Then I remembered. I was in Stacey's caravan. Sherry was beside me. She began to cry.

Dad said, 'Get up, we're going.'

I sat up, holding on to Sherry. It was too dark in the room to see. 'Is Stacey here?' I whispered.

'Don't worry about Stacey.'

'What about the baby?'

'Put her in her room.'

I got up and Sherry cried louder. 'Mumma! Mumma!' I didn't want to let her go. I didn't want to leave her crying.

'But what about Stacey?' I said. 'Is she coming?'

'Move it.'

I carried Sherry into the room with the blue light. I put her in her cot. She stood, holding her arms out to me. 'Mumma! Mumma!'

'Shhh,' I said. 'Shhh, Sherry.' I wished Stacey would come and pick up Sherry and give her milk and hold her. 'Shhhhh, Sherry.'

Dad stood outside the door. 'Come on, Justine.'

I walked to the truck, Sherry crying behind me. 'Dad,' I said, 'where's Stacey?' I looked out at the half-built house, silver in the moonlight. I couldn't see Stacey anywhere.

'Get in the truck.'

I heard crying from outside and in.

Dad turned on the engine and we drove away from Stacey Worlley's caravan.

Later, when I lay down on my bed and closed my eyes, I could still hear crying. I sat up and the room spun, the way it did the day Dad taught me how to shoot. I got up in the dark, went to the toilet and vomited.

25.

When I looked through the kitchen window the next morning, I saw a heavy grey light all around Pop's Three. It came down over the walls, the yard and the back-house. The curtains to the back-house were closed. Dad was still sleeping. The night before, he hadn't said a word all the way home. He hadn't said goodnight. It was as if I wasn't there.

I crossed the yard and went to the run to check on the chooks, closing the gate behind me. 'Here, chook chook chook,' I said, and they gathered around me to see if I had food. I threw them seeds from the drum, and they came very close and pecked the dirt at my feet. I sat on the ground near the water dish, holding out my arms. 'Chook chook chook,' I said. I wished they would come and sit on my shoulders and perch on my hands and cluck to me. I wished Cockyboy would use the hooks on his claws to guard me; he could show them to the enemy. *Leave Justine alone!* 'Hey, chook chook chook,' I said. 'Hey, girls; hey, girls. Hey, Cockyboy.' Cockyboy looked at me with his head on the side. 'I won't hurt the girls,' I told him. 'I won't hurt the ladies. I'm your friend, Cockyboy.' I wished the run was full of yellow babies and that they would all come around me and squeak and chirp. There would be so many all I could see would be yellow, as yellow as the sun, and I wouldn't hear anything but the squeaky chattering of the baby chicks all wanting me to touch them and hold them and be their mother, and I wouldn't hear crying and instead of grey it would be gold.

I don't know how long I sat there. When I stood, my legs were sore and stiff. I walked out of the chook run down to the gate. There was nobody around; Pop's fire was black coals and smoking stones. I climbed through the fence and followed the trail that went into the trees. The crying came with me. Sometimes it was Stacey's and sometimes it was Sherry's and sometimes it was a third voice I didn't know. When I was in the trees the crying became softer, until it was a hum, no louder than the sound of my footsteps on the way to my hideout.

Kirk and Steve and me hadn't been down to our hideouts since Dad had come home. I straightened the wall of branches, then I found more, thick with dry leaves, and stacked them one on top of another against the pole-tree until you couldn't see through them. I found Pop's old towel, half-buried in the dirt, and shook it out, before spreading it over the roof. I made a door that could be pulled closed so you didn't know a door was there. My hideout was as safe as Chief Puma's teepee. I picked up a stick with a point and wrote a sign in my own letters. It said *keep out* in a code nobody could read. Letters that didn't move. Every one a barb of wire in its own shape. *Keep out.*

I swept the floor inside with another leafy branch until it was smooth. I found a short, thick log and made a shelf for supplies. I carried in armfuls of dry leaves and put them on one side to make a soft leaf bed. I tidied the ring of stones and found kindling and wood, ready for a fire. The hum of crying grew softer as I worked, hardly there. I found more branches and built walls around the walls, so everything was covered and camouflaged. Even Kirk and Steve wouldn't recognise it. I grew hot as I worked, not thinking of anything but my keepout home, not Stacey and Sherry or the caravan or my dad leaning over me, *Wake up, move it!* Not remembering the drive home, Dad's emptied-out silence, as if he had left something behind at Stacey's and he was glad and quiet and calm without it, the same way he was after he shot the bullets into the cans.

I left my keepout and walked down to the river. I saw a grey kangaroo watching me through the trees, its paws up, dark eyes unblinking. There was a joey tucked into its pouch, its face turned towards me. The joey was safe in its pouch, held, nowhere else to go, his mother behind and above him. The pouch was a home and a coat and a car for the joey. I closed my eyes and felt the pouch around my body and back and legs, holding me close. I was held and I was free. When I opened my eyes I saw another kangaroo behind, then another and another, until every tree and rock and branch and bush was a kangaroo, all of them still, waiting and watching. I took a step and then every kangaroo—the mothers with joeys in their pouches, the fathers with their fists raised, the brothers and sisters still growing—turned and bounded away from me deeper into the bush. In one second every kangaroo knew it had to move, to escape the danger.

I walked along the river, dragging a stick behind me. I could hear Sherry's and Stacey's cries twined together. What happened at the caravan? What did my dad do? I didn't know the words for things—I had no answers.

Soon I came to The Choke. I watched the water flowing in one single direction. I took a deep breath. I closed my eyes, then opened them to see trees and river, then closed them. The hum of crying was so quiet that the sound became part of the Murray. I didn't belong to myself anymore. I had no mouth or eyes or thoughts. I didn't need anything to change or be different. I didn't wish Aunty Rita would come back. I wasn't waiting for a letter I couldn't read or a telephone call Pop wouldn't give me or another visit she couldn't make. I wasn't wishing it was school, so I could see Michael, be with him, have his help. I didn't need to find words, or read them. The hole inside me was filled, the same way the bullets filled the holes of the Smith—then even that smooth surface disappeared and I was part of things that couldn't be seen. I don't know how long I was there. There was no time.

26.

That night Pop didn't light a fire and we ate dinner in the kitchen. It was eggs and a tomato. When I did the dishes I checked the back-house windows for light but there was none. I hadn't seen Dad all day. He hadn't come out to get water for his shower, and when Pop called, 'Time to eat, Ray', Dad didn't answer. It was as if he wasn't there, even though I knew he was. After dinner Pop lay on his couch with his hand over his gut. 'Go to bed, Justine,' he said.

I couldn't sleep. The crying grew louder. It was Sherry and Stacey, and another voice. The cries were both inside and outside, far away and close. If Aunty Rita was here she could put her arms around me like John Wayne did to Feathers; she could put the pads to my head and send in a volt, and when I woke she'd say, *How about a walk?*

I don't know what time it was when I heard Dad go down the hall and out the front door. The glow of his headlights shone through my window. I heard the rumble of his engine turn down the Henley Trail in the direction of the pub. In my dream Sherry held my hand as Honey led us down the road.

Honey kept turning around to make sure we were there, still walking, still following. We came to a train station with a sign I couldn't read. I didn't know if a train was coming, or how long we had to wait.

⌣

At lunchtime Pop and me were in the kitchen eating toast when Dad came inside. It was the first time I'd seen him since we came back from Stacey's. His skin was without colour, like my black-and-white cut-outs. You couldn't see through the glass of his eyes. His hair looked damp. Something was gone from him, and something had been added.

'Heading off this afternoon,' he said to Pop, opening the fridge.

Surprise leaked through Pop's face, changing the lines of his mouth, deepening the tracks. He said, 'I thought you were doing a job for the Martins.'

'Changed my mind,' said Dad, closing the fridge.

Pop stood, shaking his head. Dad coughed up from his throat and spat into the sink. Pop frowned. Dad said, 'Fuck off, Robert.' He barely opened his mouth. The words slipped out the side, then he turned on the tap and started to fill the bucket for his shower. Pop puffed out air and kept his mouth shut. When the bucket was full Dad carried it towards the back door.

'When are you home again?' said Pop.

'Could be a while,' said Dad.

Pop took a breath. 'Right.'

'Problem?'

'No problem, son,' said Pop. Pop had lost something that belonged to my dad a long time ago, something that was his—Ray's—most special thing, more important to him than his truck, than the Smith, than Silver. Ray had been missing it since he was a boy in the photograph. They both knew it was Pop's fault. Dad went through the back door with his bucket. Pop leaned against the bench. He breathed out and looked at his hands.

After lunch I lay on my bed, and cut trucks into pieces. I left the metal doors hanging from the bodies, the exhaust pipes dangling from the trays. I cut off wipers and bumper bars and fenders and horns. When I heard the sound of an engine coming down the road I looked through the window and saw a police car. I jumped up from my bed and ran out the back. 'Pop!'

Pop stuck his head out of the chook run. 'What is it?'

'The cops.'

The cops had come to Pop's before. They'd been looking for Dad. A girl from Melbourne said he held her down and put his coat over her face behind the Rochy pub. It was a black-and-red checked coat and it brought the girl's world in so close she could smell it. Cigarette smoke, beer and petrol. But Mother Margy said Ray was with her that night, not at the Rochy pub, so how could he have done it? They were at the farm playing cards. A lot of the Worlleys saw him that night, they could testify. They played game after game; Mother Margy could remember Ray's last hand. She said it was the ace of spades that led the deck; she'd never forget.

The girl was from the big smoke; the wind from the city blew her in, twirling her through the air like a leaf in autumn. She had never seen the world so close as underneath Ray's checked coat; she could hardly breathe, there was no distance or space. But Mother Margy said, *Oh, bullshit, these city girls, tarts, wind blows them in, pity it can't blow them out,* and the cops drove away. Pop said, *Don't shit in your own nest, son.* Ray didn't fight him. He looked at the ground at Pop's feet. He said, *Al-fucken-right, Dad.*

The other time the cops came it was about a robbery in Albury at a house in Cobble Street. The wife said that she and her husband woke up in the middle of the robbery and caught my dad by surprise. She said my dad shot her husband with a sawn-off shotgun. The wife identified Ray but the husband said, *No, no, it wasn't him.* The wife said, *My husband had a bullet in his neck! How could he be sure of anything?* My dad said to the wife, *Bullshit. Ask your husband how he knows me, darlin'. Ask him why there's a bullet in his neck.* The wife said to her husband, *You're a coward. You know who did this to you!* But the husband wouldn't say it and he told the wife to be quiet.

When Dad came back from the police station that day, Pop raised his eyebrows at him and said, *Luck runs out, son.*

Pop looked towards the back-house. 'Jesus,' he said. He shook his head as he walked up to the house. 'Jesus Christ.'

I followed Pop down the hallway. There was knocking at the front door. 'Go into your room,' Pop said to me.

'Can I see the police?' I asked him.

'Go to your room, Justine,' Pop said. But I didn't go to my room; I went with Pop to the front door.

Pop took his handkerchief from his pocket and wiped his face. When he opened the door two policemen were standing there. One was old, with a moustache and a stomach as big as a barrel under his shirt, and one was young, with his cap low over his eyes. There were guns in their holsters, and black poles hung from their belts.

The older cop said, 'Does Raymond Andrew Lee live here?'

Pop said, 'I live here.'

'Is your name Raymond Andrew Lee?'

'No.'

'Does Raymond Andrew Lee live here?' the older cop asked.

I looked up at Pop.

He said, 'What do you need to know for?'

'Is he here?'

'You tell me what you want him for.' Pop's voice sounded shaky and dry, like the thinnest branch on the gum tree.

The older cop said, 'You better let us in, Mr Lee.'

A smell was coming from Pop. It was the same smell as when the Worlley calf's ear was cut off because of infection, the same smell. Pop's shirt and face were damp. He said, 'Wait here.'

I followed him back down the hall.

Pop called out, 'Ray!'

The policemen didn't do what Pop said; they didn't wait at the front. They followed us into the house. Ray stepped into the kitchen at the same time as the cops. He said, 'What the fuck?' He was tall, his hair shining and black, his face pale.

The older cop said, 'Raymond Andrew Lee, you are under arrest for the rape and assault of Stacey Chisholm.'

I heard Pop gasp.

'You are not obliged to say or do anything unless you wish to do so, but whatever you say or do may be used in evidence. Do you understand?'

Dad touched the inside of his mouth with his tongue. His eyes narrowed. He said, 'This is bullshit.' He leaned against the kitchen table and folded his arms.

'We're not going to talk about that now,' said the older cop.

Dad said, 'Fucken bullshit.'

The older cop said, 'Cuff him,' to the younger cop. Dad's hand shot out and hit the younger cop in the side of the head.

Pop said, 'No, son!'

The older cop had his gun out and aimed at my dad's face. He said, 'Handcuff him!'

My dad went still when he saw the gun. The younger cop pulled my dad's hands behind his back, and put the cuffs around his wrists. 'Fucken bullshit,' Dad said again. He wasn't scared. Even then.

'Son, don't . . .' Pop said.

I heard crying. Was it Stacey? Was it Sherry? It filled the kitchen, louder and louder. But nobody else seemed to hear it; only me. The cops pushed my dad down the hall, both of them behind him, the older cop with a hand on his back; they had to, or he wouldn't have moved. He would have gone to Bathurst. He would have found his friends to help him. He would have shot both cops and covered their heads with his checked coat.

I followed them out of the house. Nobody tried to stop me. Pop stayed where he was, sagging against the bench. The cries in my ears grew louder.

I watched from the front door as the cops pushed Dad down the steps and across the drive to the police car. I was waiting for him to turn his head and see me there. But he didn't. The younger cop opened the door of the police car and the bigger one put his hand on my dad's head and pushed him into the back seat.

The last I saw of my dad was the back of his black-and-red checked coat through the glass of the police car window.

I stood on Pop's front steps, the cries in my ears weaving around each other, growing loud enough to reach the forest. What had my dad done? Only the kangaroos and the emus and the possums could tell me, only the cods and the eels and the owls. They were there that night. They'd seen into the darkness of Stacey's half-built house.

When I came back inside Pop was still standing at the kitchen bench. He turned around to me. 'What happened out there, Justine?'

'The cops took Dad,' I said.

'No. At Stacey's place on Friday night. What happened?'

'I don't know.'

'You were there, Justine. If anything happened you would have seen it.' I couldn't find words to say. What did happen out there? I saw the stars, I held Sherry, I heard screaming. Dad woke me and said we had to go. I couldn't see Stacey anywhere.

I followed Pop out to Dad's truck. Pop was talking, saying words under his breath. *Ray . . . Ray . . . son . . . Christ . . . Lizzy . . . bastards . . . Stacey Chisholm! Christ! Jesus!* He got in the truck and opened the glove box. Pop took out Dad's Smith and his bullets, then he went back inside to the door that led to the gun cupboard. I listened from the top as he went down the stairs, opened the cupboard and put Dad's Smith inside it. Soon he came back up the stairs. When he saw me he looked surprised. 'Christ,' he said. If I had stood somewhere else, or gone somewhere else, what difference would it have made? The only difference I made was in the breech. That was the only time I could be felt.

All afternoon Pop sat on his camp chair in front of his fire, the edges of his hands pressed to his mouth. He stared into the flames as if they could take him back to the start, when Lizzy was there. When she might have been able to help.

⌒

On Sunday night I stayed on my bed and barely moved; if I tried to get up the room spun and I wanted to vomit. I didn't eat. Pop left me alone. When I slept it was Dad who woke me. *Get up, Justine. What about Sherry?*

Leave her, put her back in her room, move it.

27.

On Monday morning Pop said, 'I'll drive you to school.' He didn't say why. He got in the truck and said, 'Come on, Justine.'

Halfway down the Henley Trail Pop said, 'Anything happened out there, you would've seen it.' I didn't know if it was a question or an answer.

As we came to the school gates Pop looked at the other kids and parents and teachers going through the gate as if they were the Japs. His eyes widened, he looked over his shoulder and back to the front. 'Off you go,' he said.

After I got out of his truck I didn't wait for Michael at the front, the way I did on other mornings. I took a bottle of milk from the crates and went down to the shelter sheds. I kept my eyes down. When I got to the sheds I sat on the concrete and held my milk.

In the distance I saw more and more kids arriving. Soon I saw Dawn and Noreena walking towards me, holding their bottles. What did they want? We weren't even friends anymore.

When they got to me, Dawn said, 'We were looking for you, Justine. What are you doing down here?' I shrugged.

'I hate this place,' said Noreena. 'The boys piss behind the wall.' She waved her hand in front of her nose. 'Hey, Jussy,' she said.

I looked at the ground.

'Have a good weekend?'

'Did you do anything?' Noreena smiled.

'Anything fun?' Dawn asked.

There was quiet for a while.

'Anything at all?' Noreena raised her eyebrows.

My milk bottle felt damp, as if the milk was seeping through the glass.

'Did anything exciting happen?' Dawn asked.

Noreena flicked her hair over her shoulder. 'Yeah. Anything exciting happen?'

I didn't answer.

Noreena said, 'It's just that we heard . . .'

I looked up.

'What?'

'We heard your dad might have . . .'

'What?'

Noreena looked at Dawn.

'What did your dad do, Jussy?' Dawn pulled the lid off her milk bottle and took a sip. 'We heard he did something. Do you know what it was?'

'I don't know. Nothing.'

Noreena stepped closer. 'Nothing?'

'I don't know. Yeah, nothing.'

'That's not what we heard,' Dawn said.

'We heard they found Stacey in the cattle trough,' said Noreena.

We went quiet for a moment. I felt sick.

'Yeah, she nearly drowned. Her head was in the trough,' said Noreena.

The ground came up to my face. I leaned back against the shed wall.

'If her uncle hadn't come over to take a look at her taps,' said Dawn, wiping milk from her lip, 'she could have died. That's what we heard.'

'She wasn't wearing any clothes,' Noreena whispered.

Can you know and not know?

'She could hardly walk and the only thing that kept her going was her baby; she had to get back to the baby,' said Dawn. The ground tipped again. 'She had to go to the hospital for stitches. You could see her head where her hair was torn out.'

'Stacey Chisholm had nice hair,' said Noreena.

'Yeah,' said Dawn. 'Her hair was really nice. Jane Tawney did it up for her wedding.'

'She was pretty.'

'Really pretty,' said Dawn. 'I saw photos from the wedding. A professional did her make-up.'

'Stacey's a liar,' I said. It took all my strength. I had barely enough left to get up and walk away.

———

Michael didn't come to school that day. I looked at the glass square in the door for the top of his head but I never saw it. Kids talked to each other and stared at me and whispered.

28.

On Tuesday morning I pulled on the clothes I had worn the day before, then I went straight out the back. Pop hadn't let the chooks out of the run yet.

I opened the gate. 'Hey, girls,' I said. 'Hey, ladies.' The chooks looked at me, heads moving from one side to the other trying to understand why I was there. It was always Pop who opened the gate in the mornings. 'Come on, girls,' I said. 'It's me letting you out this morning. Pop's not up yet.' I lifted my arms and shoo-ed them through. 'Come on.' I scooped up a bucket of the good seed from the drum and scattered it over the grass. Pop didn't like me doing that; it brought the rats. 'Here, girls; here, ladies.'

I sat cross-legged on the grass as the chooks pecked at the good seed in the dirt around me. 'Hey, girls; hey, ladies,' I whispered. Cockyboy pecked at the seeds on the outer circle, checking the fence line and the back-house and the drive, as if this time it was me he wanted to guard. I didn't want to leave the chooks. I didn't want to go to school. Pop called from the kitchen. 'Get a move on, Justine, or you'll miss the bus.'

'He'll get seven years for what he did,' said Matt Dunning as we walked up the path to class. 'Seven years, easy. Maybe more. It's up to Stacey; she can choose.'

I didn't know what to say. I didn't know what was happening, what they were talking about, and I did know at the same time. I felt myself shrinking, pulling myself in, layer by layer, so I hardly existed. Only the outside existed. The bell rang for class. I looked around for Michael. What if he didn't come? What if he was at the hospital for another day? I didn't think I could stay at school if he wasn't there. But then I turned and saw Mrs Hooper opening her car door at the school gate. I wanted to run down to the car. There was a lump in my throat. I could only stand and watch and wait. The crutches came out first then Michael followed. When he was on his feet he turned and saw me waiting. He came up the school path as if he wasn't heading for the school—he didn't care if the school was there or not; the school could have caught fire behind me, the building in flames, and he still wouldn't look—he was only heading for me. From the street outside the school Mrs Hooper lifted her hand and waved. She looked sad.

When he was close I looked into his eyes; they went down deep, like green tunnels. Even though my dad left Stacey in the cattle trough he let me look. As we walked to class Michael didn't ask me anything about my dad, or what happened at the caravan. He didn't always need words either; he had learned other ways.

Michael and me sat at our desk and Michael opened his map book at the desert. The sun came over the dunes. The sand was in waves as if a wind had blown over the surface. There were small purple flowers growing in the sand. There was a picture of a camel with rope from its nose. 'Mrs Turning,' said Michael. I stayed close to him all day. The only time I couldn't see him was when I went to the girls' toilets. He leaned against the wall, waiting for me.

At lunch Matt Dunning and Brian Lawson came over to us at the benches. Matt said, 'Barry Grock's dad went to jail four years ago for carjacking, and he's still there.'

Brian said, 'If you fight back they keep you there forever, but if you don't fight back the other prisoners take you down.'

Michael picked up his crutch and swung it into Brian's shin.

Brian jumped back. 'Hey!' he said, rubbing his leg.

'Stick you!' said Michael.

'Freaks,' said Matt as they walked away.

29.

At the end of the last week of school it was the Christmas concert. I walked to the bus stop and waited at Pop's rock. Pop didn't come to the concert; he would only visit Sandy. He told the chickens and the walls and the esky and the fire and his White Ox, *Can't trust anybody. Learned that the hard way.*

In the afternoon the whole school was in the hall to do the Christmas play and the songs. Nobody wore their uniforms; everyone wore red and green shirts and shorts and dresses. There were rows of chairs in front of the stage. The parents and grandparents came into the hall, everyone taking a chair. The hall was filled with the whispering parents and grandparents and brothers and sisters, waiting for the concert to start.

The kids from Mrs Turning's class came out from behind the curtain. The room, though full, was still; everybody was waiting. Michael stood beside me. I could see his mother and father and his little brother, Nicky, in the front row, holding each other's hands. Sabine raised her stick, everyone took a breath, lifting our chins to follow the stick. Sabine nodded at us, mouthing the words, 'Holly and the Ivy'. Mr Briggs played the piano. *The holly* and the ivy, when they are both full grown . . . Everybody around me sang so loud I didn't know if I was singing or not. Though I moved my mouth to the words I could remember, I didn't know if I was singing. I didn't know what was my own sound.

But I heard Michael. He sang loud for his mother and father and his brother as they watched him from the front row, their faces alight and open. Michael didn't care who laughed, who stared, who called him names, *spastic elastic hooper drooper crutches retard.* He sang as loud as he could, as Sabine waved her stick, her dress bright in green and red, her mouth wide, part in smile, part in song. Michael nudged me. I knew the code of his movements. I took a deep breath, turned to face the front and sang. *The holly and the ivy, when they are both full grown, of all the trees that are in the wood, the holly bears the crown!* My voice and Michael Hooper's floated through the windows of the hall, out over the school, and the town of Nullabri, over the trucks and semis and utes along the Murray Valley Highway. *O the rising of the sun and the running of the deer, the playing of the merry organ, sweet singing in the choir.* Higher and higher our voices rose, floating over the police, over my dad in custody in the city, over Stacey Worlley in the caravan. *The holly and the ivy, when they are both full grown, of all the trees that are in the wood, the holly bears the crown.* Until everyone who heard lifted their heads and said, 'It's Justine and Michael Hooper. Can you hear them singing? Justine and Michael Hooper!'

⌒

After the concert Mr and Mrs Hooper came to their son and took his shoulders and said, 'Well done! Well done, son.'

Nicky held onto his brother's leg.

I stood to the side and looked at the ground. Did Mr and Mrs Hooper know about my dad? Did they know what happened? Everybody else did. I kept my eyes low.

Michael said, 'Justine, come here!'

Mrs Hooper said, 'Hello, Justine, how are you?'

'You're a good friend of Michael's,' said Mr Hooper. 'He's going to miss you in the holidays.' I couldn't say anything or look at him.

Mrs Hooper stepped towards me and put her arms around me. I went stiff. She pressed me to her.

30.

Every morning since Dad went away, when Pop first woke up I saw more of the track between Burma and Siam as if it had been laid on him in the night. It ran from his eyes to his chin, down his neck, then under his clothes and down his legs. The Eastern Bullet could have used his body to transport ammunition. Pop told his cigarette and his tea and the radio. *Death Rail was right, Lizzy, and for what? Bastards.* We sat at the table and breathed in the smoke from his White Ox. The kindest animal was my friend too.

———

Aunty Rita didn't write me a letter and Pop never came into the house carrying anything for me from the letter box. I took her numbers down from the fan and tried to read them. I didn't know if they were backwards or forwards. She never rang on the telephone to speak to me. Even on Christmas Day she didn't ring. Kirk and Steve came around and we ate chicken wings and did a toast to Dad. Relle said, *Even when he's not here, the bastard's here.* When she wiped the tears away from her eyes she left smudges of make-up like green wings out the sides. Kirk said, *Cops are pigs*, and Steve pulled out his pocketknife and cut the bark off Pop's tree.

All day I waited for Aunty Rita to call on the telephone. *Is Justine there? Put her on, Pop, the little beauty, tell her it's her Aunty Rita*. No new pyjamas wrapped in brown paper arrived for me; it was as if Aunty Rita's visit had never been and Aunty Rita wasn't real. Pop never spoke her name.

When Relle and Pop went inside, Kirk, Steve and me took it in turns to drag on a White Ox. We didn't fight about it. We all knew how to suck back the smoke, as if the kindest animal had shown us himself. For one moment, at the top of the suck when our heads were full of smoke, there was no trial, no father in custody, and the words 'sexual assault' didn't drift from the kitchen.

—

On Christmas night I dreamed about Aunty Rita. We were swimming at The Choke when the banks on either side of the river reached for each other, squeezing the water out from in between. The land was choking the water. I watched the Murray spill over the red gums, covering the highest branches. Aunty Rita waved to me across the rising water. *This way, Justine!*

The next day was Boxing Day. There were beer cans lying on their sides around the fire and pink wrapping paper in the grass from the necklace Kirk and Steve gave Relle.

'Where is Aunty Rita?' I said to Pop as we gathered kindling by the fence. Pop had a White Ox balanced on his lip. The smoke never stopped coming out of him; he was like a house on fire, smoke drifting from his ears and eyes and out the top of his head, wrapping around his face so I couldn't see into his eyes.

Pop said, 'I don't have a daughter. There is no bloody Aunty Rita.' He picked up a stick and threw it in the wheelbarrow.

I said, 'Yes, you do.'

He said, 'No, no . . .' He turned away, muttering words I couldn't hear.

'Yes, you do,' I said, standing straight. I did what my pop said. He was the one to tell me. There was no Ray and no Donna and nobody else. But my Aunty Rita said she would call me, said she would write. What happened to her?

'I have a son and that's enough,' he said. 'Even that's too much.'

'You do have a daughter, Pop.'

'Shut up, Justine.'

I said, 'You do.'

'Justine!'

'You do!'

'You're heading for trouble.'

'You do. Her name is Rita.'

'Don't say that name.'

'Rita!'

'I'm warning you!'

'Warn me!' I shouted. 'Warn me! Warn me!'

'That's enough!'

'Rita! Rita! Rita!'

'No daughter of mine!'

'Rita! Rita! Rita!'

Whack! Pop hit me across the back of the legs with a stick. 'Shut your mouth!' he shouted.

'No!' I couldn't stop. 'Rita! Rita!' I threw down my branches and ran to the house and into my room. I put my face on my pillow. Pop did have a daughter. Pop couldn't choose not to have Rita because she wasn't natural. It was too late; he already made his choice. I heard crying from inside and outside at the same time. The back of my legs stung.

I looked up to the blade of the fan and I couldn't see the corner of Aunty Rita's paper. I couldn't remember if I had put it back or not. I didn't even check; I didn't care. Maybe it had ended up in Pop's fire. What would I do with those numbers? They were in the wrong order; I could never call them. I got up from the bed, went to the window and looked at the road outside. John Wayne pulled The Miracle Horse in tight circles, waiting for me, gun in the air. *I'm going to Missouri with every bull I can lay my hands on. You coming?* I leaned my head against the glass. He could save people or he could kill them. He could blow the head off anyone. He could take out a bull or a man or a horse with a broken neck. He could look straight into the eyes of his target and pull the trigger.

31.

It was the first day of fourth class. My shoes were so tight I had to walk with my toes curled. 'Why are you walking like that?' Pop asked me.

'My shoes,' I said.

'What about them?'

'They're too small,' I said.

'For Christ's sake,' said Pop. He drove us into Nullabri and we stopped on Main Road outside Whyte's. Pop looked up and down the street as if he was checking for the enemy. Then he got out and I followed him into the shop.

'Hello, Robert,' the shoe lady said. The shoe lady's body was in tight rolls that pushed out her shirt. She wore lipstick and her hair was in a high, stiff ball on top of her head.

Pop nodded. 'Pearl.' He looked away from her when he said it, as if he was in trouble.

'Don't see you out and about too much these days.'

Pop scowled. Everyone in the town could be a Jap.

'What can I do for you?' she said, glancing at me.

'It's Justine. She needs new shoes.'

'Right,' said Pearl. 'Hello, Justine.' She smiled at me. 'You've grown. You must be . . . nine now. Ten?'

'Ten,' I said.

Pop said, 'Haven't got too much time.'

Pearl shot Pop a look. 'Take a seat,' she said to me. 'School shoes, dear?'

I looked at Pop.

'School shoes,' he said.

'First day back, isn't it?'

'Yes,' I said.

'Better get a move on,' said Pop.

Pearl looked at Pop over her glasses. 'Leaving it all a bit late, aren't you, Robert?'

'Could you just get the shoes, Pearl,' he said, as if he was scared the shelves of sandals and boots and sneakers might take him prisoner.

'Of course,' said Pearl, pressing her lips together. She went through a door at the end of the shop, and came back with a box. She put the box on the ground, opened it and pulled out a pair of brown school shoes with a buckle, and tiny holes in the shape of a bow.

She looked at the shoes I was wearing and shook her head, undoing my laces. 'Try these, dear,' she said, passing me the new ones.

I slipped my feet into the shoes. There was so much room for my toes. I moved them up and down. There were no laces or Velcro to catch the dirt and cotton. You could choose how tight to do the buckles.

'Walk around a little and see how they feel,' said Pearl.

I stood up and walked around the shop.

Pearl said, 'Look in the mirror, dear.'

I looked in the mirror and the buckles glowed, the brown leather was strong and shiny.

Pop said, 'Alright, alright,' and opened his wallet. 'How much?'

Pearl checked the tag on the box. 'Twenty-nine dollars,' she said.

Pop said, 'Jesus!'

Pearl said, 'Robert,' and looked at him over the tops of her glasses.

He said, 'Alright, alright,' and gave her the money.

Pearl turned to me and said, 'How about you keep the new shoes on for your first day.' She picked up my old shoes with the ends of her fingers. 'And I'll take care of these.'

'Thank you,' I said.

Pearl followed us to the door. 'You enjoy those shoes, dear.'

As I crossed the road I turned and saw Pearl still standing there. She waved to me but her face looked sad. My new shoes didn't pinch or dig and they were soft under my feet as if each foot had its own bed to sleep in. I said, 'Thank you, Pop.'

He said, 'Highway bloody robbery,' and started the truck.

I wriggled my toes and looked out of the window at the Nullabri soldier. I wanted to wave to him. I was going to see Michael; we would be starting fourth class together and I was wearing new shoes.

Pop pulled up at the school and looked around at the other kids and parents and teachers moving towards the gate. 'Out you get,' he said.

I got out of the car. 'See you, Pop,' I said, but he was already pulling away.

'Justine!' I heard. 'Justine!'

I turned and saw Michael getting out of his car. When he waved at me he almost knocked Mrs Hooper with his crutches.

Nicky tried to hold on to one of his legs as Michael swung himself up the path towards me. 'Justine!' he said. 'Justine!' His voice was loud and groaning and happy, and he didn't care how it sounded or who looked as he shouted to me across the school yard.

Michael and me walked up to the fourth-class room together. Other kids glanced at us then looked away. They didn't do or say anything to us. They didn't come close. The room was full of laughter and talking, and Michael and me were part of it. We chose a desk in the middle, and Michael took out his books and put them underneath. I put my school bag beside his. Michael said, 'No more Mrs Turning.'

'Thank God.'

'I prayed every night.'

'And God listened.'

A woman came into the room carrying a pile of books. She wore flat white shoes and a cream dress. Three of the books slid to the ground. 'Oops!' she said and smiled at us. She bent down to pick up the books and put them back on top of the pile, then she stood and smoothed her cream dress. 'Hello, everybody,' she said. 'I am Miss Suzette Frost.'

There was Mrs Turning, Mrs Shendigging, Mrs Thurgood, Mrs Dalley and now there was Miss Suzette Frost. Every kid was quiet, staring at her. She wore little white earrings and her cream dress had a collar made of lace. She turned and wrote letters on the board. *ettezuS tsorF.* She faced us and said, 'Oops,' again. She turned and wrote *ssiM* at the front of her name.

'Miss Suzette Frost,' Michael whispered.

'Good morning, fourth class,' she said.

'Good morning, Miss . . .' Nobody knew what name to use.

She said, 'Miss Frost—please, you can call me Miss Frost.' Her voice was full of air and nerves.

Every kid was quiet. Matt and Brian and every other boy.

Miss Frost said, 'Welcome to fourth class. We're going to go around the room and I want each of you to tell me one thing about yourselves, so we can get to know each other. I'll go first.' Her smile would go then come, then go then come again. 'I am from the city and I have never been to Nullabri before this year, but I am engaged to a farmer so . . .' She shrugged, smiling. 'Here I am.'

The class was stunned. A teacher had never spoken to us before about why they were here. Nobody was sure what it meant.

'What about you?' she asked Kelly Dwyer in the back row. 'Can you tell me your name and something about yourself?'

Kelly looked around the room. She shrugged her shoulders and said, 'My name is Kelly and I'm fast at running. I can beat my brothers.'

'Thank you, Kelly, thank you,' said Miss Frost. 'That was lovely. Thank you.'

Danny Orbolt said he barracked for the Tigers. Gregory Kent said he rode in the muster for the first time this year. Jeff Yulen said he won the log-splitting competition at the Rochy Show. When it came to Michael's turn Miss Frost's face was serious. She said, 'What about you? Can you tell me your name?' Somebody laughed.

Michael said, 'I am Michael Hooper.'

Miss Frost's face was still serious.

'And can you tell us something about yourself, Matthew?'

'It's Michael,' said Michael.

'Sorry?' Miss Frost looked scared.

'It's Michael. My name is Michael.'

Miss Frost was trying so hard to understand him her face creased. More kids laughed.

Someone said, 'Pass.'

I said, 'It's Michael.'

She turned to me. 'I am sorry, what did you say?'

'His name is Michael.'

'Oh, I am sorry, Michael.' She touched Michael's hand and smiled. 'Hello, Michael.'

Michael said, 'The special thing about myself is that I hate repeating my name.'

Miss Frost looked confused. She said, 'Oh . . . it's lovely to meet you, Michael.'

'What about you?' she said to me.

'Justine,' I said, without looking at her.

'Can you speak up, please, in a big, brave voice so I can hear.'

'Justine!' I said, too loud. I heard more laughing behind me.

'And can you tell me one thing about yourself, please, Justine?' What one thing was there? A quiet opened like a pit. I couldn't look up, away from it. It was as dark as the ditch around Steve.

Michael said, 'She's funny.'

'What's that, Michael?'

'She's funny.'

'Did you say Justine is funny?'

'Yes.'

Miss Frost looked at me, surprised. She said, 'Oh, good. Good. I like funny people. My fiance is funny.' She smiled at me, touched my hand and went on to Shannon Patrick, who said it was easy to ride a bull; you just put a ring through its nose.

⁓

The class was cool and quiet in the morning but by the end of the day it was hot and noisy. Matt and Brian became louder and the girls giggled. This term we were studying local wildlife and Miss Frost pinned a big picture of a Murray cod on the wall. The cod had a body the shape of a barrel, with a wide mouth and small eyes set forward. Miss Frost said the cod was a predator and ate everything it could and might even eat a duck. Matt said, 'Like someone else I know', and threw his rubber at Alan Burns. Everybody laughed. Miss Frost pulled at her lace collar and said it certainly was hot today. Miss Frost told us the cod was part of the river system and was a bottom feeder and Greg Morecroft said, 'Alan Burns and him both.'

'Please, class! Please!' said Miss Frost. The bell rang and she went to lunch with her cheeks flushed and papers sliding from her hands.

'She'd be better in a kindergarten,' said Michael.

'With no boys,' I said.

———

At the end of the day Mrs Hooper was out the front waiting for Michael.

When we got to the gate she said, 'Hello, you two. How was day one?'

'Ground zero,' Michael said.

'That bad?' said Mrs Hooper. 'Oh dear. I guess we have to give it time.' When Mrs Hooper said that—*we have to give it time*—it was as if Michael didn't go to school by himself; his mother was there too.

'Justine, would you like to come to our house on Friday after school? I think Michael found the holidays a bit long without you,' Mrs Hooper said. 'We could take you home before dinner.'

I looked at my feet. I wasn't sure what I said.

Michael said, 'That's a yes, Mum,' and grinned at me.

'Good,' said Mrs Hooper. 'Good. That's something to look forward to.'

—

I sat on the school bus home that afternoon, my face close to the window. In four days I would be going to Michael's house. I had never thought about going to his house before. Dawn and Noreena always went to each other's houses. I had never been to anyone at school's house and nobody had been to mine. I heard Worlley cousins laughing and shouting as the bus passed over the potholes. *Something to look forward to . . .* Was that why the river flowed to the sea? Was that why the rain fell on the Yolamundi dirt? Was that why Michael and me were friends? *Something to look forward to.*

Every morning I did up the buckles of my new shoes and there was so much sunshine outside my window I couldn't see behind it.

32.

Cock-a-doodle-doo! *Good morning, Cockyboy!* I looked through my window; it was Friday morning and the sky was pink.

———

At the end of the day Michael's mother came to the gate carrying Nicky, Michael's little brother. 'Hi, kids,' she said. 'How was school?'

'Okay,' said Michael.

'How is Miss Frost settling in?'

'Useless,' said Michael.

'Useless!' said Nicky.

'Oh dear,' said Mrs Hooper. 'That's not good.'

'But nicer than Mrs Turning,' said Michael.

'A lot nicer,' I said.

Michael and me sat in the back seat with Nicky as Mrs Hooper drove us back to Michael's house. Nicky pulled Michael's hair. 'Mum! Tell Nicky to get lost!' he said.

'Oh, come on, Michael, he just wants to play—he hasn't seen you all day.'

The car was smooth with no dirt or bark or papers or butts on the floor. I could feel Michael beside me, his body shaking and pushing and jerking as if it was trying to tell me something. Nicky pulled Michael's hair, and Mrs Hooper sang along to the radio as she drove. *Nothing could be righter, than you in my arms, you in my arms, hmmm, hmmmm . . . nothing could be righter . . . my sweet love . . . hmmm, hmmmmm.*

We turned off the highway onto Moruna West Road. 'Not long now,' said Mrs Hooper. Soon she stopped the car at a house made of white bricks with no rubbish or piles of wood or pieces of car in the driveway. The windows had boxes of red flowers in rows. When we opened the doors of the car a black cat came down the side and rubbed itself against Michael's leg. Michael picked up the cat and said to me, 'This is Betty and she is a bitch.' He kissed her on the head. The cat purred.

'Michael!' said his mother. 'Don't use that word. Sorry, Justine. Betty is not a bitch. She's just fussy.'

I couldn't talk.

Inside Michael's house there were yellow flowers in a vase, there were pillows and a coloured blanket on the couches. There were paintings on the walls of trees and clouds. Everything was swept and wide with no dirt in the cracks.

When we went into the kitchen I saw a whole wall covered in Michael's paintings and drawings, all the way up to the ceiling. I saw his lion, his train, his dogs and cats and cods and emus. I saw his Antarctica and his maps. I saw his writing and his bridges and his buildings. My face felt hot. I couldn't swallow.

'Coming, Justine?' Michael said.

I followed him through the kitchen to his room. Michael pushed open the door. His bed had pictures of blue boats sewn into the sheets and pillows. There was a poster on the wall of the planets that led to the sun. He had shelves with books and a construction set. There was a fish tank full of goldfish, with real seaweed and a pretend sunken boat. 'Come and have a look,' said Michael. I watched as a turtle kicked up from the sand and swam to the surface.

'That's Keith,' said Michael. 'And sometimes he tries to eat the fish.' Michael dropped some food into the tank and all the fish swam to the top, their mouths opening and closing. Michael put his hands into the water and lifted out the turtle. 'Sit with your legs crossed,' he said to me. Michael rested his crutches on the bed and lowered himself to the floor. I sat too. We leaned against the bed and Keith crossed our laps. When I touched his leg, his head went into his shell. Michael said, 'He's still getting to know you.' I knew all Michael's words and sounds—it wasn't hard. The teachers at school could have learned too; then they would have put Michael in the A reader group, not the Fs with me.

Michael set Keith back in the tank and took out some books from his shelf. There were pictures of animals and planets and volcanoes with lava. Mrs Hooper opened the door. 'Hey, kids,' she said. She smiled at us and put a plate of watermelon on the floor between us. Then she left.

Michael said, 'You're quiet,' and I couldn't say it was because he had too many things. He had Keith and fish and books and watermelon on a plate. He had things to look forward to. If the other boys at school knew he spoke and was clever, they would be his friend and then he wouldn't need to be my friend—he was only my friend because there was nobody else.

I couldn't speak or say it. I was just a friend because nobody knew what I knew about him.

'What's the matter?' said Michael. 'Why aren't you talking?' I shrugged. 'Betty wants to sit on you,' he said.

He passed me Betty and the cat went across my lap like a warm silk blanket and purred. Michael picked up a piece of watermelon and passed it to me, but I shook my head—I wasn't hungry. Michael took a piece for himself and when he tried to eat it the juice went down his chin. He wiped his face and laughed. He threw a piece at me and I laughed and then I took a piece and I could eat it. It tasted sweet and cold and clean. Betty climbed off and stretched. Michael took down his construction set and I made a floor for the garage. Michael said, 'You can drive these cars with crutches. You press on the accelerator with the end of one, and the brake with the other.'

'And you go faster than any other car.'

'So fast you can't see the wheels.'

'And there's a hole in the roof to store the crutches.'

'And a straw that comes out of the dashboard.'

'And when you go to a petrol station you fill a bucket with strawberry milk that's hidden in the dashboard.'

'That's what the straw is for.'

'Yeah,' I said.

'And there are robot arms on the steering wheel that feed you.'

'Chips.'

'Yeah, chips,' said Michael.

'And it dips them in sauce on the way to your mouth.'

'Yeah,' said Michael. 'And then it wipes your mouth.'

'Yeah.'

⌣

We went into the kitchen and Mrs Hooper said, 'How was school today, Justine?' I looked at her yellow shoes with no Yolamundi mud caked into the heels. 'Everything okay?'

Mrs Hooper was waiting for an answer. I took a breath. 'It was good,' I said. My voice sounded scratched.

'She's shy, Mum, I told you,' said Michael.

'Well, that's okay,' said Mrs Hooper. 'I'm just asking.'

'I like school when Michael is there,' I said.

Michael and Mrs Hooper looked at me, their eyebrows raised.

Mrs Hooper smiled. 'He likes it when you're there too,' she said.

'Thanks, Mum,' said Michael. 'Glad you can speak for me.'

'Sorry,' said Mrs Hooper. She looked at her watch. 'We better get you home, Justine,' she said.

I followed Michael through the house and out to the car. 'Bye, Betty,' I said as the cat wound around my legs. The air was soft. There was pale and changing light in the branches and the window boxes, and in the grass and the sky.

⌣

Mrs Hooper drove the car and Nicky sang. *Every colour of the rainbow, pink and green and blue, shining just* for *me.* The same piece of the song, over and over until I did see every colour in the rainbow and they shone just for me.

When we came to the top of the Henley Trail, I said, 'You can stop here.'

'Which is your place?' said Mrs Hooper. 'We'll take you there.'

Nicky pointed at the houses. He said, 'That one? That one?'

'Here is okay,' I said.

'But, Justine . . .'

'Just drop her here, Mum. She wants to walk the rest of the way,' said Michael.

'But, Michael . . . Are you sure, Justine? It's not far, is it?'

'No,' I said.

'Please, Mum,' said Michael. 'Can we stop here?'

'Alright, then. You don't have to walk for long, do you?' She looked around at the houses. The trail kept going into the bush. Pop's was too far to see from here.

'No,' I said as I opened the door.

'Take care, Justine,' said Michael's mother.

———

Every Friday after school I went to the Hoopers'. And every Friday, before dinner, Mrs Hooper dropped me at the top of the Henley Trail and I walked the rest of the way back to Pop's Three. Pop never asked me where I'd been; he didn't notice I was late. Every day of the week led to Fridays at Michael's. When I couldn't talk, Michael put Betty or Keith on my lap and he always gave me food—sultanas and cheese squares, apples and oranges and bananas and Monte Carlo biscuits. He put more food into my backpack and Mrs Hooper saw and didn't take it out. On Fridays I came home with my stomach full. We built trucks from his construction set, looked at pictures in the map books and talked to the fish. We had names. We had Matt Dunny Man. We had Brian the Toilet. We had Mrs Burning. We had Miss Lost. I was Lee, and he was Hooper. We had Queen Dawn and Princess Noreena and the cod was Headmaster Prentice.

———

I stopped waiting as much for Dad to come home, stopped looking out of my window at night, stopped listening for his truck, stopped watching the back-house door thinking he would step out, that he was on the way, that it was him on the telephone telling Pop he'd be there by the end of the week and then waiting for the end of the week to find he wasn't there.

I wasn't waiting anymore but Pop was. Pop was waiting for the trial, for the sentence. Until he knew, he wasn't his bloody self, he told the Isa Browns. *Not me-bloody-self . . . bloody gut . . . Jesus, Lizzy, where did we go wrong? Bloody Stacey Worlley. What the hell will they give him for it?*

33.

On Monday Mrs Hooper was at the gate waiting for Michael. She smiled at me. I lifted my head, and tried to smile back, then looked down at my feet. Mrs Hooper said, 'Justine, would you like to stay with Michael this weekend?'

Michael said, 'You want to, Justine?'

I kept my eyes on the ground. I didn't know.

'We were thinking you could come over on Friday and I could take you home on Sunday morning. Of course, I would want to ask your grandfather's permission. It has to be okay by him,' Mrs Hooper said.

When I was with Michael and his family it was as if I didn't have a Pop. I couldn't fit them into the same world. One Justine ended when Mrs Hooper dropped me at the top of the Henley Trail, and another Justine began on the way back to Pop's Three.

Michael and Mrs Hooper were both looking at me, waiting for me to speak. I didn't know what to say. How would Mrs Hooper ask for Pop's permission? Nobody had ever asked for it before. A whole weekend with Michael? More than Friday afternoon? What would happen?

Michael said, 'Don't worry, Justine. Today you can think about it and then you can tell Mum if you want to come.'

My eyes pricked as if there was sand inside and Mrs Hooper touched my arm. 'Good idea, Michael,' she said. 'Justine, you think about it. Michael wants you to camp with him in the back garden and Mr Hooper and I certainly don't want to camp with him. I need a bed!'

⁓

At the end of the day Michael said to me, 'Do you want to come on the weekend, Justine?'

My chest felt tight.

'I'll look after you,' said Michael. 'Mum will only give you food you like to eat. Do you want to come?'

'Yes,' I said. I felt the growing ridge of my tooth with my tongue.

'Good,' said Michael. 'That's good!'

⁓

I was at home with Pop when the telephone rang. Pop was painting a chicken box with creosote to keep out the rot. I was close enough to pick it up. I didn't think it would be Aunty Rita, but I didn't know. It kept ringing. But if I picked it up Pop would say, *Justine, get your hands off it. Leave my telephone alone.*

Pop came puffing through the back door with his paintbrush in his hand. He picked up the telephone. 'Who? Oh . . . oh yes . . . oh. Friday night?' He looked surprised. 'Yes, she . . . no, she never said nothing.' He frowned at me, wiping his face with the back of his hand; creosote dripped to the floor. 'Yeah, okay . . . alright then.' His face was damp when he put down the receiver. He said, 'Who the bloody hell was that?'

'Was it Mrs Hooper, Pop?'

'Who's that?'

'My friend's mum.'

Pop grunted something then turned to go outside.

'What did she want, Pop?'

He waved his brush in the air as I followed him out to the chicken box.

'Something on the bloody weekend,' he said. 'Here, chook chook chook,' he sang to the Isa Browns. 'Look what old Poppy's fixing up for you.'

'What did you say?' I stood at the gate to the run.

'About what?' he said.

'About the weekend.'

'Uh.' He grunted. 'Here, chook chook; here, chook; here, ladies—look at your new bed old Poppy's painting up for you.'

'Pop?'

He looked up at me. 'What?'

'Can I go?'

'Go where?'

'My friend's, Pop. The Hoopers.'

Pop painted a stroke across the box. 'Back on Sunday,' he said. 'Before dark.'

'Thanks, Pop.'

I was going to Michael's for the weekend. What was going to happen? What would we do? Was it something to look forward to?

—

'Are you still coming?' Michael asked me on Friday morning.

'Yes,' I said.

'Where are your things?'

I felt hot in my face. What things?

'Didn't you bring anything?'

'What?' I said.

'Didn't you bring anything for the weekend?'

I didn't know what he wanted me to bring. I shrugged.

'But you're still coming, aren't you? You're still going to stay at my house?'

'I'm still coming.'

'Great. That's great.'

As we were walking out of the classroom for playlunch, Miss Frost said, 'Justine, can I speak with you for a moment, please?'

Michael and me looked at each other. I wanted to go outside with him.

Miss Frost said, 'She won't be long, Michael.'

Michael sighed and left.

Miss Frost said, 'Justine, have you had your eyes tested?'

'Yeah.' I looked at Miss Frost's shoes. They were flat with a bow, like ballet shoes. There was new dirt on the toes from the Nullabri puddles.

Miss Frost said, 'Your school records show that you had your eyes tested by the visiting nurse along with all the other students, but I am going to contact your parents and suggest that you have your eyes tested again by the specialist in town.'

I didn't tell Miss Frost that I didn't live with parents, I lived with Pop, who thought that town was behind enemy lines.

Miss Frost had my worksheets on the desk in front of her. She was turning them over, looking at my marks and ticks and circles. She said, 'Sometimes you do really well, and other times . . . I think maybe another eye test just to make sure everything is fine.' Miss Frost gathered up all the papers and books, her glasses slipping down her nose. 'Thank you, Justine. The school will contact your parents this week.'

Michael was waiting for me just outside the door. 'What was that about?' he asked.

'Nothing,' I said.

'What do you mean? What did she want?'

'I don't know.'

'Justine, what was it?'

I didn't want to tell him; I didn't want him to know about the breech, that I got it wrong from the start, that everything was in the wrong order. 'She said I could do better.'

Michael snorted. 'Miss Frost, get lost,' he said.

34.

Michael, me and Nicky sat in the back of Mrs Hooper's car as she drove us home that afternoon. The wind from the open windows made our hair whip our faces, and dry the spit in our mouths.

'Are you hungry?' Michael asked.

I said, 'Yes.'

'What do you feel like?'

'Biscuits.'

'Biscuits with ice-cream?'

'Ice-cream and chocolate.'

'And chocolate!' Nicky said.

Michael said, 'Let's eat until we can't move.'

'Until we have to lie down.'

'Like whales.'

'Like Headmaster Prentice.'

'Like two of him.'

We sang 'Joy to the World' through all the open windows. Nicky joined in. *Joy to the world! The Lord is come . . . And heaven and nature sing, and heaven and nature sing.* Mrs Hooper sang too. *And heaven, and heaven, and nature sing!*

Michael asked, 'What would you do if you could fly? Where would you go?'

'I would fly . . . at night. I would follow the river.'

'How far would you follow it?'

'All the way to the sea.'

'How high would you fly?'

'As high as the sun.'

'As high as the sun?'

When Michael asked me questions, he waited for my answers. He wanted to find out. He wouldn't go on until I answered. It was the opposite of invisible.

⌒

When Mr Hooper came home from work we helped him set up the tent in the back yard. The grass had been cut and the air was full with its wet, green smell.

Mr Hooper said, 'Michael, can you hold down the pole?'

Michael stood and held the pole with his arm shaking.

Mr Hooper said, 'Good job, kid.'

Mr Hooper pressed a peg into the grass and said, 'Can you knock that with the hammer, Justine?'

I took the hammer and hit the grass instead of the peg. I couldn't look at Mr Hooper.

He said, 'Try again.'

I tried again and hit the grass.

Mr Hooper said, 'Third time lucky. Go on, give it another go.'

I looked at the peg, lifted the hammer and took a deep breath. Down went the peg.

Mr Hooper said, 'Nice work.'

When I stretched the orange tent canvas to make a roof Mr Hooper said, 'That's the girl.'

Nicky tried to crawl into the tent before the walls were straight.

Michael said, 'Dad, get him out!'

Mr Hooper said, 'Relax, Michael, you have Justine for the whole weekend.'

Mr and Mrs Hooper helped make the beds in the tent. They put Michael's bed on crates to make it higher for his legs and lined it with pads of foam. They unrolled sleeping bags for us, and put pillows on the ends.

———

Mr Hooper made a barbecue and we had dinner on the veranda, looking at the tent in the middle of the green yard. Mrs Hooper said, 'David mowed it for you guys. He did a good job, didn't he?' She put her arm around Mr Hooper's shoulders.

I could hardly look; it felt dangerous, as if *good* might crack me apart like one of Pop's eggs.

There were chops and carrots and chips for dinner but the food wouldn't go down. It was hard to swallow. Michael said, 'What's wrong?' He stabbed at a carrot with his fork, and pushed chips and carrot from his plate onto the table. Some fell to the floor.

Nicky got off his chair and picked up Michael's spilled food.

'Gross!' said Michael. He had sauce on his chin.

After that I could eat; I could taste the chop, oily and salty, filling me.

Everybody was talking about the tent. Mr Hooper said it was like when he was in Cubs and Mrs Hooper said, *What about our honeymoon?* and Nicky said, *Tent tent tent.* Mr Hooper said, 'How about you kids sleep in the house and we sleep in the tent?'

Michael said, 'No, Dad!'

Mr Hooper said, 'I'm kidding, Michael—there is no way I intend to sleep in a tent tonight.'

⌒

'Mum, can you take Nicky inside now?' Michael said after dinner.

Mrs Hooper smiled. 'Sure, Michael. You guys want your dessert in the tent?'

'Yes!'

Mrs Hooper put blackberries and cream and vanilla cake in bowls, and put the bowls in a basket along with a torch. She came down to the tent with us and checked Michael's bed, pressing the foam and changing its position. 'Justine,' she said, 'if Michael is in pain in the night, or needs me, you are to take the torch and come up to the house and wake me, okay? I will leave my light on. Can you manage that?'

'Mum!' Michael frowned.

'What, Michael? This is important.'

'I won't need you.'

'Justine, can you promise me that if you think Michael is . . . uncomfortable . . . if he is in pain, you will wake me?'

'Mum!'

'Yes, Mrs Hooper,' I said. 'I will come and wake you.'

'Oh, good girl,' said Mrs Hooper. 'Good girl. Thank you.'

⌒

We sat on the ground between our beds and looked through the tent flaps. The light was softening, turning blue and purple and grey. Night was coming. The Moruna mountains beyond the trees stood in shadow. Crickets chirped. I breathed in the scent of fresh-cut grass. We ate the blackberries and the vanilla cake and drank the milk, our spoons scraping the bowls, our lips and tongues and teeth turning the cream and berries and milk in our mouths. Each taste changed the taste that had gone before, making it better.

Then we lay in our sleeping bags and shone the torch into the trees, looking for bats. The night was black now, the stars like white dust. Michael said, 'Do you know why the stars shine?'

'Why?'

'Fusion. Gases on fire. You can see them best from Antarctica.'

'Why?'

'It's too cold for wind so your telescope won't blow over. In Antarctica the stars leave trails like patterns on a shell.'

'How far is Antarctica?'

'From here?'

'Yes.'

'It's a long way. Five thousand miles. More than fifty days by boat. I will go to Antarctica one day.'

I didn't say anything; I didn't want him to go.

Then he said, 'We can go together. We'll plant our own flag.'

Yes!

'We can start at the river. It will take us to the sea.'

'We can watch the way the water changes.'

'How will it change?'

'The temperature will change, the depth, the animals that live in it.'

'The way it moves will change,' I said. 'The way it flows. Or doesn't.'

'Yeah,' he said.

'Yeah,' I said.

'Yeah.'

'Yeah.'

'Yeah!'

'Yeah!'

'Yeah!' we shouted. 'Yeah!' Then our laughter became our breath, growing slow and calm, and the sky of stars came down over us like a blanket.

'Justine, you are my best friend.'

'You are mine.'

⌒

Michael's body moved even in sleep. He groaned and cried out. His arms and legs pulled and jerked. He couldn't stop the movement. Was Michael his body? Was Michael somebody different to his arms and legs and neck and head? Was I my body? I pulled my sleeping bag to my nose and listened, in case I needed to take the torch and go up to the house.

⌒

In the morning the sun was shining on the tent, turning it gold. Michael said, 'Can you help me, Justine?' His legs were shaking and stuck, and it was hard for him to get out of the bed. A piece of the foam had fallen to the ground. I picked up his crutches and he said, 'Give me your arm.' I gave him my arm and helped pull him out. He said, 'Ouch! Ow! Ow!'

'Are you okay?'

'Yes.'

Then we heard Mrs Hooper. 'Are you alright in there?'

'Yes, Mum,' said Michael.

I opened the flaps and there was Mrs Hooper with the bright sun of morning behind her.

She held Michael's arm as we walked slowly up to the house. Michael gasped and puffed. He was shaking more than yesterday.

Mrs Hooper said, 'Are you okay, darling?'

Michael said, 'Don't call me darling. Yes, I am okay.'

'Alright, alright.'

We went into the kitchen. Mrs Hooper gave Michael pills and a glass of water. I watched as she stirred oats in a pot with a wooden spoon. She mashed a soft pear and put it in the porridge, and then she dripped over the honey. Me and Michael took our bowls outside and ate in front of the tent with Nicky. Porridge fell in the grass and the ants climbed on and sucked. Everything at the Hoopers' had enough to eat.

—

We played ball with Mr Hooper and he said, 'Nice work, Justine,' when I threw to him. Michael stood in front of the goal and stopped the ball with his crutch. He shouted, 'Take that, you bugger!' Mr Hooper said, 'Michael!' Mrs Hooper said, 'Where do you think he learned it, David?'

—

Nicky came to me, put his small hand on my neck and sat on me. He was holding toast. His hand was warm. He took my hair and put it over my eyes. He said, *Eyes eyes*. He touched my cheeks and said, *Tine Tine*. He tried to feed me the toast. He said, *Yours yours*.

—

When I was coming out of the toilet, I heard Mrs Hooper talking to Michael. 'Are you sure you're up to it?'

'Yes, Mum, I already told you.'

'You can stay home, watch something on the telly.'

'No, Mum, you promised.'

'I said it would depend on the night.'

'The night was good!'

'Yes, but . . . But you have to tell me if it gets worse.'

'Okay, Mum.'

'Guess where we're going?' Michael said when he saw me. 'The movies!'

I had never been to the movies before. Sometimes kids at school talked about what they saw there. Seen *Phantom?* Seen *Robin Hood?* I didn't know what it would be like; I didn't know if I wanted to go. But Michael said, 'It's *Black Beauty*, Justine. We'll be the first to see it!' I had to go.

'Okay,' I said.

Mrs Hooper drove us to the Echuca cinema. I didn't know what would be inside, what you did in there. I couldn't ask. Everybody else had been before. There were a lot of cars driving past, and people walking up and down the street. I wanted to stay in the car.

Mrs Hooper parked at the front and opened the car doors. Michael pulled himself out and I followed. We walked into the cinema with Mrs Hooper. I smelled popcorn. There was a counter with a man and a girl behind it wearing little white triangle hats. They stared at Michael. All around the walls were pictures of superheroes and ladies wearing make-up.

Mrs Hooper walked up to the counter and said, 'Two tickets, please.'

The man looked at Michael.

Mrs Hooper said, 'Is there a problem?'

The man said, 'No, no problem.'

Mrs Hooper said, 'Then I'd like the tickets, please.' Her voice was strong. It didn't belong to one small woman; it belonged to an army with tanks and cannons and spears. 'I will come in and get you settled,' she told us, 'then I will be out the front to pick you up after the movie.'

'Mum . . .' Michael sighed.

'Michael,' I said. 'Let her.'

'Not you too,' Michael said.

'Me too.'

'Thanks, Justine,' said Mrs Hooper.

Michael huffed and didn't say anything more.

Mrs Hooper said, 'Come on. You don't want to miss a minute.'

She came with us through the carpet doors. It was a big dark room with stairs going up between row after row of seats. At the front was a huge screen that took up the whole wall. Mrs Hooper whispered, 'What about here?' She pointed to two seats together with no seats on either side. Mrs Hooper took Michael's crutches and lay them in the aisle close to our chairs.

Michael said, 'Thanks, Mum. Can you go now?'

Mrs Hooper whispered. 'Yes, Michael, I am going. Enjoy yourselves.'

The seat was soft with padded armrests. The lights came down and the carpet walls and floor closed around us, like a cocoon. The whole world was gone but this one. We were joined in the darkness. It was our movie.

The shining black horse raced across the screen, faster than any other horse, stronger, more brave, and he had a friend—Joe Evans. Joe cared for him and did everything for him, there was no better friend and boy than Joe Evans. They jumped the fences, swam the dams, shared the apples. But then Black Beauty was stolen by the squire and he didn't feed him; he tied him to a cart and the cart was too heavy so the squire whipped him. I gasped. Michael groaned. It was as if Michael and me were Black Beauty—it was our backs being whipped, our legs breaking, it was us missing Joe Evans, needing him. Where did he go? I heard Michael crying and then I cried. Black Beauty had lost Joe, his good friend, the one he loved the most. How could it be? The squire said, *Useless mule! Better off dead!* Michael cried out, 'No!' and somebody said, 'Shhhh.' But then the squire died and Beauty was sold to the circus. He was so good at the tricks they taught him that Sir William sent him to fight in the war. Beauty was so brave that he charged the enemy with Gervaise on his back. But then Gervaise was killed and his friend who was drunk sold Beauty to the coal man who made him carry such heavy loads he caught pneumonia like Lizzy in 1952. Tears dripped down my cheeks. Michael put his hand over mine. What if Black Beauty died from the pneumonia? I could hardly look. But then a woman called Anna, with white hair, rescued Beauty and took him to her farm and the man helping Anna on the farm was Joe Evans! The same Joe Evans! When the mud sprayed up it was us racing across the field towards Joe, us eating the apples and us with our black, shining coat as Joe rubbed his brush over our skin. We were Black Beauty, we were Joe Evans, we were the circus and the war and the fight, and we were together again. There was no separation.

When we came out at the end of the movie, the light was bright in our eyes. 'How was it?' Mrs Hooper asked. Michael and me couldn't talk. Mrs Hooper said, 'That good, hey?'

That evening we sat at the table: Mr Hooper, Mrs Hooper, Nicky, Michael and me. Mrs Hooper put a big bowl of long noodles and meatballs in the middle of the dinner table. 'Spaghetti,' said Mrs Hooper.

'How do you eat that?' asked Michael.

'Like worms,' said Nicky.

My spaghetti flipped all the way to my mouth and sauce was on my nose and Michael and all over Nicky and the floor.

Mrs Hooper wiped the table and said, 'You have to try everything once.'

After dinner Mrs Hooper said to me, 'Justine, would you like a bath?'

I wasn't sure. I only had baths when Pop remembered. He said, *Get in the bloody bath, Justine, you're starting to stink.* Did I stink now?

'Let me show you,' said Mrs Hooper leading me into the bathroom. There were pictures of ducks on the wall, there were plastic toys in the bath and a pile of striped towels on a stool. Mrs Hooper said, 'I have the best bubble bath. It's roses. You can have the first one and the boys can go after you.' The Hooper's bath was white without a ring. 'Would you like that?'

'Okay,' I said.

Mrs Hooper filled the bath almost to the top, then she squirted in the roses. 'Enjoy,' she said. She closed the door and left me with a striped towel. I lay in the bath and swished the hot rose water with my hands so it turned around me in pink waves. I closed my eyes and I was in *Black Beauty* again, right at the beginning when he had Joe and all the things they did, the rides they took, the races, the time they swam the dam, the time they jumped the fence . . . I squeezed the sponge over my head. Beauty had to work so hard for the coal man that he got sick and was going to die. But Joe Evans came back. He cried out, *Beauty, Beauty!* and even though Black Beauty was old, and had the scars on his back from the whip, they were together and always would be. I got out of the rose bath and dried myself with the striped towel.

Mrs Hooper knocked on the door.

'Yes?' I said.

She peeked around the door. 'You can wear this if you like.' She handed me a nightdress with a blue ribbon at the front. It felt soft and smooth in my hands. I couldn't say, *Thank you, Mrs Hooper.* I couldn't say anything; the words were never there when I needed them. She closed the door. I put the white nightdress over my head. It fell down over my legs all the way to the floor and smelled of roses.

⁓

Michael and me slept in his room so Michael could get a better rest. Mrs Hooper pulled in an extra bed. We lay in the dark and Michael said, 'Beauty should never have left the Evanses. They shouldn't have lost the farm. It wasn't fair.'

'But he found his way home in the end.'

'Joe never forgot her.'

'Never.'

35.

In the morning Mrs Hooper said, 'It's time to take you home, Justine.'

Michael and me both went quiet.

Mrs Hooper said, 'Anyone would think you two hadn't had a good time.'

Michael said, 'We have had a good time, Mum. And now it's over.'

'I can't argue with that, Michael. It's true. That's life for you.'

Michael said, 'Damned life.'

Mrs Hooper frowned at him. 'Don't swear, Michael. I've talked to you about that.' She said, 'I am going to take you to your house today, Justine.'

I said, 'No, it's okay.'

Mrs Hooper said, 'Justine, it's important.'

Michael said, 'No, Mum.'

'Michael, it's the right thing to do.' We knew in her voice it was happening.

I said goodbye to Mr Hooper and Nicky. Nicky kissed my cheek and said, 'Tine Tine.' Mr Hooper said, 'Please come

again, Justine. I need practice at ball catching.' I couldn't talk.
I couldn't say thank you.

⌐

I felt my heart sinking as we drove down the Henley Trail.
We went past the houses at the top until there were no more
houses, only bush and red gums. 'Just there.' I pointed to Pop's.
I could see it clearly, as if a veil had been lifted: the broken
bricks, the trucks and tyres and woodpiles and paint cans and
pieces of truck, all lit up bright for the eyes of Mrs Hooper.
My throat felt dry. The Hoopers were from one world and I
was from another.

Mrs Hooper drove up to the front and stopped the car.
I could see smoke over the roof from the back yard; Pop would
be out the back with the chooks. Mrs Hooper turned off the
engine. 'Looks like your grandfather has land,' she said. She
turned around to me from the front seat. 'Does he have land,
Justine?'

'Yeah.'

'How much?'

'Three acres.'

'Lucky,' said Mrs Hooper. 'It's a beautiful spot. You must
be close to the river.'

Mrs Hooper opened her door and we got out of the car. We
walked up the path and I saw everything with Mrs Hooper's
eyes—peeling paint, cracks in the bricks, the hanging screen
door, broken wire. We went out the back and there was Pop at
his fire, drinking a beer with a White Ox in his mouth.

Mrs Hooper said, 'I hope we're not disturbing you, Mr Lee.
I am Michael's mother.'

We walked towards the fire. Michael was shaking and jerking and Pop looked up from his camp chair, taken by surprise. He stood and ash fell from his White Ox. I bit down on my lip. Pop had run through the jungle, hunted like an animal, he didn't have the Mauser or the brother pistols, he didn't have anything, not even food in his belly. His only friend was Sandy. When Pop and Sandy found the tunnel the Japs smoked them out and tied them to the grille. Pop didn't like visitors; the last visitors he had were the police.

Mrs Hooper said, 'Thanks for letting us have Justine; she and Michael have had a good time.'

Nobody moved but Michael; the strings of his body tugged one way and then another.

Pop came over to Michael and I didn't know what he would do, what he would say. He held out his hand. Michael took it. Pop held Michael's hand steady and said, 'Want to meet my chooks?'

'Yes,' said Michael.

Michael and me followed Pop to the chooks at the bottom of the yard. Pop said, 'This here is Missy, this is Lady, this is Cockyboy. This pretty one is the other Lady. And this is Madame.'

Michael asked, 'What kind are they?'

Pop frowned and said, 'What?'

My chest squeezed.

'What kind of chickens are they?'

'Isa Browns, best layers around.'

'How many eggs do they lay?'

Pop said, 'Ah, the Isa Browns lay all year round and plenty too. Let's have a look.'

Michael and me went with him to the chook run.

I said, 'It's my job to get the eggs.'

Pop said, 'It sure is.' The chickens pecked around us as Michael and me looked in the straw. I lifted out an egg and gave it to him.

Michael held it in his hand. 'Still warm. What do you feed them?'

Pop said, 'What?'

Michael said, 'What do you feed them?'

Pop said, 'Seed if they've been good girls. Scraps, toast. Shell grit to make the eggs tough. Justine feeds them.'

Mrs Hooper watched from the middle of the yard. Michael carried the egg out of the run. Pop went into the kitchen and came back with a carton that held twelve eggs. The eggs had shit and feathers stuck to them. Pop passed the carton to Mrs Hooper. He said, 'This week's.'

She said, 'Thank you, thank you. Justine has been such a good friend . . .' She was sniffing.

They went down the side and out to the car, Michael carrying his egg as carefully as if it was the first one he'd ever been given. He said, 'See you Monday, Justine.'

I looked right at Mrs Hooper. I said, 'Thank you, Mrs Hooper.'

———

I went back into the yard. Pop was raking the grass. I stood and looked at him, his body hooked as he dragged the rake, his head with hair only on the sides, his neck and arms lined with the track between the jungles. I went to him and put my arms around him. He stopped raking and stood hard and still against me.

36.

It took four months for the trial. There were delays. Pop could only go to Melbourne for some of the days because of his gut trouble. Since the cops took Dad, the bug had grown hungrier. It fed from Pop's lining as soon as he woke. Before he caught the train for Melbourne he told the chooks, *If I could let you at it, Cockyboy, you'd tear the bloody thing to shreds.* He left his truck at Relle's and caught the train into town. He stayed in a hostel in the city where the men slept in a row. *If I have to listen to another fella fart I'll top meself.* He made sure he was in Melbourne for the verdict. I had to stay at Relle's with Kirk and Steve until Pop heard.

Kirk and Steve and me were in the kitchen eating leftover donuts from the bakery, and Relle and Dean were smoking. The donuts glowed green and pink. Relle took a long last suck. 'They can't pin it on him,' she said, stubbing out her cigarette. 'It's bullshit.'

Kirk took a green donut from the plate. He leaned back and put his boots against the edge of the table. 'They shouldn't mess with Dad.'

they were soft and fluffy we ate them at the table with toast and jam. I cleared the plates and Pop rolled a White Ox while I got the scissors from my room. Pop passed me the *Herald* and I cut out escape vehicles while Pop smoked. Smoke filled the top half of the kitchen, like a mist. We sat under it and Pop looked at the things I cut then he looked at the ceiling, blowing smoke towards it in fresh streams.

He got up and went to the back door. I stood beside him and we lifted our eyes to the stars like silver dust shaken across the sky. Crickets and frogs sang to each other. Pop put his arm around my shoulders. He leaned against me like I was one of Michael's crutches and spoke parts of sentences '. . . only son . . . Izzy . . . the only one left. Good thing I took you in, hey? What would I do without you?' Was it me he meant? Was it Izzy, or was it the night sky above our heads?

Dad was sent to Pentridge and Pop said to forget I had a father. Let Ray do his time. It was the only way. A part of you had to *I been there, Lady, I been there, Missy—you can't count the days, are too many to count, too many bloody days.* There wasn't here for Ray to go inside Pentridge. If he moved left or right or down they stuck a knife between his ribs. What would with his secrets when they began to cook? *Stacey Worlley for it a thousand times, then the one time she didn't . . .* I didn't what the words meant—something stopped me knowing, wasn't the truth that was buried; it was me.

Dad went away I didn't see Kirk and Steve as much. The Relle came to pick them up, a week after the verdict,

---

'Boots off the table, Kirk,' said Dean.

'I don't have to do what you tell me,' said Kirk.

'Yes, you bloody do,' said Relle.

Dean said, 'The apple doesn't fall far from the tree.'

Relle said, 'He's still their father,' then she started crying.

'You're still into the bastard, aren't you, Narelle?' Dean said. He turned to Kirk and me and Steve. 'Out.'

Relle's yard was made of concrete with cigarette butts growing like little white plants in the corners. There was an ashtray on a stand, a chair and a Hills hoist, with pegs lying on the concrete underneath. Kirk held on to the top bar of the Hills hoist and swung it. Pop said he would call us as soon as he heard. 'Danny and me are going to bust Dad out after his uncle shows us how to shoot,' Kirk said.

'Yeah,' said Steve, holding on to the other side of the Hills hoist. It squeaked as he pulled down. 'We'll shoot the walkie-talkies out of the guards' hands so they won't be able to call for back-up.'

'I'll bring his truck. I'll get the keys from Pop's belt and, Justine, you can wait out the front with the doors open and the engine running. We'll drop him in Sydney to put the cops off the scent. Then he can hitch to Cairns. That's where Danny's uncle hitched.' Kirk picked a peg up from the ground and pulled it in half. He threw the pieces across the concrete. 'Cairns,' he said.

We leaned against the fence. A weight hung over us. It was as if the sky was made of the same concrete as Relle's yard. We heard the telephone ringing. Kirk looked at me.

We went back inside. Dean passed the telephone to Relle.

Relle took it. She said, 'No. No way.' She turned away from us, pressing her forehead against the wall. She hung up.

Dean said, 'Relle?'

Relle turned around to us. Her eyes were red, make-up dripped in green tears down her cheeks. 'Guilty,' she said.

Steve cried. It was as if a hand had taken hold of his face and twisted it.

Kirk said, 'Fuck.' He picked up Relle's cigarettes from the table and threw them at Dean. There was screaming but not from outside, from inside.

Late that afternoon Dean picked Pop up from the station in Echuca and brought him back to Relle's.

'How is he?' said Relle.

'Didn't say much,' said Pop. He was even thinner than when he left; there were new shadows on his face.

'Typical.'

'Did his lawyer say anything about the sentence?' Dean asked.

'Bloody evidence everywhere. Ray's a fool.' Pop shook his head and rolled a White Ox. 'Bloody Stacey. She's wanted it from him a thousand times . . .'

'How long does he think he'll get? What are they telling him?' said Relle.

'Could be five . . . could be seven. Punching the bloody cop didn't help.'

Relle started crying.

'Go out the back, kids,' said Pop.

We went out to the yard again and waited. Kirk scraped the cigarette butts from the corners into a pile. He picked out a long one and put it in his mouth. Then he took a box of matches out of his pocket and tried to set fire to the pile. 'We'll bust him

out, don't worry,' said Kirk. He lit his cigarette. 'We if we have to.'

Pop called from the kitchen, 'Justine, time to go.'

When we got back to Pop's Three, Pop said, 'Brin Justine.' He lay on his bed and drank beers until didn't eat or turn on any lights or watch television. night he called for me. I stood at the door. 'Bloo Pop said, pulling himself up to sitting.

I said, 'Are we going to visit him in jail?'

He said, 'Jail is for crooks, not kids.'

'Is Dad a crook?'

Pop sighed. 'I suppose he is. Stupid bloody at the clock on the cupboard. 'Jesus. How l lying here? Let's go out and ask the chooks w

He got out of bed, putting his dressing-g clothes. We went to the boxes and pulled Pop,' I said.

The chickens fluffed their feathers and of Pop's boots.

'Hey, ladies, leave your old man alone, alone. Cockyboy, tell your girls to give ol voice was soft as a song for the chickens. 'You tell 'em, Cockyboy. Ole Pop's got en shook out the straw and checked the w girls. 'Night, ladies; night, girls,' said P now, and we'll see you in the morning the sunshine, ladies.'

I stood by the stove and watched into a pan. He added butter and sal

she brought Dean. Dean looked at Pop's yard and his house and the back-house, and shook his head. *The less to do with the Lees the better,* he said to Relle when Pop wasn't there. *Bloody kids; half their blood is Ray's. That's the problem.*

Relle chewed the nail of her thumb, narrowing her eyes. *Would it be so hard for Ray to write a letter? To call them? It isn't blood in his veins; it's something else.* She said the same things over and over, as if Ray took up all the room, and she had to speak the words to let some of him out. *Not for me—I don't give a shit anymore—but for them. He is their father.*

What was it flowed in my dad's veins if it wasn't blood? Was it the same stuff that flowed in the veins of the Japs? Did that same stuff flow in my veins too? Was that why I was born breech? If I had a different father with different blood, would I be able to read? Would my mother still have caught the train to Lismore? I never had words to ask anybody the questions, so I never had the answers.

37.

Michael and me were at the school benches. 'Weather
controls things,' said Michael, taking a handful of
sultanas from his box.

'What do you mean?'

He passed me the box. 'It decides what happens.'

'What things?'

'The way the land goes. How things grow. What animals
live there. Weather decides it.' Sparrows waited for sultanas to
drop at our feet.

I thought of The Choke and its banks pressing in, trying
to touch. I said, 'The Murray is part of the weather.'

He said, 'The river?'

I nodded.

'Yeah, but the weather came first.'

'The river decides things too.'

'But the river is there because of the weather.'

'Are you sure the river didn't come first?'

'No.' Michael shook his head. 'I don't think it did.'

'But you can't be sure.' I ate the last of the sultanas. 'Do you want to see it?'

'What?'

'The river.'

'Yes.'

———

The next morning, when Mrs Hooper was dropping Michael at school, Michael said, 'Can I go to Justine's, Mum?'

Mrs Hooper looked like she wasn't sure.

'Mum, it's not fair if Justine can come over to our place and I can't go there.'

'I didn't say you couldn't go there. What day?'

'This afternoon?'

'This afternoon?'

'Yes, why not, Mum?'

'I'm thinking . . .'

'Stop thinking, Mum. Just say yes.'

'Don't be cheeky, Michael. This is short notice.'

'Please, Mum.' He put his head on the side. 'Say yes?'

———

Mrs Hooper dropped us at Pop's Three after school. 'I will pick you up at five, Michael. You need to be here out the front at five. Is that clear?'

'Clear.' Michael nodded.

As soon as Mrs Hooper drove away I took Michael down the side of the house into the yard. We stopped at the chooks and I threw them the good seed. 'Here, Missy; here, Lady; here, girls,' Michael called. Cockyboy strutted around the edges. 'Matt Dunning,' said Michael.

'Not as bad,' I said.

I pushed open the gate. Michael swung forward on his crutches. The path was narrow and rose up on the sides. We went slowly. I didn't help him. The land and the forest and trees and the long puddles in the grass shone with a deeper green. Being with Michael took away the old Yolamundi and made a new one. We were looped together.

The sun was on us, and I could hear Michael breathing hard behind me. It was a hot walk. We came to the trees and the path disappeared and Michael's crutches caught in sticks and thick grass but I didn't help him. We stopped and Michael looked up at the sky and the branches. It was as if we had arrived from a long way away, and we were seeing the trees for the first time. As if we couldn't speak the language and had never seen a cloud or a red gum or a kangaroo before. Everything was new to us. The knots in the bark, the trunks like bulbs, their twisted branches. The white cockatoos, their yellow crests moving back and forth, the clouds covering the sun, the leaves rustling, the ants across the ground, the flies that hovered over the puddles, the spiders suspended in their webs—all new. We kept going, not speaking, only seeing, until we came to the river, wide, rippling and muddy, birds pushing up from the surface, wings spreading. We were quiet, listening. Michael said, 'It's still, but it's moving.'

'Come further,' I said. I knew it wasn't easy for Michael to walk the path. The crutches caught in the roots and his feet slipped and stumbled. I heard him breathing more heavily, I heard the crutches slipping on the stones, but I didn't help. At last we came to The Choke. 'Look,' I said. 'See how much closer the other bank is?'

'There must have been a change,' he said.

'What do you mean?'

'The earth changes. The plates shift. Maybe that's why the river is narrower here.'

Even the earth changed. 'The banks try to stop the water,' I said. 'But they can't. It goes over the top. Floods. The water keeps moving.'

'What happens to the trees?' Michael asked.

'They keep growing,' I said. 'Underwater.'

Lorikeets and cockatoos and kookaburras called to each other, two or three at first then more joining in, five and six and seven, then a hundred rose up louder and louder, flying out of the branches, screeching and squawking. Michael and me lay on our backs and screeched with the birds.

We sat up and looked out over the water to the far bank. He said, 'You're right, Justine. The river came first. The river decides things.'

Michael had shown me his home and a mother who gave me a rose bubble bath and a brother who gave me toast. He had shown me a tent, cut grass and spaghetti. He had shown me *Black Beauty* and which circle to tick for the right answer. I had shown him the Murray River. We were even.

We walked back slowly. Michael said, 'You could start there, at the river, and keep going and if you never left the water you could make it to Antarctica. You'd look for the channels. One leads to another.'

'You'd build your own boat.'

'Yes,' said Michael.

'That way you'd know it was strong enough to make it.'

'Strong enough to cut through ice. It would have a telescope for nights.'

'You'd arm it,' I said.
'In case of enemy invasion.'
'Brian Lawson.'
He snorted.

38.

The Worlleys left me alone. Pop said jail made Ray more dangerous to the bastards. *Don't worry about that; it's who you know.* The Worlley cousins looked through me on the bus as if I was invisible. Was I real? Did I have arms and legs and a body like other people? I knew I had a mouth. Kirk said my teeth had grown in like bent forks. Pop said, *Justine's teeth do the same job as everyone else's. Leave her alone.*

Kirk held up two forks and made them talk. He said, 'I'm Justine. Have you met my teeth?'

I grabbed the fork from his hand and held it at his face. 'Fuck off, Kirk.'

'Killed by a fork,' he said. 'Ha ha!'

—

After Dad received his sentence Pop's gut trouble was even worse. He drank beer in the mornings, he didn't collect the eggs, and some days he wouldn't light the fire. It was cold the whole day. I wore all my clothes and put the towels on my bed at night. Pop said, 'Bring me a beer.' He held his gut and said,

'Haven't you taken enough, you bastard?' He drank the beer and looked towards the window and shook his head. He shook it and shook it and shook it.

On Saturdays if there was a John Wayne movie on the television I found the channel and we watched it together. Sometimes there were three in a row: John Wayne as the Ringo Kid, John Wayne as Quirt, John Wayne as Davy Crockett. We saw John Wayne shoot the Plummers, the Mexicans and Laredo. We watched him ride Starlight, Duke and the Miracle Horse. We saw him kiss Feathers, Maureen and Sophia Loren. Pop smoked and drank beers and I ate Frosties. When I went to bed I looked through the window and saw John Wayne walking the fence lines, with his sawn-off shot gun ready to fire. I held up my 9mm in the darkness. *We're on the same side, big man.*

Michael was going to Sydney for Easter. He said he didn't want to go but his parents had business there. I missed him. Pop held his gut from the start of Easter to the end, and didn't light the fire once. There was nothing to do but wait. The day before school went back, the telephone rang. Pop picked it up. 'Who?' he said. He held out the receiver. 'For you, Justine.'

'Hello?'

'Justine, it's Lara Hooper—Michael's mum.'

Pop was watching me. 'Hi,' I said.

'Justine, we'd really like to see you. Michael, I mean, would like to see you.' I heard Michael shouting in the background. I couldn't hear what he was saying. Mrs Hooper sounded upset. 'Can we come and pick you up?'

'What is it?' said Pop.

'It's Mrs Hooper. She wants me to come over.'

'Who?'

'Mrs Hooper.'

'Be home for tea,' said Pop, and then he walked outside.

'Yes,' I said into the telephone.

'Thank you, Justine. I appreciate it.'

⌒

Nicky and Michael weren't in the car when Mrs Hooper picked me up outside Pop's. 'It just seemed easiest for me to come and get you myself,' Mrs Hooper said. 'Michael's waiting for you.'

It was quiet in the car. We didn't talk. I looked at the long sticks of wheat that lined the road ahead, which ran straight until it was too small to see.

When we arrived at the house I followed Mrs Hooper inside.

'Michael! Justine's here.'

Michael came out of his room—his eyes were red.

Mrs Hooper said, 'You two can go outside if you like. I'll bring you some apple juice and chocolate cake. You like chocolate cake, don't you, Justine?'

'Yes,' I said. I didn't understand why Michael's eyes were red or why he wasn't in the car or why I was there.

I followed Michael through to his back yard, to the mulberry tree with its leafy branches hanging down in a circle, like a green dress. We sat on the swing seat under the branches. He said, 'Thanks for coming to my house.'

I said, 'What's wrong?'

'We're moving.'

'Where?'

'We're moving to the city.'

'What city?'

'Sydney.'

'Why?'

'So I can go to a different school.'

'Why?'

'One with facilities.'

'What's that mean?'

'I don't know. Other kids like me.'

'Oh.'

Michael pressed his crutch into the dirt and swung the seat.

'When?'

He kept sticking his crutch into the ground before the swing reached the top, so it jerked and bumped.

'Two weeks.'

'Oh.'

There were tracks in the grass left behind by Michael's crutch. My eyes stung. When I opened them the mulberry tree wobbled as if rain was coming down over its dress of leaves. The swing went still.

—

That night I sat with the chooks a long time—Missy, Lady and Lady, Madame and Girl, and Cockyboy. They pecked around me, near my feet and fingers. Missy climbed over my crossed legs onto my lap and Cockyboy let me touch her and hold her. Clouds from a storm that had been caught in me came out my nose and eyes and mouth. Tears dripped onto the feathers.

—

I knew it wasn't his fault but if I talked to him again I could never go back to Pop's Three or to school or anywhere. There would be nowhere for me to go. At school I turned away from him but he took my shoulder and he turned me around; he never cared who was watching or listening, he didn't care about his voice that stretched and tugged the words, how loud his breathing was, the noises he made. He said, 'We can still talk to each other on the telephone. We can write.'

I said, 'No.'

Michael stood in front of the school, in the middle of the hard path, his body racked and jerking, his face wet with tears. His dad came fast up the path, his face full of worry, eyes only for Michael, and he didn't see me, as if I wasn't there. I ran behind the shelter sheds until Michael and the Hoopers were gone.

———

Where were they held, the things we had done? Who knew we had done them? Who knew about the tent and the blackberries, Antarctica and *Black Beauty*, trucks with lifts, cars without brakes, archaeology? I closed the door on those things and it was as if they had never been. But just before I slept the door swung open, I couldn't stop it, and Black Beauty galloped across the field towards Joe Evans, the wind in his black mane. Joe held out his arms, and called, *Beauty, Beauty!* and Joe and Beauty were together again. Only before sleep did Michael and me go to Antarctica, where there were no footprints but ours, where it was only Michael and me crossing the ice to plant our flag. Just before sleep, in those last seconds, it was a new Yolamundi, with red gums and cods and cockatoos we saw for the first time, as if we had come from a place far away, and all this was new. But the next day would come and it had never happened; the seat beside me in class was empty.

Part Two

39.

It was my first day at Echuca High School. I walked along the Henley Trail to the bus stop. Grass had grown tall around Pop's rock; you had to dig to see it. I didn't look at the other kids when I climbed onto the bus. As I sat in a seat at the front, blood came out onto my rag. I'd had my rags three times. At first I thought it was Pop's gut trouble spread to me. I lay on my bed and I didn't do cut-outs and I didn't do anything. I held my hand over my gut and waited for the bug to finish. But when there was blood on my underpants I knew it was my rags; I was thirteen. Julie Rigney said most girls were thirteen when they came. The skin of the sky seemed to grow thicker, like rubber. It couldn't be cut open. It made no difference if the sun was shining when my rags came; there was a weight over the sky.

When I was in sixth class I heard Julie Rigney tell Annette Manns that getting your rags meant you could have a baby. Did the blood become the baby? But you needed a man to have a baby. That's what made it. Everyone knew that. But you must need the blood too; it was both, put together. I only washed the rags and the underpants when Pop was out at the shop, or at Sandy's, or at the pub; I hung them on the fence where the sun shone the brightest so they dried before he came home. If there was no sun I hid the used rags under my bed.

———

I saw Worlleys on the bus, sitting down the back, but they left me alone. Everybody did. No one said anything to me about my dad. He'd been in Pentridge for three years now. Even though Dad was away Pop said he was more dangerous away than on the outside. *It's who you know and your old man will know a whole new set, don't worry about that.*

My legs wobbled against the seat as the bus drove over the potholes. I pressed my nose to the glass and looked for emus through the trees. When the bus came to the high school in Echuca I saw more kids than I'd ever seen in one place before. They stood and ran and played in crowds. They had come from Nullabri and Shep and Yolamundi and Moama and Moira and Moruna and Rochy and Ridscombe, and all of them were together here, and they knew each other. I knew some of the kids from Nullabri Primary but I didn't join them. They had grown, their bodies had changed; they weren't the same. Everyone had full, fat bags on their backs. I didn't know what was inside the bags. Mine was empty. Every kid was wearing black shoes. It was like a field of black birds. I looked at my feet. I wore white sneakers, one with a red star, one with a hole where the star had come off. They were turning brown with Murray mud.

The high school buildings were brick and there was an upstairs. I could see rows of windows. There were different paths to choose, different doorways, different steps. A lot of kids were with their mothers. The mothers straightened their uniforms and tried to kiss them goodbye and the kids pulled away as if they didn't want anyone to see the mothers kissing them or smoothing their hair. *No, Mum, come on, don't,* they said, pushing them back, and the mothers smiled and tried to hold them at the gates. *Bye, Mum, bye,* the kids said, and then they joined each other.

I walked towards the gates, my bag knocking against my back. Pop said, *Learn how to bloody read.* When he didn't have his glasses I couldn't help him read the words on the top of the newspaper. I couldn't read out the ingredients on the cake box. I couldn't read the date. He said, *Come on, Justine, learn. Everybody knows how to bloody read.* I wanted to learn how to read. I would have liked to know the order of Aunty Rita's numbers, and if she ever did write me a letter I wanted to be able to read it. But it didn't matter how hard I tried; words were different for me than for other people. The sounds, when I made them, were wrong. Unless Michael helped me, other kids laughed. My throat felt tight. My eyes pricked. Michael was gone.

There were words across the top of the main high school building. *Erad ot wonk. Erad ot wonk.* There was nothing to hold on to; I felt dizzy. I looked at the words again. *Erad ot wonk.* What was that? Was it a joke? I couldn't read the sign. I could have stood there all day looking at it, trying to read it, and I still wouldn't know what it said. If Michael was here he would have helped me. We would have been together. We would have had his crutches as weapons to hold up to the other kids. I kicked at the ground. Why was I thinking of Michael when he wasn't here? For three years I had learned not to think of him, to keep the door closed as long as I could. Only in the last minutes before sleep did it open. Not on the first day of high school.

Erad ot wonk. It was wrong. Stupid. I turned and walked away.

40.

I went to the river near the bridge that crossed to Moama—the bridge I'd crossed with Aunty Rita three years ago. It had been that long since I'd seen her. I climbed down the bank where the grass grew long and thick. I sat down near the water and watched the paddle boats go up and down the river. I could feel the damp, cool mud through my skirt. I picked up a stick and drew in the dirt. *Erad ot wonk.* I changed the letters around. *Erad to knwo.* I didn't understand. I changed them again. *Dare ot knwo.* They still didn't make sense. I changed them again and again. I tried them in every different order. *Dare to know.* I snapped my stick-pencil in two and threw it into the river. *Dare to know.* Know what?

Birds stepped through the water, lifting their knees, sticking their beaks in for fish. I stretched my legs and sun streamed across my knees. I leaned back on my arms and listened to the sound of water and wind and birds. My breathing became slow. I was made of water like the river, leaves like the trees, feathers like the birds. I don't know how long I sat there. Was it as long as school? I got up and walked beside the river. Soon the path became too thin and I climbed up the bank to the road that led back to Yolamundi.

John Wayne as the Lucky Texan came with me. He rode in front on Duke the Miracle Horse and I rode Silver. We let our reins hang loose in the sun and rode slow because the horses were hungry and there wasn't lunch in the bag, or dinner until we set up camp. The Lucky Texan's gun was slung over his shoulder; it bumped and swung as he rode, his hat low over his head. It was going to be a long ride. My stomach growled.

I heard a car coming along the road. I turned and saw a white station wagon, its body long and close to the ground, dust rising up around its wheels. When the car came close to me it slowed down, and a man leaned out. I didn't look at him. He slowed down even more. 'Hey, there,' he said.

I turned around and saw Jamie Worlley. I hadn't seen Jamie Worlley since before Dad went away. He'd joined Brian Chisholm in Goonyella to work in the Queensland mines. He'd been gone all this time, but he was here now, and instead of a boy he was a man, and he was driving a car. I kept walking, looking straight ahead. The last time I'd talked to Jamie Worlley he pushed me onto my back and lifted my skirt.

Jamie said, 'Justine?'

I wished I had the Lucky Texan's rifle over my shoulder.

'Is that you, Justine?'

I walked faster.

'Hey, Justine, are you mad at me?'

I didn't answer.

'Hey, Justine,' he said, his voice softer. 'I'm sorry about the last time I saw you. I was an idiot. Are you going home? Why don't I give you a lift in the Valiant?' He slapped the side of his car with his hand.

I kept walking.

'Come on, Justine. You can't walk all the way. It's too hot.'

Sweat dripped down my back under my shirt. My face pounded with heat. I stopped walking and looked at him.

Jamie Worlley smiled at me and a light came from his eyes made of electricity and sun. A strap of muscle ran along the bottom of his arm. He wore a hat like John Wayne as Sheriff Chance and his teeth shone white.

'Get in,' he said.

I looked at the road ahead. Yolamundi was a long way. If I walked it might take until night-time.

Jamie Worlley leaned across and opened his door. 'I meant what I said, Justine. I'm sorry about what I did the last time I saw you. I deserved the hiding your old man gave me.'

I got in the car.

'You've grown,' Jamie said as he drove.

There was a small skull hanging from some beads around the rear-vision mirror. The seats were black leather. There was a tear on Jamie's seat covered with grey tape.

Jamie said, 'Remember how much fun we used to have?'

My skin stuck to the leather as I lifted my legs up and down. The rag in my underpants felt hot and wet. I stole a look at the side of Jamie's face. He looked like John Wayne in *The Quiet Man*. My mouth went dry. Jamie's hands were brown on the wheel. They were a man's hands. They were like my dad's—they could lift anything. Dad could have pulled a tree from the ground if he wanted.

Jamie said, 'You look like your mum, Justine. She was blonde, like you. You're cute.'

When Jamie spoke it was as if I had no clothes on, and a feather was going up and down my skin. *You look like your mum. You're cute.* But Jamie was Stacey's brother. He used to call her Longhorn Stacey and Yolamundi cow, but he was her brother. He knew the reason Dad was in Pentridge. Why was he talking to me?

We were close to Pop's Three now. I didn't want Pop to see me in Jamie's Valiant. 'Can you stop?' I said.

'What?'

'Can you stop?'

He said, 'It's cute how you talk so quiet. Yeah, I can stop.' He drove the car onto the side of the trail, then turned off the engine. We sat in the Valiant, the engine ticking in the heat. 'You want to hang out, Justine?'

I looked straight ahead; everything I looked at through the windscreen—the trees, the sky, the birds—was covered in a layer of dust.

He said, 'We could go for a swim if you like?'

I could see Pop's Three from where we were parked. If Pop came out to get the letters from the box, he would see Jamie's car.

'Come on, Justine. Don't worry about him. Just say yes.'

Jamie was two of me. Three of me. I was as thin as one of his legs. Why did he want to hang out with me?

'Okay, don't answer—just nod your head.' He pushed my shoulder so I rocked. It took me by surprise and pushed out a smile. 'Just nod,' he said. 'Come on. Like this.' He started to nod.

I nodded.

'Great. Why don't I meet you at The Choke on Saturday, at lunchtime?'

Jamie was John Wayne when he wanted Mary Kate to sleep in his bed. 'Okay,' I said softly.

'You're cute when you're shy,' Jamie said. 'See you Saturday.' His smile came in volts from his teeth.

Jamie Worlley disappeared down the road.

I didn't walk the rest of the way to the Three; I floated.

That night, just before sleep, it wasn't Michael I saw. It wasn't Black Beauty and his friend Joe Evans. It wasn't the night in the tent, the blackberries and vanilla cake. It was Jamie Worlley. Pieces of *The Quiet Man* played like a lullaby: *He was his father's only son, his mother's pride and joy, and dearly did his parents love their wild colonial boy.*

41.

I saw Jamie again when I watched *True Grit* on the television with Pop. John Wayne as Rooster Cogburn tracked Chaney into Indian land. It didn't matter what Chaney did, Rooster found him. When the movie finished I said, 'Pop, when will it be on again?'

'I don't know, Justine—call the television, for Christ's sake.'

That night, in my bed I saw Jamie walk through the sheriff's door, holding his gun. *You owe me, Chaney.* Jamie took Mattie Ross in his arms. *It's a bold one, you are,* he said. I was Mattie Ross, the bold one, my dark hair thick and shining, my teeth straight, my cheeks pink. When Mattie Ross spoke, she knew the words to choose and the right order to put them in. *Who knows what's in a man's heart? I will not bandy words with a drunkard.*

———

The next day, my schoolbag on my back, I walked towards Pop's rock, but I didn't stop there. I kept going into the forest, to the river. I was Mary Kate waiting at my keepout for Thornton in

The Quiet Man. He would be coming home soon. *Where are my eggs? Oh, you devil, you devil! You belong to me now, Mary Kate.* I straightened my walls, tidied my towel roof, and made supplies from twigs and stones. I put a cup of river water in my esky.

I walked along the path to The Choke. I heard the same crying I had heard ever since the night Dad took me to Stacey's. I walked down to the water. I took off my shoes and socks, my t-shirt and skirt. I peeled off my underpants with the rag of blood and left them on the dirt. I looked down at myself and saw the angles of bones showing under the skin. My hair tickled my shoulders, pale yellow, like straw that had been left in the sun.

I stepped into the mud at the edge of the river. The blood from the scar between my legs trickled down my skin. I went deeper and watched as the water washed away the blood. I went deeper still so that the water was up to my neck, and then I flipped and lay on my back, looking up at the trees. I let the air out slowly and my chest sank, water flowing over me. When I breathed in again my chest rose. I half closed my eyes against the light of the sky. Sometimes I was the tree, sometimes I was Mary Kate, and sometimes I was the cockatoo on the branch. I could choose. The crying was so soft now that I could hardly hear it.

When I sat on the bank to dry, blood from my scar dripped into the spider holes in the ground. I brushed river dirt from my knees and ankles. The sun was warm on my shoulders. A kookaburra laughed above my head as I was getting dressed. Wind moved through the trees. Another kookaburra answered.

I walked almost all the way to Pop's Three, then turned around and walked back again. I wasn't looking for my dad anymore, waiting for his truck to come down the road and save me. I was waiting for Jamie's white Valiant instead, its fins on either side of its long low body.

When my feet were sore from walking up and down the trail, I went home and waited for Pop to cook dinner. He made ham and egg and cheese with macaroni. I ate bowl after bowl until the pot was empty. Pop rolled a White Ox and said, 'Jesus, Justine.'

When I went to bed that night, the scissors in my dream cut two red waves with a white line down the middle, like a road. At the top there was a tooth left behind by the dogs. It was Jamie's scar. I dug in my fingers and pulled out the tooth, rolling it from side to side in my hand as if it was a bullet. Jamie said, *Give it back*, but I said, *No, it's mine*.

———

In the morning I went out to see the chooks. I sat down on the floor of the run and threw out handfuls of seed. Pop said, *Not too much of the good stuff, Justine. Costs a bloody fortune*, but I did it anyway. 'Hey, girls; hey, ladies. When is Saturday? How long till Saturday comes, hey, madams?' I asked the Isa Browns, 'Do you know Jamie Worlley? Do you know him, girls?'

I found my swimmers in my cupboard, stretched and worn thin. I was glad my rags were finished. How do you swim with rags? I looked for wood for Pop's fire so I could light it myself. I dragged branches across the fence, my skin prickling and damp with the heat. It was summer, the start of the school year but not for me. *Erad ot wonk*. What could I do with those words?

Every day I said to Pop, *What day is it today?*

Wednesday . . . Thursday . . . Friday . . .

What day is it, Pop? What day is it?

At last his answer was Saturday.

Pop put two plates of toast with eggs on the table and we dipped the toast in the egg. Pop smoked and drank tea. I said, 'Can I have a cup?'

'Of what?'

'Tea.'

'Bloody hell, you're growing up,' said Pop. He put in two sugars and so much milk the tea was almost white. I took a bite of toast then a drink of tea and one went with the other as if they should never be apart. I sat beside Pop, holding my warm cup, as we breathed the kindest animal.

—

After breakfast, when I was hanging out Pop's washing, Relle came over with Steve. 'I spoke to him,' she said.

'What? When?' said Pop.

Relle glanced across at me. 'Can we go inside?'

Pop and Relle went inside, while Steve and me waited in the yard. Steve pulled at the clothesline Pop had strung from the kitchen window. 'Where's Kirk?' I asked him.

He said, 'With Jamie Worlley. He's back in town.'

My heart sped up. 'Jamie Worlley? What's he doing with Jamie Worlley?'

'They got pissed last night.'

'What?' I didn't know if I had heard right. Why was Kirk with Jamie?

'Jamie's getting him work at the mine if he wants it. All Kirk has to do is say he's eighteen and he can go. That's what Jamie did and it worked. He makes a thousand dollars a week.'

My stomach felt light and sick. 'What are they doing now?' I asked Steve.

'Who?'

'Kirk and Jamie.'

'I dunno. Hair of the dog.'

'If Pop finds out he'll kill him.'

'He'll never find out. He'll be home soon; he has to help Mum get the trailer onto the back of the car.'

'Right,' I said. Had Jamie forgotten he was seeing me today? Why did Jamie want to be friends with Kirk? Did he not care what had happened to Stacey?

'I could lie about my age too,' said Steve.

Pop's shorts flapped in the breeze around our heads.

'What for?'

'To go to the mine with Kirk. I could save enough to get Dad out of Pentridge.'

I knew that nobody would believe Steve was eighteen; he wasn't like Kirk. He was small and thin, like Relle.

'Yeah, you could,' I said.

Steve poked at a pair of Pop's shorts with a stick. 'Even Jamie reckons Dad didn't do it.'

'Did he say Dad didn't do it? Is that what he said?'

'Nah. But he wouldn't be getting pissed with Kirk if he thought Dad did it, would he?'

I didn't know the answer. Pop and Relle came out the back. They sat down on the camp chairs and smoked. Relle said, 'Fucken justice system. Where's the justice? Stacey Worlley spent her life chasing him, then when she got what she wanted look what she did to him.'

Pop said, 'Ray could have stayed away.'

'Who would have stayed away? You tell me one guy you know would stay away from what she was offering.'

'Not bloody Ray, that's for sure.'

'Not any man,' said Relle.

They smoked and sighed and looked at the unlit fire. When would they leave so I could go to the river? At last Relle stubbed her smoke out into the grass. 'Come on, Steve, let's go. Got to get the trailer sorted then get to work. Those logs aren't going to count themselves.' Relle worked at the sawmills now, taking inventory. She said working with men and chainsaws was better than making pies with bitches.

'See ya, Justine,' said Steve. They walked out to the car. Relle never looked at me; not even once.

After they were gone I pulled on my swimmers—they felt loose in some places, and tight in others. I pulled my dress over my head. 'I'm going to see Dawn,' I called out to Pop.

Pop said, 'Good, darlin'. Be home for tea.' Pop was glad I lived with him on his Three. Since Dad went away he let me drink tea, he let me light the fire and throw in the wood.

———

As I walked down to the Murray, questions rose like bubbles in my chest. Why was Jamie drinking with Kirk? They used to be friends before the fall-out, but I was the first to touch his scar, not Kirk. It was me Jamie picked up in the Valiant. Or did he pick up Kirk too? What were they doing together? Why did he want to be friends with Kirk *and* me? Why not just me?

I closed my eyes as I walked the path, feeling Silver's warm, strong body beneath me. My rifle swung over my shoulder. I sang, *He robbed the rich, he helped the poor, he shot James MacEvoy, a terror to Australia was the wild colonial boy.* It was the first song John Wayne heard when he came to Innisfree. Light moved through me. My stomach felt shrunken and tight. I couldn't breathe as deep. The feather pushed its way along the top of my skirt, moving up under my shirt.

I came to my keepout. Mary Kate said, *Who gave you leave to be kissing me?* Thornton answered, *So, you can talk!* Mary Kate said, *Yes, I can, I will and I do! And it's more than talk you'll be getting if you step a step closer to me!*

I swept the floor of my keepout with a branch of leaves. Every time Mary Kate pushed the broom her long green skirt danced across the dirt. I watched my branch-broom stir up the dirt then smooth it, seeing my green hem darken. Thornton would be home from mustering soon. He would leave his secrets behind him. He would be home for a long time—two months or three months before he had to leave again. He would teach me things. We would drive to places in his car. I would make him lunch. Sometimes he was Jamie and sometimes he was Thornton and sometimes he was Ray. His skin became other skins, as if it was elastic. He was Rooster Cogburn, he was Jamie, he was the Quiet Man and he was my dad.

I walked to The Choke; every time the river was the same, and every time it was different. The water was always moving between the banks, even if it was slow, it never stopped flowing. I didn't know what time it was. Was it lunchtime? I tried not to think about Kirk and why he had been with Jamie. Why was Jamie friends with Kirk? But he wouldn't say Kirk was cute. He wouldn't go for a swim with Kirk, would he? I wasn't sure. Was it crying I could hear? Whose voices were they?

I started to scrape dirt into the shape of a chair, with a back and sides. I gathered stones and sticks and made the arms of the chair. *Sean Thornton, the men of Innisfree bid you welcome home.* As I worked, my hum became a song. *And that was how they captured him, the wild colonial boy.* The chair could fit Mary Kate and Thornton and that's all. There wouldn't be room for Kirk or Steve. There was a tree nearby to tether the Miracle

Horse and Silver. I put my arms around the trunk, my cheek against the bark. Thornton said, *There'll be no locks or bolts between us.*

'Hey, Justine!'

I looked up and saw Jamie coming through the trees. He smiled at me. My heart thumped. I needed to go to the toilet. I stepped away from the tree. I didn't know whether to push down the chair I had made.

When Jamie was closer he said, 'Nice day for it.'

His eyes were so blue, I couldn't look.

Jamie turned to face the river. He hadn't seen the chair. He was wearing jeans and his legs were strong like my dad's and his hands were in his pockets. His hair was light and came over his collar at the back. He was wide across the shoulders. I felt as if I wasn't there; only he was there. He said, 'G'day, cutie.'

The feather brushed the insides of my arms.

He said, 'You ready for a swim?'

'Yeah,' I said. There was no spit in my mouth.

Jamie unbuttoned his jeans and pulled them down. He was wearing shorts underneath. He unbuttoned his shirt and took it off and I saw the scar and the tooth in the middle left over from the dogs. Jamie had grown up around the scar, the scar was the centre; it decided how tall he grew, how strong he became, what he did.

Jamie stood shimmering in the sunlight. 'Coming in?' He held his hand out to me. It was big, like my dad's. When my hand was inside my dad's, it looked small, like a baby bird in a nest.

I pulled my dress over my head. My hair caught in the button. I kept pulling at it but couldn't get the dress over my head. I couldn't see out from under the dress. My face felt hot. It was dark. I felt the same as when Dawn and Noreena talked to me, or when I didn't get the words and letters right at school. Stupid. I wanted to turn around and run back to Pop's Three with the dress still over my head. Never pull it off. Stay in my room with the dress over my head forever.

Jamie said, 'Don't move.'

I kept as still as I could as his fingers brushed against my neck. He was standing so close I could hear him breathe. The feather went up the back of my legs, stopping behind my knees. Then it was light again and the dress lay on the dirt beside us.

Jamie took my hand—he didn't look at my swimmers hanging loose and old, and tight in places. We climbed down the steep side. When we came to the bottom we slid into the brown river water. It felt cold; I stood up with my arms crossed around me. Jamie said, 'Justine, you are so cute.' The feather tickled under the bum of my swimmers.

He went under and I couldn't see him. I looked around but he was nowhere. I looked across to the bank on the other side, but all I saw was water and reeds and the trees. It had turned quiet. I looked back at the bank we had just climbed down. Where had he gone?

Suddenly I felt my legs grabbed and Jamie came up laughing. 'Gotcha!' he said.

I splashed him and screamed and it came out like any other girl in the school playground—a girl like Dawn or Noreena.

Jamie swam close, put his back to me, and said, 'Climb on.' He patted his shoulder. 'I'll take you for a ride, little mermaid.'

I put my hands on Jamie's shoulders. He dived under and I held tight. We went down deep where it was cold and black, my hands on his shoulders as he pulled me deeper through the water, moving through the darkness on our way to our underwater home. If we kept swimming we would push through the same dirt that buried my dad's secrets, that buried knowing. We would push through it, our faces and bodies and feet bursting through the dirt and there we would be on the other side, and nothing would be hidden, everything would be clear and known in the light.

My chest felt tighter and tighter. Jamie kept swimming deeper. I thought my chest would burst, then he pushed up from the bottom and we came through the water into the dry world. We sucked back the breath. Jamie kicked up and lay on his back and I trod water, watching him. Pieces of him rose and sunk. He flipped back up. 'Smoko?' he said, and swam to the shore. I followed and he put out his hand for mine as we climbed out.

When we were on the bank Jamie shook the water from his hands and took his cigarettes from the pocket of his shirt. When he went to sit down on the edge, I took his hand and led him to my chair. He said, 'Is that for us? Justine, you're so cute.'

We sat down in my chair and Jamie took a cigarette out of the box. He offered me one but I shook my head. 'You can have some of mine,' he said. He leaned against me while he smoked. He passed me the cigarette when it was halfway down and I took a small puff. I held the smoke in my mouth then blew it out, and didn't cough.

When Jamie leaned forward to put the cigarette out in the dirt, I saw his scar. 'You can touch it if you like,' he said.

I didn't move.

'Come on, it won't bite. Remember? Touch it.'

Jamie took my fingers and put them against the scar. My mouth felt dry. I ran my finger down the red waves and up the middle and Jamie shivered. I took my hand away. Jamie said, 'Don't stop.'

But I did stop. I didn't want to touch it anymore.

Jamie leaned against the back of our chair and the dirt fell flat and we did too. Jamie laughed. He said, 'It was good when we were kids, remember?'

'Yeah,' I said.

He sat up. 'How old are you, Justine?'

'Thirteen. Fourteen soon.'

'Soon?'

'A few months.'

'How old do you think I am?'

'I don't know.'

'I'm nearly twenty. Bit older than you. Do I scare you?'

'No.'

'No?'

'No.'

'I can't hear you.'

'No.'

'Louder.'

'No.'

'I still can't hear you. Do I scare you?'

'No!' I shouted. 'No! No! No! No!' A cockatoo screeched in the sky.

'That's better,' Jamie said.

We sat and looked at the water. I wanted to ask about Kirk, but I didn't want anything to stop or change. I didn't know if I wanted to hear the answer.

Jamie pushed at the dirt at our feet until he made two small hills. He said, 'Weird coming back here. A lot of shit's gone down.' I wasn't sure if he was talking to me or to himself. 'Been nice seeing you, Justine. You're different to . . . the others.'

I swallowed. What did he mean I was different? To who? To Kirk and Steve?

He looked at his watch. 'We'll do this again.' He turned to me. 'You want to?'

'Yes,' I said.

'Cute.' He shook his head. He stood and stepped into his jeans. As I watched him thread the end of his belt through the buckle, the feather flew down between my legs. Jamie put out his hand and pulled me to my feet. 'There's nothing to you, Justine,' he said. 'Not like some of the girls in this place.' He laughed to himself. 'I could pick you up and throw you.' He didn't let go of my hand as we walked through the bush to where he'd parked the Valiant. I couldn't swallow or speak. The feather kept tickling under my swimmers. When we came to his car he said, 'I'm heading into town. You want me to drop you home?'

'No,' I said.

He said, 'I'll find you and we'll set something up.' He got into his car and turned on the engine. 'See you, Justine,' he said through the open window.

'See you.'

'Jamie.'

'What?'

'See you, Jamie,' he said.

I felt heat on my cheeks. 'See you, Jamie.'

'That's better.' He revved the engine hard, smiling at me, then he turned onto the road and was gone.

I went back to my keepout and made Thornton sandwiches of sticks and dirt. I poured him a beer of Murray water and after he drank it we had a rest on the keepout floor. The feather tickled me to sleep and there was no crying. It didn't come at all. I heard birds and breeze and water. I stayed and stayed in my keepout home. I had a letter box made of sticks and Aunty Rita sent me a letter. It said, *Friends make the difference. Dare to know.*

When it grew dark I walked back to Pop's Three, my stomach growling and empty. I felt clean and light. Jamie's smile had taken away everything all the way back to my first mistake. There was no breech, no split, no Donna, no Michael, no Stacey, no Pentridge, no Echuca High. Jamie had rubbed out all the wrong words I had written and read and spoken, and made me new, like an empty page.

42.

That night the feather came out from under my pyjamas and drew pictures of Jamie and me as we walked the streets of Dublin. It was *The Quiet Man*. Jamie put his fists up at the enemy and said, *I'm mad enough to kill.* In my dream the scar on Jamie's back became the road to Stacey's half-built house. Sherry called, 'Mum! Come home!' I held her in my arms and said, 'Won't be long now.'

In the day I was either at the river or walking the Henley Trail looking for the Valiant. When I heard a car coming I stood at the side and waited, my heart pounding. When it wasn't him, I felt empty and flat. It was a long time between cars. I went down to the river to fix my keepout. For five days I watched the road and waited, and worked on my keepout home. I built shelves that reached the ceiling, dug a hole to hide supplies, and shaped a window with a bark frame. The Quiet Man in Dublin became Sheriff Chance in Arizona. I was Feathers or Mary Kate or Mattie Ross. I was in the river with Jamie underwater, riding on his back deeper and deeper until we pushed through the dirt and came out on the other side where nothing was hidden.

It became hard to eat. Sometimes I was dizzy. The world outside of Jamie was finished. Aunty Rita and Michael had never been. There was no Black Beauty or Joe Evans. Nobody missed anybody else. Nobody was separated. I didn't need answers or letters or words.

⸺

On Saturday morning I was on the trail when a car came. *It won't be him it won't be him this time I won't look because it won't be him.* For the first time I didn't stop or turn around. The car slowed down beside me, and Jamie said, 'You're hard to find.'

I didn't know how to stop walking.

He said, 'The silent treatment, hey?'

I kept going.

He said, 'Justine, stop.'

But I couldn't. I had been walking for so many days, up and down, I didn't know how.

'Justine, come on!' His voice was sharp. At last I stopped. He said, 'That's better. Let me look at you. I've missed you, cutie.'

The feather tickled me under my skirt.

'Are you busy tonight?'

I shook my head and wiped sweat from my lip.

He said, 'Good. What about I meet you right here, right here at this spot?' He looked around at the trees and road. 'We'll go somewhere. We'll get fish and chips and eat them at the river, how does that sound?'

I nodded.

'Good,' he said. 'Well . . . at five. Okay?'

'Okay,' I said.

'Ah, she speaks.' He tipped back his head and laughed, and the volts came from him and lit up the road so that I could see all the way to Innisfree.

———

I walked back to Pop's and found him in the kitchen. He said, 'Come and feed the girls with me.' We went down to the run and took handfuls of the seeds that cost a bloody fortune out of the bucket and scattered them around the grass. Pop said, 'Hello, girls.' He looked at me as I was changing the water and said, 'Justine, you are growing up.' He took three eggs out of the hen's boxes, held them up to me and said, 'Want some lunch?'

'Yeah,' I said, and even though my stomach was light and sick I swallowed every yellow liquid bite.

Pop burped and rolled a White Ox. 'Good thing I took you in, Justine—someone to share the eggs with.'

I wiped yolk from my chin and he grinned at me.

I said, 'What's the time, Pop?'

'One o'clock,' he said.

The next time I asked it he said, 'What's the bloody difference what the time is? Going somewhere?'

'Yes.'

'Where, for Christ's sake?'

'Dawn's.'

'When?'

'Five o'clock. Just before.'

'I'll let you know when it's nearly five, okay?'

'Okay.'

'How will you get there?'

'Her mum's picking me up at the rock.'

'On the trail?'

'Yeah.'

'How is her mum?'

'Okay.'

'Nice you're seeing Dawn again,' he said. 'Eat your toast.'

I dragged my toast across my plate and waited for nearly five.

43.

Pop never did tell me the time. He sat on the camp chair near his fire, threw crusts to the girls and drank beers. There were empty cans all around his feet. He smoked and talked to the flames. 'Bloody hell, Ray. What were you thinking? You weren't bloody thinking, that's the trouble.' He got up and went down to the gate that led to the river. 'You old bastard, Cockyboy,' he said. 'I know, I know, they all belong to you, ole bastard. Come here and talk to me.' I didn't want to say, *Is it nearly five yet, Pop?* I just waited until he went inside for a beer, then I left.

I walked along the trail to the place where I had last seen Jamie. I didn't know what time it was. I kicked around at the grass until it was flat and then I sat down. I crossed my legs, and put my chin in my hands. Jamie was Stacey's brother. He wasn't in Yolamundi the night I was in Stacey's caravan; he was in Goonyella at the mines with Brian. He didn't see what happened to Stacey. But he knew Stacey wasn't with Brian anymore. She couldn't be a wife anymore. She couldn't be on her own out there. Did Jamie think my dad did it?

I heard crying and put my hands over my ears, trying to rub out the sound.

When I looked up I saw the white Valiant coming along the road. I jumped to my feet. The crying stopped.

The car pulled in close to me. Jamie leaned over and spoke through the open window. 'Sorry I'm late,' he said. He opened the passenger door. 'Get in.'

I got in the car. It smelled of ash and petrol. Jamie looked at me; there was electrical light around his face. It was too bright to see into his eyes. He drove out onto the road. One side was the river and the other side was Yolamundi. There were trees all around us. Eagles flew in high circles in the sky. I wanted to keep going. Keep driving through the trees, sitting beside Jamie, eagles in the sky. He drove out onto the highway.

'Where are we going?'

'To pick up some beers,' he said. He touched my knee. The feather tickled up to my underpants. 'That okay?'

'Yeah.'

He drove to the Yolamundi pub and parked in the street outside. 'Back in a minute,' he said.

I watched as he went inside. I saw Noreena's mother, Mrs Rimes, come into the car park on her way back from the shop. I slid down against the seat and didn't sit up again until she was gone. She knew where my dad was; everybody did. *It's all or fucken nothing with your father,* Relle told the boys. *Free as a fucken bird, or locked up in a bloody cage.* Everybody knew.

At last Jamie came out of the pub through the back door, carrying three paper bags. He got in the car. 'Wasn't too long, was I?'

'Yes.'

'Getting cheeky on me, now, huh?' His smile made me dizzy.

Jamie drove down to where the Murray flowed through Yolamundi and parked at the river car park. He got out of the car first, carrying the paper bags, and opened my door. He bowed to me, and said, 'Princess.' I didn't know where to look. We walked down the path to the water. The river was running wide and brown. I saw the black roots of red gums in the banks where the waterline was low. Willow branches trailed in the shallows. Every tree leaned towards the river, as if it was calling them to come closer. We sat down on the bank. Jamie said, 'Nice to see you again, Justine.' Jamie's legs were like two long roads you could travel down; you could slide off the ends of his boots and then keep going further. He leaned back on his straight, strong arms. 'Nice to see me again?' he said.

'Yeah.' It was hard to talk.

Jamie leaned over and kissed my cheek, light and dry, like wings. Blood rushed through my body. Jamie turned away and pulled a can of beer out of one of the paper bags. He said, 'This is for me.' He pulled a big green bottle from another bag. 'And this is for you.' He lifted the ring from the lid of his beer, then he unscrewed the top from the green bottle and put it in my hands. He said, 'Here's to you.' He took a long drink from his beer. 'Your turn, cutie.'

Pop had drunk all his life and so had Dad. I had seen Kirk and Steve drink beer at Pop's when Pop was sleeping, but this would be my first drink. I put the green bottle to my mouth and tipped it back. The drink exploded in my throat. I coughed and choked and the drink came out on my chin. When I wiped it away Jamie said, 'You are so cute.' A flame moved from my throat to my stomach, warming the skin as it passed. It was like drinking a hot Mintie. Jamie said, 'What do you think of that? Nice?'

'Nice.'

'Should be bloody nice, cost enough.' He wiped more of the drink from my chin with his thumb and finger. 'Nah. You're worth it.'

I took another sip. Now I knew why Pop drank when his bug was feeding; the drink would burn it down.

I saw some boys coming along the river path. It was Jamie's cousin Lachie, and another guy I didn't know. What were they doing here? Did Jamie know they were coming?

'G'day, Jamie,' said Lachie, looking at me. Lachie would be fifteen by now. He was carrying a tape recorder.

The other guy was almost as big as Jamie. Jamie said, 'G'day Stu.'

Stu said, 'Getting started without us?'

'Yep,' said Jamie. 'Cheers.' He tipped his can towards them. I took another swallow of the hot mint drink. Lachie and Stu sat down beside Jamie. Did Jamie want them to stay? Didn't he want it to be just the two of us?

Jamie passed Lachie one of the paper bags, and the boys pulled out cans of beer. Lachie pressed a button on the tape recorder and it started to play. *What was it, baby, did my love let you down? What was it, baby, when I came to town?* I closed my eyes and saw Dad coming through the trees, the Smith tucked in his belt. *What was it, baby, that made you so blue? Didn't you know, baby, my love was true?* Dad took my hand, pulled me towards him and said, *My special girl*, while the music played. *Oh, baby, when we touch, I know you are mine, when I feel your lips, baby.* When I opened my eyes Lachie was looking at me, as if he knew something that I didn't.

Lachie and me used to play together. He went down the yellow slide behind me. The bubbles were in his hair too, on his back, across his shoulders. Lachie knew what my dad did to Stacey. He never left for Goonyella like Jamie did; he'd always been here. I moved back, further behind Jamie, taking small sips of the green drink. I wondered why Lachie and Stu were there, why it wasn't just Mary Kate and Thornton.

Jamie stayed close, squeezing my hand.

Lachie said, 'Caught thirty bloody cod at once last time it drained. Not with a line. We speared them. Lazy bastards.'

Stu said, 'Cod gut fucken stinks. You ever notice that? Stinks like a dead man.'

Jamie said, 'Tastes sweet but. Sweet as.'

I needed to do a wee. The picture had changed. It started with me and Jamie and now it was a picture for more Worlleys and somebody else. I tried to stand, but stumbled. Lachie said, 'Had a bit to drink, Justine?'

It was the first time I'd heard Lachie say my name since we used to be friends. I said, 'No.' My voice sounded loose, loud, as if it belonged to someone else.

Jamie said, 'Going somewhere?' I didn't want to tell him I needed to go to the toilet, but he guessed. 'Ladies' room?' I nodded. 'Don't be long,' he said softly.

I took a deep breath and walked away from the river and into the forest. When I couldn't see them or hear them anymore I found a big tree, pulled down my underpants and squatted. The wee came out in a hard stream. I looked up at the top of the tree and saw the sky turning slowly, in a circle. I looked down and watched the pathways the wee made through the dirt, drowning ants and a beetle. I wobbled and almost fell as I moved my feet. When I was finished I shook up and down, then I pulled up my underpants and walked back.

I couldn't hear what they were saying, but I could hear them laughing. I saw a beer can land at the edge of the water. The boys were big—they were all one thing, and I was another. I wasn't big enough. Suddenly I didn't want to go back to them. I wanted to go to my keepout. It wasn't far from here. The boys wouldn't see me leaving. I could load my rifle, climb on Silver's back and ride along my friend, the Murray. I could drink from the river so that the hot mint was washed away, and my legs would be steady beneath me and my voice would be my own again.

'Hey, Justine!' It was Jamie; he had seen me. 'Hey!' he called out. 'Look who's here!' I saw Kirk and Steve coming down the path from the other direction. Had Jamie invited them? Kirk saw me and looked as surprised as I was. He lifted his hand.

My brothers were here—now it was Lees and Worlleys, the way it used to be. Three of them, and three of us. I felt my legs grow steady. I breathed out and walked back down to the riverbank. Kirk raised his eyebrows. He looked from me to Jamie. 'What are you doing here?' he asked me.

'Same thing you are,' said Jamie. He was bigger than Kirk. He was the only one who could buy beer, the only one who didn't go to school anymore, the only one with a job at Goonyella mine. Jamie held beers out to Kirk and Steve. He patted the ground beside him and I sat back down.

Shadows passed across Kirk's face. He was my big brother; he knew Pop wouldn't want me here. They had never seen me with a drink before. They knew Pop would never let me. They were boys and I was a girl.

The music played. *I can't love you if you won't stay, sweet angel, let your love come my way.*

Kirk sat down on the other side of Lachie and Stu. They all began to drink and talk at the same time. It was Lees and

Worlleys again; I wasn't by myself anymore. Kirk and Steve knew Pop's rule, they knew I was thirteen. They knew I was younger than all of them, that there was nothing to me, that Jamie could pick me up and throw me.

I leaned back against Jamie. *Let go into my arms, girl, you know you can, let me hold you, girl.* I took another drink. Jamie's body hid me, like a shelter. Even though he was talking to the boys, he was with me. I could feel it in the kiss on my cheek. Even with the picture changed—now a picture of Worlley and Lee boys drinking beers—the kiss stayed. I put my hand over my cheek. Everything was warm. My throat, my face, gut, legs, arms all warm, as if I was melting. There was nothing that had gone before, nothing and nobody lost.

Kirk watched me from narrowed eyes as he drank. He turned to Jamie and they talked and laughed and looked at the river and threw in a stone. 'Be good to get out of this place,' said Kirk.

'Yeah, it's a big country. You don't know how big till you go there.'

'Would you ever drive it?'

'Shit, yeah. Not in my fucken car. I'd end up sleeping in the desert.'

'For a month.'

'Yeah. No girls up there but. Oh, there's girls, but they're old. There's no young ones.'

'Shit.'

'Yeah, shit's right.'

'Shit.' Steve repeated Kirk's words, doubling them, trying to make them his own. It was only me who knew he never could. Me and him.

Jamie whispered to me, 'How are you feeling, cutie?'

It was getting dark. The green flames of the drink jetted through me, warm and minty. I said, 'Good.' He turned my cheek to him and kissed it again. I saw Kirk and Steve watching. Our eyes met.

In one look I saw our years together; our hideouts, our times at the river, our father in prison, our plans to bust him out. Steve turned away but Kirk kept his eyes on me. I saw all the times Dad didn't answer Kirk's questions, look at him, teach him to shoot, teach him anything, anything at all. Dad left Relle for my mum. Everyone knew. Jamie knew. Lachie knew. Pop knew. The whole of Yolamundi knew it was my mum he chose and it was Kirk's mum he left behind. Kirk drank from his beer and threw another stone into the river. I saw all the days without Dad in his face, in the twist of his mouth, in his flat eyes. All the days of wishing Dad would show him how to shoot, how to drive, how to fight, what to say, when to laugh. Kirk had to pretend every day that he knew, but he had no clues, it was all pretending. It was the same as me trying to read; he had to guess. The only person he knew more than was me.

The music played a song about a stairway. Kirk and Steve and Jamie sang some of the words. I closed my eyes and watched the stairway as it curled around the stars. You never knew if it would keep going, but it did, up and up and up, higher and higher.

When the song finished Kirk got to his feet. He crunched his empty can under his foot and threw one more stone into the water. I looked up at him. 'See ya, Justine,' he said. His eyes glittered. I couldn't answer. The mint drink softened my words so I couldn't speak a single one. Not *Don't leave me here, please, Kirk.* Not *Take me with you.* Not *I am not big enough*. I couldn't do anything. Kirk smiled at me, his shining eyes part Dad's, part Relle's, and he left me there. Steve was behind him, in the same place he had always been. Even though they were my brothers they were only half.

44.

Now it was only Jamie, Lachie, Stu and me. I could see the river in the moonlight, covered with tiny waves. I could hear the music it played, as if a tiny bell was tied to the crest of every ripple.

'More?' Jamie said to me. Without waiting for an answer he put the green bottle to my lips.

I could see the outline of trees on the other side of the Murray. If my secret boat was waiting for me I could have untied it and rowed to the other side. I could've kept going. The boys talked but I didn't listen. I didn't know all the voices. Who was here? There was another voice now, a man's voice, like Jamie's. Who was he? They were talking about cars and speeds and which car was the fastest if you pressed the accelerator. Lachie said he could prove it. Jamie said, *You're on,* and the other guy said he'd set a watch and Lachie said the Ford had a bigger engine and Jamie said, *Fuck that, the Ford could do twice that.* I drank more and stopped missing Kirk and Steve, stopped wishing they had stayed. All I had to do was drink. Jamie pulled me in closer; I could feel the places where our bodies were touching through my jeans and shirt. I listened to the bells of the river and the voices. Jamie had me in his arms and it was enough. I was part of things, and didn't need to find words, nobody asked me to speak any.

When I closed my eyes I saw Jamie's scar under his shirt, two red waves parting so that you could see the line in the middle. The boys kept talking. They said, *That fucken highway, coppers every time, fuck did you hear what happened to Sean? Coppers booked him once then got him again ten minutes down the road.* They spoke to Jamie as if he was the boss, like my dad; they wanted him to laugh, to like what they said. Nobody told me to get lost, nobody said my teeth stuck out. Nobody said I was too thin or thin as a stick or was a skeleton or was a rake, because I belonged to Jamie. He squeezed my hand, and it was as if our fingers had a language not made of words, a language even I could speak. Jamie passed me the bottle. It didn't hurt anymore when I swallowed.

Everything was there together at the same time. Jamie's scar, the talk of our bodies, the bells of the river, the night sky, the voices of Jamie's cousin and friends, all part of the one blanket that wrapped itself around me. It was as if I had always been cold since the start, since the breech and the split, when I made my first mistake, and now I was warm.

———

In my dream I held Sherry in my lap. She smiled and tugged at my hair, moving her small fists up and down to music—the bells of the river, the song from the stereo. I heard voices. I saw stars. The stairway took me to heaven.

———

The next time I opened my eyes I saw a star shoot across the sky. Nothing could get in its way. Not the other stars or planets or comets or the distance itself. The star saw where it wanted to go, pushing through the black, leaving a trail you could see from Antarctica. I tried to lift my hand so I could show Michael—'Look, look! Michael, look. The star knows where it's going. Can you see? It's the star that decides'—but I couldn't move. I felt myself picked up and carried. Who was carrying me? Was it Dad? Was it Pop? The night sky wobbled and bounced over my head. I felt sick and wanted to vomit. I heard a car door opening. Someone put me into the car then climbed in beside me. I lay stretched out in the back. 'Michael, Michael, did you see the star?'

I vomited hot mint. 'Oh, shit!' someone said. I heard the car door open, I was lifted out and I vomited more onto the ground. My throat was on fire. What was I doing here? The thoughts were in pieces, hard to hold on to, like words on the blackboard. I was lifted back into the car.

—

I heard a cry. The light of the moon showed me Stacey's half-built house; piles of bricks and corrugated iron and planks and a concrete mixer. There was a weight above me. I saw my dad in the moonlight tearing Stacey's clothes from her body. I saw him hit her across the mouth as the weight above me grew heavier. I was being crushed. I saw my dad over Stacey, his body attacking hers, as if he was hungry and Stacey was the dinner. I saw the cattle trough, her hair in the water, my dad's hand over her head. I heard music. *You are mine, till the end of time, so kiss me, baby.*

I saw my dad at the hospital and Lizzy was in the bed in her final moment, before everything changed and was lost, before she took the best part of Ray with her. Lizzy wasn't in hospital because of the pneumonia—she was there because of the bones my pop broke when he came back from the war, the sound of gunshots in his ears, the train tracks laid in his face, the bug in his gut. He had to give it all to Lizzy. She was the one he loved.

Something tore. I was choking, as if the banks of the river were closing around my throat. I couldn't keep going, couldn't move forward. I heard a man groan. 'Fucken Lees.' I cried out and knew the third voice belonged to me.

Not a word had yet been spoken. Nothing had been born. Not a single mistake had yet been made. It was right at the start. It wasn't alive and it wasn't dead. Then there was a tiny light, like a spark. The first mistake shone like a jewel, and it was mine.

⌒

'Wake up, Justine. Get out.'

I didn't know where I was. Who was talking to me, shaking me? 'Wake up. Get out of the car,' said Dad. Somebody was crying. Was it Stacey? But it wasn't Stacey's caravan.

I opened my eyes. It wasn't my dad telling me to wake up; it was Jamie Worlley. The cold air hit my face. Jamie was pulling me out of his car, his engine running. My arms and neck ached. He put me down on the ground. I looked up and saw Pop's house. I tried to speak, 'Jamie,' but no sound came from my mouth. Jamie got back in the car. He closed his door and I watched him drive away. The ground swayed. My hands and knees stung as I dragged myself forward. My back felt twisted. Vomit bubbled in my throat. It hurt me to move, hurt to breathe.

I don't know how I pulled myself up Pop's front steps, how I opened his door.

—

'You alright, Justine?' Pop stood over me. 'You getting up?'

'Yeah,' I said. But no sound came.

'What?' said Pop.

'Yes,' I croaked, 'I'm getting up.'

'Jesus, Justine! You been drinking?'

'No, Pop.'

'What did I tell you about drinking?' He pulled back the covers. 'Jesus, what were you doing last night?'

'Nothing,' I said.

'Bullshit nothing. You stink. What did you get up to?'

'Nothing, Pop, nothing.' There was fire in my gut and between my legs. I leaned over and vomited onto the floor.

'Oh, Jesus,' said Pop. 'Get up, Justine. Get out of bed.'

It was hard to move. My back ached. I vomited again, on the blanket. My head was throbbing. The room spun.

Pop said, 'Where's Dawn?'

'Dawn?'

'Did she make it home?'

'Yes,' I said. 'Yes.'

'Jesus,' he said. 'Bloody little idiot. Where were you?'

I didn't know the answer. I didn't know anything. I fell back against the pillow.

'No, you don't,' said Pop. 'Get out of bed and clean this up.'

But I couldn't move.

Pop said, 'For Christ's sake.' He left the room.

My throat burned. It stung between my legs.

Pop came back into my room carrying a glass of water. He helped me sit up in the bed and he put the water to my lips. He smoothed a cool cloth over my forehead. I closed my eyes and heard him mopping the floor.

45.

I didn't want to see Jamie again. When I tried to remember what happened with him the night at the river I felt sick. Knowing was buried. If I could dig deep enough I might reach it. But buried alongside knowing was something I didn't want to find. It belonged to Stacey and Sherry. Even if I uncovered it, shovelling the dirt away from where it lay, I couldn't give it back to them alive.

After the night at the river with Jamie, words became harder to find; I was like Pop, the sentences only came for the chooks. *Here, ladies; here, girls; it's Jussy—it's Jussy, girls, your friend who would never hurt you, not you, not the chooks.* I changed their water and turned the straw so it was soft for their nests. *Here, Girl; here, Missy; here Lady and Lady; here Madame and Cockyboy—it's Justine, your friend.*

Even when Mrs Mulvaney said, *A treat for you today, Miss Lee,* I couldn't answer. I bought the bread and Mrs Mulvaney looked at me with a smile that pulled her face to the side, and she put an eclair in the bag anyway. But I didn't care if I ate it. I didn't go to school a single day. I walked through the trees to The

Choke. I sat on the bank and closed my eyes; I saw the bright light of the single shining star and nothing more. I listened for the bells, and then it wasn't only me in the world—I was the river and the light and the bells and the red gums, and there were no words to be spoken that I couldn't find. The crying stopped. After the night with Jamie I was more and more in my keepout home.

—

One night there was a knock at the door. I opened it and saw Relle. She looked straight past me. Her eyes were red and her make-up was smudged.

Pop said, 'Relle, what is it?'

'Kirk's gone,' she said, passing Pop a note. I hadn't seen Kirk or Steve since the night with Jamie. I was glad; I didn't want to see them.

Pop held the note far from his face and read. 'The mines? Christ. The boy's not eighteen. They'll kick his arse if they find out.'

Relle sniffed. 'He reckons he'll send money.'

'Don't hold your breath.'

She groaned. 'Steve'll be lost without him.' She didn't see me standing there. 'So sudden,' she said to Pop. 'Like father like fucken son.'

—

I was looking for clothes to wear in my cupboard when a pile of my rags fell out onto the floor. How long had it been? I put my hand on my gut; it felt hard and pressed against the elastic of my skirt. Was it full of the blood that hadn't come? I found pants in the cupboard that used to be Kirk's and wore them.

What happened if one day all the blood of the rags came out at once? I rubbed my hard and growing gut as I walked the fence line. 'You better come soon, rags, you better come soon.'

⁓

Summer finished and my gut grew bigger. The ground squelched as I carried bread and cold bacon and milk down to the Murray. Everywhere was wet with the rain of autumn; my knees were dark with mud, my socks damp in my shoes. The grass shone with puddles that didn't end. All night the rain fell on Pop's tin roof. The land was green with rain and Murray water. Flooded roads were blocked with signs I couldn't read. The bridges were closed. 'Need bloody stilts,' said Pop, lighting a White Ox. Still my rags didn't come.

⁓

I was at the supermarket in Nullabri and Pop was parked outside. I was there for bread and matches. I stood in front of the fridge with the cheeses and the butter. I looked over my shoulder—the aisle was empty. I took the cheese and put it in my schoolbag then I took a thin, cold sausage from the meats, and jam and honey from the shelf. My stomach growled and was full at the same time. I ate the food later in my keepout, dipping the sausage in the jam and the honey. I ate mouthfuls of cheese, washing it down with river water from the cup of my hand.

I stole more—from the Yolamundi shop and from the supermarket in Nullabri again while Pop waited outside. I took oranges and butterscotch and more sausage and a can of beetroot. I stole Jax salt biscuits and tomato sauce. I built up supplies in the keepout, covering them with bark and leaves. I squirted tomato sauce onto the Jax and when the biscuits were finished

I smashed the can of beetroot against the rocks but it wouldn't open. I needed Dad's Smith. *Only point it at the thing you want to kill.* I put the unopened can on my shelf; I could use it as a weapon. I sat in my keepout, jam sticky on my cheeks, the taste of cold sausage in my mouth, watching through the branches. I was as still as the tawny frogmouth in the tree—couldn't tell if I was tree or tawny. I saw a wallaby. I was a hunter like the Comanche Indian. The forest and the Murray were my camouflage. I threw my spear. The wallaby bounded away. The world outside my keepout was gone. Summer was a long time ago.

I was always back at Pop's for tea. He boiled eggs and fried eggs and scrambled eggs and poached them, and I ate every egg. He didn't ask about school. No letters came. He didn't make me go.

One night I took the matches from the jar. I pulled in branches from the other side of the fence. I crumpled the paper, lay the sticks and struck the match. Then I sat back in Pop's camp chair and watched the flames burn bright. It had been a long time since there had been a fire. I warmed my hands, holding them open at the flames as if I was surrendering like Regret in *The Comancheros*. I lay my hands across my gut of hardening blood as the flames warmed my wet knees.

Pop stepped out the back door. His hair was knotted, his eyes puffed. 'Smelled smoke,' he said. He came slowly down to the fire carrying a beer, and I got off his camp chair and sat on the stool. Pop sat down and the flames turned his face orange. He held out the palms of his hands to the heat as if he, too, surrendered.

It was just Pop and me now. The back-house at the bottom of the yard was locked and nothing could escape, and Dad, far away, couldn't escape either. Pop and me weren't waiting for him anymore.

Later I helped him peel and chop and stir the onions. Our eyes watered and stung. Pop said, 'Hold your bloody nose.' He put butter over the egg and the onion, and it mixed with the yolk to make a sauce for our chicken. Butter and chicken oil dripped from our chins as the flames crackled, keeping us warm.

'Doesn't get better, hey, Jussy?' said Pop, taking a sip from his beer.

'No, Pop.'

46.

I was in the kitchen the next morning, doing the dishes when Pop asked me to fill the kettle. As I turned to take the kettle from his hands Pop looked down at my stomach. Between my skirt and skivvy there was a small gap like a smiling mouth. Pop frowned. Bubbles dripped from my wet hands. Pop was staring at my stomach. His mouth dropped open. I put the kettle on the bench and tried to pull the skivvy down over my gut. Pop couldn't close his mouth. He went from my stomach to my face. He said, 'Justine . . .' I wiped my hands on my skirt, pulling my top down again.

Pop stepped towards me and hit me across the back of my head. 'Jesus, Justine! Jesus! What have you been doing?' I didn't know what I'd been doing; I wasn't sure. 'For God's sake!' He hit me across the back of my head again and I fell forward over the sink. I felt dizzy. I had to grip the sink. My gut wriggled and jumped. He said, 'Not you too, Justine—the whole bloody world, but not you! Get out of my sight!'

I sat on the bed and put my hands on my stomach. It moved as if Pop's bug had crawled inside and grown huge. I lay down, pulling the covers up to my chin. I couldn't get warm. *The whole bloody world, but not you.* What did Pop mean? What had I done? I lay on one side and then the other. It was raining outside. I knew something but it was in the shadows and wouldn't come into the light. Something I had done to my pop that he hadn't wanted me to do. Something that the whole bloody world had done before to hurt him. The Japs, Aunty Rita, my dad had all done it, and now I had done it too. I stayed in bed a long time. The rain didn't stop. Soon the house would be underwater, like the trees caught in The Choke.

———

When it was night Pop came into my room and sat on the edge of the bed. 'You'd think I'd learn,' he said. He rubbed his forehead and sighed. 'Who did this to you?'

I shook my head. I didn't know what I was saying no to.

'Justine,' he said, 'who did this to you?'

I didn't know. But at the same time I did. It was something that happened the night at the river.

He said, 'Justine—who?'

I remembered the night in pieces—the water, the stars, the car, a weight above me—but what was done to me? Was it what Julie and Annette meant? I started to cry. I didn't know things, but I did know them.

Pop put his hand on my face, gently. 'Oh, Lizzy . . .' he said. 'Jesus.'

Later I heard him talking on the telephone. 'G'day, Narelle,' he said. 'Relle, can you put Steve on? . . . G'day, Steve—do you know what Justine's been up to? . . . Put your mother back on . . . Why didn't you tell me, Relle?' Then there was no talking. Pop put down the telephone. He came back into my room.

He said, 'Justine.' He shook his head and looked at his feet in slippers then back up at me on the bed. 'Have you been with Jamie Worlley?'

I wanted to vomit.

'Justine?' he said. 'Tell me.'

I shook my head.

He said, 'Relle told me, Justine.'

'What does Relle know?' I asked. Tears rose up around my voice, trying to drown my words. Relle had never seen me, never looked at me even once in her life.

'She talked to Steve. Steve knew. They saw you. Steve said they couldn't stop you. You were with him, weren't you? Jamie Worlley?'

I shook my head. Pieces were missing. It was the breech. I didn't understand. The cloud of that night. Stacey, Sherry, my dad, Jamie's car . . . I didn't know.

Pop was crying. 'Jesus, I'm too old for this, Lizzy,' he said. 'Help me . . .' He got up and left.

I heard him go to the laundry and take beers out of the esky. I heard the creak of the screen door as he went outside to drink. My gut kicked and moved and growled with hunger.

47.

I sat beside Pop in his truck that grumbled and stopped and started as he drove down Dray Road. 'Why do I have to go?' I asked him.

'You do what I say from now on, Justine. Shut your mouth.'

My stomach pressed against my dress. I felt sick. We were on the way to the Worlleys. The Mauser sat between us, leaning against the seat like a third passenger. I didn't know if it was my friend or my enemy. Was Pop going to shoot Jamie? Ian Worlley? Mother Margy?

Pop turned into the Worlleys' road, past the cows and the dam with the car and the island for the geese, then down to the caravans. There were two more than there had been when we were last here. There were tyres in a tower. Pop stopped the truck in front of the circle. Mother Margy came out of one of the caravans. She wore a long purple dress that hung around her feet like a tent.

'Jesus,' Pop whispered to himself, 'Jesus, it's Margy.' When Pop was friends with the Worlleys it was Mother Margy who fed him the most. She said the war took the meat from men's bones and didn't give it back. 'Jesus,' Pop said again, then slowly he picked up the Mauser, opened his door and climbed out. He stood beside the truck holding the Mauser with its barrel pointed at the ground.

Mother Margy nodded at Pop. 'Robert,' she called across to him. Then she looked past him to me sitting in the truck.

'Where is he?' said Pop.

'Who?'

'You know who.'

'If it's Jamie you're after, he's not here.'

'Where is he?' said Pop, changing his grip on the Mauser, lifting it higher.

'Nowhere. You better go.'

'Or what?'

'Or there'll be trouble.'

'There's trouble already. My Justine's in trouble.'

'Rob, I'm telling you to go.'

'I'm not going until I see your boy.'

'Leave it alone, Rob.'

'Do you know what he did to her?'

'Got a fair idea.'

'She's fourteen. Thirteen at the time.'

'I know, Robert. Jamie's a bastard. So is your Ray.'

'Stacey's not a bloody kid.'

'Stacey can't look after that daughter of hers now. A lot of days she can't get out of bed.'

'That's up to her.'

'Ray nearly killed her. That wasn't up to her. You get out of here, take Justine with you.'

Pop said, 'Jesus. Margy . . .'

'Take your stupid bloody gun and your granddaughter and go home,' she said. 'And I never saw you.'

Pop looked around the circle of caravans. There was nobody else here. I heard the sound of crying. It was the same crying I had been hearing since the night Dad took me to visit Stacey. A little girl stepped out of the door of the last caravan. Pop and Margy turned to look at her. She stood on the top step in pink underpants. Her hair stuck up from the top of her head in a ponytail. Her face was red with crying. It was Sherry. Tears came down her face. 'Nanna, Nanna, Nanna! Where's Mummy? Nanny, where's my mummy?' Sherry's cry rang out over the circle of caravans, loud enough for Stacey to hear where she lay in her half-built house.

Pop looked at Mother Margy, who looked back at Pop.

'Mummy! Mummy!'

They were both old. Their hair grey, their faces lined, eyes hidden in the falling skin, their bodies leaning, tired.

Pop turned and walked back to the truck.

48.

The next day Pop said, 'We're going into town.'
'What town?' I asked him.
'Echuca. Get your shoes on.'
'What for?' Pop hated Echuca.
Pop said, 'Just get in the truck.'
'What for, Pop?'
He said, 'Haven't you bloody worked that out yet? Get your shoes on.'

I didn't know what he meant. As I bent to pull on my shoes my gut pushed up against my chest. What was I meant to work out?

I held on to the window ledge of the truck as Pop drove, and looked out for the trucks as they came in the opposite direction. The trucks had twenty wheels and carried logs from the Yolamundi forest. The drivers knew the direction they were travelling; they could keep going, they had everything they needed in the truck. I turned and watched until they were gone.

When we came into Echuca Pop drove to a house with a sign out the front that I couldn't read. Pop parked the truck and we got out. I followed him into the house.

We sat in a room with chairs around the wall and a small table in the corner, with magazines and a box of books for children. There was a long counter on one side with a lady wearing a white dress working behind it. Pop sat beside me; he smelled sour. Even though it was a cold day Pop's face was damp with sweat. As he rolled a cigarette, his hands shook. Strands of White Ox fell from his fingers. Pop put the rolled cigarette in his shirt pocket. It was as if Pop only belonged to the Three, not to the world outside, and trying to join it made him sweat and shake. The lady behind the counter said, 'Robert Lee?'

Pop stood, dropping his keys. I picked them up and passed them to him. 'Come on,' he said to me.

The lady in the white dress pointed to a door, and we went through. A man as old as my pop was sitting at a desk. He wore a suit with a tie around his neck and glasses with thin metal frames on his face. I couldn't tell the difference between glass and skin. He held out his hand and said to my pop, 'Mr Lee, I'm Dr Manning.'

Pop nodded. 'This is my granddaughter, Justine.'

The man glanced at my gut, his face serious. 'Perhaps I had better examine Justine first, then you and I can speak after the examination, Mr Lee.'

'Alright, then,' said Pop, and left the room.

I was alone now with Dr Manning. The doctor looked over his glasses at me. He said, 'Do you know why you are here?'

I looked at the legs of the desk and the doctor's shoes.

Dr Manning said, 'You are here because of your own actions, your behaviour. It's important you understand that. Can you take off your underwear and get onto the examination bed for me, please, Justine?' He pulled back a curtain and showed me a thin bed on steel rails, covered with a white sheet.

I pulled off my underpants and held them bunched in my hand as I climbed onto the bed. I didn't understand what he meant by my behaviour and my actions.

Dr Manning put a sheet over my legs. He said, 'Lie down, please.'

I lay on my back, my gut pushing up to my throat.

Dr Manning lifted my top and felt my stomach with his long, cool fingers. He measured my gut with a tape measure and wrote some things down on a piece of paper. He took a rubber glove from a box. 'Knees up, please,' he said, pulling on the glove.

I lifted my knees and Dr Manning reached in between my legs and pushed his fingers into me.

I gasped. Dr Manning twisted his fingers. My stomach rose higher, as if it was trying to move away. I closed my eyes tight; from behind my lids I saw the walls of Jamie's car and tasted vomit and hot mint.

Dr Manning pulled out his fingers and peeled off the glove. He said, 'You can sit up now.'

I pulled down my skirt and sat up on the bed.

Dr Manning said, 'You're five and a half months pregnant, Justine.'

I felt dizzy. *Five and a half months pregnant.* What did he mean?

Dr Manning helped me down from the table. He said to me, 'Please wait outside while I speak with your grandfather.' He spoke into a machine on his desk, 'Send in Mr Lee.'

A voice came through the machine: 'Yes, doctor.'

Pop walked slowly, carefully back into the room, his face pale. There were damp circles under the arms of his shirt. The nurse stood at the door. I went out and Dr Manning closed the door behind me.

I sat in the waiting room and a mother came in with a little girl. The mother took the little girl to a box of books in the corner. The mother pulled out some books. 'You play with those, Tilly, while we wait to see the doctor,' she said. She sat back on her chair and the girl looked up at me with wide eyes.

Soon Pop came out with Dr Manning and they went to the counter together. Dr Manning said to the lady in the white dress, 'Please give Mr Lee the information brochure we have for St Jude's.'

'Of course, doctor.' The lady passed some papers to Pop. Pop took money from his wallet and paid her. I followed him out of the doctor's house.

The papers the nurse had given Pop flapped against his chest as we crossed the road. 'It's going to be taken care of,' he said.

I didn't know if he was telling me or the road. 'You'll go to the hospital when it's time. Then it will be over and done.'

We got into the truck. My stomach rippled and bumped.

'You won't be gone long.' Was he telling himself, or me?

'Where am I going, Pop?'

He turned the key and didn't answer.

Five and a half months pregnant. It was like it was happening to somebody else and that other person knew and understood what it meant, but I, Justine, did not. Something was between me and knowing, like the veil that covered Stacey's face when she married Brian Chisholm. I put my hand on my gut. I didn't want there to be anything in it. I only wanted it to be me.

When we got home, Pop put the papers from the doctor on the kitchen table. I saw a picture of a brick building with a cross on top and two nurses walking along the path in front smiling. Underneath that was a picture of a woman holding flowers and a baby. Pop said, 'You need to sign these, Justine.' He picked up one of the papers and took a pen from the jar on the window sill. 'Here.' He put his finger on a line. Then he crossed the kitchen to fill the kettle at the sink.

Without Pop's finger to keep it still, the line moved. I couldn't do it. I left the pen and papers on the table.

Pop set the kettle on the stove. 'That's the girl,' he said, pushing the papers into the shelf under the knives and forks. 'Come and get the eggs.'

49.

The trip to Dr Manning was the last one. Nobody saw me after that, not even Steve; Relle and him never came over anymore. I stayed at Pop's and I didn't even go with him in the truck to do the shopping. When I stood up to fix the aerial on the television I could feel Pop staring at my gut. It pushed out my jumper like a white balloon. Later I found a checked shirt of Dad's in the laundry, long and wide enough to hide it.

The rain fell as my stomach grew and the Murray rose higher between its banks. The news said it was the highest rainfall of the winter. Pop looked at the radio and said, *You don't need to tell me, mate.*

I built a truck outside my keepout at the river. I made the sides and the cabin with branches, and built a bed in the space behind the steering wheel. I brought down all the clothes that wouldn't fit and made them into pillows and a roof and a mattress. I hung a green-and-red lorikeet feather from my mirror. I watched from the cabin as the rain fell. Emus moved through the trees, lifting their feet over the roots and pecking at the grass. *I've a mind to kill.* I raised the Smith and shot my dinner.

I made a spear and stood in the shallows, watching for the cod. I saw one moving more slowly apart from the others, as if it wasn't as strong, as if its body wouldn't do what it needed. I took aim, my spear hovering over the slow cod that couldn't even make its own body do what it wanted. I held my spear and looked at my target, the thing I wanted to kill—*only one of you will die today, which one will it be?* I stabbed the cod with my spear. I didn't know what to do with it when I pulled it from the water. I put it on the bank. It wriggled and jumped and flapped. Tears came from my eyes. It was a long time before the fish was still. Dirt covered its scales. I tried to gut it but I tore the meat.

The Murray flooded. The water spilled over and came up higher over the red gums that held on and held on and didn't break, weren't washed away, weren't even scared. I was always wet, my socks damp inside my sneakers, my pants soaked, my jumper heavy with rain and river.

I stayed with my river-truck at my keepout home more and more, coming up to the house later and later. I knew the path in the darkness. Silver came with me. John Wayne on the Miracle Horse followed behind. Pop never asked where I'd been. He drank beers inside and didn't light the fire. He told the chooks about me. *Silly bitch. Our Justine. Even her. Sometimes I wonder. I should be laying in the jungle alongside the bloody sleepers, a train over my head.*

———

At night it took me a long time to roll over. I tucked clothes under my gut so it didn't fall to the side and tear my skin. I couldn't sleep. I didn't do cut-outs. I closed my eyes and made pictures of my truck and the Murray at The Choke. I watched the banks trying to touch. I watched the water flowing faster the longer it rained. I only spoke to the chooks. I said, *Hey, chook chook chook.* I changed their food and raked and gave them new straw. *Hey, girls!* I sat in the chook run and let them come around me. *Hey, girls; hey there,* I said, *hey there.* I said, *My behaviour, Madame; hey, Missy, my behaviour, my actions,* and Missy came right to me and sat in my lap against my gut and she rested there and her warm body under my hands was the only thing dry.

50.

One day Pop looked at the calendar on his wall and said, 'We leave Monday.' I didn't know what day it was anymore; I never asked.

I said, 'Where are we going?' I was on my way down to the keepout; I had supplies in my backpack for the truck: bread and a can opener and bottle tops for bullets.

He said, 'Bloody hospital. It's time.'

'Where is the hospital?' I asked him.

'Don't you listen to anything I tell you? Geelong,' he said. 'Bloody miles away. I want you to have a bath before we leave.'

'Why?'

'Because you stink.'

⸺

Two days later, in the morning, before I'd left the house, Pop filled the bath.

I said, 'Is it Monday?'

He said, 'It is.'

'I don't want a bath.'

'And I don't want you covered in river dirt when you get to the hospital. Pregnant is bad enough. Get your clothes off,' he said, and left the bathroom.

I undid the buttons on Dad's shirt. It was hard to step over the sides of the bath; my gut took my balance, and my breath. I didn't want to look down. I pushed the water in the bath around my sides with my hands, and rubbed the soap over my arms and neck and across my swollen chest. The Murray dirt made a ring around the bath the same as the one around the house. I traced it with my fingers, smudging the dirt, and wrote words. *Erad ot wonk*. My gut wriggled as if there was a lizard trapped inside. I wished I could pull open a lid, like the one in Pop's can of beer, and let it out.

There was a dress and coat on the sink in the bathroom with tags from a shop. The dress had flowers on it, a yellow collar and long sleeves. Pop must have bought it for me. It was a dress Mrs Turning might have worn.

'Hurry up, Justine, let's get moving,' Pop said from the other side of the door.

I held on to the taps as I pulled myself up from the water. After I was dry I put the dress Pop had left for me over my head and pulled on the coat. When I bent over to put on my sneakers, I could hardly breathe.

I went out and got in the truck with Pop.

'I've put some of your things in a suitcase,' said Pop. 'It's in the back.'

I didn't know what he would have packed. I didn't do my cut-outs anymore. I didn't fit any other shoes or clothes. I didn't have Aunty Rita's numbers anymore. Everything I wanted was at my keepout.

'Pray she makes it,' Pop said. He turned the key and the truck coughed. 'Christ, not today.' He tried the key again and the truck started. 'Thank God,' said Pop.

We drove for hours. The highway didn't end. I leaned against the seat and slept, the acid in my throat rising from my gut. When I next woke I saw tall buildings in the distance and a long, high bridge. Pop said, 'When you're done you can come home.'

My gut cramped as if it was being stuck with the same spear I used to catch the cod. *When you're done.* I knew what those words meant, didn't I? I was going to the hospital to have a baby, and then I would be done. I knew what the words meant, but they belonged to somebody else, not to me. My back and legs ached.

After we crossed the bridge Pop checked his map. 'Where the hell?' He looked up at the road ahead, then at his map again. He wiped sweat from his forehead. 'Where the hell is the place?'

We drove in a circle past the same shop, the same bus stop, the same fence. He took another road and there was the sea.

'Stop,' I said. 'Stop, Pop!'

'What is it, for Christ's sake?'

'Stop, Pop. Park there.' I pointed across the road at a car park on the cliff. 'Then you can look at the map.'

'Alright, al-bloody-right.' Pop pulled over into the car park and stopped the truck. He looked up through the window at the sea and shook his head, then turned his map upside down, holding it back from his face.

I got out of the truck, my hands around my gut, and walked to the rail. I breathed in the clean, salty air and looked out to the ocean. It was as wide as the sky, and moving. This was where the Murray led, where all the rivers in Michael's map book led—this was the way to Antarctica. I breathed in deep. My gut wriggled and kicked.

'Justine!' Pop called. 'I found the place on the bloody map.'

This was what surrounded the world. I breathed it in one last time.

'Justine, get a move on!'

He drove us down a quiet street with houses on both sides. At the very end was a building with two levels. I recognised the building—it was the one on the papers Dr Manning's nurse had given to Pop.

'St Jude's,' Pop said. 'Saint of the bloody hopeless is right.'

He parked the truck on the road outside the building. There were no other trucks; Pop's was covered in Yolamundi dirt, tied with twine, its mesh tray full of straw and hardened with chook shit. As we stood on the street looking up at the brick building, Pop seemed to shrink. He held my suitcase in one hand and gripped my arm with the other.

We walked up the steps to the doors.

'Bloody Geelong,' he said. 'Better than the bloody city, I suppose. Leave that to bloody Ray. Pentridge, for Christ's sake. Jesus!'

Pop pushed open the doors at the top of the steps and we went inside. There were women in white uniforms behind a desk. They didn't smile at my pop as we crossed the tiles. The biggest one said, 'I am Matron Carting. Your name, please?'

Pop said, 'This is my granddaughter, Justine Lee.'

Matron Carting checked her book. 'Here she is. Justine Lee. You're late—you were due here on the fifteenth. My notes say Justine is past her due date.'

'Thought I'd keep her out of trouble as long as I could,' said Pop. He sounded like he was scared of getting in trouble himself.

The matron frowned. 'If you'd like to say goodbye to your grandfather, Justine, we can take you to the ward.'

My pop turned to me. 'When this is done you can put it behind you. Start fresh.'

'Okay, Pop.'

He squeezed my hand. He was brown and lined, marked with the tracks that ran between the jungles. Everything here was white and smooth. 'I'll come and pick you up when it's over.' I watched as he turned and walked out the doors.

51.

Matron Carting took me into a room with six beds. There were girls lying in four of them. The girls lay on their sides or up against the pillows. They were reading or sleeping and one was knitting a scarf. All their guts were big like mine. They looked up at me.

'This is your bed,' said the matron. 'This is your cupboard. You can unpack your things. The nurse will come around and examine you before dinner. The bathroom is through that door.' She pointed. 'Dinner will be brought in at six.' She left the room.

Another girl came through the bathroom door. She held her gut with her hands. 'I can't stand this,' she said.

'Should have thought of that nine months ago,' the girl knitting the scarf said.

'Too busy enjoying myself, wasn't I?' the girl said, lying down on her bed.

The knitting girl snorted. 'Weren't we all?' She turned to me. 'My name is Leslie. And that's Mona. Over there, snoring her head off, is Lucy, and that's Debbie.' The girls said hi and I looked at the ground.

Leslie said, 'You're a bit young to be here, aren't you?'

I sat down on my bed. I didn't unpack the suitcase. I lay on my side and wished I was done and could be in the keepout with a pouch of Pop's White Ox.

'How old are you?' said Leslie.

I didn't answer.

'Don't be shy, we're all in the same boat.'

'Some boat,' said Mona.

'How old?' Leslie asked.

'Fourteen,' I said.

'*What?*' said Leslie.

'Are you kidding?' said Mona. 'Did you say fourteen? I thought seventeen was bad.'

A woman in a white dress and white hat came into the room.

'Hi, Nurse Patty,' all the girls said at once.

'Hello, ladies,' said the nurse. 'I hope you're all being good.' Nurse Patty checked the clipboard at the foot of my bed. 'Hello, Justine,' she said. 'I'm Nurse Patty. I'm a trainee.'

'Our *favourite* trainee,' said Leslie.

'That's only because I spoil you.' Nurse Patty smiled.

'And because the others are horrible,' said Leslie. 'Nurse Undine . . . horrible.'

'Nurse Withers,' said Mona. 'Now there's someone who needs to be spoiled.'

'Shhhh,' said Nurse Patty. 'Don't scare Justine.' She started to pull the curtain around my bed. 'Behave yourselves.'

'Bit late,' said Mona and they all laughed. Nurse Patty rolled her eyes at me.

She looked at the clipboard. 'Your history says you were due . . . yesterday, could that be right?' Nurse Patty's face was smooth with white skin and pink on her cheeks. Her hair was dark, each strand as thick as cotton, and shining. It was tied up with a blue ribbon like a strip of sky. 'Can I have a look at your belly, Justine?' She lifted my dress. My gut rose up white and round as the moon. 'Sorry, my hands are cold,' she said, rubbing them together. 'Nothing worse.' Nurse Patty put her hands on my gut. I watched it move. 'You've got a live one,' she said.

I didn't want a live one. I only wanted to go back to my keepout home, back to my river-truck, my ammunition.

Nurse Patty pressed my gut from the bottom to the top. 'Baby's head is in the right place,' she said. 'Like they say, nice and low, ready to go. You came to St Jude's just in time, I'd say.'

Baby's head is in the right place. I knew there was a baby in there, but when Nurse Patty used the word it was a surprise. As if, at the same time as knowing, I didn't know. Didn't want to know.

Nurse Patty pulled down my gown and put the blanket back over me. She wrote something on the clipboard. 'You are young to be here, Justine. Oh dear . . . I'm sorry this happened to you.' She touched my stomach.

I looked away from her, towards the window too high to see through.

Nurse Patty sighed. 'Whoever did this to you is a bastard. I don't know if I'm meant to say that or not, but it's the truth. Fourteen years old . . .' She clicked her tongue. 'They'll find a home for it, that's the only good to come of all this.'

A home for it. I hadn't thought about it being something that needed a home. It was a lump in my gut that Pop said would soon be gone. It wasn't anything.

Nurse Patty smiled. 'It won't be long now, Justine. Then all this will be behind you. You can start again. You can go back to school. You can think about what you want to do with your life.'

Her voice was smooth, without cracks or damage, as if it had come from another country, not Yolamundi. I grabbed her hand as she turned to leave.

'Oh, Justine. I have to finish my rounds or I'll be hung, drawn and quartered.' She took my hand from hers. 'Tell you what, I'll come check on you first thing tomorrow morning, okay? I'll make it my special mission.' Nurse Patty pulled open my curtain and left.

52.

That night I woke with rag pain in my gut. Sour water rose in my throat. I rolled to the other side, and water leaked down between my legs. I closed my eyes and saw the Murray thick with cod, running through Yolamundi all the way to the sea. I wished I was there. Minutes passed. I heard the other girls snoring from their beds. I put my hand on my stomach. It bumped against me as if it was trying to push my hand out of the way. The rag pain was gone. I slept on the wet mattress as the river flowed through me, pouring from my scar onto the hospital mattress.

I was woken again by a pain that moved across me like a wave on the Murray after a storm. I held my breath and rolled over. Acid bubbled in my throat from the weight of my gut. I heard nurses talking outside the door. I tried to sit up and more water came out from between my legs. Were my rags coming? I felt sick. I lay back down on the bed. My gut thumped from the inside as if one of Pop's chicks was tapping on the shell. I lay and listened to the soft snoring of the other girls. I breathed in time to their noisy breaths, in and out, until I slept again.

When I next woke I saw the first light of day through the window. Behind it I saw a wave of pain rolling towards me; not made of water but of dirt. I groaned.

'Justine? Are you alright?' It was Leslie from the next bed.

I was bunched up tight, biting down against the pain. Then the wave passed over me and was gone. I took a breath.

'Justine? Are you okay?'

I opened my eyes. In the distance I saw another wave made of ground, and stones and dirt rolling towards me. The wave was bigger than the ones before. I cried out and vomit burned my throat.

'Justine, I'm going to get the nurse!'

I was underneath a wave made of mud. Could a wave be outside and inside? Could it be both? Like knowing and not knowing?

I heard Leslie leave her bed. 'Matron! Matron! It's Justine!' she called. I wanted to stop her. I didn't want the matron to come. I wanted to be alone, by myself at the river, empty of the thing inside me so I could lie on my back in the water, my gut flat.

I saw another wave coming towards me, rising out of the ground, as big as a mountain, then it came down hard, breaking over me. My mouth clamped shut. I was crushed underneath.

'Justine? Justine, we need to move you. You're having the baby.'

I lifted my head and saw a nurse I didn't know. She was old with black wings on her head and the cross around her neck. She shook her head at me. 'This is what happens, Justine. A baby. Never mind the pain.'

A baby? I didn't want a baby. I wanted it to be gone, out of me.

I saw another wave coming, made of dirt and stones, big enough to finish me.

'Justine, come on. Get up. Come on.'

I had to stand. There were two nurses now; they pushed me up but I was dropping, falling into their hands as the wave rolled over me.

'Okay, onto the bed.'

They lifted me onto another bed. I watched the ceiling change as they rolled me along the corridor, the wheels bumping over the ground. Another mountain came thundering towards me, as if it wanted to crush me again. Two nurses I didn't know hovered over the bed. They were old like Mrs Turning, their bodies in layers under their black costumes. They knew what happened with Jamie Worlley. It was wrong. It was my behaviour. The mountain of stones and froth and churning earth crashed over me. I was under it alone. There was no one that I knew. Nothing to save me.

The nurses wheeled me into a room and put a sheet over me. Another wave came, carrying the pain of a thousand rags all at once, and I screamed as the acid burned holes through the skin in my throat. Then, over the top of me, beside the faces of the matron and the nurses I didn't know, was Nurse Patty. She said, 'Oh, Justine,' and I could see she wanted to cry, and so I cried instead, in place of her, and she took my hand and said, 'Justine, you have to breathe.'

I heard the words outside of me but there was nothing I could do. I was in a battle, holding my breath was the only way to stay alive.

'Justine, hold my hand, squeeze my hand as hard as you need. Breathe this time.'

I opened my eyes and Nurse Patty said, 'With me, okay?' and she took a breath and let it go, so I did too.

I went deep into the heart of the mountain. It didn't care that I was there. Nobody did. I was in there alone. 'Aren't you needed upstairs, Nurse Patricia?' One of the older nurses said to Nurse Patty.

'Dr Rogerson said he'd rather I had the experience in the birthing ward, Nurse Undine,' Nurse Patty answered.

'Alright then,' said Nurse Undine as if she knew Nurse Patty had won. 'Her ankles, please.'

Nurse Patty tied my ankles to steel pedals. 'I'm sorry, Justine,' she said softly, keeping her eyes on my face.

Another wave bore down on me.

'Shhh,' said Nurse Patty. 'It will be okay, Justine.'

There were no windows in the room. It was as if the room had left the hospital and was just a room on its own, not part of Yolamundi or Geelong, not belonging to anywhere, just a room with me inside it in a battle. The doctors and the nurses could come and go, while I couldn't. The pain and me, in a war like the one Pop fought against the Japs. This was what changed him; this was what took the meat from his bones.

Then the shape of the pain changed. 'Nurse Patty, I need to go to the toilet,' I told her.

'You don't need to go to the toilet,' said Nurse Patty. She looked excited. 'It's the baby.'

'No, it's not,' I said. 'I need to use the toilet!' I couldn't talk anymore. I sat forward and went to the toilet. Then the pushing stopped and I lay back, panting like a dog.

'That's it, Justine,' said Nurse Patty. 'You're doing well.'

Nurse Undine gripped my leg. 'Not yet,' she said. Nurse Undine placed her hand on my stomach. She leaned in and looked between my legs. She pushed her fingers up between them, and pressed down. 'She isn't to push. Wait till I say.'

'I need to push, Nurse Patty,' I said. 'I need to push.' But the words were broken. It was as if I was being pushed from the inside. I made sounds I'd never made before—screaming and grunting. I didn't want it. I didn't want it inside me or outside me. I wanted to be in my keepout. I wanted to drive my river-truck to the sea.

'Push now,' said Nurse Undine. 'Hard as you can.'

Nurse Patty was beside me, looking down between my legs. There was sweat on her face and her cheeks were pink. I held her hand and squeezed when another push came. 'That's it,' said Nurse Patty. 'That's it.'

The baby was tearing me as if it held a knife in its teeth. I didn't want it to come out. I didn't want to see it or push it.

'Now again,' said Nurse Undine. 'And keep pushing this time, even when you want to stop. One more big one.'

I pushed. The other people in the room moved around like ghosts outside of me. They didn't count. Only Nurse Patty's hand in mine counted.

I felt it holding me open, I was prised apart, splitting like my mother before me. It was the breech—first I did it to her, and now it was being done to me, like punishment.

'I can see the head now,' said Nurse Undine. 'The next contraction should see us there.'

I pushed again, the biggest push of my life, and then something rushed from me, wet and slippery as a Murray eel.

Nurse Patty gasped. 'Justine,' she said. There was crying in her voice. 'You did it.' There were tears in her eyes.

'What?' I asked, my voice croaky.

'The baby is here, you funny thing,' she said. She put her hand on my forehead.

I lifted my head and saw Nurse Undine holding the outline of a body. I watched as she laid it on a tray.

'They're weighing him,' said Nurse Patty.

I couldn't see his face, only his outline, his side. I heard crying.

'It's a boy,' said Nurse Patty.

'Patricia . . .' Nurse Undine warned.

'A boy?' I said.

'Yes. Do you want to see him?'

'Patricia, that's enough!' Nurse Undine said.

Did I want to see him? Did I? 'Yes,' I said.

Nurse Undine huffed. 'Look what you've started,' she said to Nurse Patty.

Another wave was coming. Was it more? Was it another one?

'It's the placenta,' said Nurse Undine. What was that? Was it another baby?

'It's okay,' said Nurse Patty. 'Just the last bit, Justine, then it will all be over. One more push.' I started to cry. I couldn't hold on. The baby cried louder than me. It was a boy. 'Come on, Justine, nearly there.' I pushed and then something slid from me, smaller than the baby, and at last I was empty. I heard more crying.

'Can I see him?' I asked.

Nurse Undine was carrying the baby, wrapped in a white blanket, to a glass box.

'It will do you no good to see him, dear. And it won't do him any good either.'

A tall man wearing a white coat came into the room. 'Nurse, you are needed in ward eight. All hands.' He spoke quickly.

'Is it the Smith girl, Dr Rogerson?' Nurse Undine asked.

Dr Rogerson nodded. 'I'm afraid so.'

Nurse Undine put the baby into the glass box.

'Help this one wash up, Patricia,' she said. 'Nurse Withers will be back in a moment.'

'Yes, Nurse Undine,' said Nurse Patty.

Nurse Undine left, and Nurse Patty and me were alone in the room. 'Can I see him?' I asked her.

'Oh, Justine.' Nurse Patty chewed at her lip. 'Nurse Undine is right.'

'I want to see him,' I said. I kept my eyes on the baby in the glass box. I had never thought of the baby as a boy or a girl or a person. It had been something growing in me, but not a person.

Nurse Patty shook her head. 'I don't think so.'

'I want to see him,' I said. 'Nurse Patty, can I see him?'

Nurse Patty looked towards the door. 'Oh dear,' she said. I tried to stand.

'You stay there,' she said, pushing me gently back down.

'Please, Nurse Patty . . .' My voice was worn and quiet.

'Oh dear, how can I say no?'

She crossed the room to the glass box and she wheeled him to me. He was wrapped in a white blanket. His blue-grey eyes were open. I sat up and leaned down to him. He looked at me and started to cry and I felt where he had been inside me, now empty. It was as if the whole time he had been there I hadn't known it—I only knew it now. And now he was out of me in the glass box and when I looked at him I wasn't as young as before. I had been fourteen, but I was older than that now.

Nurse Patty said, 'Justine, you are still bleeding.'

I lifted the baby from the box and held him to my chest and I grew even older, as if years were passing. I grew older than Mrs Turning, older than Nurse Withers or the matron, older than my grandmother Lizzy. I was the oldest holding the youngest. I kissed his round cheek and his forehead. I closed my eyes and breathed him in and even though I didn't have a mother it didn't matter now because I was one.

'Justine!' Nurse Patty held out her hands.

I could've kept looking into the baby's eyes for a long time. I didn't want or need to stop. He went on behind his eyes, the way Michael Hooper did, as if the eyes were only the surface and by looking into them I could go to a world where there was room. Where I was needed.

'Justine,' said Nurse Patty. 'Come on.' She put her hands on him.

I said, 'Can I give him a name?'

'Oh dear,' said Nurse Patty again, looking towards the door.

'Can I?'

Nurse Patty sighed. 'Oh well, I don't see the harm . . .'

'What should I call him?'

'Whatever you like,' she said. She patted my shoulder. Then she looked at the door. 'Be quick, Justine.'

I didn't know what to call him. What names were there? What names for boys did I know? I closed my eyes. Black Beauty ran towards Joe Evans. He was the horse's best friend. Joe never gave up. In the end he said, *I knew we'd be together again, Beauty.* 'Can I call him Joe?'

'Whatever you like, Justine.'

'Joe Michael?'

'Yes, you can call him Joe Michael.'

'Thank you, Nurse Patty,' I said.

'That's no problem,' she said. She wiped more tears from her cheek. 'You have to give him back to me, Justine.'

'Do I, Nurse Patty? Do I have to?' The baby didn't belong in a box; he was too new to the world. He belonged with me, the one place he knew.

'You do.'

'But . . .'

'Justine, you have to give him back.'

'Alright,' I said. I held him one more minute, and all the warmth of life was in the hold—there was nothing missing or wanting. It was as if the baby Joe had lit Pop's fire inside me and made me warm.

'Justine? Justine, you have to give him back to me now. I am sorry . . .'

I gave him to her.

Nurse Patty laid the baby back in the glass box then she checked the sheet on my bed. I kept my eyes on the baby in the box; I'd never had anything before, and now I had a baby.

'Lie down now, Justine. We need to clean up this blood.' She ran to the door. 'Dr Rogerson!' she called. 'Matron!'

I was in a dream with the baby. Things around him went cloudy. Only he was sharp and clear. I could see his eyes from where I lay. I didn't care about the bleeding or Nurse Patty moving quickly around me, or Dr Rogerson coming back into the room. I didn't care when Dr Rogerson cleaned me, looking between my legs; I didn't care when Nurse Withers took the bloody sheets from under me, or when Nurse Patty left the room. In the dream I was with the baby, with Joe. We were together. It was my job to look after him so he wouldn't be alone. So he wouldn't wonder what he had done wrong. In the dream it wasn't hard. It was easy. It was the right way and I knew it, for the first time.

But then Nurse Undine went to my baby in his box and began to wheel him out of the room. He couldn't see me anymore and my dream was broken. He was taken away from me. He started to cry as Nurse Undine wheeled him through the door. 'No, no!' I cried out.

Nurse Withers rolled me over and put a needle in my backside.

53.

When I next woke I was in a different room. I saw pink roses through the window, growing towards the glass. All the beds were empty except the one beside mine, where a girl lay sleeping. I put my hand on my stomach; it felt soft and empty.

Everything was slow. I heard sounds coming from outside the room, metal on metal, wheels, voices. The room was quiet. I kept listening. I took a breath and let it out slowly, and then I heard him. Not a sound outside me—a sound inside, a crying and calling.

The girl in the bed beside me sat up. 'When did you have it?' she asked.

I closed my eyes to see the baby's face again. His eyes were shining grey like the Yolamundi light, shot through with the blue of sky. There wasn't an end to them; they kept going, like water. I sat up, awake now.

The girl said, 'You lost a gallon of blood. That's two milk bottles. I lost a lot too, but not as much as you—I heard the nurses. You're lucky you're still alive. What's your name?'

I turned my face away. I had to listen for Joe Michael.

'I'm Candy,' she said. 'It's not my real name, but I like it more than Margaret. I'll go home tomorrow. Once they can stop the milk from coming.' She pressed her hands on her chest. 'It's disgusting. And it hurts like hell. They'll give me a pill soon and it will stop like magic. What did you have?'

I didn't want to talk. I wanted to listen for Joe Michael.

'I had a boy,' she said. 'They told me he's already got a home. The mother and father were waiting for me to have him, providing everything was normal.' She sat up in bed and drank from a glass of water. 'Ten fingers, ten toes.' She held up her hands, spreading her fingers. 'I asked Nurse Undies if they'll ever tell him about me, or will they trick him and say she was the mother, and Nurse Undies said they wouldn't tell him, that he deserves a good start no matter where he's come from.'

Candy had a lot to say. I had nothing. Words were in my head, but I couldn't speak them. *He's already got a home.* It was as if I was only understanding now, even though I'd known all along. Mrs Turning said I was slow; was this what she meant? Things were taking time to catch up. Candy knew her baby had a home. What about my baby? I wished I could hold him again. I put my hands to my chest; it didn't hurt like Candy's. Did I have milk? I wished I could see my baby. I wished it more than anything. Did somebody else want him? Had they been waiting? Why did Candy know and not me? I closed my eyes to hear his cry; it was still there, calling for me from inside. I had to go to him. I had to find someone to help me.

'Where is Nurse Patty?' I asked Candy.

'Who?'

'Nurse Patty.'

'I don't know any Patties. Is she nice?'

'Yes,' I said. 'Yes, she is.'

'I only get the mean ones,' she said. 'Like Nurse Undies. Or Nurse Withered-up. I wish the milk would stop. It's awful.' She squeezed her chest. 'I wish they'd give me that pill so I can get out of here. I've got a job waiting for me. It's in the business park just outside town. I'll be answering the phones. It's a new system; they have twenty phones ringing at the same time. I'll get my licence soon.'

I could hear Joe crying, calling for me, under the other hospital sounds. Nothing had ever called for me before. Joe wanted me more than anyone. I was his only one, and he was mine. I wished I could be with him. I wished I had Pop's Mauser. *That baby belongs to me, nurse. Give him back.*

Nurse Undine came in and looked at the clipboard at the end of my bed. 'I need to check your pad, Justine,' she said. She lifted my sheet and checked between my legs. 'You need to keep changing these, you know. You need to stay clean and dry to prevent infection.' She tapped a white box of pads that had been sitting beside the bed. 'Your mother will need to have plenty ready. It goes on for a while. Go to the bathroom now and give yourself a wash with soap and water. You need to do that every day, twice a day. Hot water and soap. Go on.'

I got out of the bed and Nurse Undine showed me to the bathroom. There was a shower with a plastic chair underneath it. I sat down in the chair and listened. I could still hear Joe calling me. I wished I could hold him.

When I looked down I saw blood smeared on the white plastic of the chair. But I didn't want to turn on the shower in case it muffled the sound of Joe's cries. I had only ever said *I love you* to Silver. I wished I could say it to the baby, into his ear. I'd say it over and over. *I love you, Joe. I love you, Joe. I love you.* It didn't matter what he did or where he went or what happened to him, he'd always know it, because I told him so many times, so deep into his ear that he'd never forget. *I love you, Joe. I love you.* The words would be a song. *I love you I love you I love you, Joe, I love you* and the song would never end, it would be under all sounds, all movement, all change, the way his crying was now.

The nurse called through the door, 'Go on, get the water going. I don't want to have to come in and do it for you.'

I turned on the tap, and water dripped over me, but I kept my head out for the sound. 'Joe Michael,' I whispered. 'Joe Michael, where are you? Are you still here?'

———

That night Nurse Patty came to me for the first time since I'd had the baby. Her face was as smooth as ever and she wore a white ribbon in her hair. I sat up straight in the bed. 'Justine,' she said. 'How are you? I wanted to come sooner but Nurse Undine kept me busy.' She sat down on the side of my bed and looked into my eyes. 'Are you okay? You did so well.'

'Where is my baby?' I asked her.

She frowned. 'Oh, Justine . . .'

'Where is he, Nurse Patty?'

Nurse Patty put her hand on mine. 'You don't need to worry about that,' she said.

'Did they find a home for him?'

She shook her head. 'No . . . no they didn't. Not yet. But, Justine, I'm not sure that—'

'So he's here? He's still here—in the hospital?'

'Yes, he is, Justine. He is alive and healthy. You don't need to worry about a thing.'

He was still here! My baby was still here at St Jude's! He wasn't with me in the bed, I couldn't see his eyes or hold him or smell his skin, I couldn't sing to him or feed him milk, but he was here, in the building. Breath that had been trapped inside since Nurse Undine took Joe Michael finally left my body. 'Could you take me to him?'

'You know I can't do that,' Nurse Patty said, fiddling with the hem of my sheet.

'Why not?'

'It's against the rules.'

'Why?'

'Because ... because ... Justine, you gave him up for adoption.' She looked at me. 'You can't see him. You know that, don't you?'

'No.'

'Hasn't anybody explained it to you?'

'I didn't give him up.'

'Yes, you did, Justine. That's why you're here at St Jude's. Because you gave him up. Don't you understand that?'

'I don't know. I want to see him. Why can't I see him?'

'He's going to be adopted. You gave him up.'

'But I didn't. I didn't give him up!'

'You wouldn't be here if you hadn't given him up. There's no point in you seeing him. The baby belongs to the hospital until he is adopted, and then he'll belong to his new parents.'

I *had* heard it, *did* know it, but understanding had been buried. Now I understood, only now. 'But he's mine, Nurse Patty. Joe Michael is mine.'

'He's not yours, Justine. I mean, he was yours, but you're so young, with your whole life ahead of you.'

She went to touch my cheek but I pushed her hand away. What whole life was ahead of me? I had never known about it. Everything that had been was finished, over, and now there was Joe Michael. He was the thing that had come. He was the whole life. I wished I had a gun. I would make Nurse Patty put her hands in the air. Then I'd take my baby.

'But he's mine. I had him, Nurse Patty.'

'Yes, you did. But you are too young to take care of a baby. You need to take care of yourself first. You need to finish school and grow up. Make a life for yourself. Find a nice man to marry.' She smiled at me. 'Then you can have a baby of your own.'

But I had a baby of my own now. It was the one thing I did have. 'Can I see him?'

She shook her head. 'I'm sorry, Justine—it's just not possible.' Her mouth went flat and firm. Not possible . . . but if I wanted it why wasn't it possible? Why did everybody else choose what was possible for me?

I turned away from Nurse Patty. I wanted to listen for Joe Michael. I closed my eyes. It was a better way to see him. His face, his small nose, the bow of his lips, his small ears.

'Don't be like that, Justine. We're friends, remember?' I heard the crackle of paper as she pulled something from her pocket. 'I've brought you lollies.'

The sound came between me and the baby; I didn't want lollies. Blood trickled from between my legs onto the pad. I wished Joe was here. John Wayne as Quirt held the gun at the face of the enemy. *I only want what's mine.*

I heard Nurse Patty leaving. I know she wanted me to say goodbye, as if we were friends, but I didn't want to. She knew where Joe Michael was. She could hold him, kiss his head, sing to him. She could have taken me to him.

54.

In the morning, when the breakfast nurse wheeled in the trays, she said to Candy, 'Your mother will be here in an hour. You can pack your clothes into your suitcase.'

'At last!' said Candy, throwing back her covers. She pulled her white gown over her head. 'I feel like I'm getting out of prison.' She took a yellow dress from the cupboard. 'I took the pill,' she said to me. 'And the milk has just about stopped. I put pads in my bra just in case.' She stepped into the dress. 'Imagine if I leaked when I was walking down the street. Disgusting!'

Matron Carting came into the room with a lady who wasn't a nurse or a doctor. The lady had a necklace of white beads around her neck and wore a brown suit. She said, 'Hello, Margaret.'

'Hi, Mum,' said Candy.

'Are you ready?'

'I need to use the toilet before I go,' said Candy.

'Don't dawdle, Margaret. I'll be at the front desk waiting for you.' Candy's mother left the room.

Candy looked at me. 'It'll be your turn soon.'

I knew Candy meant my turn to leave, but she didn't understand. Leave for what? I didn't want to leave. Candy came and sat on the side of my bed. She glanced over her shoulder. There was no one in the ward but us. 'They keep the babies on the top floor. You can go up the stairs. They took me there to give the baby the early milk. If you want to see your baby, go at night—there's only one nurse on duty and she has a lot of babies to check.'

My baby was upstairs? He was here?

'Thank you, Candy,' I said.

'Only go at night, otherwise there's visitors—the mothers and fathers coming to choose a baby.'

'Thank you.'

She squeezed my hand. 'Good luck.'

Candy walked out of the room. The babies were upstairs. Joe Michael was upstairs.

———

I stayed in bed that day, waiting for night to come. A new girl was brought into the ward. She lay on her side, the blanket pulled up to her ears, and never spoke. When she woke she cried. I watched the light change outside the window. I turned from the clock to the changing light. Night was close now. The other girl woke and cried and slept and cried. The nurse pulled a curtain around her, then she went behind the curtain so I could only see their shadows bending and reaching.

I lay on my back and listened to the voices coming from the corridor. Once, when I was at the Worlleys' farm, I saw a cow with its calf hanging from its backside. The calf's tongue was blue and the cow twisted and turned, trying shake out the baby. The cow had been trying to push out the calf for a long time;

it was too big. The cow moaned, her eyes rolling back in her head. The cow that looked so wide from the outside must have been small on the inside, its bones a trap that the calf couldn't pass through. The cow wanted to be close to her baby, to lick him clean, to smell his coat, to help him walk, but it didn't matter how far she turned around, she couldn't reach to help him out; she was like a dog chasing its tail. The calf's tongue turned blue, its eyes closed, its long, damp legs stuck out under its chin, one across the other. *Is it alright?* I asked Ian Worlley. Nobody answered. Later they cut the calf out in pieces to save the cow. Only the cow was saved.

———

At last the night nurse drew down the blinds and dinners were brought into the ward. I pushed the tray away.

'You need food,' said the nurse. She smiled at me. 'If you want to leave this room and go home you'll need food in your stomach.' She was nice. Not as pretty as Nurse Patty, but nice. Nurse Patty hadn't come back since I saw her the last time. 'Come on, it isn't that bad. It's meant to be chicken Maryland, but let's just say it's chicken with mash.' The nurse helped me to sit up in the bed.

If you want to leave this room . . . I did want to leave this room. Tonight, to see my baby. I stuck my fork into the chicken.

The new girl who had taken Candy's bed had stopped crying and was sitting up against her pillows. She had no colour in her cheeks and had not eaten any of her dinner. There was nobody else in the ward. I said to the girl, 'They keep the babies upstairs. Yours will be there too.' She turned to me, her face blank. 'You can go and see your baby,' I said. 'It's upstairs.' She turned away from me.

Later, after the dinner trays had been cleared, a nurse came and helped the other girl to the toilet. After she left, the sounds of the hospital settled. Soon it would be time. My heart began to race. What if I couldn't find the way upstairs? What if they'd already found a home for Joe Michael? He had ten fingers and ten toes like Candy's baby. What if he was gone? *Please don't let him be gone.* When I found him I would take him from here. He didn't belong in St Jude's. I was his home. He belonged with me.

The only light in the room was coming from the corridor outside. I sat up. Blood came from between my legs, heavier than my rags. I got out of the bed; my scar stung. I felt swollen. I closed my eyes against the pain; I could hear the baby crying. It went from loud to soft then louder again. He was calling for me.

I went to the door; just as I was about to step into the corridor two nurses walked out of one of the other wards. They were talking and laughing, looking at a chart. I held my breath and waited. When I couldn't hear the nurses anymore, I looked out again. There was nobody there. Further down the corridor I saw another door. I walked as quickly as I could to the door and opened it. I was in a concrete stairwell. I closed the door behind me.

I climbed the stairs in the darkness, the concrete cold under my bare feet. My heart beat fast. What would happen if a nurse saw that I wasn't in my bed? They would come after me; they would stop me from seeing Joe and he would be taken. Joe would be given away. I started to run.

I pulled open a door at the top of the stairs and heard voices and babies crying. Candy was right—this was where the babies were kept! I put my head into the corridor. I could see a nurse at the far end. She was measuring something into a bottle, with her back to me. Then she went through a door and was gone. I could hear babies crying, but muffled, as if they were behind a wall.

I stepped into the corridor, following the sound of babies crying. When I saw a nurse coming I went through the nearest door into a cupboard of folded towels. I held my breath. When I opened the door of the cupboard the nurse was gone. I went on down the corridor towards the sound of crying. I came to a set of double glass doors with numbers on a sign. I pushed open the doors and there they were, the babies.

There was nobody guarding them but I knew the nurse would be here soon. I walked along the rows of babies in their cots. What if I didn't know him anymore? What if he had forgotten me? Then I saw him. My baby! Joe Michael! He was sleeping, his face softer than any face living. He wasn't yet in the world, but he wasn't inside me either. He was between worlds. *My baby.* I would know him anywhere. I picked him up as gently as I could and held him to me. He woke and looked at me and there was nothing between us, as if he was still in me, and yet he wasn't, he was here, in this world. I put my face to his soft hair, and he curled into me as if he knew me, knew my voice. 'My baby, my little baby . . . little Joe, hello, Joe, little baby.' They were the best minutes of my life. 'Little Joe, my little one, I am your mother.' They were the minutes that contained my dream. 'Little Joe Michael, baby Joe, baby Joe, sweet little baby Joe.' It was as if I had been empty up till now. The baby was mine. Nothing had ever been mine before. My own body wasn't mine, but the baby, here, now, in my arms was mine.

He snuffled against me and cried softly. 'Oh, little Joe, little baby Joe.' I rocked him up and down, bob-bobbing as if I was a human sea, the perfect size for my baby, who could let himself go in my arms and be rocked by me, Justine, his one and only mother. We both knew we didn't have long, that we had to work fast. We were stamping ourselves on each other; even after life was finished, we would be forever Justine the mother, and Joe Michael the son.

'Hey! What are you doing?' A nurse came through the doors. 'What on earth? Give me the baby! Give him to me!' She tried to take my baby from me. But Joe Michael was mine. He'd been in my stomach, I made him and carried him and pushed him into the world.

He started to cry, and I started to cry too.

The nurse pulled Joe Michael from my arms. I had to let him go, I didn't want him to be hurt. Joe Michael cried louder. The nurse called, 'Nurse Withers! Nurse Withers! Come quickly!'

Nurse Withers came charging towards me, black wings flapping. 'What were you thinking?' Her cold hand was pressed to my back as she took me down the stairs. 'You could have hurt him!'

I couldn't speak. I would never have hurt him—never! But I couldn't find the words, even for my baby. I could only cry for him, and long for him and wish for him to be in my arms.

Back in my bed Nurse Withers gave me a pill and waited until I swallowed.

55.

When I woke the next morning I was the only one in the ward; the other girl was gone. Nurse Undine came into the room. She was cold and hard as sink metal. 'After breakfast you can change into the clothes you were wearing when you first arrived. Your grandfather is on the way to take you home.'

I pulled my dress over my head. It hung down in folds over my empty stomach.

—

Matron Carting led Pop into the room. He was pale. The tracks in his face reached all the way to the end. He said, 'You got everything?'

I didn't answer. I was numb.

When the nurse gave him pads for me, Pop's hands shook. He was all made of dry sticks, like kindling. He tried to take my hand but I pulled away. Joe Michael never stopped crying; I had to listen.

Pop and me walked to the glass doors of the hospital; Joe was on one side, the world without him was on the other. Through the doors I saw Pop's truck parked on the road out the front. Once I was in the truck I would not see Joe again. I knew it now; *Erad ot wonk*. Nothing came between me and knowing anymore. Pop pushed open the doors and we walked through. Joe's cry grew sharp as a knife. When I came to the edge of the road I stopped.

Pop said, 'Come on, Justine.'

I didn't move.

'Come on. Be bloody hours before we get home.'

Still I didn't move.

'Get in the truck.'

'No.'

'Justine, get in the truck.'

'No.'

'Get in the bloody truck.'

I pulled away from him. 'No!'

'Justine!' He pushed me towards the truck.

'No!' I screamed. 'No! No! No!' Joe was there, inside the hospital. He belonged to me. I never had a baby before; I didn't have anything. 'He's mine!' I shouted. 'He's mine, he's mine!'

'Get in, Justine!' Pop pulled open his door and threw me against the seat so hard my nose and chin hit the dashboard. Pads fell from his hands onto the road like bread for the birds. People passing on the street stopped and looked, then turned away.

'No!' I screamed.

Nurses coming out of the building saw us, a woman in a dressing-gown and a family of children stared.

Pop got in the truck, reached over me and locked my door. The truck screeched as Pop drove onto the road, bumping over the kerb. Pop was driving me away from Joe Michael. There was nothing I could do. I was leaving him. He was alone in the cot in the hospital without me. My baby! A weight came down over me. Pop kept driving. There was nothing I could do.

He said, 'You can go back to school. See your friends. Have some fun, hey?'

I looked out of the window; I saw the same trees, the same roads and cars and buildings, the same sky, but everything had changed. The world was not the same. I had a baby.

I put my hands on my stomach and leaned against the seat. I wished I could push him back inside. This time I would understand that it was my baby I was carrying. I would put my hands over my stomach and sing to him, *The birds in the sky, singing just for you*, and he wouldn't come out until it was safe. I wouldn't go to St Jude's. I would go somewhere else, where I could hold Joe Michael in my arms, where nobody could stop me.

We drove on and on. Pop said, 'That bastard's back in town, living at Stacey's place, but he won't bother us . . . Don't go near him, Justine.'

I heard my pop, and I didn't hear him. I didn't care what he said. Didn't care who was in town. Didn't care about anything.

When we got back to Pop's Three there was the line of dirt around the house, there was the ash of Pop's fire, the empty back-house, my bedroom with its window to the end of the road. What did any of it mean now? What had it ever meant?

⌣

Early in the morning, when there was still a moon, still a star in the sky, I woke from a dream. It was baby Joe: his blue-grey eyes were open and he was looking for me. He searched the walls of the hospital, the sides of his cot, the corridors, the stairs, the bathroom, the ceiling, the faces of the nurses, the doctors, the other girls in their beds, but none of them was me. I was the only one in the world who he wanted; there was nobody else who would do. The dream changed and I was inside Donna. It felt warm, my head was in water, I could breathe through slits in my neck, the way cod do. I heard the beat of her heart through the water. Donna had her hands over my body; I could feel the pressure through her skin. 'You better turn soon, baby,' she said, rubbing her hands over me. 'You better turn soon.' I could smell Dad's White Ox and the eggs frying and I could hear Cockyboy and the chooks clucking in the yard.

———

The light was bright through my bedroom window when Pop knocked on the door. 'Justine?' he said. 'Can I come in?'

Pop opened the door, carrying a plate. 'Brought you breakfast.' Pop tipped the plate; he'd made a face, with two yolks for the eyes and a piece of bacon for the mouth. He pushed the pillow up behind me. 'Sit up, Justine,' he said, setting the plate on the bed. 'The girls miss you. Even old Cockyboy misses you.'

I turned away from him.

'You have to have a bath, Justine. And you can take these aspirin.' He held out a box of pills. 'They'll make you feel better.'

I didn't want to feel better.

Pop stood and looked at me. 'You'll need to bloody eat.' He shook his head and left the room.

I slept then woke and couldn't tell the difference. I was in the room with the wave of dirt thundering towards me, then the wave rolled over me, and with its force the baby pushed its way through my scar, splitting me, finishing me, the old Justine, so a new one was born. Justine the mother. My baby was here! He was here! Then I opened my eyes and saw that he wasn't here, he wasn't here. The crying came again, and I slept, returning to him in my dream.

All that day I heard the baby, Joe Michael, calling for me. His voice was all he had. It was his weapon, his protection from danger, and he was calling for me every minute.

I got out of my bed and pulled on the same dress and coat I'd been wearing when I came home from the hospital. I would sing to Joe Michael at my keepout—my song would be carried by the river to the sea, to St Jude's in Geelong, where Joe Michael lay in his box, and he would hear me, and then he would drink his milk and sleep, and know I was his mother.

I went to the toilet and saw the pad was covered in blood. It stung and burned when I tried to do a wee. I thought I would fall into the same hole the baby had come through. I was at the edge, looking down.

I took one of the pads from the bag and put a clean one in my underpants, then I put the rest in my schoolbag. I put the bag on my back. My chest felt tight and hard.

I went out the back door and stood on the step. I looked across at the fence line, at the clouds in the sky, at the gate. I breathed in the air and listened. I could hear him more clearly outside. I stood for a long time then I turned and went back inside.

Pop lay in his bed, mouth open, a hand over his gut. His face twitched.

There had never been anyone else. Not my dad, not my Aunty Rita, not my mother, not Nurse Patty—there had only ever been my pop. It was Pop who sat with me the first night Donna left, Pop who introduced me to the big man, Pop who collected the eggs with me, so we could eat our dinner on our knees at his fire. I brought him beers from the esky and he made me tea with milk and sugar, and we looked after the chooks. So many chooks we had cleaned for and spoken to and fed. But it was Pop who had taken my baby. He was trying to give him away. The only thing that was mine. I didn't have a horse and I didn't have a friend and I didn't have a mother, but I had a baby, Joe Michael, and Pop was trying to take him from me. I picked up his belt from the floor, unhooked his keys and left the room.

One of the keys was for the truck, one was for the front door, one was for the back-house and one was for the cupboard that held the guns. I separated the key to the cupboard from the others, holding it tight. I took a kitchen chair and opened the door to the stairs. I felt hot and wet. The stairs were as dark as they had been the night I went down with Kirk and Steve all those years ago. Where were my brothers now? Where had they ever been?

I went down the stairs, one hand against the wall. I put the chair under the cupboard, climbed up and put the key in the lock. I pulled open the door and put my hands inside—there was Pop's Mauser and the brother-pistols. I could feel Dad's Smith tucked behind them, wrapped in the cloth, the way it had been the day he taught me how to shoot. The same box of bullets sat beside the gun. My hands shook so much that as I took them out I thought I would drop the gun.

Leaving the key in the lock I climbed down from the chair and put the gun and the box of bullets into my schoolbag. Then I went back up the stairs and out of the house.

I couldn't keep up with my own shaking as I crossed the yard. My teeth chattered. I couldn't see straight. I stopped and took the gun and six of the bullets from the bag. I pushed the bullets into the six empty holes in the cylinder. *You need to know how to look after yourself. So when you say,* Fuck off, *they'll know you mean it.* My dad's one lesson.

I walked towards the gate, my legs weak. I couldn't feel the ordinary ground. It rose up to me as I walked, then fell back behind me. I gripped the gun. I was at the chicken run. I heard Cockyboy clucking. Electricity charged my hands. I was shaking as if I was the gun and the bullets were loaded in me. I opened the door of the run. Cockyboy jumped from his perch and came towards me. Showing me who was boss. He had the same look in his eye as Mrs Turning. As Dr Manning, as the nurses, Withers and Undine. He was another one against me the way Relle and Kirk and Steve were against me. The way Dad was against me. I raised the gun and looked into Cockyboy's black-pip eyes. I pulled the trigger and shot a bullet into his head. Blood sprayed from his neck like water from a hose. I shot another chook, Missy, and I was released. Blood splattered the walls of the shed and the dust and the sleeping hens, Lady and Lady and Madame and Girl, who started and jolted and looked at me, their feathers rising from their skins. I blasted them one after the other, the hens taking it from me, taking it for me, taking what had been put in me, the only creatures in the world who ever had, the hens who never did anything against me, never hurt me, never stuck anything into me, never against me, the hens, all dead, in pieces in Pop's shed, their blood on my face and on my hands and on their enemy the gun. They took it for me, dying on the run floor in feathers and blood, all dead, my sweetest friends, the chooks.

I ran through the gate towards the trees, my breath heaving in my chest. The trees rose up around me like ghosts. I kept running. There was my river-truck made of branches, there was my keepout where I had my blanket, my torch, my biscuits and my matches. I pushed open the door and was home again. I vomited onto the floor, then I fell against the gun, wrapping myself around it, cold as bone, my face sticky. I cried. It was death all around, my face stained in blood. It was the end of things, because I had lost the beginning.

———

I held on to my weapon, and slept without moving. I didn't see the clouds passing over the bright face of the moon. I didn't feel the damp of the forest floor, or hear the owl calling. Sleep was a valley and I was walking its darkest path, where nothing can be reached or saved. When I was too tired and too weak to go any further, Silver came to my side. She stood over me, snorting her warm breath against my cheek, ready to fall to her knees so I could climb up onto her back. There were blankets tied to her saddle, and supplies, there was hot tea and eggs to eat with bread. Silver and the gun guarded me.

———

When I next woke the gun was still in my hand, my fingers stiff around the handle. I sat up and took the box of bullets out of my bag. Dad didn't teach me how to read or write or speak or make friends or look someone in the eye—he taught me how to use the Smith. *They're all the same. Every single last one, rich or poor, black or white, old or young, they all want it.* I opened the gun's cylinder and pushed in six more bullets. *You don't ever want to find yourself looking into a gun from the wrong end. Chances are it'll be the last thing you see.*

I left the keepout and walked down to the river. Birds with long hooked beaks flew away as I came close. Clouds of insects separated and trees pulled back their branches.

I stood at the edge and looked at the water. It had stopped flowing. The banks of The Choke had tightened. The water had nowhere to go.

I put the gun to my head, my finger on the trigger.

56.

In the quiet of the Murray I heard my baby calling for me—his one and only mother. The same way I had called for Donna the day she left, the same way Sherry had called for her mother when Stacey couldn't get out of the bed. Slowly, my hand shaking, I lowered the gun. There wasn't anybody who could take my place for Joe Michael, there wasn't anyone else he wanted. The way I had wanted Donna. I closed my eyes and felt her arms around me, holding me to her, rocking me, whispering words I didn't know, dancing with me across the floor, nobody in the world but us.

I folded the Smith back in the cloth and put it in the bag. I kneeled and took a long drink from the river. The water cooled me and soothed my throat. I splashed more over my face, washing the blood from my hands. My head stopped pounding. I looked up and saw that the river was moving, flowing forward, it hadn't stopped. The banks were the same distance apart as they had always been. I breathed in deep and my breath flowed out and forward. My breath and the Murray. I closed my eyes and saw the hole the baby had come through. It was the same ditch that surrounded Steve. I looked over the edge. It wasn't dark; it was light.

I put my schoolbag on my back and walked up to the Henley Trail, then I left the trail and went through the trees. I took the same path that the Worlleys and the Lees used when we were young and would run between the farm and Pop's Three. All our tracks had disappeared, the grass had grown thick, new young red gums grew in the way, but I knew where to go. My bag was steady against my back; it had only ever been empty and now it held a gun. There was throbbing between my legs, as if a heart was under the pad. That was where the baby had come from, where I was split; it throbbed and burned but I didn't want it to stop—it kept me joined to him. I walked in time to its beat as I headed for the Worlleys'. Night was coming. It was a circle that didn't stop turning.

I came to the dirt road that led to the Worlleys' caravans. I stopped. The slide was bright yellow, the bubbles flew as we slid, the Worlleys and the Lees, there were so many you couldn't tell which was which. The fall-out happened in a single night. *Tight bastard . . . The Japs took your balls, old man . . . Fucken money.* And then we weren't the Worlleys and the Lees anymore, and it was war. I kept walking, one foot in front of the other.

—

Stacey's half-built house was outlined in silver, the way it had been the night I was there with Dad. The moon was full then too. Bricks were in piles around the concrete square, there were planks not yet laid, bags of concrete, torn and spilling, glass broken. I saw two cars without wheels, I saw engines and a fridge and an upside-down bath. Jamie's Valiant was parked outside

Stacey's caravan. I heard cries and couldn't tell one voice from another. Was it Joe Michael? Was it Stacey? Was it Sherry?

I stood behind one of the cars and took the Smith from my schoolbag. I was shivering. I thought I was going to vomit. I walked closer to Stacey's caravan. All Sherry's toys were gone; now it was car parts and sheets of iron and fallen bricks. The cries in my ears grew louder. I held on tightly to the Smith as I listened for the cry that belonged to my baby. My little baby, Joe Michael. Then I heard it, a cry just for me. I took another step towards the caravan and out came Jamie Worlley.

He stepped down from the front door and unzipped his jeans. He was tall, his shoulders broad. I heard him piss into the dirt. He was like my dad. Jamie and my dad could have been the same. He zipped his jeans and turned to go back inside. I stepped out of the shadows. 'Jamie,' I said.

'What the hell?'

I held up the gun with both hands. *Only point it at the thing you want to kill.*

'What are you doing here?' Jamie said.

I had to find the words. *Which one of you will die today?*

'I came to see you.'

'What do you want?'

'I had a baby.'

'So I heard. Fuck off, Justine.' He turned to go into the caravan.

My hand was charged, as if Pop had put his jump leads against it and turned the key. All that had been taken from me was in the force of my finger as I pulled the trigger and shot the ground near Jamie. *Bang.*

'Fuck!' Jamie's voice shook and jumped.

'I need you to help me.'

'P-put down the gun, Justine . . .'

'No.'

'Please . . . Please, put down the gun.'

'I said *no!*'

'Okay, okay. What is it . . . why are you here?'

I shot the other side of his feet. 'You can help me,' I said, my voice new and strong for Joe Michael.

'Fuck! Fuck, Justine. Jesus. What the . . .'

'Take me to my Aunty Rita.'

'Rita? Who . . .' He shook his head. 'I don't understand . . .' Jamie never took his eyes off the gun.

'My Aunty Rita.'

'Your aunt?'

'Yes,' I said. The gun was steady; even if I had taken my hand away it would still be there, suspended, ready to shoot.

'Justine, please, can you put down the gun?'

'No,' I said. 'Take me to her.'

'Where is she?'

'Sydney.' I stepped closer to his face.

'Okay, okay, Sydney.'

'Gladesville. Tarban Creek. Take me.' I lifted the gun, as if the gun itself had a voice to add to mine. *Do it, Jamie.*

'Okay!' he said. 'Okay.'

'Now!' I shot the Smith at the side of his head.

'Okay! I need to get money. Please, just let me get some money. I got to get keys. It's inside, we have to go inside.'

'Get the money,' I said. 'But, Jamie, if you don't do what I want I'm going to kill you.' I wanted to kill him, leave him as bloody and dead as Cockyboy on the floor of the chook run. But that wouldn't stop my baby crying. 'Do you understand? I'll kill you.'

'Okay. Okay, Justine.'

I followed him as he stepped into the caravan. The television was on; people clapped. There was a picture on the wall of Stacey holding Sherry. She was smiling and holding her yellow rabbit. They were both laughing and Stacey was whole, happy, her face wasn't in the trough with pieces of her hair missing, and she could get out of bed and look after Sherry another day, the way she was before my dad took me to visit.

'Get your things and get in the car.'

Jamie picked up his wallet and his keys from the kitchen bench. I followed him outside to the car, my gun pointed at his back. It was the same white car, the Valiant, but this time I got in the front seat, not the back, and this time I was holding a gun.

Jamie turned the key and started the engine. He drove down past the Henley Trail, past the Yolamundi pub to Nullabri, then onto the Murray Valley Highway. I knew I was heading further away from Joe Michael, and the distance pulled at me, twisting my gut. Soon we were on the Sturt, heading for Sydney. Every second made me ache but I would not drop the gun. We weren't turning back.

———

The highway was long and straight, line after line down its middle. After a long time Jamie said, 'Justine, put down the gun. I am getting you there.' But I didn't put down the gun. Outside the car the bush was thick—there were a lot of places to hide a girl in the bush. Jamie's strong hands were on the wheel, and when I looked at them as he drove, the night we were together came back to me like pieces of a puzzle. With every hour of road, every white line behind us, I knew more. I was fourteen now, I had a baby, I had been pregnant, it happened in the back of Jamie's car, after the hot mint drink. Kirk and Steve left me at The Choke with Jamie and his cousin, Lachie, and their friend, Stu, and another guy I didn't know.

We had watched the river and I had been listening to the boys talking. I had drunk from the bottle Jamie bought for me, and then the next thing I knew I was vomiting in the car, and after that Jamie was on top of me. It was hard to breathe, I tried to push him off but I had no strength. There was a dream of my dad, a dream of Stacey, but what was happening to me wasn't a dream. I was torn apart, peeled back like chicken off the bone.

Jamie helped the baby come into me. It happened that night. I didn't want Jamie to do it, I didn't ask for it, but now that he had done it I would take it. It was mine. With every mile I knew more. Knowing woke and found a voice, pushing through the dead, dry ground like a body back to life.

My father was in Pentridge for what he did to Stacey Worlley. I was there with him that night. Jamie Worlley was Stacey's younger brother, and it was Jamie Worlley who had hurt me. Joe Michael came from them, from Jamie, from Dad, from Stacey, from Pop, he came from the mistakes they had made, but Joe Michael was not a mistake.

We kept driving. I could stay awake holding the gun, and I could know the truth, for Joe Michael I could do it. Hours passed. Inside the car it was still. Jamie's arms were steady. I kept my eye on him and the gun and the bush outside. I never put down the gun for one second. When I needed to piss I did it onto the pad. We only stopped for petrol. I stood close to Jamie with the gun to his back.

'I need to piss,' he said.

'Go over there.' I pointed to some grass beside the wall.

'Fuck.'

'Do it there or nowhere,' I said.

Jamie pissed beside the wall.

———

The highway stretched on. The sun rose, lighting the sky with gold and grey and pink, mixing like the paint of a picture by Michael. My friend Michael, who I'd missed every day since he left. Who helped me and waited for me. Who shared his house and his family with me, protected me, knew me and wanted to know more. My friend Michael. Who wanted to write to me, but I told him no, because I could never read a single word. Whose name I gave to my baby. It was morning, there were still stars in the sky, fading, soon to be gone. Joe Michael's call mixed with the call of birds. I had never had a reason before, and now I did have one. I saw it in the light of the rising sun.

———

We were outside a brick building with hedges all around it like walls. Jamie stopped the car. 'It's here,' he said.

I kept the gun pointed at him and looked at the building.

'Now what?' he asked.

I couldn't read the sign; I saw the letters, I could see they were words, but I didn't know.

'What does it say?'

'What does what say?'

'There,' I pointed. 'The sign.'

'Gladesville Hospital.'

That was where Aunty Rita worked. Tarban Creek—Gladesville Hospital.

Jamie took cigarettes from his pocket. 'What happens next?' he asked.

'Now you can go.'

'That's it? I'm not going to hear from you again?'

'No. That's it.'

'What are you going to do in there?' He looked at the hospital through the car window.

'Find my Aunty Rita.'

'What if she isn't in there?'

'I don't know . . . This is where she works.'

He looked at the wheel then up ahead and through the glass again. 'Do you want me to wait?'

'No,' I said.

'Justine,' he said, 'if you need me to wait here, I will.'

I shook my head. 'No.'

'If she isn't here, if she's somewhere else, I'll take you there.'

I shook my head.

'Are you sure?'

'I'm sure.'

I looked into his eyes and saw a tunnel. I saw his sister, Stacey, in the tunnel; I saw Sherry calling for her mother from Margy's caravan. I saw bottles of see-through drink and the rusted car rising from the Worlley dam. I saw the long red scar on Jamie's back that never came from a dogfight.

'Your old man nearly killed Stacey that night. He's where he belongs . . . fucken Pentridge.'

I waited. I didn't move or speak.

He stubbed out his cigarette, then he looked across at me. 'I s'pose you think I belong there too . . .'

I didn't know where Jamie belonged. I didn't say anything.

'Is that what you think, Justine?'

I had no answer for him. He opened and closed his hands around the steering wheel. 'Do you want me to come with you? I can if you need me to.'

'No.' I put the gun down on the seat.

He picked it up, turning it over in his hands. 'You don't need it anymore?'

'No,' I said, pushing open the door.

He put the gun into the glove box. 'Good luck, Justine.'

I got out of the car then watched as Jamie drove away.

57.

I walked up to the entrance of the hospital. A nurse in a white dress was coming down the steps in the other direction. I stopped in front of her. 'I am looking for my aunt.'

'Your aunt?'

'Her name is Rita,' I said. 'Rita Lee. She works here. At Tarban Creek.'

'I haven't heard it called that in a long time.'

'That's what my aunt calls it.'

'Then she's been here a while,' the nurse said. 'Come with me.' We went through the doors of the hospital to a front desk. There were other nurses inside, and doctors, and people wearing pyjamas. The nurse went behind the desk and looked at a folder, running her finger down the page. 'Rita Lee, did you say?' she asked. 'And she's on the staff here, right?'

'Yes.' I started to feel as if I might fall. I hadn't had anything to eat or drink in a long time. It was burning and wet between my legs. My dress stank.

'Rita Lee . . . let me see . . .' The nurse pointed at a name on the folder. 'Okay,' she said. 'She's here.'

She's here. I had wanted it to be true, needed it to be true, but until now I didn't know if she would be here. My knees felt weak as we walked to another part of the hospital and up a set of stairs. There were signs and numbers but I couldn't read any of them. Letters jumped before my eyes, my arms ached from holding the gun. I could only just hear Joe Michael now, his cry was so weak and tired. *Birds in the sky, birds in the sky. Wait for me, Joe Michael!*

The nurse took me to a desk. 'Rita Lee on duty?' she said to the man behind it.

The man said, 'Place doesn't run without her.'

'Somebody wants to see her.'

The man, who was as old as Pop, said, 'And who might that be?'

'Rita Lee is your aunt, right?' The nurse turned to me.

'Yes,' I said. I was dizzy.

'You'd better take a seat, love,' she said.

'I'll call Rita,' said the man.

'She'll be here soon,' the nurse said to me. 'Hang on.'

Then she disappeared and I closed my eyes. When I woke up there was my Aunty Rita but I didn't know if it was a dream.

Her hair was dark and shining, her eyes were blue with the traces of my dad. She was the same and she wasn't. She said, 'Justine . . .'

I took her hand and held it tight in mine. She was here. 'Help me.' It came out dry and croaky.

'What is it? Justine, are you okay? What's happened?'

'Help me.' Joe Michael's cry was faint now. I could hardly hear it. Was somebody taking him?

'Come with me.' She led me out of the waiting room and through a door, into a room with a bed and a chair. She closed the door behind us. 'What's going on? Are you okay? Sit down.'

I sat on the side of the bed. 'Rita, you have to help me.'

'Justine, are you hurt? Is Pop here?'

'No.'

'You came alone?'

'Yes. Rita, you have to help me.'

'What is it? What's wrong?'

'I had a baby.'

'What?'

'I had a baby.'

Aunty Rita's mouth dropped open. She looked down at the front of my dress. Her mouth closed then opened again.

I said, 'Aunty Rita, I had a baby.'

'When?'

'Five days ago.'

'Five days? What are you talking about?'

'They're trying to take him from me. But he's mine. Rita, help me!'

'Whose baby?'

'My baby.'

'But, Justine, who is the father?'

'He doesn't have a father.'

'But how did you get pregnant?'

I was quiet.

'How, Justine?'

'Jamie Worlley.'

'Jamie Worlley?' She frowned. 'Does he know?'

'Yes. But it's my baby, Rita. He doesn't want it.'

'Is the baby with Dad?'

'No—Rita, we have to hurry. He isn't with Pop. He's in the hospital.'

'What do you mean? Where?'

'St Jude's. In Geelong. He's mine, Rita. But Pop put him up for adoption. We have to hurry. They are going to take him from me. But he's mine!'

'Okay, okay,' she said. 'Calm down, Justine.'

'Aunty Rita, the baby is mine. I am his mother.' I had never spoken the word out loud before. *Mother.* Could that be me? It was me.

Aunty Rita got up from her chair and walked around the room. She put her head in her hand. She sat back down. 'Does Pop know you're here?'

I shook my head. 'Pop doesn't want the baby. But he can't decide. Only I can decide.' I hardly recognised my voice. It found the words and could speak them without the gun in my hand.

'We have to tell him you're here. That you're okay. Justine, are you okay? You're bleeding!' She looked at my dress.

'I want my baby!' There were no other cries anymore but his. 'Rita,' I said. 'Rita, help me!'

'I need to speak with Dad. We need to get the doctor for you.'

'No!' I said. 'No, Rita!'

'Calm down, Justine.'

She went to the sink and filled a glass with water.

'Not Pop,' I said.

'Did he hurt you?' she asked, passing me the water.

'No,' I said. 'But the baby is mine. Please, Rita, can you find him?'

She looked at me. 'You want this baby?'

'Yes,' I said.

'You're fourteen.'

The wave was coming, it spoke what it wanted to, without waiting. 'How would you know how old I am? How would you know anything? You lied. You said you would write to me and

be my aunt! You said you would ring me on the telephone an
you never did. Not at Christmas. Not when Dad went to jail.
Not once! You never did anything!'

'Don't shout. What are you talking about?'

'Where did you go?'

'Nowhere. I've been writing to you. I've written to you every
month.'

'No, you didn't.'

'I did, Justine. And I tried to call. Lots of times. When Ray
went to prison I got in the car and drove down. Pop wouldn't
let me stay. He said if I stayed to see you he wouldn't give you
my letters and he'd tell Ray and Ray would make trouble—for
me and for you and for everybody. He never told you I came?'

'No.'

She shook her head. 'Dad . . .' she said. 'I am sorry, Justine.'

Aunty Rita had tried to see me? She had been writing
to me? Why would Pop hide her letters? Why would he do
that to me?

'You didn't forget?'

'No, I didn't forget, but I thought I would only make trouble
for you if I tried any harder. I wrote every month. I didn't know
what else I could do. I knew how much Pop needed you.'

'Please, Aunty Rita . . . there was nowhere else to go. Nobody
to help me. I want my baby.'

Aunty Rita walked around the room some more. She looked
out of the window. She looked at the telephone on the table.

'Aunty Rita!' I said. My strength was thin and running out.
'They will take him from me, give him away. Please!'

She said, 'I have to speak to someone first, Justine. I have to
make a phone call. Can you let me do that?'

'Naomi?'

'Yes, Naomi.'

'Your girlfriend?'

'Yes, yes, my girlfriend.'

She opened the door of the room. She led me out and sat me on a chair against the wall then went back into the room. There were nurses walking up and down. There was a man in pyjamas with a tank behind him on wheels. I felt dizzy. I took off my coat, rolled it up and held it close. *Baby Joe Michael, wait for me.* My chest ached. Between my legs stung and burned. I heard some of the things Aunty Rita was saying. 'Naomi, Justine is here. She says she's had a baby . . . I don't know. What do I do? . . . Okay . . . Okay. Yes, I'm going to. But, Naomi, what if . . .? Okay, okay. I love you.' She came back to the door. She said, 'Justine, come in. I am going to call the hospital.'

'Okay,' I said.

'And then you are going to see the doctor here.' She rang some numbers on the phone. 'I need the number for St Jude's Hospital in Geelong.' She spoke into the receiver. 'Yes . . . yes, thank you.' She dialled more numbers.

She said, 'Births and adoptions, please.' She said, 'To whom am I speaking? . . . I believe there has been a misunderstanding . . . No, no, that's a mistake; Justine Lee is the baby's mother and I am her guardian and speaking on her behalf . . . Is he still at the hospital?' Aunty Rita looked at me and nodded.

I fell onto the floor and Aunty Rita called a doctor.

Naomi came. She was small with light hair the same colour as mine. 'Hello, Justine, I'm here to make sure you are okay.' She helped me onto the bed, then she took my temperature and felt my stomach. She said, 'I am sorry about this, Justine, but we need to have a look at you.' She was gentle with me. She said, 'I have heard so much about you.' She checked between my legs, and when Aunty Rita came back inside she said, 'Justine is going to be fine. She needs medicine, and she needs to recover—she has a fever—but she'll be okay.'

Aunty Rita looked at Naomi and squeezed her hand. 'Thank you.'

Aunty Rita gave me a cup of tea, a bowl of porridge and some toast. 'You have to eat, okay? Let's get that much straight.'

'Okay.' I ate everything she gave me, and then she took me to the bathroom. 'You can take off that dress and we'll find you something clean,' she said. Then she passed me soap and turned on the tap in the shower.

The water came down over my head like hot and steaming rain. All the dirt and the soap and the blood washed away in a circle down the plughole.

Aunty Rita looked in. 'Here's a towel,' she said, and it was a new white towel, with letters on the side that I couldn't read. Aunty Rita gave me clean underpants and everything was white without marks. She gave me a top and some pants with a string.

Joe's cry was soft in my ears and I sang to it under my breath, I had to wake him. *The holly and the ivy when they are both full grown of all the trees that are in the wood the holly bears the crown . . .* Any piece of song I could find, like a breath to light the fire. *Stay, Joe Michael, stay.*

—

Aunty Rita drove us back to Victoria. It was the same road I had taken with Jamie only the day before. I pressed my coat to my chest as if it was Joe. *Wait for me, little baby.* I put my nose to the window. I slept and woke, my shoulder stiff against the seat. Aunty Rita said, 'Have you thought about what you want to do, Justine?'

'Look after Joe Michael.'

'But you can't live with Pop and the baby. You can't . . . It's not going to work.'

'I am his mother,' I said.

'I know you are, but you're only fourteen. You're going to need help. Have you thought about that? How you are going to do this? Pop can't help you. Where are you going to live?'

I looked at her. She was my aunt. She didn't choose it, but she was my father's sister. 'With you.'

'With me?'

'Yes. Here. In Sydney.'

She sighed. 'You know I live with—'

'Naomi.'

'Justine, this is happening very quickly. I'm not sure if—'

'I am sure. Joe Michael is my baby. And that means you are his aunt.'

She sighed again. 'Great-aunt.'

'Okay,' I said. 'Great-aunt.'

58.

Matron Carting was stern, her mouth hard. She said, 'It is not customary.'

Aunty Rita said, 'I am sure that is the case, but Justine's voice needs to be heard in all this.'

'In order to review her file I will need Justine's signature,' said the matron. 'You can sign here.'

I took the pen but I couldn't see where to sign. The lines changed places.

Aunty Rita touched the page. 'Here, Justine.'

I took the pen to where her finger was. I didn't know if I could do it.

'Justine?' said Aunty Rita.

I felt like I was going to cry. If I couldn't read they wouldn't give me Joe Michael. I was standing in front of the same wall Mrs Turning made me go to. If I couldn't write, couldn't read, how could I have a dream?

'Justine, can you sign it?'

'No.'

'Why not?'

'I can't.'

'But why not?'

I shrugged.

'Come on, Justine, what is it? You can read and write, can't you?'

'I don't know.'

'What do you mean you don't know? Justine, tell me, can you read?'

I had never told anyone, never said it. It had been a secret that couldn't be spoken, but I had to tell it now to my Aunty Rita. She had to know how wrong I got it, all the way back to the start. 'The letters are backwards.'

'Backwards? What do you mean?'

'The wrong way round. Not in the right order.'

'Have you had your eyes checked?'

'Yes. There's nothing wrong with them.'

'But the letters are backwards?'

'Yes.'

'Justine, have you been tested for dyslexia?'

'I . . . I don't know.'

'Christ,' she said. 'Justine . . .' Aunty Rita pressed her fingers to her own eyes. 'You have to learn how to read, Justine.' Then she turned to the matron. 'Justine couldn't have signed your forms, Matron Carting—she can't read or write.'

The matron frowned. 'I will need to look into the matter further.'

'There is no matter,' said Aunty Rita. 'The baby does not belong to the hospital.'

'Where is Joe Michael?' I asked.

The matron left the room.

'Justine, I need to speak with Dad—with Pop,' said Aunty Rita.

'I want Joe.'

'I need to speak with your grandfather, Justine. He's your guardian. I can't do this without speaking to him.'

'Why?'

'He's been looking after you all this time. Not me.'

'He tried to take my baby.'

'I can't help you without talking to him. You will need to speak to him too, Justine. We're not hiding. There won't be any secrets.'

Secrets were stories that couldn't be spoken, things people did that couldn't be told. Secrets put Lizzy in the hospital. Secrets put Stacey's face in the cattle trough so she couldn't be a mother. Secrets put my dad in prison. 'Okay.'

I was so close to Joe, but still so far away. His cry came and went; was he still here? I didn't know how much longer I could wait. My arms and legs were falling away from my body. I was weak.

There was a telephone just inside the door. Aunty Rita dug in her pocket for money and dropped it in the slot. She dialled the number for Pop's Three. When he answered she looked at me, then turned away, the receiver to her ear.

'Dad, it's me, Rita. Justine is with me . . . Yes . . . Yes, she's okay. She should still be in hospital, you know. She should be recovering. They should never have sent her home . . . I know it's not your fault, that's not why I'm calling. She never signed the adoption papers for the baby . . . No, she didn't, Dad—she can't write; she can't write her bloody name. Who signed them? . . . I know her age, Dad . . . She wants to keep it . . . I know . . . I know you can't. She can stay with me. We can help . . . Calm down, Dad, I'm not taking her away from you. She wants this baby.' Aunty Rita handed me the telephone.

'Justine?'

'Yes.'

'What are you doing?'

'I want my baby, Pop.' Tears fell down my face.

'You're fourteen.'

'I know.'

'You can't look after a baby.'

'Yes, I can.'

'How are you going to do that?'

'He's mine. I can do it.'

'For Christ's sake,' he said. I heard his voice shaking. I closed my eyes. I saw him standing at the doorway, his thin and trembling body, his gut, the smoke from his White Ox, his kindest friend, rising around him. I saw him watching the big man without me—my one and only Pop.

'Pop, I . . .'

'What?'

'I want this.'

'A baby?'

'Yes.'

'Sounds like you've made up your mind.'

'Pop . . .' I didn't want to say goodbye to him. There was a lump in my throat. I gripped the telephone. 'Pop . . .'

'Jesus . . .'

'Pop, can I do this?'

I heard him mumble words that weren't clear.

'Pop?'

'What is it?'

'Can I do this? Can I have this?'

'You'll need help. You can't do it on your own.'

'Pop . . .'

'What?'

'If I have help, can I do it?'

'You're asking me? I thought your mind was made up.'

'I am asking you, Pop.'

He sighed. 'Justine, if you have help . . .'

'Pop, Rita will help—Rita and Naomi.'

There was quiet. 'If this is what you want.'

I said, 'It is, Pop. I love you, Pop.' I gave the telephone back to Aunty Rita.

'Dad, let us come and see you,' she said. There were tears in her eyes. 'As soon as things are sorted. Please . . . let us come. Bye, Dad.' Aunty Rita hung up the phone and wiped tears from her cheeks. 'Justine, do you want to speak to your father? Do you need to talk to Ray?'

Ray was my dad; he rode a horse called Silver and knew how to use a gun. It was the only thing he had shown me. He couldn't show me anything else. 'No,' I told Aunty Rita. 'I don't want to speak to him.'

59.

The nurse passed me my baby, wrapped in a white blanket. I looked into his sleeping face. I was holding the middle of the warm world. There was nothing else to need. 'My baby, my little baby, Joe Michael.'

When Aunty Rita saw the baby she cried. 'Oh, Justine, Justine, he is beautiful. My God. How are we going to do this?'

I kissed Joe's cheek again and the smell of him was clean and new and sweet. The need for anything to change or be different disappeared and all that I needed was baby Joe Michael. He was my family. Just as the water that flowed between the banks of the Murray knew its direction, I knew mine. I held Joe Michael warm and close against me. I kissed his forehead. Joe Michael opened his eyes. They were made of warm grey light, and in them I could see beyond my own reflection to my dream.

'That's early for a first smile,' said the nurse. 'You don't see that every day. Aren't you lucky?'

I looked up at her, into her eyes. 'Yes,' I answered.

Acknowledgements

Special thanks to Clare Renner, Carmie Isaacs, Kim Kane, Sue Walsh, Richard Walsh, Gail Jones, Alec Patric, Jane Palfreyman, Christa Munns, Ali Lavau and Elise Jones.